The Lotus Eaters

The Lotus Eaters

Tatjana Soli

St. Martin's Press

New York

This is a work of fiction. All of the characters, organizations, and events portrayed in this novel are either products of the author's imagination or are used fictitiously.

THE LOTUS EATERS. Copyright © 2010 by Tatjana Soli. All rights reserved. Printed in the United States of America. For information, address St. Martin's Press, 175 Fifth Avenue, New York, N.Y. 10010.

Map of Vietnam copyright © Gaylord Soli

www.stmartins.com

Library of Congress Cataloging-in-Publication Data

Soli, Tatjana.
    The lotus eaters / Tatjana Soli. — 1st ed.
        p. cm.
    ISBN 978-0-312-61157-6
    1. Women war correspondents—Fiction.   2. Americans—Vietnam—Fiction.   3. Vietnam War, 1961–1975—Fiction.   4. War—Psychological aspects—Fiction.   5. Ho Chi Minh City (Vietnam)—Fiction.   6. Vietnam—Fiction.   I. Title.
    PS3619.O43255L67 2010
    813'.6—dc22

                                                                                    2009045697

First Edition: April 2010

10 9 8 7 6 5 4 3 2 1

For my mom,
  who taught me about
  brave girls crossing oceans

For Gaylord,
  with love and gratitude

. . . we reached the country of the Lotus-eaters, a race that eat the flowery lotus fruit. . . . Now these natives had no intention of killing my comrades; what they did was to give them some lotus to taste. Those who ate the honeyed fruit of the plant lost any wish to come back and bring us news. All they now wanted was to stay where they were with the Lotus-eaters, to browse on the lotus, and to forget all thoughts of return.

—HOMER, *The Odyssey*

ONE

The Fall

April 28, 1975

The city teetered in a dream state. Helen walked down the deserted street. The quiet was eerie. Time running out. A long-handled barber's razor, cradled in the nest of its strop, lay on the ground, the blade's metal grabbing the sun. Unable to resist, she leaned down to pick it up, afraid someone would split his foot open running across it. A crashing noise down the street distracted her—dogs overturning garbage cans—and she snatched blindly at the razor. Drawing her hand back, she saw a bright pinprick of blood swelling on her finger. She cursed at her stupidity and kicked the razor, strop and all, to the side of the road and hurried on.

The unnatural silence allowed Helen to hear the wailing of the girl. The child's howl was high and breathless, defiant, rising, alone and forlorn against the buildings, threading its way through the air, a long, plaintive note spreading its complaint. Helen crossed the alley and went around a corner to see a small child of three or four, hard to tell with the unrelenting malnourishment, standing against the padlocked doorway of a bar. Her face and hair were drenched with the effort of her crying. She wore a dirty yellow cotton shirt sizes too large, bottom bare, no shoes. Dirt circled between her toes.

The pitiful scene begged a photo. Helen hesitated, hoping an adult would come out of a doorway to rescue the child. She had only days or hours left in-country. Breathless, the girl staggered a few steps forward to the curb, eyes flooded in tears, when a man on a bicycle flew around the corner, pedaling at a furious speed, clipping the curb and almost running her down. Helen lurched forward without thinking, grabbed the girl's arm and pulled her back, speaking quickly in fluent Vietnamese: "Little girl, where is Mama?"

The child hardly looked at her, the small body wracked with sobs. Helen's throat constricted. A mistake, stopping. A pact made to herself that at this late date she wouldn't get involved. The street rolled away in each direction, empty. No woman approached them.

Tired, Helen knelt down so she was at eye level to the child. In a head-long lunge, the girl wrapped both arms around Helen's neck. Her cries quieted to soft cooing.

"What's your name, honey?"

No answer.

"Should I take you home? Home? To Mama? Where do you live?"

Rested, the girl began to sob again with more energy, fresh tears.

No good deed goes unpunished. The camera bag pulled, heavy and bulky. As she held the girl, walking up and down the street to flag attention, it knocked against her hip. She slipped the shoulder strap off and set it down on the ground, all the while talking under her breath to herself: "What are you doing? What are you doing? What are you doing?" The child was surprisingly heavy, although Helen could feel ribs and the sharp, pinionlike bones of shoulder blades. The legs that wrapped viselike around Helen's waist were sticky, a strong scent of urine filling her nostrils.

A stab of impatience. "I've got to go, sweetie. Where is Mama?"

She bounced the girl to quiet her and paced back and forth. Her mind wasn't clear; why was she losing her precious hours, involving herself now, when she had passed hundreds of desperate children before? But she had heard this one's cries so clearly. A sign? A sign she was losing it was more like it, Linh would say.

A young woman hurried across the intersection, glanced at Helen and the child, then looked away.

The orphanage was overflowing. Should she take the girl home with her? Once they abandoned this corner, she would be Helen's responsibility. Could she take her out of the country with Linh? What had she been thinking to stop? Was it a trap? By whom? Was it a test? By what?

Helen stroked the girl's hair, irritated. She had a heart-shaped face, ears like perfect small shells. A bath and a nice dress would make her quite lovely.

Ten, fifteen minutes passed. The idea of this being a sign seemed more stupid by the minute. Not a soul came, nothing except the tinny, popping sound of guns far away. Helen toyed with the idea of putting the girl back down. Surely the family was close by, was searching for her. No harm done in keeping the girl company for a few minutes. Not her responsibility, after all. When she began to kneel to deposit her back on the ground, the girl's arms tightened to a choke hold around her neck, and Helen, resigned, strained back up. All wrong; a terrible mistake. A proof that she was failing. Linh would be worrying by now, might even try to go out to find her.

Helen bent and fished for the strap of her camera bag, putting it on the other shoulder to balance the weight. Maybe it *was* a sign. Insane, but what else could she do but take the child with her?

Halfway down the street, a woman's voice yelled from behind them. Helen turned to see a plain, moonfaced woman with thin, cracked lips stride toward them.

"Are you her mother?" Helen asked, guilt welling up. "I wasn't trying to take her—"

The woman yanked the girl out of Helen's arms, eyes pinched hard. The girl whimpered as the mother swatted her on the leg and scolded her.

"She couldn't tell me where she lived," Helen said.

But the mother had already turned without another glance and stalked away. The girl looked over the mother's shoulder, dark eyes expressionless. In a few more steps, they disappeared around the corner.

For the briefest moment Helen felt wronged, missed the weight on her hip and the sticky legs, but then the feeling was gone. How had the mother been so neglectful anyway? It rankled that she had not been thanked or even acknowledged for her effort. But with the shedding of that temporary burden, the old excitement buoyed up in her again. The possibility of the girl disappeared into the past. She'd better pull herself together. She picked up her bag, checked her watch, and ran.

On a normal day the activity in the streets so filled her eye that she hardly knew where to turn, torn whether to focus her camera on the intricate tableaus of open-air barbers on the sidewalk cutting their customers' hair, or tea vendors sweating over their fires and flame-blackened pots, or ink-haired boys selling everything from noodles to live chickens to cigarettes, or old men with whisk beards as peaceful as Buddhas playing their endless games of *co tuong*. And, too, there was the endless flotsam and jetsam of the war: beggars and amputees thronging everyplace where foreigners were likely to drop money.

But today streets were vacant, the broken windows and smashed doors like gouged-out features of a face once familiar. The people gone, or rather hidden, the streets deformed by their absence.

Helen's Saigon had always been about selling—chickens, information, or lovely young women, it didn't matter. It had once been called the Pearl of the Orient, but by people who had not been there in a very long time. Saigon had never been Paris, but now it was a garrison town, unlovely, a stinking refugee shantyville filled with the angry, the betrayed, the dispossessed, but she had made it her home, and she couldn't bear that soon she would have to leave.

Closer to the center of town, there was activity. Gangs of looters ranged through the city like gusts of wind, citizens and defeated soldiers who now in their despair became outlaws, breaking into stores they had walked past every day for years, stores whose goods they coveted.

Helen hurried, sucking on the drop of blood at her fingertip, but couldn't help her excitement, stopping to look, framing the composition in her mind's eye: teenage boys, some in jeans, some in rags, breaking a plate-glass window; a crowd inside a ransacked grocery, gorging themselves on crates of guava and jackfruit; a young girl with pink juice running down her face and onto her white blouse. It had always fascinated her—what happens when things break down, what are the basic units of life?

Hours late. Helen walked faster, touching the letters in the top of her bag, letters that she had wasted the whole morning begging for, that undid the last bit of her foolishness, her wanting to stay for the handover. She hoped that Linh would have taken his antibiotic and morphine in her absence but guessed he had not. His little rebellion against her. He had forgiven her and forgiven her again, but now he was drawing a line.

At the central market, unable to stop herself, she held up the camera to her eye, shooting off a quick series—a group of men arguing, then carrying away sacks of polished rice, bolts of cloth, electric fans, transistor radios, televisions, tape players, wristwatches, and carton after carton of French cognac and American cigarettes. She was so broke she could have used a few of the watches herself to resell stateside.

Wind blew from the east, a tired, rancid breath carrying across the city the smells of rotting garbage and unburied corpses. The rumbling to the north might have been the prelude to a rainstorm, but the Saigonese knew it was the thunder of artillery, rockets, and mortar rounds from the approaching Communist armies. Her brain hot and buzzing, all she could think was, What will happen next?

The looters, figuring they would probably be dead within hours, were careless. They fought over goods in the stores, then minutes later dropped them in the street outside as they decided to go elsewhere for better stuff. Even the want-stricken poor seemed to realize: What good is a gold watch on a corpse?

Helen walked through the torn streets unharmed as if she weren't a foreigner, a woman; instead she moved through the city with the confidence of one who belonged. Ten years before, she had been dubbed Helen of Saigon by the men journalists. She had laughed, the only woman from home the men had seen in too long. But now she did belong to the ravaged city—her frame grown gaunt, her shoulders hunched from tiredness, the bone-sharp jawline that had lost the padded baby fat of pretty, her blue gaze dark and inward.

Ten years ago it had seemed the war would never end, and now all she could think was, More time, give us more time. She would continue till the end although she had lost faith in the power of pictures, because the work had become an end in itself, untethered to results or outcomes.

She stopped on Tu Do, the old Rue Catinat, shaken at the gaping hole of the French milliner's store. The one place that had always seemed impregnable, a fortress against the disasters that regularly fell upon the city, Annick guarding the doorway with her flyswatter in hand. But the doorway was deserted, the plate-glass window shattered. Inside, crushed boxes, flung drawers, but not until she turned and saw the two rush-bottomed chairs, empty and overturned, did she believe the ruin in front of her.

When life in Saigon grew particularly hard, Helen would go to the store, enjoying the company of Annick, the Parisian owner, her perfectly coifed dark blond hair, her penciled eyebrows and powdered cheeks, the seams of the silk stockings she insisted on wearing despite the heat. She had been the only female friend Helen had all these years.

At first Helen had not understood the Frenchwoman's talents, did not understand that the *experiénce coloniale* made her a breed apart. Annick was an old hand at Indochina, having thrived in Saigon for two decades, coming as a young bride. When her husband died she had confounded her family in France by staying on alone.

The two women would retire to the corner café and drink espressos. Helen sat and endured Annick's scolding about neglecting her hair and skin when only hours before she had been out in the field, working under fire. Helen smiled as the Frenchwoman pressed on her jars of scented lotions, remedies so small and innocuous that they made Helen love her more. Had Annick finally gotten scared enough to leave everything behind and evacuate?

In the smashed display window, the red silk embroidered kimono Helen had been bargaining for was untouched, although the cheaper French handbags and shoes had been stolen. The Vietnamese always valued foreign goods over Asian ones. Helen hadn't worked a paying project in a while; her bank account was empty. Her last batch of freelance pictures had been returned a month ago with an apology: *Sad story, but same old story.* But that would be changing soon. The silk slid heavy and smooth between her fingers.

She had worn down Annick on the price, but the kimono was still extravagant. This was the game they played—haggling over the price of a piece of clothing for months until finally Helen gave in and bought it. Annick refusing to sell the piece to anyone else. Feeling like a thief, Helen undraped it from the mannequin, making a mental note of the last price in piastres that they had negotiated; she would pay her when she saw her again. In Paris? New York? She couldn't imagine because Annick did not belong in any other place but Saigon.

The whole city was on guard. Even the children who usually clamored for treats were quiet and stood with their backs against the walls of buildings. Even they seemed to understand the Americans had lost in the worst possible way. The smallest ones sucked their fingers while their eyes followed Helen down the street. When her back was to them, she heard the soft clatter of pebbles thrown after her, falling short.

Helen picked her way back home using the less traveled streets and alleys, avoiding the larger thoroughfares such as Nguyen Hue, where trouble was likely. When she first came to Saigon, full of the country's history from books, it had struck her how little any of the Americans knew or cared about the country, how they traveled the same streets day after day—Nguyen Hue, Hai Ba Trung, Le Loi—with no idea that these were the names of Vietnamese war heroes who rose up against foreign invaders. That was the experience of Vietnam: things in plain view, their meaning visible only to the initiated.

The city had ballooned in size, overwhelmed by refugee slums, the small historical district with the charming colonial facades hiding miles and miles of tin sheds and cardboard shacks, threats of cholera and plague so frequent hotels swabbed the sidewalks in front with ammonia or burned incense, both remedies equally ineffectual. Garbage collection, always sporadic, had been done away with entirely the last few weeks. In some alleys Helen had to wade ankle-deep through a soupy refuse, banging a stick in front of her to scare away rats.

A dark scarf covered her hair so she would attract less attention, but now she also wore a black cotton smock over her T-shirt to hide her camera. Soldiers had beaten up a few reporters already. Paranoia running wild. A camera a magnet for anger. The South Vietnamese soldiers, especially, were bitter against the press, blaming the constant articles on corruption for stopping their gravy train of American money. Not an exhibitionist people, they didn't want evidence of their looting, their faces splashed across world papers, ruining chances of promotion at home or immigration abroad. Helen pitied them as much as she feared them. They were mostly poor men who had been betrayed along with everyone else abandoned in Saigon. If one was rich or powerful, one was already gone. Only the losers of history remained.

At the alley that led to her building, Helen folded the kimono into her lap and bent down into the stall as she did most days. She lifted a camera and took a quick shot, already thinking in terms of mementos. *"Chao ba. Ba manh khoe khong?"* Hello, Grandmother Suong, how are you?

The old woman stirred her pot, barely looking up, poured a small cup of tea, and handed it to Helen. She felt deceived, tricked into loving this Westerner, this crazy one. People gossiped that she was a *ma,* a ghost, that that was why she was unable to go home. "Why waste film on such an ugly old woman?"

"Oh, I only take pictures of movie stars." Grandmother smiled, and Helen sipped her tea. "Read the leaves for me."

Grandmother studied the cup, shook her head, and threw the contents out. "Doesn't matter. You don't believe. These are old Vietnam beliefs."

"But if I did, what does it say?"

Grandmother studied her, wondering if the truth would turn her heart. "It's all blackness. No more luck."

Helen nodded. "It's good I don't believe, then, huh?"

The old woman shook her head, her face grim. Gossips said they saw the Westerner walking through the streets alone, hair blowing in the wind, eyes blind, talking to herself. Heard of her taking the pipe.

"What's wrong, Grandmother?" They had been friends since the time Helen was sick and too weak to come down for food. People walked over from other neighborhoods just to sit at these four low stools and eat *pho,* because Grandmother Suong's had the reputation as the best in Cholon. During Helen's illness, the old woman had closed her stall and climbed the long flight of stairs to bring her hot bowls of soup.

"The street says the soldiers will be here tomorrow. Whoever doesn't hang a Communist or a Buddhist flag, the people in that house will be killed."

"Oh, I don't know. I've heard those rumors—"

Grandmother gave her a hard look. "I don't have a flag."

Helen sipped tea in silence, watching the leaves floating through the liquid, imagined them settling into her doomed pattern again and again against the curved bottom of the cup. The future made her weary.

"The way it works, from what I know of what happened in Hue and Nha Trang, is that the women scouts come in before the soldiers. They go through the streets and hand out the flags. Then you hang them. Welcome the victors and sell them soup."

The old woman nodded, the furrows in her face relaxing as if an iron had passed over a piece of wrinkled cloth. "They season very differently in Hanoi than we do." She rapped her knuckles lightly on the back of Helen's hand. "Listen to my words. They are killing the Americans, even the ones without guns and uniforms. Their soldiers and our own. All the Americans leave, but you stay."

Helen shook her head as if she could dislodge an annoying thought. "Linh is hungry."

"I took him soup hours ago. You are too late. War is men's disease."

Helen finished her tea and set the cup on the crate that served as table. The old woman filled a large bowl with soup and handed it to her as she stood up. "You eat to stay strong."

"Did you read for Linh?"

The old woman's face spread into a smile. "Of course. He pretends he doesn't believe. That he is too Western for such notions. For him there is only light and long life. Fate doesn't care if he believes or not."

Helen dropped lime and chilies in her soup.

"*Da, cam on ba.* Thank you. I'll bring the bowl back in the morning."

"Smash it. I won't be open again after today."

"Why, Mother?"

"*Chao chi. Toi di.* I'm going to the other side of town so maybe they forget who I am. Not only Americans but ones who worked for Americans are in danger. No one is safe. Not even the ones who sold them soup."

Helen stood in the stairwell, a cold, tight weight in her chest making it hard to breathe. She was afraid. Not so afraid of death—that fear had been taken from her years ago—but of leaving, having failed. Time to go home, and the thing that had eluded her escaped. Always it had felt just around the corner, always tomorrow, but now there would be no more tomorrows. Grandmother's words of doom had spooked her. *More time, give us more time.*

Her reputation had waxed and waned with the course of the war. Never a household name synonymous with Vietnam the way Bourke-White and Higgins were in their wars. Or the way Darrow had been. At thirty-two already middle-aged in a young man's profession, but there was nothing else she was prepared for but war. Her ambition in the larger world had faded until there was only her and the camera and the war. She knew this war better than anyone—had been one of the few to live in-country continuously, out in the field, taking every risk. She wanted to stay for the end, cover the biggest story of her career, especially now since the news services and the embassy were insisting that all Americans leave. The holy grail, an exclusive that would fill both her depleted reputation and her bank account. But what if the promised bloodbath did happen? There was Linh. She would not endanger him.

Chuong, the boy who lived under the stairs, was again nowhere in sight. Helen paid him daily in food and piastres to guard the apartment and do errands. Mostly she paid him so the landlord would allow the boy to sleep in the stairwell, so Helen could be sure he ate. The small networks of connection falling apart. His absence was unusual, and Helen climbed the stairs, trying to ignore her sense of dread. *No one is safe. Not even the ones who sold them soup.* The old woman was usually accurate about the manic mood swings of the city. What if the city itself turned against her? Rumor swirled through the streets like burning ash, igniting whatever it settled on. She could still feel the bony rap of Grandmother's knuckles on her skin.

Inside her apartment, Helen put the bowl on the floor, slipped out of her shoes at the door, and set them next to Linh's. She threw off the smock, pulled the neckband of her camera over her head, and laid the equipment on a chair. The camera was caked in dust. She would have to spend most of the evening cleaning the lenses and the viewfinder. The shutter was capping exposures, so she'd have to take it apart. A long, tedious evening when already she was dead tired.

She pulled off her T-shirt and pants, the clothing stiff with sweat and dirt. The laundry woman had stopped coming a week ago, so she would have to use a precious bottle of Woolite from the PX and wash her undergarments herself in the small basin in her bathroom. She tugged off the black scarf and shook out her hair, standing naked in the dim room for a moment, enjoying the feeling of coolness, the air touching her skin. Outside, she had to protect herself, had to become invisible. No hair, bared throat, absolutely no hint of cleavage or breasts, no hips or buttocks or bared calves were permissible. When she had first gone into the field, a veteran female reporter, happy to be on her way out, advised her to use an elastic bandage wrapped over her bra to flatten the outline of her breasts. Even in the cities it was advisable to wear pants with a sturdy belt, the woman said, because it was harder to rape a woman in pants.

It had all come down to this. Losing the war and going home. Her heart beat hard and fast, a rounding thump of protest. Would she go home, missing what she had come for?

Helen picked up the kimono and quickly slipped it on. In the darkened mirror, she tried to see the effect of the robe without looking herself in the face. The war had made her old and ugly, much too late for any of Annick's lotions to make a difference. She pulled a comb through her hair and started to take out the hoop earrings in her ears but decided against it.

"Is that you?" Linh called.

She heard both the petulance in his voice and his effort to conceal it. "I'm coming." Tying the sash of her kimono, she went to a cabinet for a spoon and picked up the bowl of soup.

In the bedroom doorway, she stood with a grinning smile that felt false. Lying in bed, staring out the window, he did not turn his head. The soft purple dusk blurred the outline of the flamboyant tree that had just come into bloom. Impossible to capture on film the moment of dusk, the effect of shadow on shadow, the small moment before pure darkness came.

"I brought soup, but Grandmother said she already fed you."

"I worried."

She could tell despite his hidden face that his words were true, but what she didn't know was that since he had become housebound, he spent the hours while she was away imagining her whereabouts, visualizing dire scenarios. Each time he heard her walk through the door, he said a quick prayer of gratitude, as if torturing himself in this way saved her. Too close to the end to take such risks, and yet he was helpless to stop her.

"I was trying to get home, but things kept catching my attention."

She came forward in the dim room and sat on the edge of the bed to eat. She bent over him and kissed him gently on the lips. No matter that they had been together years, always a feeling of formality when they first saw each other again, even if the separation had been only hours. It had something to do with the attention Linh paid to her, the fact that he never took anyone's return for granted. The feeling disappeared with his quick smile, the way he always reached out a hand to establish touch. He wore old pajama bottoms, stomach and chest swaddled in gauze that had a dull glow in the room.

He was unhappy, and she was the cause of his unhappiness, and yet she was perfectly willing to bull herself through the conversation as if the feelings underneath their words didn't exist. *Why did someone fall in love with you because you are one thing and then want you to be something else?*

"I had many things to do today, my love."

"The old crone read my fortune. Always the same—plenty of luck and a big family." The remark made to sting.

When Linh turned to look at her, she noticed how sharp his cheekbones were, how his eyes were unfocused by pain. She caressed the half-moon scar on his cheek with her fingers. Whenever she asked how he got it, he changed the subject.

"You didn't take your shots?" she said.

"Forgot."

With his infection, unsafe even to be still in the country. When Linh reached out his hand, she saw a belt twisted around his wrist. "What happened?" She held his hand and unwound it, feeling the cold heaviness of the flesh underneath, the welts left behind. She rubbed briskly, willing the disappointment from her face.

"I was just bored, fooling around. Eat your soup."

She looked at him. But this wasn't the time to confront. Just shrug it off, move on. "I'll change the dressings and give you a shot. Then I'll front you a game of Oklahoma gin." Linh was tall, slender, with the finely etched features of the warrior princes of Vietnamese legend, perfect until one's eyes traveled to the scar that formed a half moon on his cheek and the ribboned skin on the wrist that he couldn't leave alone, an ache. Both of them full of scars.

"Sit with me a minute. Tempting me with cards?" He fingered the sleeve of the kimono. "You couldn't resist?" Equally appalled and in love with the fact that she could think of a kimono while their world was about to be lost.

She buried her face in his neck for a moment. Her only rest anymore when her eyes were closed, the images stopped. His skin felt hot and damp against her cheek. Fever. "Annick is gone." They were both still for a moment. "A day, two at the most. Then I'll achieve my goal—'Last American Woman Reporter in Vietnam.'"

"We should leave now. While there is time."

"Martin is still promising the city will never go," she said. "There might be more time." The American ambassador had lost a son in the war, and the end would force him, too, to face things he didn't want to face. Better anything than that. "You distracted me," Helen said, jumping up and going through the room to her film bag. She fumbled inside it and held up a thick envelope. "Guess what this is?"

"Then we're ready. Let's go now."

Linh swung his legs to the floor and sat doubled over, hands gripping the bed frame.

"Yes. Your 'Get Out of Vietnam Free' card. Now you have two letters, Gary's and the embassy's. Insurance. But I had to sit through a two-hour lunch listening to how the press are tools of Hanoi. No wonder we lost." She stood at the side of the bed, bouncing up and down on the balls of her feet, shaking her arms, trying to release tension.

"And what did you reply?"

"That photographs can't lie. I said, 'Make sure Nguyen Pran Linh gets to America, and as a bonus, I'll leave.' The country is going to disappear, be hidden behind a wall, and then the real stuff will start. All they want to talk about is identity cards, jumbled paperwork. How they have five different names on file for you."

"We need to leave now," Linh repeated.

"Not a moment past 'The temperature is 115 degrees and rising,' and the playing of 'White Christmas.'" This was the clumsy radio signal for the beginning of the evacuation. She ran her fingers over his forehead, trying to brush away furrows of fever.

Linh smiled. "Does it strike you as an obvious signal? I predict the whole of the NVA Army is bent over radios waiting for it. A great cheer will go up."

"Soon."

"If you want to stay, we'll stay." He touched her hand. "You're shaking."

"Tired."

He understood that this was an untruth, that she was afraid and running, and if he made the wrong move he would lose her. "Lie down."

"First things first." She readied the needle, gave him the injection.

Reluctant, knowing she had hours of camera repair work, she stretched out against him, shivering despite the heat.

After Linh had fallen into a drugged sleep, she got up and counted the ampoules of antibiotic and morphine left. A day's supply, bought at triple the normal going rate on the black market. But there was no more bargaining. By next week, there wouldn't be a black market for medicine at any cost.

Two days ago at the French hospital, the doctors had cleaned out Linh's wound while he sat on a rough wood bench in the hallway, the rooms all filled to capacity, no drugs available. The doctor told Helen she was on her own finding penicillin and gave her a list of what would work in a pinch. The bullet had gone in at an angle and torn tissue on its way. The doctor left the young nurse with a needle and told her to suture him up. She was inexperienced, and the stitches were wide and irregular.

"Take him home if you want him to recover. We have no medicine, no food. They are abandoning patients," she whispered.

Helen nodded, hired a cyclo on the street while two orderlies dressed in rags helped Linh out the door and down the stairs. His arms were outstretched, one on the shoulder of each man at his side, cruciform.

On a regular schedule, Helen swabbed out Linh's wound, relieved that it had finally stopped draining. The skin was swollen and red around the bullet entrance and exit wounds. It had taken her a full day of scouring the city to get untampered-with antibiotic in sealed bottles. From her days in the field, she had learned the signs that things were starting to go bad—the pallor of the skin, the sticking sweat that didn't dry. Linh was okay so far, although the fever troubled her. It was her fault he was wounded in the first place.

They had driven to the outskirts of the city to photograph what President Thieu was officially denying: that three million people had taken to the roads, refugees flooding into Saigon, that the South Vietnamese army was blocking entrance, trying to quarantine the city like a ship at sea. Thieu was blaming everyone else for his decision to abandon the Highlands. The mob scenes up the coast in Danang—airports overrun, people hanging on to the outsides of planes, weighing them down so they could not take off, women and children trampled—made everyone paranoid about the same disaster happening in Saigon.

From Martin down to her own contact at the embassy, the Americans were dazed by their impending loss and again forgot the Vietnamese. Negotiation was still considered an option, although the North Vietnamese made it clear they weren't interested. Helen had been trying to sell pictures about the plight of the demoralized SVA, but Gary had told her bluntly that after '73, when the American soldiers pulled out, Asian against Asian didn't make the front page. The world was bored by the long, brutal, stupid war. Until a few months ago, there had been only a skeleton press in the whole country, but now reporters flooded in, waiting for the handover so they could write up the finale and fly back out.

Linh had been angry the last few months, angry at the government's ineptitude, and, Helen suspected, angry at America's coming betrayal. A fait accompli that the North had won, the least the government should do was facilitate a peaceful handover, avoid a panic where more of the population would be hurt. The government paid lip service to preserving peace and order even as the authorities scrambled like rats to abandon the city. Linh's usual gentle temper gone, he insisted on proving Thieu's lies. "Turning soldiers' guns against their own people."

The cab had dropped Linh and Helen blocks from the barricades, and they slowly walked through the alleys to come up behind the SVA soldiers, the last vestiges of the government's power, armed and facing a sea of refugees. Men, women, and children dying from lack of food and water, and many, having nothing to lose, tried to break through the blockades of concertina wire and bullets.

They had been warned that no one could help them if they got in trouble. Linh flaunted the danger, and Helen got caught up in his anger as well. She was taking pictures of the crowd when there was a surge of people to the left of them. A young soldier who looked no older than fifteen panicked and unloaded a clip from his automatic rifle into the crowd. The recoil shook him like a giant shaking him by the shoulders, and he turned sideways in his effort to hold on to the gun. A bullet ricocheted off the wall of a building.

Linh kept walking, stumbled, walked on. This is the way one survived. The mind shuts down. He kept walking, swatting at the smudge of blood that was growing on his shirt, walking on as if he would die walking.

"Linh!" Helen cried. She saw the blood and pulled him down on the sidewalk, lifted his shirt. The wound was at the side of his abdomen. She pressed her finger against the hole and could feel metal as he grimaced. Relief that it hadn't gone in deep. Helen used his shirt to bandage it. She rubbed her bloodied hand against her pants. Ironic, given all the times they had gone on far more dangerous runs, but Helen, now as superstitious as the Vietnamese, knew there was only a certain quantity of luck in each person's life, and they had remained past theirs.

Now Helen woke up on the apartment floor, her hand rubbing against her leg, shaken by yet another nightmare. She got to her feet, stiff, and walked to the map hanging on the wall. After all this time the idea of Vietnam was still as distant now as it had been to her as a young girl when her father studied maps of French Indochina. She barely recalled his face, confused if her memories were her own or pictures of him, but she did remember him letting her trace the outlines of countries with her fingertip, and from that gesture, she had felt the conqueror's feeling of possession. Now she had spent ten years in a country, South Vietnam, that had not existed on his maps, yet none of it was hers. Within a very short time—days, weeks, months?—it would disappear once more.

She had not imagined herself outliving this war. The country deep inside her idea of who she was; she would tear out a part of herself in leaving it. Darrow had seen to that. He said she would never survive the way she had been, and she changed, gladly. The girl she had been lost in the Annamese Cordillera, the untamed mountains that rose up behind the Central Highlands and folded themselves all the way back into Laos.

They had been out photographing a Special Forces reconnaissance mission when he woke her before dawn. The patrol was still out, and they watched the sun rise up out of the east and color the western mountains from a dull blackish purple to green. So many shades of green, Darrow said, that Vietnamese legend told that every shade of green in the world originated in this mountain range. The emerald backbone of the dragon from which the people of Vietnam sprang. Until then she had been blind, but when she saw those mountains, she slipped beneath the surface of the war and found the country.

Linh sighed in his sleep, and Helen laid a hand on the thin, strong muscle of his arm, willing away bad dreams. The way his dark eyes followed her the last few days made her nervous. As if he suspected her heart. Long ago she had become more ambitious than feeling. She had fallen in love with images instead of living things. Except for Linh.

He moaned, and her nails cut red half-moons in her palm.

Her brother's death brought her to the war, but why had she stayed? Wanting an experience that wasn't supposed to be hers? Join a fraternity that her father and brother firmly shut her out of? What did all the pictures in the intervening years mean? The only thing in her power now was to save Linh. It angered her, his refusal to leave without her. An emotional blackmail. But she supposed that finally the last picture would get taken, even if it wasn't by her.

She picked up the camera and saw her face in the dusty lens, her features convexed. Was she to be trusted? She would kill for him, but would she also stay alive for him? An hour before dawn, her equipment clean and ready to go, her insides buzzed, a cocktail of lack of sleep and nerves. She fell asleep on the floor beside the bed.

They woke to the crumping sound of mortars on the edge of the city. She rose and was in motion, a prickling of adrenaline that she recognized when an operation was about to take place. Heating water for tea, swallowing a handful of amphetamines, she sponged herself off and packed a small carrying bag. Next to the door, she set down two battered black cases filled with film she had taken over the last week.

The last three years no one was much interested in pictures of a destroyed Vietnam. So Linh and she did humanitarian aid stories and began covering the ensuing crisis in Cambodia for extra money. Now Cambodia was off the list with the Khmer Rouge takeover. But when the actual fall of South Vietnam came, a photo essay recording the event would be very much in demand.

She had photographed the stacks of blackened corpses in Xuan Loc, had gone all over the city getting shots of the major players in the Saigon government, Thieu and returned Vice President Ky, who swore to stay and fight this time, while at their personal residences movers stacked valuable antiques— blue-and-white porcelain vases, peaceful gilded Buddhas, translucent coral and green jade statues carved into the shapes of fish and turtles—in the yard for shipment out of the country. And, of course, she had roll upon roll of the doomed people who had no special privilege, no ticket out. Looking at those faces, she felt a premonition like a dull toothache. Maybe inside these two cases she had finally pinned it down. Maybe these two cases would redeem her part in the war.

She stood by the window drinking tea, looking at the overcast sky, roiling clouds in varying shades from light pewter to the muddy, brownish gray of scorched earth. The breeze had turned sharp, the smell of rain and thunder promising a strong monsoon shower. Saigon was loved precisely because it was so unlovable—its squalor, its biblical, Job-like misfortune, its imminent, hovering doom.

At the sound of a creaking bedspring, she turned and saw Linh awake.

"What are you thinking?" he said.

"Time to go to the airport. Our bags are here. Your papers are on top."

"We agreed you would go to the docks, get shots of the boat evacuation. Then the airport."

"Does one more shot matter?" She spoke so faintly he could hardly hear her.

"Either they all matter or none of them did."

She nodded, unconvinced. "I have a bad feeling."

"We have plenty of time." He was reeling her back, gently, from wherever she had been.

Jittery, she moved over to the bed and unwrapped Linh's dressings. Skin puffy and inflamed, hot to the touch. It puckered over the nurse's crude stitches like yeasted dough. Helen bit down hard on her lip as she rewrapped him. A new hollowness around his eyes.

"Another shot of antibiotic even though it's early," she said. "I'll be back by noon. Leave the radio on. Listen."

Linh nodded but seemed distracted, and Helen feared he was getting worse. She helped him up to the bathroom and then back to bed. She would have to hire a cab or cyclo to move him. She placed a pot of tea and a cup in a chair next to the bed.

"I should skip Newport, and we'll just get started."

"Go," Linh said. Then he began to sing: "'I'm dreaming of a white Christmas. . . .'"

She smiled, but her mind calculated potential problems each way. She assumed she could get out at any time but worried Linh was getting too weak. The trip would be hard on him until he reached a medical facility.

"Hurry," he said. "Go have your final affair with Saigon. No regrets."

She opened the refrigerator, the only one in the building, and filled the pockets of her smock with rolls of fresh film. At the door she pulled the neck strap of her camera over her head, then buttoned her smock.

She opened the door but stood, still undecided. "If I'm late, have Chuong help load everything on a cyclo and go ahead. I'll meet you at the airport. Do you hear?"

He was silent, staring at the ceiling.

"Linh?"

"If you don't return, I stay," he said.

"Of course I'll return." The halfhearted ploy failed; he would not let her off so easily. "You just be ready."

"You got it, Prom Queen."

She pretended she had not heard him, banging the door shut and running down the splintering wood stairs that smelled of cedar and the sulfur of cooking fires. She was out into the street before she registered the continued absence of Chuong in the stairwell. That was what she had come to dread most, the continual disappearance of what she most relied on.

A cyclo stopped at a busy corner, and Helen jumped in before the driver could protest. After a wheedling argument, he grudgingly accepted three times the normal rate to go down to the Saigon River. People had decided to come out of hiding despite the twenty-four-hour curfew and the frequent pops of small-arms fire all around. A mile away from the port, the cyclo driver jumped off his seat and refused to go any farther. When Helen complained, he pointed a crooked finger to the solid wall of people. She got out, telling him she would pay double again his going fare if he waited an hour for her. Without a word, he calmly turned around and headed back downtown. Time more precious than money for once.

A rumor went through the crowd that two men had fallen into the water and had been crushed between evacuation boats. The fetid air smelled of unwashed bodies and fear. As Helen stood deciding whether to risk plunging into the crowd and getting caught out for hours, she spotted Matt Tanner behind a concrete barricade with another photographer. In the false camaraderie of shared danger, she was happy to see him. He waved her over.

"Madhouse, huh?" Tanner was tall and slope-shouldered, with a narrow, wolfish face, and when he laughed, which was seldom, he showed a forbidding mouthful of jagged teeth.

"This is new blood, Matt Clark. We're the two Matts."

"It doesn't look good," she said.

"Are you staying on, too?" the new Matt asked. He was young, with white-blond hair in a ponytail and wearing a black T-shirt with astrology signs all over it. She didn't like the vultures dropping in now and made no effort to hide it.

"Heading out this afternoon." Watching the crowd, Helen rubbed her hand along the rough concrete of the barricade, which was already crumbling. Cheap, South Vietnamese government-contract stuff that had been undercut for profit so much that it was already disintegrating back into sand from the constant humidity. For what USAID had paid for it, it should have been stainless steel. She looked down and saw a smear of red. The jagged edge had reopened the cut on her finger.

Tanner pulled out a handkerchief and wound it around her finger. "No need to shed blood. This isn't even your country."

"I forgot."

"The airport's worse than this. ARVN shooting at the crowd. Especially Vietnamese with tickets out. Hurt feelings and all, huh?"

"I hadn't heard that." A mistake to come. The embassy had told her it would be at least a week if not longer before the real squeeze began. Wishful thinking.

"If I wanted my ass out I'd head for the embassy, *di di mau,* quick quick. My guess is that it's today, and they're not announcing to avoid a panic. The hard pull is on."

Helen shook her head. She disliked the way he looked at her, the smugness of his smile. The press corps knew all one another's secrets, like an extended, dysfunctional family. Tanner used the long fingernail of his pinkie to scratch the inside of his ear.

"I meant to ring you up. Do you still have that Vietnamese working for you?"

"His name is Linh."

"A couple of us are staying on for the changeover. Cocktails on the roof of the Caravelle to toast in the victors. Macho stuff. We need someone to translate."

"He's going out with me." She looked Tanner in the eye, daring him.

He squinted back. "You two married?"

Everyone had suspicions but didn't know. Helen shrugged.

"Then, honey, I'd get there yesterday fast."

"Why are you staying?"

"Miss the biggest story in the world? You're right. Crazy." He looked out as the crowd swelled, then drew back. "To be frank, I'm thirty-five and haven't won the Pulitzer yet. If I don't come out of this place with it, it'll be damn hard to win back in Des Moines. I'll gamble being dead."

Her desire was to stay, work her way down to the water as the bodies were fished out, record the faces desperate to leave, but she found Tanner's reasoning so distasteful it made her decision clear. She bit the inside of her cheek as she put the lens cover on. The time she had banked on to get Linh to the airport was gone.

"Sorry you're going to miss the party," the new Matt said.

"Me, too."

Tanner looked at her hard. "Take care of yourself. You know, you've paid your dues already, right?"

Helen made her way back toward downtown, fighting against the stream of evacuees. A rushing river of people, each intent on his or her private fate, blind to those around them. Even though Helen stood a full head taller than most of the Vietnamese, she had a hard time avoiding being pushed back toward the docks. Men and boys shoved with their arms and shoulders; a middle-aged woman knocked Helen hard in the shoulder with a cart loaded up with belongings. Did they really think they'd manage to escape with their lives, let alone with television sets and curio cabinets? But she understood the instinct—too hard to let go of what had been acquired with such difficulty.

What did she herself take? What did she have to show for ten years of devotion? A kimono, cameras, a few old photos of a life now gone?

Farther away from the docks, the pull of the traffic lessened. People eddied around her as if she were a rock in a stream. Her body ached, spent and tired. She tried to flag down a cyclo, but all had been commandeered by families to haul away household belongings. So she began the long walk home. It was only ten o'clock in the morning.

By the time she walked through her own building's door, she felt as if she had been up for days, not hours. It had taken her twice the usual time to retrace her way home. On the first step of the stairway, the boy, Chuong, stood, his eyes big at the sight of her. He was one of the few plump street children, actually bordering on fat, and Helen felt chagrined that it was her money that led to his overindulgence in food. His red-striped T-shirt pulled tight across his belly.

As she opened her mouth to speak, they both heard a loud thud overhead as if something heavy had been dropped. They looked at the ceiling, but there was no further noise.

"Where did you disappear to?" Helen asked. "You've been gone for days."

"Many important things. This morning soldiers come to building. Looking for good American things to steal. I tell them everything already stolen. Just old Vietnamese man dying upstairs. They go away."

"Good," Helen said, fear feathering along her back, a quick shiver. Just as likely Chuong had led them to the building in order to "liberate" her things. She no longer trusted the boy, and now it was simply a matter of figuring out how dangerous he was. "You did good."

The boy held his ground on the bottom step like a cranky landlord.

"Oh . . . I'll pay you now." Helen pulled out a thick roll of piastres, as soft and crinkled as tissue. As they lost value each day, it took more and more paper, small, tumbling stacks, to get anything done. "Here. This will buy as much as your old salary."

The boy looked at the bills in her extended hand, unimpressed, licked his index finger and smoothed his eyebrows. "Very bad soldiers. Kill anyone who lie to them."

Helen took the rest of the bills out of her bag, paying out again as much. The piastres were almost all gone, but she figured they would be worthless to her soon anyway.

"Very good. You not number-one liar like other Americans."

Helen did not bring up the delicate matter that she was paying him even though he had not been there for days. To save face, she should press him on the point, but she had lost her will. For his part, he showed none of the gratitude he had when she first helped him, years ago. Now she received only a smirk. Before she could ask him to commandeer a cyclo for them, Chuong jumped off the step and brushed past her, out the door.

Inside her apartment, the air was blue with the opulent scent of incense. Linh sat stiffly in a chair by the window. He never turned his head at her arrivals, and she always felt a small disappointment at this indifference.

"How're you feeling?" she asked.

"Did you get your pictures?"

"Sure." She put her arms around his neck. "I got them." Instead of sweat and ointment, his skin smelled of soap. "Were you up?"

"Better. A shower and some packing."

She knelt next to his chair and stared out at the flutter of red blossoms in the heavy, wet wind. The twisting gray branches bent under the corpulent flamboyant flowers, crowded so tightly not a hint of green leaf was visible.

"The rains are early this year," Linh said. "The tree is blooming early."

"The same time as last year. And the year before."

"It seems early," he said.

"I wish we could stay in this room and never leave it," Helen said.

A gun lay on the floor next to the wall—the source of the sound she had heard in the stairwell. But she wouldn't ask, just as Linh didn't press if she got the boat evacuation shots. The usual delicate dance they did around the truth. Her truth was she longed to hide in this room, become invisible. As if the flimsy papered walls and thin door could save them. Out on the streets, without her camera, she felt vulnerable. No one knew of her panic attacks.

What internal price she paid for exposure. Preferable to be shot through a door or curtain and to have the source of death anonymous and to die in privacy and alone.

Helen went to the table and mechanically labeled the rolls of film she had taken the day before. Nothing extraordinary. Or rather the extraordinary had become ordinary. Linh had repacked the film cases much better than she. On top lay a folded white shirt, as perfect as in a store display. When she saw the hopefulness of the neatly creased folds, a fresh shirt to begin a new life, she had to turn away. And then it took over as if steel had entered her bones. Everything, including love and fear, squeezed out of her body, and all that was left was determination.

"Chuong told me about the soldiers," she said.

"What soldiers?"

"They came in downstairs. He sent them away."

"No soldiers came. I watched from the window since you left."

Helen nodded, still surprised at her own naïveté. "Were you going to guard the apartment?" she asked, pointing her chin toward the weapon.

Linh studied the gun as if seeing it for the first time. "If they came, I planned to kill myself."

Helen sucked in her breath. No matter how long she had been in Vietnam, she still took things lightly, like an American. Linh's quick acceptance of the worst case reminded her that it was not as hard to be brave with the promise of helicopters waiting to whisk you to safety, to home.

"We're going now."

She gave Linh the last two shots of morphine, hoping it would last till the embassy and American doctors could give him more. She put on her smock, retied a scarf over her hair.

As she picked up the two cases, the corner of one gave out, spilling out film rolls. The cases were worn and battered, the cardboard corners turned mushy. Helen had patched them with electrical tape, the only thing that didn't disintegrate in the humidity. "Just a minute," she said, running to get more tape and wrap the corner.

"Why don't you get a new case?" Linh's face set in impatience. The case was just another example of her difficult ways, her willfulness that was putting them both in danger. Yet he knew if he pushed at all, like a high-strung horse, she would balk.

"I know. I will," Helen said, using a knife to cut the last tail of tape off. Like everything else, it had been provisional, meant only to last out her time there, but like everything else, the provisional had become permanent. Linh slung their tote over his good shoulder. She locked the thin wood door of the apartment, leaving the lamp with the red shade burning, and hurried down the stairs, but Linh took the steps slowly, stopping briefly on each landing. By the time she reached the stairwell, the journey before them had changed as in a fairy tale, grown difficult beyond imagining.

Outside, they plunged into a stream of people and were carried along. The ruttish noise deafening. Families argued over which direction to go, children cried, dogs barked, and on top of it all was the impatient blaring of horns as vehicles tried to force their way through. Far in the background, like the steady thrum of a heart, the sound of bombs exploding. The image of a bloodthirsty army approaching closer and closer made each person jog instead of walk, push instead of wait. Like a fix, Helen ached to pick up her camera and start shooting. What was the point of living through history if you didn't record it?

Linh walked steadily, but his limp was more pronounced with his weakness, and there was a pallor to his face, his skin wet with a sweat that didn't dry. Helen took a deep breath to keep her panic down, her mind calm. The biggest part of her job as a photographer to make the minute calculations between getting the picture and getting killed, a skill that she took refuge in, honed into instinct. Yet she had ignored her instincts, following the embassy's assurance that things would unravel slowly. Cutting that timeline in half had still been too lenient. Yesterday, when she had been told the city wouldn't be lost, that all Americans and dependents would get out in time, she should have run to the airport.

Down Tan Da, a street usually full of restaurants, metal bars were pulled across all the doors and windows.

Hard to walk close to the buildings because of the mounds of garbage, hard to walk in the street without being run down. Helen moved ahead of Linh, navigating the easiest path through the debris that littered the street.

Broken glass crunched underfoot. People dropped or abandoned things as they went. Clothes everywhere, plastic bags bulging with household goods, pieces of furniture and old rusted bicycles, a sewing machine and a frayed bedroll.

Helen guided him to the wall of a building, and Linh crouched, holding his side, and took deep breaths, huffing out air through his open mouth. She watched him suffer and hated herself more each minute.

"You okay?" she asked.

"More air."

She felt his drenched shirt. "Give me the bag."

"You already have the cases."

"We'll move faster."

Linh nodded and handed her the tote.

The traffic stopped ahead, some kind of checkpoint. Helen helped Linh into a doorway of a building and left the bags with him.

Five minutes later, she came back, her face stern as she grabbed the bags. Linh noticed her hands trembling. "Come on, let's turn around. Some ARVN colonel types are trying to catch deserters. Executing them on the spot. I don't want them getting hold of your papers."

They retraced a block and headed down a side street off An Dong Market. Along the sides of the road, more and more old people squatted on the ground, their faces closed down with despair. Children shivered at street corners despite the heat, eyes blinking hard and hands holding tight to whatever toys or clothes they carried, separated from their families. Almost a Danang. It always seemed to come to this moment in a war when the strong fought to survive and the weak fell. Civilization a convenience for peacetime.

Inside her head, a clock ticked off the minutes they were losing. Her shoulders already hurt from the weight of the film cases. Everyone knew Ambassador Martin was delusional, hiding in the embassy, afraid to call it quits. But Helen had calculated that when the hard pull finally came, the U.S. military wouldn't dare leave until every American and all the related Vietnamese staff were taken out. They could never afford that kind of bad publicity. Days if not weeks of flights. Not like the British embassy that flatly abandoned its Vietnamese staff. Impossible to anticipate the breakdown of the city within hours, having to make it all the way on foot, with bags and a weakening Linh. It wasn't supposed to fall apart like this.

Two blocks over from An Dong they turned up another street parallel to the checkpoint, weaving back and forth through alleys to avoid soldiers, wasting precious energy. Helen got lost and left Linh several times while she rechecked major street names. Halfway up Tran Hung Dao, at the front of a loose crowd of people, gunfire sounded behind them. The crowd panicked, trampling those in front, and Helen was shoved hard against her back, knocking her down on her hands and knees. She reached for Linh, and together they scrambled to the sidewalk, pressing themselves behind an overflowing garbage bin. Linh sat on the sodden ground, chest heaving.

Helen moved to the front of the trash bin and looked back south to the head of the street. There were about ten men, drunk and swigging from liquor bottles. Dressed half in uniform, half in civilian clothes, unclear if they were ARVN trying to melt into the civilian crowd or the local *coi boi,* cowboys, thugs, masquerading as soldiers in order to loot with less interference. They fired into the crowd and laughed as they watched people trample over one another in their desperation to flee.

One of them was dressed in a satin shirt that hung down over camouflage pants with army boots. He pointed a rifle at a group of women cowering on the opposite side of the street from the garbage bin. The men surrounded the girls, pulled one away from the rest and pushed her into the deep alcove of a doorway.

Helen looked up and down the street, hoping for some diversion to rescue the woman. Nothing she could do without getting herself and Linh killed. The always present "white mice," city police, usually on every corner, now nonexistent.

Her only means taking out her camera, ready to shoot.

An older woman from the group, a mother or aunt, screamed and ran forward toward the alcove, and one of the soldiers shot her. Captured on film. The curse of photojournalism in a war was that a good picture necessitated the subject getting hurt or killed. Helen blinked, tamped emotion.

The men gathered the rest of the women together, guns trained on them, probably planning to execute all witnesses. A frame. The girl from the alcove ran back into the group, face bloodied, pants torn. A frame. One of the men with an angry blade of a face. Frame. He jerked his head around, making sure no one saw what they would do next, and then his eyes locked on Helen across the street. A frame. And another.

"*Dung lai!* Stop!" he shouted, and the men abandoned the women and ran across the street with their guns aimed. The women, forgotten, clambered away.

Helen stood up. "*Bao chi.* Press. The press is to have protection."

Everything went black. When she came to again, she was flat on the ground, the rough surface of the street like nails in her back, her face covered in a warm liquid that turned out to be her own blood. The one who had rifle-butted her in the head screamed and pointed to the camera with his gun, but he seemed far away, everything seemed very far away, and Helen separated from herself, detached, amused by the absurdity of his shooting a camera. Didn't he realize there were always other cameras? Her only thought that these men must be soldiers because normal street thugs wouldn't care about pictures. Another soldier, his face round and childlike, with a sprinkling of acne across the cheeks, came and held the point of his rifle so close to her temple she could feel the heat from the muzzle, could tell it was the one used on the dead woman across the street.

Time unraveled. Had she passed out again? She finally found it, a sense of peace after all these years; for whatever reason, she was unafraid, and wasn't that something remarkable for a poor little scared girl from California? Maybe it was no worse than closing a book. But then everything tunneled again to the present. Again, she was on the street and sick to her stomach. The asphalt under her head, tar from the street, garbage, and the acrid smoke of a fired gun, although she no longer remembered one firing, and she felt a childish fear that she would die in a foreign place.

The Vietnamese believed the worst way to die was far from home, that one's soul traveled the earth lost forever, but this place was as much her home as California, she had lived out some of the most important moments of her life here, and if that didn't qualify a place as home, what did? She knew retired military men who had come back to live in Vietnam, married Vietnamese women, and fathered children, with no intention of ever leaving, who still considered Ohio home. That was wrong. California was infinitely far away. California was gone. Even her dreams were shaped by this land—rice paddies stretched flat to the horizon, mountains and jungles, fields of green rice shoots and golden rice harvests like rippling fields of wheat, lead curtains of monsoon rain, bald gaunt hides of water buffalo, and, too, Saigon's clotted alleyways, the destroyed tree-lined avenues, the bombed-out, flaking, pastel villas, even their small crooked apartment with the peacocks and Buddhas painted on the door. The battered, loving, treacherous people. Her heart's center, Linh. An undeniable rightness in ending here.

A blinding flash of white, an explosion, and when she looked up at the soldier with the child's face, he was gone, or rather partly gone, half his head and neck scooped away, and then he toppled, bouncing up off the pavement an inch before settling back down to the earth. The thugs were silent, suddenly sobered, a pack of feral dogs, and with the capriciousness of the violent, one by one they turned and jogged away.

Helen pulled herself up and turned her head, a tendril of pain curling up her neck, and saw Linh sitting braced against the wall, legs tucked against his chest, the gun from their apartment balanced on his knees. What toll had been exacted from him in saving her over and over again? A roll of the dice. Helen knew the soldiers could have just as easily decided to shoot them.

Her last bit of shiny luck used up, now there would be only the rattle of her empty bag with each step.

The women returned and surrounded their shot friend. Taking her remaining camera out of one of the cases, Helen went over and crouched, taking pictures of the outstretched woman. Staring up at the lens, eyes dark and empty, hiding a secret. One of the women moved a hand in front of her. Without thought, Helen batted it out of the way. Risking her own and Linh's life, she'd earned this one and took the shot. Her due. The women enclosed their friend. After a moment, a wail.

Now Linh struggled to get up on his feet; no protest when Helen lifted the two black cases and their tote. They ran.

After a block, they slowed down to a walk, and after another few blocks they both stopped to catch their breath. They hobbled. A small spot of blood spread on his shirt.

"I need water," he gasped. They searched the surrounding storefronts in growing desperation, and in that panic, that low point, she heard the beating of helicopter wings, as beautiful as a piece of music, and she craned her neck to see over the buildings. The sound was still far off. She smashed the glass door of a restaurant, went to the bar, picked up a glass from a neat row of them turned upside down, and filled it with water from a clay cistern on the counter.

The spot of blood had doubled in size. She pulled out a clean T-shirt from her bag. "Hold this against it." When he finished the glass, he quickly turned away and retched. She picked up the film cases again but left the tote behind, unable to bear the weight on her shoulders and neck any longer.

They walked, this time more slowly, so slowly that any of the old people along the streets could have kept up.

Her head throbbed from the rifle butt, and she fingered a crust of dried blood in her hairline. Should she discard the two black cases to keep moving on? But it was as if she were abandoning each person captured on a frame of film. She remembered one shot in particular, a baby that had been trampled by the crowds of refugees on the outskirts of town. The guards had set up barriers right next to the body without touching it. He lay on his side like a small animal curled up in leaves in a forest. Myriad stories like this. This human being already gone, except as a dark spot on a lighter background of negative. If the print were published, the child would achieve some kind of immortality, however flimsy. Each of those kinds of pictures diminished the taker.

Helen hefted the straps higher on each shoulder, skin rubbed raw, and kept walking.

Linh held an arm across his stomach and picked up a walking stick lying in the street.

"Put your hand on my shoulder," she said.

They walked down the center of main thoroughfares now, incapable of taking the more roundabout route of small streets and alleys. Luckily, hardly a vehicle was on the road anymore. If soldiers or *coi boi*s came upon them now, they would be unable to run away. The traffic thinned even more as they approached the residential section where the American embassy was located.

Here the streets appeared deserted, and she felt cheered that the hardest part of the ordeal was nearly over.

Linh collapsed against the trunk of a large tamarind tree. The neighborhood was old here; the branches arched over the streets in an umbrella of shade. Many of the trees on other streets had been chopped down to make room for tanks. A pair of helicopters came in, and Helen saw them clearly now down to the runners, heard the throbbing of one as it hovered over the embassy grounds, waiting for the first to land.

"We're close now," she said and squeezed his hand.

He leaned against the tree, holding on to it to stay upright, his face as wet as if he had just doused it with water. The blood spot on his shirt was as large as an outstretched hand. He gave her a stiff nod.

"We can't stop again," Helen said. "Next stop is inside."

This was as bad as her worst patrols, each step an act of will, the urge to lie down overwhelming.

A block away from the embassy, a new noise joined the cacophony of helicopters and distant artillery. A silky, rustling sound, constant yet changing like the rolling of the ocean. Helen and Linh turned the last corner and came to a standstill.

A sea of bodies spread before them, not an inch of ground empty, bodies limited only by the buildings they were crushed against, from the front of embassy gates to the other side of the boulevard. Not a static, passive crowd, but a turbulent ocean of people eddying around motorcycles and islands of stacked suitcases, people surging and dashing themselves up against the solid metal gates of the embassy front like waves crashing against the rocks of a forbidding coast, breaking and falling back onto themselves.

Helen stood, numbed by the sight of Americans locking themselves away, fleeing. She glanced at Linh, who barely registered the turmoil around him. If he lost consciousness, it would be over for both of them.

"Give me the gun," she said.

Too weak to argue, he handed it off to her. If anyone used it, it would have to be her. Helen took off the safety and placed her index finger on the trigger. In all her years in-country, she had never carried a weapon, had refused to make a decision to defend herself. Yet Linh had just killed to save her.

Shouldering her way into the back of the throng, moving toward the side entrance, her fingers firmly locked around Linh's wrist, she figured even if they made it inside, the film cases would have to be sacrificed at some point along the way. But not without a fight.

The first people who felt the pressure of her pushing turned with angry glances but shrank away once they saw her.

She looked down to her blood-covered smock, realizing it wasn't her own blood but the child-faced soldier's. Her stomach flopped. She wanted to rip the smock off, but there was hardly room to lift her arms. If she released her grip on Linh, he might go down under the feet of the crowd. So she let go her grip on the gun, dropping it into her smock's pocket, and reached up and pulled the black scarf off her head. She wiped dried blood off her face, wiped the smock, then let go of the scarf and watched it suspended between the bodies of people before it disappeared from sight as if in quicksand.

In the hot wind her hair blew, and the faces around her registered the fact that she was an American, or at the very least a Westerner, and more compelling than resentment was their realization that staying close might be a ticket out. "Make way for the dying American, make room for the dying American." And so Helen and Linh were surrounded and nudged through the crowd, and after two hours they were pressed into the grillwork of the side gate.

She felt delivered, grateful for the Marines with their crew cuts and black-framed glasses, elated at the sight of their uniforms and reassured by the M16s across their chests that rendered her own attempt at self-protection ridiculous. Almost delirious, head throbbing, legs like paper, she realized that she was still on the wrong side of the gate, the guards so overwhelmed they didn't see her.

All around her voices were raised to the highest pitch—pleading, Vietnamese words falling on deaf ears, begging in pidgin English for rescue. People bargaining, trying to bribe at this too-late hour with jewelry and gold watches and dirty piastres pushed through the bars of the gate, valuables flung inside in this country where wealth was so scarce.

A man close to Helen held out a baby. "Not me. Take my baby. Save my son." He would pay one million piastres, two million, and as he met silence

on the other side of the gate, he cried and said five million, five million piastres, money that he had either amassed over decades or stolen in minutes. He
opened a sack and shoved bundles of the bills through the gate to obligate
his son's protectors, unaware that to these Americans his money was worthless, less than Monopoly money, that these soldiers were scared of this dark-
faced mob, unable to grant safety even to one baby, that all they wanted was
to protect the people already inside and escape from this sad joke of a war
themselves.

Helen's arm jerked down as Linh collapsed behind her, his legs buckled,
and she screamed in Vietnamese, forgetting, languages blurring, then realizing her mistake, screaming in English, "Let us in. I'm American press."

The Marine's head turned at the sound of her words. "Jesus, what's happened to you?"

"Let us in."

"Open the gate," he said, motioning to the guards behind him.

As the gate opened, more Marines came to provide backup, aiming automatic rifles into the crowd.

The guard put a hand against Linh's chest. "He can't come."

"He works for the American newswires. He's got papers."

"Too late for papers," he said. "Half the people out here have papers."

"Damn you," Helen screamed. "This man was just wounded saving my
life."

"Can't do it."

"He's my husband."

"I suppose you have a marriage certificate?"

"He stays, I stay. And if I get killed by the NVA, the story of the embassy
refusing us will be in every damned paper. Including your name."

The guard's face was covered in sweat, already too young and tired and
irritable for his years. "Shit, it doesn't hardly matter anymore. Get in." He
came out a few more steps, grabbed Linh, then Helen, and flung them inside like dolls. The man with the baby tried to grab Helen's arm, but the
Marine punched him back into the net of the crowd. As they passed through
the gates, five or six Vietnamese used the chaos to rush in. They scattered
into the crowd, invisible like birds in a forest, before the guards could catch

them. Guns fired, and Helen hoped they had been fired into the air. No more blood on her hands this day. With a great metallic clang, the gate shut again.

The lost opportunity frenzied the crowd outside. Heads poked over while Marines stood atop the walls, rifle-butting bodies off.

Inside was crowded but calmer. Americans stood by the compound buildings while Vietnamese squatted on every available inch of grass.

They were searched and patted down. "Ma'am, you'll have to turn that in."

Helen looked at the guard bewildered until she realized they had found the forgotten gun in her smock. Not only that, but she had managed somehow to keep both film cases. The guard led her over to the compound swimming pool, where she tossed it in to join the fifty or sixty guns already lying along the bottom.

"I need a medic," Helen said.

The guard nodded and went off. Helen grabbed Linh's shoulders and supported his weight as he lowered himself and stretched out on the ground. The front of his shirt was soaked in blood. Several minutes later an American in white shirtsleeves came over with a black kit. "You hurt, miss?"

"Not me. Linh was wounded a couple of days ago. He's bleeding."

The man helped unbutton Linh's shirt and unwrapped the bandages. "I can clean him up, but he needs attention from doctors on ship."

"How long before we go?" Helen said.

"They'll call you."

Helen nodded.

"How about I look at that bump on your head? Looks like you might need some stitches yourself. Don't want a scar."

Hours passed. Helen and Linh sat on the grass, propped against the film cases. Papers were being burned inside the compound buildings, the endless secrets of the war, smoke and ash drifting in the air, settling on the people, the ground, on top of the water in the pool like a gray snowfall. After the adrenaline wore off, Helen was bone-weary. She nibbled on a few uppers, then brought warm sodas and stale sandwiches from the makeshift food service operating out of the abandoned embassy restaurant.

"We made it," she said. "Happy, happy."

"Still in Saigon. We just managed to crawl into a new cage." Linh held his side, his face drowsy with dull pain.

Helen leaned in close to him. "I pushed it too far, but it all worked out. No damage done."

"No damage."

"When I took the picture of that woman, I was angry that the shot might get ruined. And then I thought, What have I become?"

Linh shifted and grimaced at the pain. "Just be with me."

"I want to."

"You didn't start this war, and you didn't end it. Nothing that happened in between is your fault, either."

Helen's face was expressionless, tears running down it, without emotion.

"You don't believe me." He wiped her face dry, but already her attention was slipping away. "None of it had anything to do with us. We're just by-standers to history."

The sky darkened. Linh's head rolled to one side as he fell into a deep, drugged sleep. People near Helen worried about the Marines being able to keep back the crowd outside. The Vietnamese going out were classified as dependents of the Americans, although for the last decade the Americans had depended on them to survive in this harsh country. Traitors by association. The number of people per flight was minuscule compared to those waiting, like taking water out of a bucket an eyedropperful at a time.

The noise from the helicopters was deafening, but in between Helen could hear the distant rumblings from Gia Dinh and Tan Son Nhut, a constant percussion that matched the throbbing in her head. The noise much closer than this morning; lifetimes seemed to have passed in the intervening hours. Linh trembled in his sleep.

An embassy employee walked by, and Helen stopped the man. "How much longer? This man needs medical attention."

"Could be all night." He looked at her sternly, tapping his pencil on his notepad for emphasis. "Americans are being boarded now. Especially women. Go inside. He'll be taken care of later."

In the convoluted language of the embassy, trouble. She woke Linh, tugging him onto his feet, harnessing the straps of the film cases around her neck. They joined the end of a long line going up the stairs to the roof. She flagged one of the Marines guarding the entrance. "I need to get this man on a helicopter."

"Everyone takes their turn."

She rubbed her forehead. "No. He's been shot. He's going to die without medical attention."

"There are a lot of people anxious to get on the plane, ma'am. I don't have any special orders concerning him."

A rumpled-up man with a clipboard came up. He was in his twenties, with a beaten-up face that looked like he hadn't slept in a week.

"I'm Helen Adams. *Life* staff photographer. This is Nguyen Pran Linh, who works for *Life* and the *Times*. He's wounded and needs immediate evacuation." Helen figured under the current circumstances no one would find out about her lies, the fact her magazine had pulled her credentials. Weren't they trying to kick her out of the country, after all?

He scribbled something on his clipboard. "Absolutely." He scratched his head and turned to the Marine. "Medical evac. Get someone to escort them to the front of the line. And get someone else to explain why to everyone they're bumping in front of. Tell 'em he's a defector or something."

"You're the first person today who's actually done what he said," Helen said.

"I'm a big fan of yours, Ms. Adams."

"I didn't know I had any."

"You covered my older brother. He was a Marine in 'sixty-eight. Turner. Stationed in I Corps."

"Did he—"

"Back home running a garage in Reno. Three kids. The picture you took of him and his buddies on the wall. He talked about meeting you. I've been following your work since."

"Thank you for this. Good luck," she said.

"We're going to need a whole lot more than luck."

One Marine carried the film cases and another half-carried Linh up the jammed staircase. They went through a thick metal door and more stairs, waited, then climbed up a flimsy metal ladder staircase and were on the roof. The air filled with the smells of exhaust and things burning, a spooky camp-fire. To the north and west, Helen saw the reddish glow of hundreds of fires and the few streaks of friendly red tracers going out against the flood of blue enemy tracers coming in. The odds visibly against them. The throbbing of her head had become a constant buzz, but she didn't want to take anything, wanted her mind to keep clear.

The helicopter jerked down onto the roof, landing like a thread through the eye of a needle, and her body went rigid. The beating rotors and the screaming of the engine so loud, the Marines shouting unintelligible board-ing instructions that she didn't have time to explain to Linh. His eyes flut-tered half-closed. A young man from one of the wires stood next to them, going out on the same flight.

The Marines signaled their group to move out, and they crouched and ran under the hot rotor wind. At the helicopter door, Helen grabbed the young newsman's arm.

"Get these to someone from *Life* on board the ship."

"Sure. But why?"

"I'm going out on a later flight." Until the words fell out of her mouth, she hadn't accepted that she had made room for this possibility.

The Marine started heaving the film bags on, the tape coming loose and hanging off like party streamers. "Hurry up, people. Ma'am, get on."

Helen backed away. Her stomach heaved, sick in soul.

"Look after him," she yelled to the stranger. "His name is Nguyen Pran Linh. He works for *Life*. Get him a doctor immediately."

Linh looked up confused, not comprehending Helen wasn't boarding. When he did, he struggled back out of the helicopter. "You can't—"

"Stop him!" Helen screamed, backing away, blood pounding in her ears, sick that she was capable of betraying again. The Marine and the young man forced Linh back inside and buckled him in. She watched as, weak as a child, he was strapped into the webbing, saw his head slump to the side, and was relieved he had passed out. She ran to the helicopter, crouched inside, begged a pen and scribbled a quick few lines on paper. She put his papers and the note inside a plastic bag, tied it with a string around his neck, the same way she had handled the personal effects of countless soldiers.

In front of the waiting men, Helen bent and put her lips to Linh's forehead and closed her eyes. "Forgive me. *Em ye'u anh.* I love you."

Back out on the landing pad, the wind whipped her hair and dug grit into her skin, but the pain came as a relief.

The Marine stood next to her. "Get on the next helicopter out. Everyone here is not going to leave."

"What about them?" she said, shrugging her shoulder at the great filled lawn below.

"Better a live dog than a dead lion. And they eat dogs in 'Nam."

The helicopter's door closed, and the Marine crouched and guided Helen back to the doorway, and he shook his head as she made her way back down the stairs.

Helen stood on the lawn and watched the dark bulk of the machine hover in midair for a moment, the red lights on its side its only indicator. Because of the danger of being fired on, the pilots took off in the dark and used projector lights on the roof only for the last fifteen feet or so of the landings.

A mistake, she thought to herself, a mistake not to be on that helicopter. Wrong, wrong, wrong. Her insides tingling electric as if there were bubbles running through her blood.

As much as she had prepared herself for this moment, she was at a loss. What was she looking for? What did she think she could accomplish? If she had not found it yet, what were the chances that a few more days would change that? She had always assumed that her life would end inside the war, that the war itself would be her eternal present, as it was for Darrow and for her brother. The possibility of time going on, her memories growing dim, the photographs of the battles turning from life into history terrified her.

Blood had been shed by one side; blood had been shed by the other. What did it mean?

The helicopter swayed and the nose dipped, a bubble of shuddering metal and glass, and then it glided off across the nearby tops of buildings. Safe. Tiny and fragile as an insect in the night sky. Helen felt bereft, betraying Linh, and all she could hope for was the cushion of delirium before he realized what she had done.

The Vietnamese on the grounds of the compound grumbled about the length of the wait, complaining that the Americans were not telling them anything but "It'll be okay. You'll be taken care of." When they protested their thirst, the Marines directed them to the pool. The sight of Helen standing outside on the grass reassured those close-by—obviously the evacuation wasn't over until every American, especially a woman, was gone.

Helen dreaded a repeat of the mob scene outside, the potential for it to turn violent, and made her way to one of the outer concrete walls of the compound and lay down on the cool, dead grass under a tree. The roaring grew quieter and quieter, the calming outside conflating with her state inside, until she almost felt herself again. In the middle of chaos, she slipped into a deep sleep and woke up to rusty clouds of smoke passing the faint stars and moon.

She took her camera, attached a flash, and began taking pictures. The Vietnamese watching her grew visibly disgruntled. A journalist wasn't a real American; everyone knew they were crazy.

In the early hours of the morning, when many of the evacuees had fallen into a disjointed sleep, Helen noted a thinning in the ranks of Marines on the grounds of the compound.

An hour before dawn, the last perimeter guards withdrew, and as Helen followed, taking pictures, the barricade slammed down and was bolted—a final rude barking of metal—locking her and everyone else out. The first to notice the lack of guards were the people still outside the embassy, who had never gone to sleep, who remained frantic and now tore at the gates. The people inside the compound heard the roar and rushed the building only to find tear gas and a steel wall between them and escape.

Canned dreams and cynical promises crushed underfoot like bits of paper.

The outside gates were scaled and burst open from the inside as the last he-licopters loaded on the roof. People poured in, flooding the compound in a swell of rage. Helen took a picture of a Vietnamese soldier aiming his machine gun at the disappearing helicopters, pulling the trigger, tears running down his face. Bullets sprayed the night air now tinged by dawn to the east. Understand-ing that their chance was gone, the crowd destroyed and looted. Helen watched a small Vietnamese woman haul a huge desk chair upside down on her head out the compound driveway. A man left with a crate of bagged potato chips.

A shabbier conclusion than even Darrow had foretold.

Now she walked through the same gates unopposed, ignored, made her way home down the deserted streets as if in a dream. Too incredible that the whole thing was finally over. Rumors were that the NVA would arrest any Western journalists and shoot them on the spot, the "bloodbath" that the Americans warned of, but she figured the reality would fall something short of that.

She came alone to the moon-shaped entrance of the alley, puddled from rain, then entered the narrow, dark throat of the cobbled path. At her crooked building, she looked up and saw her window lit, the red glow of the lampshade, and her heart, not obeying, quickened. Their old signal when Darrow had come in from being in the field. Except that he had been dead seven years now. With Linh gone, time collapsed, and it felt strangely like the start of the story and not the end. Exhausted, Darrow would be sleeping in their bed, damp from a shower, and she would enter the apartment and go to him.

She reached the lacquered Buddha door and found the brittle wood crushed in at knee level as if someone had kicked it hard with a boot. After all this time to finally be broken now. No one bothered stealing from this build-ing. She wondered if Chuong had done it in spite after they had left. She ran her fingers over the worn surface, now splintered, touching the peacocks and the lotus blossoms that signified prosperity and long life and wisdom. She looked at the various poses of the Buddha in his enlightenment. Saigon in utter darkness this last night of the war. A gestating monster. Her letter to Linh had been simple: *I love you more than life, but I had to see the end.*

This was the way one lost one's homeland. The first things lost were the sights, then the smells. Touch disappeared, and, of course, taste was quick to follow. Even the sounds of one's own language, in a foreign place, evoked only nostalgia. Linh had no memory of the final helicopter flight over Saigon. No feeling of this being the end of his war. When he tried to recall anything, he saw, or rather felt, the beating of the rotors overhead in slow motion, like the pulsing of the wings of a great bird. A heartbeat. Darkness, then blinding light, then darkness. A strong mechanical wind that drove small bits of stone and dirt into his skin as he was pushed into the belly of the bird. Her broken face.

There was the familiar lifting of the helicopter, stomach dropping into feet, but for the first time he didn't feel his inside righting itself after gaining altitude. He feared he might be dying, afraid that in lifting off from the embassy roof, his soul had dropped away. The images of his family, mother and father, brothers and sisters, Mai, Darrow and all the countless others, all passed before his eyes. And Helen had slipped between his fingers at the last minute, lost. Idly he wondered as he flew through the night if it might not be better to die right then.

The American ship rose and fell with the waves, but despite his fever, Linh held on to the railing. After the doctors had bandaged him up, he slowly made his way on deck. The sick room reminded him of a coffin. The medication they had given him made him faint-headed, but he had to see the sky, breathe the air.

He squinted to see the last of the dim landmass like the humped back of a submerged dragon through the hazy air, but the ship had already begun the long journey to the Philippines. He could not tell if it was the shadowy form of land on the horizon or merely the false vapor of clouds.

Superstition held that if one traveled too far from one's birthplace, one's soul would fly out and return home, leaving one nothing more than a ghost, but if that were true the whole world would be filled with nothing more than wanderers, empty shades. Women's superstition.

He felt an isolation that would grow to become a new part of him, an additional limb. Among the Americans on board, he was a Vietnamese, but even among the refugees, he had little in common. Most were happy to have escaped. Some had sacrificed everything, including families, to be on board. But he had never taken sides. His only allegiance was to Helen, and she had forsaken him.

A young man walked up to shake his hand, and Linh had a dim memory of his face aboard the helicopter. A full, childish face with skin too tender and unformed for a beard.

"Shouldn't you be down below?" the young man said. He had been moping around for hours, sorry for himself that he had missed the war and thinking of how to make an interesting story of the little that he had seen. When he saw Linh, his eyes lit up with possibility.

"Do you know where Helen is?" Linh's legs were shaky, and he gripped the railing to keep standing.

"Not to worry. I gave the cases to a reporter from your office. They're being transferred as we speak. I had no idea who she was. Man, she's a legend."

"Is she on board?" Linh repeated, sterner, closing his eyes with the strain of thought in his addled brain.

"No, not on this ship at least, no. Isn't she staying to cover the changeover?"

Linh said nothing, simply looked into the opaque blue surface of the water. He had suspected that she might try such a thing, but he never guessed that she would try it without him.

"I just arrived in Saigon two weeks ago." He glanced at Linh hopefully.

Linh remained silent. Over the years, he had doubted her love, if that love could only exist in war, if she insisted on staying partly because their love was only possible in his own country. But now he knew that she did love him. Clear now that she was as dependent as any addict on the drug of the war. He had underestimated the damage in her.

"I mean, I hurried! Left the day I graduated college." He laughed. "And I missed the whole damned war."

How would Linh manage to get back to her?

"Maybe we can talk? Later? When you're feeling yourself? Fill me in. What it was like? I found out who you are. You've worked with everyone."

Linh made a sweeping gesture with his hand, letting go of the railing, his legs slipping out from under him.

The young man grabbed him as he was about to slide under the railing. "Watch it there, mister! You're coming with me down to sick bay." He took Linh's arm. "That was close."

"I'm fine," Linh said, although it was obvious to them both he was too weak to stand alone.

"Sorry, but I'm responsible for you. Don't worry about her. Rumor is she's charmed. They'll probably be kicked out of the country within twenty-four hours. She's well-known. The Communists don't want any bad publicity."

Linh closed his eyes and saw sun-bleached fields of elephant grass, the individual blades prostrating themselves, bowing over and over in supplication. That was how one survived, and yet Helen had never learned to bow.

"What they don't want are any witnesses to what happens next."

Angkor

1963

Once there was a soldier named Linh who did not want to go back to war. He stood outside his parents' thatched hut in the early morning, the touch of his wife's lips still on his, when he smelled a whiff of sulfur. The scent of war. This part of Binh Duong was supposed to be safe. He had heard no shots, but nothing remained secure for long in Vietnam.

Mai's voice could be heard rising from inside the hut, defiant, rising, the song tender and lovely among the tree leaves, threading its way through the air, a long, plaintive note spreading, then the flourish of the trill in the refrain that they had rehearsed over and over. An old widowed man, coming out from his hut on the other side of the river, stopped at the sound, which was like a bow gliding across a reed, recalling his own beloved wife's face, a tight rosebud from forty years earlier.

> For the river, we depend on the ferryboat
> For the night, on the young woman innkeeper
> For love, one suffers the fate
> Of the heart . . . I know that this is your village.

The war was a rival stealing her husband away. Mai peeked through the door and sang clearer. Wanting to lure him back into her arms. As if they were in their school days again, and she could seduce him to miss classes and go to the river for the day, listening to her songs. The war would end soon. If she could only keep him with her, he would be safe.

Ca, Linh's youngest brother, appeared at the side of the hut and mimed Mai's performance, putting his hand delicately to his cheek and holding his legs primly pressed together while throwing out his hip like the French chanteuse in Dalat they had made fun of. Linh and Mai burst out laughing.

Mai's tears too painful, Linh had forbidden her to see him off, her belly large with their first child. A boy, the midwife had predicted, because of how high she carried the baby—tight under her heart.

The night before, the family had performed the play Linh had written, and the villagers had stomped the ground and hooted and gotten drunk in approval. Linh still felt a warm tingle of pleasure in his hands and face at the thought of its success, but Mai had not let him enjoy a minute of it. The roaring audience demanding she sing her solo four times had emboldened her, and she wanted to leave for Saigon that very day.

"How can I leave? A deserter? They shoot deserters."

"They shoot soldiers, too." Mai held her belly, a hand at each side, and took deep breaths with her eyes closed, a new habit that unnerved him. "They have no time with poor soldiers like you. In Saigon, we'll use false names. After the baby is born, I'll get a job singing."

Linh didn't know what to do; he wanted to be a simple man, but fate pulled like a weight on his shoulders. He steeled himself with the thought that he was going off to fight so there would be no war in his son's future. Mai didn't understand that the families of deserters also suffered. Nor did he tell her that her sister, Thao, was already on her way to Saigon, even though her voice was many shades rougher than Mai's. If she had known, the earth would have broken open with her wails, and Linh couldn't deal with women now.

This is how history unfolds: a doubt here mixed with certainty there. One never knew which choice was the right one. . . .

He tested the air again to catch the reek of fired weapons, but the odor was gone. Had it been real or only his imagination?

At thirty years old, Linh had already been in the army for four years. He had joined the northern army, then escaped to the South only to be conscripted by the SVA. A lackluster soldier. Sick of the war, but an able-bodied man had no other choice if he wished to stay alive. The flowing robes of a poet suited him better than the constricting uniform of a soldier.

Mai thought he should become a singer, a kind of matinee idol, to make the women swoon. She did not acknowledge how the years of soldiering had changed him—the slight limp from a piece of shrapnel in his foot when he was tired; the look in his eye, a new uncertainty. He was like a man with a golden tongue who is suddenly asked to conduct business in an unknown language.

His father had been a scholar, a professor of literature in Hanoi, and in his youth, Linh had shown a passion for writing poetry and putting on plays. But the war squeezed out everything else. Every young man was forced to take sides, either the northern or the southern army. Sometimes, over the years, one ended up fighting for both sides at different times. A paradox, he would later discover, the Americans could not accept.

Wounded in the foot, for a time he gladly traded in his gun for an army clerical job near his family. The workload was light, his paperwork never collected, and pretty soon he no longer bothered with it but went back to plays. A romantic young man, always dreaming, he hoped he had somehow slipped between the cracks, been forgotten. He and Mai planned their escape to Saigon, but he couldn't tell her he delayed because he was afraid. After almost a year, his father's bribe money ran out, and his company had informed him it was time to pick up a gun again.

Linh posed in front of a mirror in his uniform, playing the part of soldier. Squaring his chin. He wanted to look brave but thought he looked more confused than anything else.

Mai's fears were partly true. The last time he had left he had not seen his

family or his new bride for two years. When he left now, there was no knowing when he would see them again. He lifted the large bag of rice cakes Mai
had given him. Her instructions were to come back before the cakes were all
eaten.

The Americans had started to join the SVA on missions as advisers. Giant, they towered above Linh and the other soldiers as they handed out sticks
of gum and cigarettes. Linh learned to recognize the Americans because
they smiled more than the French, and because of their perfect, straight,
white teeth. Always impulsive, Linh immediately decided these new foreigners were an improvement over their old masters.

The advisers stood with their legs spread apart, feet planted in big boots,
and hands on their hips, nodding and conferring with Linh's captain, Dung,
who everyone knew was a fool. He wore a long white silk scarf around his
neck, copied from some old American movie, and the majority of his attention was spent in keeping it clean. Jaws snapping with chewing tobacco, the
Americans stood over the felled bodies of two Viet Cong, their bodies as
small and gray and lifeless as river birds, their tattered black shorts barely
covering their thighs. Did it escape everyone's notice that the South Vietnamese soldiers more resembled their enemies than their allies? After all his
years in the army, Linh still could not bear to look at the dead, and he hurried off to check supplies.

The first American Linh met was Sam Darrow, a tall, birdlike man who
didn't smile like the others. Darrow, slouched over, still stood taller than the
other Americans. Thin, he had sharp limbs that jutted out from his rolled-up
sleeves, the skin stretched across large, bony wrists. His thick-framed glasses
were a part of his face, head moving from side to side like a bird's, as if trying
to add angles to what he saw. Linh stared at the name, DARROW, and another
name, LIFE, stenciled on his jacket. Cameras that Linh had only dreamed about
owning hung from around his neck, one on an embroidered Hmong neckband, one on plain leather.

"Come on," one of the advisers yelled. "Take some snaps of us."

Dung checked his hair in a small gold mirror that he pulled from his pocket. He preened as Darrow sauntered over.

"I don't think . . ." he said.

"Don't worry about thinking," the adviser said. "Take a picture."

"You got it."

Darrow took off the lens cover and carefully checked the film. Then with a barely perceptible flip of the middle finger, he opened the aperture all the way so that the film would be overexposed, ruined. For the next ten minutes, recognizing what Darrow had done and the fact that none of the others had a clue, Linh could barely breathe as he watched Darrow pose Dung all around the camp, even going so far as to have him mug over the bodies of the two corpses. "That should do you," he said, rewinding the film, snapping the cap back on, smiling at last.

"Does America train in war better than it trains in photography?" Linh said.

Darrow smiled. "A smart guy."

"I'm Linh. Tran Bau Linh."

"You, Linh, are a sly one. How about if I ask Dung over there to assign you to help me today? Keep our little secret?"

The company decided to make camp that night about half an hour from Linh's village, planning to move out in the morning. They had not even gone to sleep when the first bombs went off nearby. The new advisers used their shiny new radios to call in for an air bombing of the surrounding area. Linh would never talk about the events of that night. The memory burrowed deep inside him and remained mute.

This is how the world ends in one instant and begins again the next.

The only way Linh knew how to make the journey from his old life to a new one was to take one step, then the next, and then another. Now, when there was nothing left to save, he deserted. No longer caring what they did to him, he continued on the highway south, unmoored, for the first time in his twenty-five years of life utterly alone. Each day he ate one of Mai's rice cakes, until the supply began to dwindle, and then he broke them in halves, and as the number grew smaller still, he broke the cakes into quarters and eighths, until finally he was eating only a few grains a day of Mai's cakes, food that tasted of her and no one else, and then finally even that was gone.

During his first months in Saigon, he wandered the streets, working as a waiter in a restaurant, a shoeshine boy, a cyclo driver. No family, the things that had weighted his life buried. At night he felt so insubstantial he held his sides to make sure he himself didn't blow away like a husk. The smells and tastes and sounds of the city entered him, but they did not become a part of him. His only thought was to earn enough for food and shelter, no more. By accident, he had lodged into an eddy of the war—to think of the future or the past was to be lost again.

In this vacuum, he grabbed for the lifeline of attending English lessons every Tuesday and Thursday afternoon on his neighbor's balcony. Although he was already fairly fluent from his father's lessons, Linh went because it made him feel like a child again. Too, there was a more serious purpose: Linh's father had been proficient in both French and English, telling his sons that in order to defeat them one must always know the language of one's masters.

The teacher needed the small amount of piastres she earned giving lessons to support herself and her parents. She was a pretty young woman, the shape of her face reminding him of Mai. The hours he spent looking at her were like balm, and he made sure not to let his English exceed hers. Her mistakes charmed him. Instead of using "Don't," she said, "Give it a miss." "Don't go down the street" became "The street, give it a miss." Dreaming of Mai, he wanted to give waking a miss.

In those first terrible months he listened to his sweet-faced teacher conjugate verbs: *I am, you are, he is.* The plan he came up with was to rejoin his unit in the army and volunteer for the most dangerous missions. Possibly managing to get killed within months if not weeks. *We are* peaceful, *they are* the enemy. *We* kill; *they* die. Honorable and efficient death. And yet although he was no longer afraid, he did not go.

On a day neither too hot nor too cold, when the sky was clear, and the sweet-faced teacher smiled at him on the stairs, Linh passed the office of an

American news service and stood rooted to the spot as he recognized the name *Life,* handwritten on paper and taped to the window. A talisman from the day his real life disappeared. Give it a miss, his first thought, but instead he took this as a sign and walked in. He found a large American man hunched over his desk, his face shiny with sweat, staring at a stack of papers.

"You have a job?" Linh said. "I am a good friend of Mr. Darrow."

Gary, the office manager, looked like the heat was boiling him from inside out; his potbelly pushed against his belt. He looked up at Linh and gave him a wide-toothed smile. "I didn't know Darrow had any friends." Always, he thought, in the nick of time, look at what the cat drags in. Within ten minutes, Linh was hired. That afternoon they were on a cargo plane bound for Cambodia.

Gary chewed away rapid-fire on his piece of gum, mopping at the sweat that literally poured off him with a big, soggy handkerchief. "Man, this is good. How did you find us? That office is just a temp space. This is like fate, kismet. If it wasn't for you, it would be me lugging around his stuff." Gary figured the young Vietnamese man's reticence covered up something unpleasant that he would have to deal with later, like a criminal record. Too bad, he couldn't worry about that now. He had a new assistant.

Linh said nothing. He stared out the cargo door at the jungle rushing beneath them, giving no sign that his stomach was in his feet, that this was the first time he had been in a plane.

They drove the empty, hacked roads, dust flying like a long sail of sheer red silk behind them, hanging suspended in the coppery sky.

"You're right, absolutely. Enjoy the ride," Gary said, agreeing with the continued silence. "People talk too much anyway." He was a man who didn't let his ego get in the way of the job. People didn't question him as much if he acted like a cowboy and so he did just that. How could he operate if the staff guessed that he sweated each assignment, felt like he was sending off his own children? Unfazed by Linh's silence, he had changed his mind about him being a criminal. Probably something far worse. The whole damned country was shell-shocked as far as he could tell. At least he had maybe bought himself a few weeks of peace from his prima-donna photog.

By the time the jeep reached Angkor Thom, the sun throbbed like a tight drum in the late afternoon. Villagers were handling a jungle of equipment—cords snaking over the dirt; large sheets of foil scattered along the ground, heating already hot air to scorching; tripods splayed like long-legged birds; film floating in coolers; and in the middle of it all, directing the chaos like a maestro, stood Sam Darrow.

Gary handed Linh a bottle of lukewarm Coca-Cola and promptly forgot him, leaving him standing in a group of Cambodian workers. One man, Samang, grumbled that the sodas had been dumped out of the coolers so that there was more room for the film. His brother, Veasna, tapped him on the calf with the leg of a tripod. "Complainer. But not when there is a tip."

Linh sat in the shade, apart, and watched as Darrow painstakingly looked through his camera set on a tripod, moved away to make an adjustment, looked through the finder again, and at last pressed the cable release to snap the shutter, taking exposure after exposure of a bas-relief overhung by a cliff of rock that cast shadows on it. The joke among the workers was why so many pictures of a rock that hadn't moved an inch in thousands of years? Linh calculated it would take more than an hour to go through a roll of film at that rate, the job potentially endless. Darrow made minute changes after each frame with infinite patience. Three men held a long piece of reflector foil, changing the angle an inch at a time.

During a break, the workers collapsed into the shade. Samang gossiped among his coworkers that the Westerners would kill them by working through the heat of the day. Darrow bellowed out a laugh and with his long strides moved to greet the new arrivals. He was even taller and thinner than Linh had remembered, as if his figure had attenuated during the months that had passed. Or had Linh's misfortune bent him? Made him smaller in the world? He recognized the American's large bony wrists.

Earlier at the office, Gary had drummed on his desk in joy when Linh said he had worked with Darrow. Everyone in the know avoided working with his star photographer, and Gary had been on the verge of locking up the office to go hump equipment himself when Linh turned up. He would not look this gift horse over too closely. Past assistants quit because Darrow insisted on covering the most dangerous conflicts, carried too much equipment, and worked them endless hours.

"You're as red as a lobster!" Darrow said.

"The climate's killing me. Look who I found!" Gary used a flourish of hands as if producing Linh out of smoke, trying to cover the sham. "Nguyen Pran Linh. Am I good or what?"

"Sure." Darrow smiled and offered Linh a cigarette and a piece of gum. This was a land of nuance, the outright question of where they had met before unspeakably rude. Content to wait, Darrow dipped his bandanna in the cooler water to wipe his face. The afternoon had been long and peaceful, but with the sound of Gary's jeep he felt a black weight descend on him. He cocked his head, moving slightly side to side, trying to place Linh. "How are you, my old friend?"

"Why don't you make foil shields for each side instead of lighting only from underneath?" Linh took the cigarette and lit it quickly so the shaking of his fingers would not be noticed.

Darrow let out a big laugh. "My technical expert from Binh Duong. Of course."

Linh smiled but said nothing.

"You really do know each other?" Gary asked.

"Why would you bring someone who I didn't know?" Darrow said.

Gary looked back and forth between the two men. "You're one funny guy. That's what I love about you. He's going in with you to the delta and Cu Chi. Lots of good stuff there. Cover stuff, you know? Another Congo. How can one man be so lucky? Chop, chop."

"Got it." A mixture of feeling angry and tired, and something else—a strange, gauzy sensation that Darrow recognized as fear. Did Gary sense that he was hiding out? Trying to forget about Henry? That he was waiting for something? A sign that things were safe again? Why didn't Gary go hump through Cu Chi and risk getting his ass blown off? Instead he pimped another inexperienced local off the street as his assistant. Darrow's business was faces, but he hadn't recognized this one—Linh had changed so drastically. The guy had been dipped in hell.

"So how much longer, you think?" Gary asked as they walked back toward the jeep.

"Till I get the picture." He played Gary, pulled his chain, unfairly resenting the push. After all, it wasn't his fault—this crisis of nerve. Henry broke the illusion that they were charmed because they carried cameras instead of guns. It would pass. Darrow had been through it before. Just a matter of waiting it out. The accumulation of deaths and horrors and jitters that got him. The curse of curses was that he was good at war, loved the demands of the job. What was frightening was he had developed an appetite for it. Like a starving man staring at a table of food, refusing to eat on moral grounds; appetite would win, and his shrewd boss counted on that.

Gary stopped in front of the jeep, and in a gesture of bravado slammed his hand down on the trunk. He barely kept himself from wincing and crying out in pain. "It's going down now, man, and you should be the one getting it. This old pile of rocks will still be here when the war's over."

Darrow wagged his head. "Did you know that the French who discovered Angkor asked the peasants who was responsible for creating it? They answered, 'It just grew here.'" More and more it seemed to him a possibility just to sit out the war where he was.

Gary wiped his face and shook his head. "That's truly crazy."

"You never know."

"How's that? Who cares about this tourist crap? Just hurry back home, okay?" Gary tapped the driver on the shoulder to start the motor. "And take it easy on this new guy. My hunch is that he bullshitted me to get the work. Let's put it this way—there's no waiting line for the job."

"Sure you don't want to spend the night? Hang out a couple of days?" The truth was he liked Gary's callousness, his will to do anything to get the picture, because that was the way Darrow used to be. And he didn't want to be alone another night, and didn't have much faith in Linh as a drinking buddy.

"Yeah, that's right. That's what I want to do, hang in this godforsaken place—Angkor What?"

"The gods will strike you for that."

"Add it to the list, baby. I don't care how good the stuff is you're smoking. Get me back to Saigon with air-conditioning and ice cubes. Headquarters is busting me about hiring women, you think you have problems?"

"I'm hurt. Thought you'd want to watch a genius in action." Darrow slapped his palm against the jeep hood.

"Don't take a week? Right?"

"Hurry, Gary. Get out of here before the sun goes down and the monsters come out."

After the jeep had left, the silence settled back down on the place like dust, but the black weight that was the suck and pull of the war had arrived, and it pressed down on Darrow's shoulders. He should tie himself down to one of the big stones to keep himself there, to avoid Gary's siren call. He smiled into the shade where Linh was standing. Too bright; he couldn't make out Linh's expression. The day he met him had indeed been dipped in hell, Darrow assigned to cover the joint operations as American advisers walked the SVA through a basic search mission. When they were fired on, the advisers called down airpower, but it dropped short, falling on them and civilians. A free-for-all clusterfuck. The SVA panicked and started firing on their own people, on civilians instead of the enemy, who had probably long retreated. The next day as they reassembled, the man assigned as his assistant was AWOL, nowhere to be found. He had seemed an unenthusiastic soldier. Perhaps he had used the chaos as an excuse to slip away. Perfect, Darrow laughed out loud, finally the type of assistant he deserved.

For the next week, Linh lived in the jungle side by side with Darrow. They rose at dawn, ate a simple breakfast of rice, fish, vegetables, and the dark Arabic coffee Darrow had become addicted to in the Middle East, insisting on brewing it himself. They worked all through the day with a crew of a dozen men, including the two brothers who were his favorites, taking hundreds of exposures, spending hours to light a subject, sometimes to the point of sending Veasna shimmying up a tree to strip foliage that was blocking the sun. One day, Veasna spent five hours picking half a tree away, leaf by leaf. He came down dehydrated, and Linh fed him glass after glass of water while Darrow hurried to get the right late afternoon light.

Darrow figured at that rate, he could spend the rest of his natural life photographing the grounds and never have to see another dead soldier. Yet at night they could hear thunder on the horizon, the war's pulse, beckoning.

The two men shared a small room like a monk's cell, crowded by a mountain of photographic equipment Darrow insisted on cleaning and moving it into the room each night so none of it would be stolen. Veasna usually stayed behind to help clean, while Samang hurried to town to chase women.

"So, Boss," Veasna said. "You get me good job?"

"I'll certainly put in a word for you in Saigon," Darrow said.

"No, Saigon. I stay number one in Cambodia."

"But there's nothing here. No war."

"Less competition then."

Often Darrow stumbled across Linh in out-of-the-way corners, writing on scraps of paper that he quickly put away when approached. He caught glimpses of words and was surprised they were in English. His little AWOL friend a never-ending mystery. Nights in the stone city, when the workers returned to the village, seemed haunted to Linh. Darrow worked away, oblivious to his surroundings, the obsession of his work keeping him from the luring obsession of the war, but Linh felt ill at ease in this mausoleum. In the stillness, the place swarmed with gliding shadows. He, Samang, and Veasna took their meals in the village. Veasna talked about how the Cambodian traditional life was being ruined by the royal family, how they needed to return to the roots of the village, the communal life of the family. He said Samang had gotten corrupted by spending time in Phnom Penh. Linh stayed to drink tea and talk with the other Vietnamese and Cambodians on the project. Many talked of broken families, hardships, and escaping across the border to avoid being conscripted into the army.

The first night Linh came back too early and saw a woman from the village leaving Darrow's room. The lamplight outlined her figure as she stood out-side, as full and rounded as the carved *apsara*s on the walls of the temples. Darrow came to the doorway and pulled on the cloth around her hips, reel-ing her back inside. After that, Linh made sure he did not come back till midnight.

"Where are you so late?" Darrow asked when Linh came in.

Linh did not like this man's disingenuousness.

"Found a girlfriend?"

"I'm married."

"Sorry. Of course not." Darrow nodded. "Stay for dinner sometimes. I like conversation. And I cook."

"You have friends."

Darrow smiled. "Lovely, huh? My God, lovely. Naked, she's the replica of the ancient statues here. Brought to life. As if no time had passed since this place was built."

One hot afternoon, the air as heavy as stone, Linh sat alone on a terrace far away from where they worked. They had been up since before the sun to capture the light on the buildings at dawn. Sleepy, eyelids weighted, Linh heard only the stillness, broken by the occasional shrill cries of the monkeys who scampered across the warm stones in search of offerings of fruit. The monkeys were feared. They bit and sometimes were rabid, and the workers trapped them and roasted the healthy ones for meals.

He had knotted a piece of jute rope and slipped his hands through the circle, then proceeded to twist so that the rope bit a tighter and tighter figure eight around his wrists. At each tightening, he felt a burning and then relief, his mind filled only with the white-hot sting of his wrists instead of the deeper pain that was always there. So preoccupied by heat and pain, he did not no-tice Darrow passing by.

Darrow disappeared and then returned minutes later, drenched with sweat. "How about it?" he called to Linh from across a courtyard. Pretend-ing ignorance, he climbed the stairs in his big, loping gait, carrying two beers. Linh was so dazed he did not notice Darrow's heavy breathing, did not know that Darrow had run back to his room like a madman, torn open a cooler, grabbed two beers, then run back.

Bound, he nodded, too late to hide the fact of the rope.

Darrow leaned over with a knife and cut the twisted rope between the purpled wrists. Acting as if it all were the most normal thing in the world, he then pried the caps off the bottles and handed one over. He'd noted the freshness of the scars when Linh first arrived. Darrow knew the wreckage of war. "Let's talk."

Linh rubbed his hands against each other, felt the tug of his callused palm, blood slow like sand through his veins.

"You were Tran Bau Linh last we met. An SVA soldier."

"That man is dead. Now I'm Nguyen Pran Linh."

"Okay."

"I shouldn't have lied that I'd worked for you."

Darrow rubbed his face. "A cursed day, the day we met."

"Yes."

"Does this"—Darrow waved his hand at the rope—"have to do with that night? You disappeared."

Linh looked away. "I do good work for you?"

"Best assistant I've had."

"Is that the price to keep my job? To tell you?"

Darrow took a long sip of his beer and looked across the nearby jungle. "You don't trust me yet. That's okay."

"You're happy here?" Linh asked.

"Like getting a chance to explore the pyramids. Gary's a good guy, but he doesn't get it. I've had enough war, you know? Hell, of course you know. Just can't quite get around to quitting. So whatever your reasons for being here are, okay by me."

Linh took a slow sip of his beer. "You think you are in a peaceful paradise here. But you're hiding in a graveyard. Their violence is simply past, ours is happening now. Each stone laid in place here is laid on top of blood. Violence all around you, but you don't recognize it. It's easy for you—you don't belong here."

"I didn't make the war. I was just a mediocre photographer, headed toward wedding shots. War made me famous."

"What about duty?"

"Far as I can see, you don't belong, either. Officially disappeared." Darrow stared at him. "So why not run?"

Linh bowed his head and was silent so long Darrow thought he would not answer.

"From what happened to me, there is no running. 'Which way I fly is hell; myself am hell.'"

Darrow was speechless at his Milton-quoting, AWOL soldier-turned-assistant. What in the world more would he find out about this man?

On their day off, Linh woke to the usual smell of cardamom-scented coffee being brewed but then smelled something else—sweet like the French bakeries in Saigon. He found Darrow outside nursing a skillet over an open fire.

"Pancakes," Darrow said, not turning. "My wife sent me a box of mix. It even has dried blueberries in it. And a bottle of Vermont syrup. Get a fork."

"You're married?"

"She thought it would make me homesick. You know how women are."

"I'll never get over my wife's love."

Darrow looked at him. "I'm sorry . . ."

Linh waved away the apology. He didn't want to be one of those people who couldn't stand another's happiness. "She would make my favorite, *banh cuon,* rice cakes, each time I left."

When breakfast was ready, Linh looked down at the golden cake on his plate, the brown puddle of syrup.

"Dig in!" Darrow said.

Linh took a bite and gagged. The texture and the sweetness and the flavor, all peculiar. He poked at the blue pools of fruit in the cake with the prongs of his fork and felt queasy.

Darrow ate a stack of five cakes, along with cup after cup of coffee. "This takes me home."

When he turned away, Linh threw the pancake into the bushes behind him. When Darrow turned around again and saw the empty plate, he smiled and plopped another on it, despite Linh's protests. "You're turning more American by the minute."

Later in the morning, Veasna had a question about drop dates, and Darrow was nowhere to be found. After searching for an hour, they finally tracked him down to where he stood in front of the carved stone face of Avalokiteshvara, the Buddha of Compassion. Motioning Veasna away, Linh watched Darrow study the sculpture—blank, unseeing eyes, serene smile of the lips, the chips and cracks and lichen, shadows that changed the expression as the sun crossed it—until nightfall. Linh could work with such a man.

At his usual late hour, Linh returned from the village and stretched out on his mat. Darrow, as always, wide-awake and reading. Glass of scotch at his side, he insisted Linh join him with a small glass. Linh wet his lips with the alcohol—he would have drunk it even if it was poison to please—then closed his eyes and felt the walls spin. When Darrow came across interesting parts in his book, he read them aloud, regardless of whether Linh, muddled with drink, had fallen asleep or not, so that Linh acquired his knowledge of Mouhot's history of the ruins in dreamlike segments. He would never be sure if the stories were real or his imagination.

The king of Cambodia, along with an entourage that numbered into the thousands, went elephant hunting through the dense forests northeast of the great lake, Tonlé Sap, in the year 1550. In some places, passage was so restricted that his slaves had to cut away vegetation and trees in order to pass through. They came upon a particularly thick, overgrown place through which they could make no progress. Finally they realized these were solid stone walls beneath the dense foliage—the outer wall of Angkor, rediscovered by the Khmers after having been forgotten since the twelfth century.

One day when work had finished early, Darrow rounded the corner of a building and ran straight into Linh, who quickly stuffed a scrap of paper away into his pocket. "What are you writing all the time?"

"Nothing. Scribbled poems, stories."

"Really?"

"I used to write plays."

"Let me read them? You write in English, don't you?"

Linh looked down, his skin flushed. "Sometime, yes, maybe." His hand a firm *no* over his pocket. When he came to his room to go sleep that night, he found a new thick spiral notebook and a package of ballpoint pens on his mat.

Finally, the last picture taken, exposures packed away in their cans, Darrow could not prolong the inevitable any longer. Finally he would go. He would not starve himself any longer, but must gorge himself on war. On their last day, as the trucks were loaded, he walked among the workers, handing out small gifts. Veasna and Samang were nowhere to be found. Since Linh had taken the morning off, Darrow went into the village alone with only a translator. He hoped to catch a glimpse of the young woman who came nights, who fed him the soft-fleshed jackfruit and mangosteens, but knew he could not ask for her. He wanted to make the brothers a farewell gift of an old Rolleiflex that he had taught them to use. Unable to find anyone, Darrow had the translator question the villagers. Long minutes of back-and-forth, indecipherable, while Darrow sat on a rock, sweating and swatting at flies that he hadn't noticed while he was under the spell of his work. A shaking of leaves, and the young woman appeared from behind a banyan tree. She leaned against the trunk and rubbed her hand against her thigh, a smile on her lips, and Darrow felt twice as bad about going. Finally a shrug from the translator.

"What?" Darrow said in a raised voice. His irritation, a breach of etiquette. The girl's hand dropped from her thigh, and she hurried away. Screw the camera, more than anything else he had an overpowering urge to run after her for one last meeting.

"Samang die of snakebite two days ago. Veasna is in mourning." The brother had been climbing the side of an overgrown wall of the ruins when a cobra lurched out and bit him in the thigh.

Darrow slapped at the air. "Why didn't anyone tell us? We have anti-venom. A doctor is only a few hours away."

"He die fast. Not want to bother you."

Shaken, Darrow returned to the camp, slammed his belongings into bags, the spell of the place broken—the girl, the temples, the pancakes—all of it ridiculous and driving him crazy; he just wanted to get back to real work.

Linh walked in and considered him.

"You heard about Samang?" Darrow snapped.

"It is sad."

"Not sad! Stupid. Ignorant. It didn't need to happen. Forget this place."

"Samang could have been working on other job when the snake found him."

"But he wasn't. He was on my job."

Linh picked up his bags. "I'll go check equipment on the trucks." He turned away, then turned back. "He was very lucky, doing his duty, earning to support his family. You should give the camera to Veasna. If he does well, he can earn money. That is all that matters to Samang now."

Darrow snorted and shook his head. He shoved a heavy case out the door with a hard push of his foot. "I hope *I'm* not as lucky as Samang." He grabbed a towel and wiped off his face, put his glasses back on. "Damn unlucky in my book."

"And then there is the young lady you entertained. Their sister-in-law. Widowed with two small children to feed. It would be thoughtful to give her some money so she could do something besides sell her body to foreigners."

The Europeans, upon finding Angkor, refused to believe that the natives could have built the original temples. Briefly they entertained the thought that they had found Plato's lost city of Atlantis.

The young woman dropping pieces of warm fruit into Darrow's mouth had given him a false sense of understanding that was lost again, that did not transport to the modern world, where a syringe and a dying man were separated more by fatalism than actual distance. He felt like that ancient king hacking through the jungle, stone walls of his own treasure barring his way.

Before leaving Angkor, Linh dropped a sheath of torn-out notebook paper on Darrow's lap.

During the reign of King Hung there lived two brothers, Tam and Lang, who were devoted to each other. They were orphaned at a young age and came to live with a kind master who had a beautiful daughter. As they grew up, both brothers came to secretly love the girl, but the master gave her hand in marriage to the older brother, Tam. The young man and woman were blissfully in love, so much so that Tam quite forgot about his younger brother, Lang.

Unable to stand his unhappiness anymore—the loss of the two most important people in the world to him, and his jealousy at their happiness—Lang ran away, and when he finally came to the sea and could go no farther, he fell on the ground and died of grief, and was changed into a white, chalky, limestone rock.

Tam, realizing his brother was gone, felt ashamed of his neglect and went in search of him. In despair of not finding him, he stopped when he reached the sea, sat down on a white, chalky, limestone rock, and wept until he died, changing into a tree with a straight trunk and green palm leaves, an Areca tree.

When the young woman realized that her husband was gone, she went in search of him. Worn out, she finally arrived at the sea, and sat down under the shade of an Areca palm, with her back against a large white chalky rock. She cried in despair at losing her husband until she died, and changed into the creeping betel vine, which twined itself around the trunk of the Areca palm.

"Yours?"

"A famous legend of Vietnam. As best as I can remember. So you begin to understand where you are."

"It's sad. Tragic."

"These are our national symbols. We are a people used to grief. Expecting it even."

When they returned to Saigon, Gary paced the office with a summons from ARVN headquarters demanding Linh's immediate appearance. The identity papers he had submitted were all faked. "I knew it. I knew you were too good to be true. Who's Tran Bau Linh? Huh? They think he's a deserter from the SVA."

"Hell if I know. Linh's worked for me the last year."

"How's that since I introduced you a few weeks ago?"

"A year. I'll go down and talk to ARVN. You know with a little grease, they won't care."

Linh followed Darrow outside. "How we met . . ."

"We've worked together for a year."

"You are sure?"

"Want to go soldiering again?"

"No."

"A little flattery and some pictures of the boss go a long way. I noticed how late you stayed out so you wouldn't run into my friend." Darrow squinted in the sunlight, breaking into a grin. "We make a good team. No one is exactly begging to work with me."

When Linh became Darrow's assistant, the war was small and new. A bush war, a civil war in a backwater country. The American presence was the only thing that led Darrow there, a reluctant last stop before retiring from the war business.

They sat in the gloom of rubber trees in Cu Chi, the Iron Triangle region, after a firefight. Linh had stood up to get the picture, before Darrow knocked him down, and small bits of shrapnel had nicked him in the face and neck. Even the Leica he had been shooting with had been damaged. Darrow bent over the medic, making sure he cleaned out the half-moon-shaped nick on his cheek. "Now you have a beauty mark. Women love scars."

"I can fix the camera," Linh said.

Darrow took a long drag on his cigarette. "Don't see how."

Linh picked up spent shell casings and a metal fork. Darrow watched him, amused.

"Where'd you learn that? SVA doesn't teach that kind of stuff."

Linh shrugged.

"You're the onion man. Peel back a layer and get another mystery."

"No mystery."

"I've read the NVA train photographers to work under any field conditions," Darrow said.

"I've read that also."

Darrow laughed. "They pose shots. Making heroes. Unlike us. We're showing the truth."

The rest of the company was out of earshot, but still Linh spoke softly.

"Make believe that a man's father, a professor at the university in Hanoi, fought the French to free our country. And the French became the Americans. And the Nationalists became the Communists. And pretend the son learned to fix a camera with casings and a fork for the North, but that he found their promises to be lies. He escaped but was made to fight for the SVA. And pretend that after all this time fighting, all he wanted was to flee the war. If this was true, would you take this assistant?"

"Why doesn't he run away?"

"He is tied to his country." Linh rubbed his hand over his wrist.

Darrow took another drag on his cigarette, handed one to Linh. "This man has suffered enough. I'd be proud to work alongside him."

Linh turned away. He could not help feeling he had lost face by telling so much, and yet he knew the Americans expected this, needed this abasement to feel comfortable.

"Question?" Darrow said. "This imaginary man who worked in the North, did he ever see Uncle?"

"I imagine . . . yes." The more one told, the less real the story seemed.

"Where?"

"Outside Hanoi. Visiting a friend who served as a guard. A tiny village, just a few huts strung along a canal. A small vegetable garden, and he was bent over the rows for hours, weeding. All alone. He was only in his fifties but was sick with TB and looked ancient. Just a glimpse. He was just an old man weeding his garden. Hidden because he was in plain sight."

They went out with an LRRP (long-range reconnaissance patrol) unit on patrol into a guerilla-dominated province. Darrow favored these small, specialized units who went native because they allowed him to understand the nature of the particular place better than the larger units that turned everyplace into an American base. Special Forces had agreed to let Darrow go along on the condition that there would be no mention of the mission, no pictures. He knew from past experience it was worth it simply to get the lay of the land even though it drove Gary crazy.

For days they walked in silence in the dim claustrophobia of jungle, not coming across another human being. Day melted into night that melted back into day. They lost track of time, staking out spidery trails, unable to move or talk—the only sound rain slapping against leaves.

Linh thought of the blank stone faces at Angkor staring out at nothing. Centuries passing without a single human voice intruding. Relieved by the sheer physical exertion, at night he sank down to the earth, asleep; in the morning he woke to find his hands clenched around his wrists, the skin bruised and chafed. The effect of the patrol on Darrow was unexpected. Maybe it was the time away at Angkor, sharpening his eye. After all the wars he had covered, this place spoke to him. The quality of the light on young American faces in this ancient land that was by turns beautiful and horrific. He had found his war.

The patrol spent the night in a small clearing, a village of six huts along a small tributary river. The people were kind, even killing a chicken in their honor, while the soldiers shared their rations. The chief brought out a bottle of moonshine to sip on. Leaving at dawn, they stopped by again five days later to get out of the rain and came upon only smoldering ruins. A dozen villagers dead, stinking in a thick sea of mud. Since there would be no acknowledgment that Americans were even in the off-limits province, no report of the violence. The enemy had been watching and had taken vengeance. An enemy that ruthless commanded a certain awe. Darrow realized that Vietnam was going to be a very different thing from other wars he had covered. The surface of things was just the beginning. The surface of things was nothing. Linh had it right: things hidden because they were in plain view.

Four of the soldiers disappeared down a path toward the west in hopes of finding the trail of the departing enemy. They would meet back in six hours. Darrow, Linh, and the remaining soldier retraced their steps to the original landing zone.

They waited another full day in the long elephant grass, unable to talk or play music or even start a fire to heat food. The sun beat down on their backs, the air heavy, a wet sheet, buzzing with insect energy. Linh, hidden in the tall grass, dreamed of running away. But where would he go? Finally, as protocol demanded, the soldier radioed for an extraction, although it would give away their presence and endanger the others.

And then like three lean and hungry wolves in the far distance, the missing soldiers appeared, carrying the fourth. They were struggling, exhausted, each stumbling with a leg or an arm of the fourth, now unconscious, soldier.

As naturally as Darrow had picked up the camera at the first sign of movement, he now put it down and ran through the field to help carry the wounded man. A decision without hesitation because it had been made and acted on a thousand times before.

As instinctively as Darrow going out across the field, Linh forgot his dream of running and followed him. The lines and dirt on the soldiers' faces, the dry, unblinking stare of their eyes, showed the war had already started, the suffering begun.

No one had time to notice that Linh took a picture of Darrow helping to carry the wounded soldier. He was the only one in the shot without a weapon, the only one without helmet or flak jacket. For the first time since Linh had left his village, he felt something move within him, the anesthesia of grief briefly lifted. What he felt was fear for Darrow. To survive this war, one should not be too brave.

Returning to Saigon, Darrow was gloomy. "Pictures would have shown what's going on. Now nothing. If it's not photographed, it didn't happen."

"Those villagers don't care if they were photographed or not."

"You have time to get out of this, you know," Darrow said. He still did not understand that the worst had already happened to Linh.

"So can you."

But that was not true. Darrow knew they were both caught.

THREE

A Splendid Little War

Saigon, November 1965

The late-afternoon sun cast a molten light on the street, lacquered the sidewalk, the doors, tables, and chairs of restaurants, the rickety stands of cigarettes, film, and books, all in a golden patina, even giving the rusted, motionless cyclos and the gaunt faces of the sleeping drivers the bucolic quality found in antique photos. The people, some stretched out on cots on the sidewalks, lazily read newspapers or toyed with sleep, waiting for the relief of evening to fall. This part of the city belonged to the Westerners, and the Vietnamese here were in the business of making money off them—either by feeding them in the restaurants, selling them the items from the rickety stands, driving them about the city in the rusted cyclos, having sex with them, spying on them, or some combination of the above.

The dusty military jeep came to a rubber-burning stop in front of the Continental Hotel, scattering pedestrians and cyclos like shot, and a barrel-chested officer jumped out of the back to hand Helen down from the passenger seat.

"What service," she said, laughing. "How much of a tip should I give?"

"Just promise you'll have drinks with us."

"Promise."

"We're only stationed here a few more days."

"I will," she said, and started up the steps of the hotel.

"Remember we know where you live, Helen of Saigon," the soldiers shouted, laughing, peeling away from the curb with a blaring of the jeep's horn that caused pedestrians to flinch, to stop and turn. The Americans at the terrace tables closest to the sidewalk grinned and shook their heads, but the Vietnamese out on the street simply stared, expressions impossible to read.

Linh shared a table with Mr. Bao. They both watched the scene unfolding on the street in silence, saw the tall blond woman in high spirits dusting her hands off on her pants, patting her hair back into its ponytail, the crowd parting as she moved up the sidewalk, skipping up the stairs of the hotel.

Mr. Bao shook his head, turned and spat a reddish brown puddle on the floor to the chagrin of the busboy, who hurried for a rag. "They think this is their playground."

Already tired of the meeting with Mr. Bao, how the old man spoke right into his face, warm puffs of breath assaulting him, stale as day-old fish, Linh signaled for another bottle of mineral water. "Another whiskey, too," Bao said. For a professed proletarian, Mr. Bao certainly seemed comfortable using the Continental as his personal lounge.

"Add a bottle of Jack Daniel's to my shopping list."

Linh had been working for Darrow for a year, had finally moved into his own apartment in Saigon and begun to have some normalcy in his life, when Mr. Bao showed up one night at the café he frequented. Although he didn't make clear which department he worked in, what was clear was that he had an offer from the North impossible to refuse. "Tran Bau Linh, we almost didn't recognize you. It does us good to see how you've prospered in the world since your untimely departure from the party," he said. He had the square, blunt face of a peasant. As well, he had the unthinking allegiance to the party line. Linh was surprised that they hadn't already killed him.

"We have big plans for you," he said. "You will do your fatherland proud after all."

The job was fairly innocuous. A couple times a month, he would report to Bao on where Darrow and he had been. Any frequent newspaper and magazine reader would know as much. The idea was to know the enemy. Linh made sure to bore Mr. Bao in minutiae to the point that he buried anything that could be of value. Most of their meals were spent talking of the food. If Linh chose not to cooperate, Mr. Bao made it clear that he would never hear the bullet that killed him. "You are lucky that you have a use, otherwise you would not still be here talking with me."

The sky had turned a darker gold by the time the woman came back down into the lobby wearing a blue silk dress the color of the ocean at dusk. Her heels made a delicate clicking sound on the floor as she crossed to the bar where her date for the evening, Robert Boudreau, was standing. Linh imagined the air turned cooler where she had passed. "I have to leave now," he said, getting up.

The bar was packed, standing room only, almost all men, but Helen spotted Robert in the corner.

"I'm sorry," she said. "My ride back from the hospital didn't come through. I had to bum a ride from some army officers passing by."

Robert turned with his drink and looked at her. "You clean up pretty well. I've got the prettiest girl in Saigon. That's worth the wait right there." Robert was on staff at one of the wires and had been wasting time in the front office when she came in looking for freelance work. Sensing that she was entirely overwhelmed, he quickly made himself indispensable.

He had a squat build, beefed shoulders, and a muscular chest that caused him to move with a thick, heavy grace, like an ex-athlete. Too, like an ex-athlete, there was the sense that his best days were behind him. A little too neat in dress, a little too Southern and patriotic in politics, he didn't fit in with the younger journalist crowd beginning to filter into the city. Helen was the kind of girl he dreamed about showing off back home, but coming across her in Saigon seemed on the edge of a miracle. The coup he was devising that afternoon was sweeping her off her feet, romancing her until his assignment was up, returning home with her on his arm, a salve and a cover to an unspectacular foreign career.

She grinned. Back home, she had been considered on the plain side, but here the attention of being a rarity was unlike anything she was used to.

"Have a sip of rum for the road." He gave her his glass, a heavy, square one with a solid crystal bottom that made her hand dip from its surprising weight.

"Hmmm," she said. "I needed that."

"You should come home to New Orleans with me. Plenty of the good stuff down there. I'll put you in one of those big ol' houses in the Garden District, and we can fill it with kids."

"Robert, honey," she said, batting her eyes and using a phony, thick Southern accent, "I came to Saigon to escape all that."

"Let's go. Everyone's already left for the restaurant."

They stood on the sidewalk while Robert haggled over the fare to Cholon with two cyclo drivers. Dark, lead-colored clouds had moved in and now begged against the tops of buildings, the humidity and heat so intense Helen felt as if she were walking fully clothed into a sauna. A shimmer in the air. She pushed past Robert and the drivers, ducking under the umbrella covering of one of the cyclos just as a sheet of rain crashed down. The city changed from gold sepia hues to shades of silver; the air, rinsed of its smells, recalled the closeness of the namesake river. Water beaded on the bunched flowers standing in buckets along the side of the road.

"Pay the fare, Robert," she shouted, laughing, as he climbed in the second cyclo behind her, dripping wet.

The suddenness of the rains still seemed magical to her. Not like back home, where a few drops gave warning and then slowly increased. With the blink of an eye, a sudden Niagara. The monsoon had the tug of the ocean as if it were trying to reclaim the land.

Especially in Cholon, the Chinese section of Saigon, the shower didn't slow the heavy pace of business. People simply covered themselves with an umbrella, a piece of plastic, whatever was on hand, and continued on. Both of the drivers were soon drenched but didn't bother with rain gear, their shirts and shorts soaked and clinging to their stringy frames, water squelching out from their rubber sandals, as they serenely pedaled on. When they stopped in traffic, Helen turned to see her driver close his eyes and lift his face to the sky. When the other cyclo pulled next to her, she leaned across and whispered to Robert, "He doesn't seem to mind the wet."

"Probably the only bath he gets every day," Robert said. He had been stationed in more than five countries since he started reporting, and he took pride in the fact that he remained immune and separate from each of them. He looked forward to the time when all the thrill of the exotic drained away for Helen, too.

"Don't talk so loud."

"He can't understand me, honey."

"I don't care. It's not nice."

"You're right. He's probably a cyclo driver by day, a VC operative by night. Unless he's a homeless refugee whose village we destroyed. By all means, I want to be nice for Helen."

She glared at him. "Maybe he's just a cyclo driver trying to make a living." She reached over and pinched Robert's arm.

"Ouch! That hurt!"

She giggled, not as naive as Robert thought she was but playing the part. "Stop making fun of me." The truth was Saigon was dirty and sad and tawdry, and the catastrophic poverty of the people made her weak with homesickness. She found the Vietnamese people's acceptance and struggle to survive terrifying, and she wondered again what the United States wanted with such a backward country.

"Helen, nothing is ever simple here." He guessed she was shrewder than she played, but he appreciated her tact. He was tired of the hard-eyed local women who tallied their company by the half hour.

A few blocks away from the restaurant, the traffic bottled to a stop. A snarl of cars, trucks, carts, motorcycles, and bicycles. Standing still, the air turned an exhaust-tinted blue around them. The delay caused by an overturned cart ahead. Its load of fowl—ducks, geese, swallows—spread across the street in various stages of agony. Loose, downy feathers floated into the puddles until, waterlogged, they sank underneath, creating a cloudy soup. A group of Chinese men argued in loud voices. The birds inside the bamboo cages had toppled into the street. They quacked and honked in fright. Many of the birds had been trussed and hung upside down on the sides of the cart, left alive for freshness. Now many of these were half-crushed but still alive, flapping broken wings or struggling with snapped legs and backs. The owner of the cart pulled out a half-moon hatchet and began to lop their heads off. Dirty, orange-beaked heads were thrown into a burlap sack. A thin ribbon of bright red joined the muddy river of water running down the middle of the street. The cyclo drivers looked on, no intention of moving till the road was cleared.

"I can't watch this," Helen said. Since she arrived a few weeks ago she had made an effort to avoid the ugliness in the city and now it was unavoidable, blocking her path.

"Okay, we can make a run for it. The restaurant is only a street away."

The rain lightened to a heavy drizzle, and Helen stood in the road looking at the mess of wet feathers and blood, shivering, waiting as Robert paid the fare. A dog watched from an alley and made a sudden run past Helen, swooping down and grabbing a duck. Helen saw the white underside of its belly in his mouth as the dog sped past with his prize, an old man in pursuit with a broom. Splashing up water and mud, the dog paid with one wallop to his rear end before he disappeared around the corner with his prize. The man who caused the cart to overturn agreed to buy all the birds, and the final detail of the price was being negotiated. The uninjured ducks in the cages quacked madly as the owner made a grab for them, dashed their heads on the ground, and used the hatchet, tossing the bodies into a box.

Helen ran over and motioned with her hand not to kill them. She pulled dollars out of her purse and handed them to the old man, who grinned at her and bobbed his head.

Robert came up to her. "What're you doing?"

"I want him to set them free."

"What do you think the odds are for a freed duck in Vietnam?" The ridiculousness of the situation made him feel protective of her. Maybe he could love such a woman. She would never last here long.

"He understood me. He'll take them to the country or something."

Suddenly the rain started full force again. Robert grabbed her hand, and they ran, laughing.

"One of those ducks will probably be on your plate by the time we order," he said.

They arrived at the restaurant and were forced to stand in the doorway by a grim-faced maître d' who demanded towels be brought from the kitchen for them to dry off. He stood in front of them, arms folded across his chest, tapping his foot as they waited. Helen looked down and saw he wore women's shiny black patent-leather shoes.

Robert took Helen's elbow and led her to a large table of reporters at the far end of the room. When the men at the table saw Helen, conversation stopped. Helen's wet hair fell in stringy strands; her dress had turned the dark blue of midnight. Some of the faces looked stony, others outright hostile. A few were bemused. The lack of welcome was palpable.

"You look like a goddess risen from the sea," Gary said.

"Did you swim here from the States?"

"Everyone, this is Helen Adams. She's a freelancer just arrived a week ago," Robert said.

"So now the girls are coming. Can't be much of a war after all."

"Quick work, Robert. What do you do? Wait for all the pretty ones to deplane at Tan Son Nhut?"

"Funny." Robert made introductions around the table. "And that's Nguyen Pran Linh down there. He's the poor bastard who has to help that scruffy-looking guy at the end, the famous Sam Darrow. More commonly known as Mr. Vietnam. Either the bravest man here or the most nearsighted."

The table broke up in laughter and catcalls. The awkwardness lingered.

"Don't you usually bring nurses, Robert?"

Darrow rose from the end of the table, unfolding his long legs from under the low-set table. His skin was tanned, his graying brown hair curling long around his ears. His hands smoothed out the rumpled shirt he wore. The furrow between his eyes, though, was not dislike. He just couldn't stand the sight of another shiny, young, innocent face landing in the war, especially a female one, and he was irritated with Robert for bringing her. Still, she looked pitiful and wet, already tumbled by the war, and he wasn't going to let the boys go after her. He gave a short bow, his assessing, hawklike eyes behind his glasses making her self-conscious.

"Excuse the poor welcome," Darrow said. He looked down at the table and picked at his napkin, then continued. "Helen, the face that launched a thousand ships."

"Watch out, Robert. Incoming."

Gary laughed too loud and turned away. "Where are my lobster dumplings? Get the waiter."

"I propose a toast to the newcomer," Darrow said. "Welcome to our splendid little war."

"Getting less splendid and little by the day," Robert said. He sensed his mistake in bringing her there.

Darrow raised his hand to push his glasses up on the bridge of his nose, and Helen noticed a long burled scar running from his wrist up to his elbow, the raised tissue lighter than the rest of his arm. He lifted his glass and spoke in a mock oratory:

"And catching sight of Helen moving along the ramparts,
They murmured one to another, gentle, winged words:
'Who on earth could blame them?'"

"My God," Ed, a straw-haired man with a large nose, said. "Do you have crib notes in your egg rolls or what?"

"Now he's showing off. Making us all look like illiterates."

"Fellows," Darrow said, "most of you *are* illiterates."

Everyone laughed, the tension broke, and Helen sat down. Darrow had okayed her presence. Gary passed a shot of scotch to her to join the toast. She picked up the glass and emptied it in one gulp. The table erupted in cheers.

"You flatter me," she said. "But I'm afraid you've got the wrong Helen." She knew he had taken pity on her, but she wouldn't accept it.

The white-coated waiter brought a platter of dumplings, filling her plate.

The effect of her arrival over, the conversation resumed its jagged course. "So I'm out in Tay Ninh," Jack, an Irishman from Boston said. "And I have my interpreter ask the village elder how he thinks the new leader is doing. He says Diem is very good." Grunts and half-hearted chuckles around the table.

"Oh man, looks like we're winning the hearts and minds, huh?" Ed said.

"So I tell him Diem was a bad man and was overthrown two years ago," Jack continued. "He asks very cautiously who the new leader is."

"You should have said Uncle Ho."

"Only name anyone recognizes anymore."

"So I said to him Ky was in power," Jack said.

"What does he say?"

" 'Ky very good.' "

Guffaws and groans. "So much for the domino theory. The people don't care which way it goes. No one cares except the Americans."

"The French would make a deal with Ho himself as long as they could keep their plantations and their cocktail hour. Just go off and be collective somewhere else, *s'il vous plait*."

Helen stopped eating. She wanted simply to observe and hold her tongue, but she couldn't. "I don't agree."

"What's that, sweetheart?" Ed said, eyes narrowing.

"That the people don't care. They cared in Korea. Everyone wants to be free."

"What do you think, Linh? Our mysterious conduit to the north."

Linh looked up from his plate. "I think this rice is very good." The table burst out in laughter and when it died down, he continued as if he had not noticed the interruption. "Many people in this country haven't had such good rice in years."

"Our Marxist Confucian mascot. 'Let them eat rice,' " Jack said.

"I'm sorry, but what do you know about Korea?" Darrow asked. "You're just a baby now. You could have been prom queen last year in high school."

Maybe, after all, she would not escape the night unscathed. "My father died there. Nineteen fifty Chosin. My brother was in Special Forces. He died in the Plain of Reeds last year."

Darrow refused to offer sympathy. "Half of this table is probably here out of curiosity," Darrow said. "The other half out of ambition. Of course it's *not* the excitement that draws us. We're in the business of war. The cool thing for us is that when this one's done, there's always another one—Middle East, Africa, Cambodia, Laos, Suez, Congo, Lebanon, Algeria. The war doesn't ever have to end for us."

"You're just a starry-eyed mercenary, huh, Darrow?"

A long silence followed, time enough for plates to be cleared and drinks poured, while Helen and Darrow stared at each other, then looked away, then looked back. The most arrogant man she had ever met; her face burned with anger.

"Wrong. I was prom queen four years ago."

Chortles and some hand claps. "Here, here."

"Where you from?"

"Raised in Southern California."

Robert coughed, wanting to divert whatever was happening across the table. "What do you all think of the army's estimate that the war will be over in a year?"

Darrow sipped at yet another drink. "It'll be over if we quit. Isn't anyone reading Uncle Ho and Uncle Giap? 'We'll keep on fighting if it takes a hundred years.'"

"You don't believe that? No one fights a hundred years."

"I absolutely believe that. You would, too, Ed, if you ever left your air-conditioned hotel room and slogged out in the jungle with us."

"I'll leave the heroics for you. Framed your Pulitzer over your desk yet?"

Darrow smirked, a shamed, lopsided smile. "Actually it was sent to my wife, so I've never seen it. I believe she hung it up in the john. She feels the check was the best part of the deal. Making up for my piddling salary."

Chuckles around the table. "Cry me a river, Darrow."

As curfew approached, the restaurant emptied; people hurried away with full glasses and bottles, promising to return them in the morning. The waiters pointedly stripped off tablecloths, turned over chairs. A bucket and a mop were propped at the door to the kitchen.

Jack turned to Helen. "So, should we have come here in the first place, lass?"

"To this restaurant?" She smiled. Laughter. "In the briefing today they said eighteen hundred men have died so far. Eighteen hundred, including my brother."

"It's never too late, Prom Queen. Get out while the gettin's good," Darrow said.

"So what about a country's manifest destiny? What woulda happened if America had never come?" Jack said.

"We might all end up speaking Vietnamese someday?" Robert said. Laughter.

"Vietnam's destiny has not been her own for a long time. What about the French?" Ed asked.

"The French were on their way out," Robert said.

"Only because Ho found something stronger than them," Darrow said. "If the French had never been in Vietnam, maybe he wouldn't have needed to unleash the genie from the bottle."

"And what a genie she is."

"Well, geniuses, we've figured out world politics for one night. I say we adjourn."

"Fine."

"Sounds good. Sports Club or the Pink?"

Outside on the sidewalk, the men formed a large, boisterous circle, but Linh stood off to the side. He said his good nights and walked away alone. Helen watched his slight, solitary figure move away. No matter how they patted him on the back and bought him drinks, he would always be on the outside of this good-old-boys' club.

Robert turned to Helen. "I need to go to the office. Is it all right if Jack takes you back to the hotel? I'll meet you back there in an hour or so for a nightcap?"

"Sure," Helen said, disappointed the night for her was already over, conscious that she, too, was now being excluded from the boys' club.

"I'll take her," Darrow said. He walked up and stood next to Robert, hands dug in his pockets, head hung down studying something on the sidewalk.

"No, it's out of your way, I'm sure," Robert said.

"Actually, I was . . . going that way."

Robert looked straight at him, his usual deference blown. "Where?" he said. "You don't even know where she's staying."

Darrow smiled. Everyone waited. "Everyone new stays at the Continental."

"Jack said he would take her," Robert said.

"I have a room there, too. Remember?"

"I'll go with Sam," Helen said. She gave Robert a shrugging, apologetic look, as if the choice were out of her control. "Maybe I can win a few arguments by the time we reach the hotel."

The men, entertained, realized the sparring match was over with a clear winner. Ed grabbed at his heart in mock agony and staggered on the sidewalk. Robert bit his lips together; his face reddened. Jack clapped him on the back. "Come on, we'll drop you off, laddie."

Two jeeps with drivers pulled up, and they piled in like frat boys going out on the town.

"You two be careful now. The streets can be dangerous late at night." From inside one jeep, they heard, "Easy come, easy go, huh, Robert?" Laughter as the jeeps sped off.

"Well, I've put us in the middle of a little scandal, I'm afraid," Darrow said.

"We haven't done anything."

"But we will."

"We won't." Helen stood in front of the restaurant and looked up into his face. A paper lantern behind her cast a gold light on the edge of his high cheekbone, on his glasses so she couldn't see his eyes. "That was sudden," she said.

"That's one of the keys to life here. Sudden and sublime. Sudden and awful. Everything distilled to its most intense. That's why we're all hooked."

"You don't scare me. Tell me, does the great Sam Darrow always get the girl?"

"He never got the girl. Why would he be here otherwise? The boy who can't talk learns to take pictures. Did you know you have blood on your dress?"

Helen looked down and saw the spatters along the hem that hadn't been visible when the fabric was wet. Her face tightened at the memory. "The ducks . . . and a dog running by with a body in his mouth."

Darrow bent and wiped at the fabric with a handkerchief but the blood had dried. "Can you walk in those things?" he said, pointing to her heels.

"Sure."

"I'd like to show you something. It isn't far."

"I don't know . . . we should be getting back." She didn't feel nearly as bold alone with him as she had in front of the group. She was too lonely and homesick to trust herself being attracted to someone.

"Come on. I don't bite."

They walked down the narrow, crooked streets. Storekeepers had pulled down signs, mostly ones in French, a few in Vietnamese, and were replacing them with ones written in English. Skirting around vendors on the sidewalk, Helen and Darrow occasionally brushed shoulders.

She didn't know if she liked him, but she saw a passion for the work and for the country that was missing in the others. "My presence wasn't appreciated tonight," she said.

"The boys?" Darrow said. "They're okay."

"They don't want women here."

"Wrong. They think you're a novelty. A fun toy. Wait and see what they act like when they consider you a threat."

She felt his hand at the small of her back as she stepped around some packing crates. He hesitated, then asked what had happened to her brother.

"The letter said he died a hero in a firefight. Sacrificed himself for his buddies. I loved my brother, but that doesn't sound like him."

"That would be enough reason for most to stay away," Darrow said.

"I took care of Michael while my mother worked. After Dad died. When he broke a toy, I'd glue it. Whenever he got in fights with the other boys, I'd defend him." She laughed. "I even gave him advice about the girl he had a crush on in junior high. I told him whenever he needed me, I'd always be there. And, of course, I wasn't. For the most important thing, I was nowhere near."

Helen looked down at the bloody marks on her dress, frowning. "How could I bear to live out this small life of mine back home?"

"You came too late. The good old days are all over."

As they left the main thoroughfares, they turned left, then right, then left again. They doubled back and went forward, circled, until it seemed they had gone a very long way but not traveled far at all. Darrow leading her until she was so disoriented that her only compass was his arm in front of her. A new world, or an old world hidden, only half the stores lit by electricity, and then usually no more than a bare lightbulb swinging high on the ceiling, the rest dimly illuminated by kerosene lamps that flickered and made the rooms look alive. Many of the stores barely larger than closets, a mystery to figure out what they put up for sale in their crowded interiors. One sold paper—newspaper, writing paper, butcher paper. Another store sold twine. Still another, only scissors and knives. Food vendors crowded in portable stalls. The smells of spices she could not name blended with the sweet incense burning in the stores, all of it cloying the smell of diesel and sewage and the ever-present river.

They came to the moon-shaped entrance of an alley that was flooded across from the rain. It narrowed to the dark throat of a path.

"The streets are known by the guilds on them—noodle street, sail street, cotton street, coffin street. So if you want a driver to bring you here, say you want to go to the meeting place of silk street and lacquered bowl street."

"Why would I want to come here?"

"It's this way," he said, ignoring her.

Helen looked down at the oily, pitch-black water doubtfully as Darrow stepped into it. It covered his ankles.

"They don't get around to fixing the dips and the potholes very often."

"Maybe we should do this another time. Curfew is only an hour away," she said.

Without warning he scooped her up in his arms and carried her through the puddle. Chinese and Vietnamese crowded the wide mouth of the alley, the women giggling and pointing. Helen heard men barking out comments she couldn't understand. On the other side of the puddle, Darrow kept holding her.

"Put me down now," she said. "This is stupid."

He kept holding her.

"Put me down," she said. He slowly lowered her but kept her tight against his body. When her feet touched the ground, she was still in the cage of his arms.

"If you don't stop this, I'm going to leave."

"How? Now I have a moat holding you back. You'll ruin your lovely shoes."

She sighed. "I'll take off my shoes and carry them as I run through your moat. Believe me."

"I believe you."

They entered the alley, the buildings now close together, and the lights within the storefronts dim. The darkness and closeness enveloped them; they walked shoulder to shoulder, Darrow holding her hand, and in the velvety pitch of the alley she did not let go. Not a person passed them, but there was no feeling of solitude in the night. Instead the passageway felt teeming, even crowded; it seemed to her that if she reached out her hand she would touch a body, someone pressing against the wall, holding still and waiting until the two of them passed by. For a moment, the image of the Vietnamese man, Linh, came into her mind, how he stood away from the group and went off by himself. Was he standing somewhere close, watching them now, holding his breath?

They walked in silence and came to a two-story, yellow stucco colonial building that leaned to the left as if it were gossiping with its neighbor. The facade wore faded, long ocher streaks from the rains and humidity, the patina like that of the moldering buildings in Venice. The roof and the entrance portico were tiled in a cobalt blue Chinese ceramic, the corners curved upward into points like the upturned corners of a sly mouth. An unsettling mix of cultures that created a strange beauty. The front door of the building was made of lacquered wood. On it were painted squares depicting the various scenes of Buddha's enlightenment.

"Beautiful," Helen said, tracing her hand along the panels.

"A lacquer artist lived here. When he couldn't pay his rent, the landlord demanded he make something of equal value."

Helen looked at peacocks perched atop rocks, elephants striding through bamboo, tigers crouched in palms, the great spreading of a bodhi tree, and pools of lotus blossom.

"It should be in a museum."

"That's part of what I love here. Everything isn't locked away behind glass and key, you live with history as part of your life and not just on a field trip. The legend is that he worked on it a year. And when it was done, he ran away and was never heard from again."

"Why?"

"It was during the war with the French. He couldn't make a living and marry his girl, so she married a soldier. I don't know if it's true or a folktale. But the door is real. A friend of mine lived here. I still keep the place."

"I thought you had a room at the Continental."

"That's the room that *Life* pays for. My official residence. This is my real life." Darrow opened the door and waited for her to move inside.

They walked up the shadowy stairs that leaned to the right for a few steps, then to the left, as if nailed together by someone who felt ocean swells under his feet. The wood felt light and hollow like balsa, the middle of the struts bending under the weight of each footfall with a small groan.

"Are you sure these are safe?"

"This is a very old building. They've held so far."

In front of a thin, scuffed door, Darrow pulled out an old-fashioned brass skeleton key and turned the lock. "This key only opens this door and a few thousand others in Cholon."

Inside, he flipped on a small lamp with a red silk shade with beaded fringe that gently swished against his hand. The room smelled dusty and unused, like the stacks of an old library. He sneezed and walked to the window and opened it. The room was threadbare, furnished with only an old iron bed, an armoire, two wooden chairs, and a table. The only ornate decorations in the room were a large mirror in a scrolling gilt frame and the lamp.

"That's a very feminine touch," Helen said, nodding at the red glow of the shade.

"Henry, the guy who rented this place, was involved with a Vietnamese girl. It looks like it's her taste. I let her take what she wanted, but she left this behind."

"Where is Henry? Did he go home?"

"He was home. He was American, but he loved Vietnam. The war tore him up. I'll show you some of his work—he was on his way to becoming a hell of a photographer."

"Where is he?"

"Died two years ago covering an operation in the delta. Henry was reckless. I refused to go out with him on assignments. But he knew the dangers.

That's one lesson of etiquette you need to learn here—never ask what happened to someone. The answer is usually bad."

"Not a very lucky apartment for its owners."

"Not a very lucky country. Henry gave me a key. It's the one place I could escape when I needed."

Helen went to the open window and leaned on the sill. She smelled dust and rain, heard people walking down the alley, the tinny sound of Vietnamese pop music from a transistor radio. "Are you escaping now?" she asked.

"Trapped now is more like it." And then, as if in answer, the room went dark. "Great Electric of Saigon at it again." Darrow groped his way to the table and lit a candle.

Up and down the dark street, the slow pulse of flames like fireflies appeared.

"Why did you bring me here?"

Darrow stood next to her, reticent, and stared out the window as if he were waiting for something to happen. He did not want to say it was because she had appeared scared shitless tonight, woefully inadequate for what she had come to do. Neither did he want to admit he found her beautiful.

"You see the tree in front of the building? It's bare now, but in the spring it blooms large red flowers. Henry and his girl used to have parties each spring to celebrate the tree blooming. Very *Tale of Genji,* very Asian." Darrow chuckled to himself. "Henry loved all that shit. Swore he'd never go back to the States. Said America scared him more than any war could."

"What happened to the girl of the red lampshade?"

Darrow shrugged. "I don't know. Disappeared. Found someone else. The local women don't have much choice once they start taking up with white men." Darrow justified his own actions with the native women that if not him, they would offer themselves to someone else. He treated them kindly and then promptly forgot them. The grand, futile gestures of renunciation, fidelity, bored him; he had become a practical bourgeois in wartime. "There's something lovely here, yet even as we look, even as we have contact with it, we change it. So why are you going out with that blowhard, Robert?"

"How rude. We're friends."

He poured two glasses of scotch from the armoire and handed her one. The glass was heavy, square, with a solid crystal bottom.

"Aren't these from the hotel bar?"

He grinned. "Keep forgetting to return them."

She sipped her drink in silence, listening to the outside sounds, the heaviness of the warm air moving through the room. He refilled their glasses and sat across from her.

"I like it here," she said finally. What she didn't add was that it was the first time she'd felt safe since she'd arrived in-country.

"This is the real Vietnam. When I come here, my mind slows down. . . . I can imagine what is good about the place, what the people want to keep. The Continental and the Caravelle, the air-conditioning and room boys and ice cubes, make you forget where you are. The war groupies starting to descend. Restaurants and nightclubs booming, parties every night. Saigon is their Casablanca or Berlin. It's the scene now. All these daughters of the country-club set descending with their copy of Graham Greene under their arm . . . sorry for the speechifying, I'm drunk."

Helen set down her glass on the floor. "You're saying I shouldn't be here."

"Should you?" His eyes took her in, coolly assessing. "Don't ever believe that staying here won't change you."

"Tell me what you *really* think."

"I've hurt your feelings."

"I had Robert take me to the dinner tonight because I knew you would be there."

Darrow raised his eyebrows. "Should I be flattered?"

"All they've let me do so far is human-interest features—widows, orphans, wounded soldiers. I need someone to get me out in the field."

He blinked, not wanting to admit his hurt feelings at how unromantic her reasons were. Usually the battle-weary reporter spiel worked. "Only a handful of women are covering the war. None doing combat. It's too dangerous, too spooky out there. The men don't like it, either. It's hard work. It's hard for me. I'm forty years old, I look fifty, I feel sixty."

"My brother wrote me a letter before he was killed. He said no matter what happened he couldn't regret coming. I needed to see for myself. And the only

way to become famous is to cover combat, right? I dropped out of college because I was worried it would be over by the time I graduated." Later, she would
cringe at her crassness, but at the time it had seemed daring to reveal such an
unflattering truth. How could she explain the years of being a tomboy, refusing dolls and dresses, always hanging out with the boys? Her father and Michael shared the idea of soldiering, and she had been left out. She cried when
she had to stay in the kitchen with her mother, told to bake cookies. Michael's
taunts as they went out shooting—*You can't come, you can't come.*

Darrow knelt in front of her. He liked her a little less now, so it made it
easier to seduce her.

"No one can say I didn't try. Go out with me on patrol tomorrow. You'll
have your own bite of the apple. You're going to get it anyway . . . right?"

"Right."

This girl, filled with ambition and doubt and passion. Like himself. Utterly unlike his wife, who was cool, clear, and sharp—a constant obstacle to
his doing what he loved. A mystery why she had married him just to make
him guilty over what he did. Their arguments ran in circles like a dog chasing its tail: *It's the only thing I'm good at,* he'd shouted, but the truth was it
was the only thing that made him feel alive.

"Are we fine? I mean, things between you and me?"

Helen reached and gently pulled off his glasses. Despite her playacting, she
was terrified by what she saw in the hospitals, and the idea of turning down a
man she wanted tonight seemed ridiculous. What if she were gone tomorrow,
like Henry? She frowned. "Is there something between you and me?"

He put a hand on each side of her chair, and she noticed his hands shaking. That was good; neither was practiced at this seduction thing.

"Nerves. I'm steady in the field. Downtime fallout."

She ran her fingers along the scar on his arm. "How'd that happen?"

He shrugged. "An angry husband."

She laughed.

"I think it was Algeria. Hard to remember one from another. We should
discuss this. Are we open about it, or do we try to keep it secret?"

"Cat's a little out of the bag."

"True. But are you prepared? A married man's mistress?"

He folded the glasses into his shirt pocket. With his index finger he lightly traced her upper lip. Pressing harder, he went down her lower lip, pressing on the fleshy bottom till it spread into a dark flower. He kissed her.

"You're beautiful," he said.

She was not beautiful, but she did not correct him. She let it go that she was beautiful enough for that moment.

"Tonight is just ours. Nothing to do with tomorrow, okay?" he said.

She nodded and pulled away from him, stood up, and walked across the room to the mirror. Back home time seemed to stand still; she was always impatient, restless. In Vietnam everything moved at a flash speed that had nothing to do with normal life. She tried to hold her breath and become as still as the room. "You didn't ask why I came here tonight."

"I figured you'd tell me if you wanted to. I'll find out soon enough."

"Robert said you were one of the charmed. He said everyone tries to stick close to you because they think they will be safe." As the words came from her mouth, she realized how foolish she sounded, like a child.

"Poor Robert still believes in the Tooth Fairy."

"I already asked him to help me. He refused."

"Well, good for him."

"He said you have no morals. That you'll do anything for a picture. That you would have no scruples about bedding a woman or letting her go out in the field."

Darrow sat back on his heels a moment, winded. He got up and moved behind her, slowly unfastening the back of her dress, one button at a time. "But you came anyway. I didn't finish the passage at the restaurant tonight. Last time I was out on a mission, the only paperback I had was a battered copy of *The Iliad*. I would memorize passages:

> "'Ravishing as she is, let her go home in the long ships
> and not be left behind . . . for us and our children
> down the years an irresistible sorrow.'"

A growl came from deep within the building, and the electricity struggled back on, first at half power, then all the way. Out of the darkness, plunged into light, she felt confused. Cheap, more like it. Dress half pulled off and her bra showing. Desire shrank. She pulled away, reached to refasten the buttons that had been undone. "We should be going. Robert will be at the hotel. . . ."

"Really? Did you suddenly get frightened of yourself?" He watched her flushed face as she moved around the room, gathering her things. Not as easy as he had thought. Was he being played? Even so, she intrigued him. Perhaps at long last he had met his match in female form? "Why is it, you suppose, that the people who are supposed to love us the most are precisely the ones who try to stop us doing what we love? Did you leave anyone behind?"

"No. If there had been anyone that important, I wouldn't have come. I wouldn't have been so selfish."

"That's where you're wrong."

"How so?"

"Sometimes you have to fulfill a promise in order to deserve the love you're given. Don't you think it's a calling to live in danger just to capture the face of those who are suffering? To show their invisible lives to the world?"

She walked past him and out the door. "I'm leaving . . . with you or without you." Down the hallway, she refused to look back, not wanting to acknowledge that if he didn't follow her by the time she reached the alley, she would most certainly be lost.

When she and Michael were kids, their favorite game was hide-and-seek. Helen would search for the most difficult hiding places possible, and time would turn into eternities; often she would fall into a daydream and forget she was playing a game. She would wait in the darkened cubby, desperately wanting to be found.

FOUR

Indian County

At the Bien Hoa Air Base, Helen stood in the shade of a metal storage shed, a faded red stenciled BEWARE above her head; the words below disappeared, peeled off by the sun and rain. The area to be patrolled was considered a cleared one, the search of some marshland and two hamlets routine, establishing presence and nation building.

Darrow rolled his eyes at her as he harangued the lieutenant colonel into taking Helen along. She heard the words *added burden* and *lack of facilities,* but then the man gave in because of a gambling debt he owed Darrow.

Waiting for the transport, Helen fumbled with her newly acquired cameras, which were fancier than the simple Instamatics she was used to. "Would you show me how to load film in these?" she said quietly, her eyes downcast.

Darrow was speechless, with no choice but to comply. He showed her basic photographic technique in the fifteen minutes it took them to load supplies.

"Where's Linh?" she asked, trying to act casual.

"He's taken off for a few days. Personal stuff."

The helicopter hovered above the ground, and the soldiers jumped and ran; Helen also jumped and ran, the soft, dull ache of the jump inside her ankles, the small bones and ligaments crushing against one another. They ran to a berm of reeds in front of the swampy marsh and crouched down on the dry land behind, waiting for the next helicopter to unload. It wasn't until the last soldier got off that sniper bullets started hissing through the air. "That's not supposed to happen," she said, as the last helicopter bucked up like startled prey, nose dipping, then disappeared over the trees.

"Shut up," a soldier hissed.

After the shudder and roar of the helicopter, the land sounded hushed and peaceful except for the percussive, insect whine of bullets past her ears. Her field of vision was reduced to the few feet between her and the berm and the tops of the far-off trees. The heat burned through her clothing; pebbles bit into her down-turned palms. The danger seemed unreal, like a movie, like being out on training maneuvers, a bored rifleman shooting blanks from behind a tree. Her heart thumped hard against her chest at the idea that there was a real live enemy hidden in front of them.

Lieutenant Colonel Shaffer crawled over to her. "Stay flat and stay here. We're going toward the tree line."

Darrow moved forward with the rest of the men, entering the waist-high marsh. She saw him as if for the first time, the truest image she would ever have: a dozen men moving out single file, visible only from the waist up, only packs, helmets, and upraised weapons to identify them; a lone bare head, an upraised camera. After he forgave a ninety-five-dollar debt to get her on board the plane, he treated her like a stranger, which hurt her feelings though she understood its necessity. Darrow turned his back on the safety of the rear position, on Helen, on thoughts of Saigon and possibly America; his whole attention directed toward the depth of the marsh, and the further depth of the jungle, the war, the secrets he still had not found. Not yet understanding what drove him, she already respected it. She felt stupid with fear.

Raising her head, she saw that the trees were eucalyptus, lined like the windbreaks back home between the citrus groves. The familiarity of the trees, malevolent in this setting, doubly disturbed her.

Home. She longed for the clean quiet of her mother's house, the mildew smell of closed rooms from being so close to the beach. All those surf days of beating sun and rolling water, dried out and happy, licking her child's lips of salt, of ice cream. The crowded boardwalk along the beach, the pink-burned tourists and the tanned locals, giggling with her friends over the browned, lean torsos of older boys playing basketball, always shirtless, always ignoring them. Walking past the restaurants with their unfurled umbrellas, their white tablecloths, and cheap bottles of wine on the table to entice customers, the waiters leathery and bored.

Her mouth was dry, air scraped the shallows of her lungs, as the reality of where she was took hold. Shivering from the foreign rush of terror, she felt a warm, wet sensation, and burned at the realization that she had peed herself. She pressed her cheek into the dirt, the lip of the helmet—a man's small but still too big—cutting into her ear. The sharp scent of burned grass combining with gunpowder and the sweetish smell of her own urine shamed her.

Nothing had prepared her for the smallness of the action. The moment-to-moment boredom. Intellectually, yes, there were people on the enemy side trying to kill them, American men might die, but that was all television stuff. Being on the flat land, pricked by the dying grass, the idea that she herself could be the target of a bullet became real. But the whole time she lay there she mostly fretted over the embarrassment of wetting herself, solving the problem by spilling the water from her canteen over part of her pants.

Minutes passed. She heard a cry in front of her. A soldier had been hit in the thigh. Helen crawled up to the group as the medic bandaged him and gave him a quick prick of morphine. Movement was better than paralysis. The boy was lying on his back, wild-eyed and jabbering.

"He's fine, mostly nerves," the medic said, shrugging. "First time out."

The soldier's lips twisted in sarcasm. "They say that to anyone who isn't dead."

"What's your name?" Helen touched the boy's hand.

"Curt."

"Shut up, Curt," the medic said. "We should call you Yellow."

The bullets stopped, and half an hour later the patrol was back together, waiting on an opened dirt road for an evacuation helicopter for one wounded. The thick marsh slime dried stiff and dark on their fatigues in the scalding air. Helen's own darkened pants went unnoticed. Against regulations, soldiers took off their flak jackets, smoked cigarettes, and wrung out socks while they waited.

Helen joined a group sitting under a tree. She took off her helmet. In her panic and then relief that the encounter was over, she realized she hadn't shot a single frame, had, in fact, forgotten all about the camera. Years later, her biggest regret was not taking the shot of Darrow in the marsh. It remained the one image etched in her mind, perhaps because she did not have the film to refer back to. Once a picture was taken, the experience was purged of its power to haunt.

Curt was talking and joking too loudly. Lieutenant Colonel Shaffer told him to keep it down. "It's not a goddamned party that you're going to the hospital."

"Oh, yes it is," Curt mouthed behind his back.

"That was a nothing." Darrow crouched a few feet from Helen and took her picture. "How'd it go, Prom Queen?"

She wiped her face and made a grimacing smile. "All right." The way he looked at her, she knew he guessed that she had frozen.

"More excitement than we expected. It's cleared till it's not, till it is again. End of lesson today. Take this ride out."

"No!" If she left now, it would be empty-handed, without a single exposure taken, the risk all for nothing.

"No bodies in the tree line. That means they retreated, probably back to the hamlet, waiting for us. It's no longer Peace Corps stuff."

"I can handle it."

"Enough for today. I'm asking, but Shaffer will order you."

Helen braced herself as the helicopter pitched, then rose. She crawled, crablike, along the corrugated metal floor over to Curt. Away from the other men, he looked even younger—clear blue eyes slightly dilated from the morphine and a child's rosy lips.

"Looks like you and me got a ticket out of there," he shouted in her ear above the roar. "Aren't we smart?"

"You wouldn't believe how I worked just to get here."

"What's wrong with you?"

She shrugged. "Where're you from?"

"Philly."

"I'm from Southern California."

"Oh man. When I get out of here, I'm going straight to Hermosa Beach and learn to surf."

"My brother went there all the time."

"Is it great?"

"Surfing capital."

She thought of the water off the pier back home, how one day she finally couldn't bear sitting on the beach with all the girlfriends. She had paddled out on a borrowed board to hoots and howls from Michael and his friends. She had tumbled in the surf, frightened, pounded against the sandy bottom again and again, but she wouldn't stop trying. The first time she got up on the board and saw the beach ahead of her, she had felt invincible. Everything had happened so fast during the firefight and now her failure was settling in.

"I can't wait," Curt said.

"Do you want me to take your picture? I'll send it to you."

"Okay."

She picked up her notebook and as she wrote his dog tag number he grew quiet.

"You promise you'll send it? Maybe to my parents in case I'm not around."

"If it's in this book, you'll get the photograph." Helen talked briskly, pretending she had not heard his last words. "They'll send it to your local paper. You'll be a hero back home."

"Fuck the people back home. This wound'll be patched, and I'll be back out in the boonies in a few weeks. I promised myself I'd go out and kill me at least one dink before I left here." He leaned back, and they both remained silent the rest of the way.

When she returned to the hotel that night, she took a long, hot shower. Her first action after returning from the Cholon apartment had been to throw her copy of *The Quiet American* in the wastebasket, but her room boy, a small, thin-shouldered boy with the long eyelashes of a girl, dug it out of the trash and put it back on the table. Inconceivable to him that a perfectly good book would be thrown out. Now he knocked and gave her a note from Robert that a group of them was having dinner at the hotel dining room and inviting her. She couldn't face them down tonight, especially not after the afternoon's disaster. She looked at the boy. "I'm done with the book. Would you like it?"

"You sell." He gestured with his hand, and she was struck by the grace of his movement.

"You sell, keep the money," she said.

He looked the book over carefully, gave a tender shrug.

"On second thought, leave it here tonight. Take it in the morning." Although she had read it at least a dozen times, she longed to lose herself in it tonight, to rest in Fowler's certainties or Pyle's innocence. To counterbalance the uncertainties of life with the sureties of a book. She had always been an avid reader, but as an adult her reading habits had changed, and only after she had reread a book many times did she claim to begin to understand it.

Her head ached. She had been lying paralyzed in a field earlier that day and now stood in this room the same night, and the two parts were not meant to fit. She slipped into slacks and a loose cream blouse. At first she put on loafers but decided instead on suede pumps. Impossible to be alone on such a night even if it meant joining Robert and that ambivalent crowd. Her saving grace was that only Darrow had witnessed her failure. She poured herself a glass of water and her hand shook as she raised it to her lips. The old-fashioned ceiling fan shuddered above her head. She stared at the shabby bedspread and remembered the glare of the sun on the paddies, making it impossible to see; the fields bleached by the fierceness of the sun. The only vivid color she could recall the red of blood on the young soldier's thigh. Darrow's point, of course, that no matter what group she traveled with, one went out alone, hand in hand with only one's own fear.

Michael. Determined to follow in their father's footsteps. To outdo him if possible. Graduated with honors. He could have done anything, but he wanted only to be in the elite corps. Because Dad wasn't. Her father would have been dismissive of what she was doing, unless, of course, she succeeded. But Michael would have been bemused and not surprised at all at his big sister, always trying to play catch-up.

She drank down the glass of water and poured another. The niggling humiliation that she had not snapped even a single picture. The second glass of water gulped down so fast it dribbled down her chin and onto her blouse so that she had to change again. When she finally managed to make her way to the hotel dining room, she couldn't hide her disappointment that Darrow wasn't there.

Ed, the straw-haired man from the previous night, grinned. "So how was the maiden voyage out, love?"

She said nothing.

"It's always a bear, the first couple times," Gary said.

"Maybe next time you can bring film," Ed said, laughing.

"You don't need film where you go, Ed," Robert said. "Everyone knows the inside of your girlfriend's thighs."

The table broke up in laughter. Helen ate quickly, not tasting her food, then excused herself. Had they known because she didn't make the rounds of the wires to sell her pictures? Or had Darrow told them?

Robert went after her and stopped her in the lobby. She had gone out with Darrow and returned with no pictures, and he hoped that mortification would give him back the upper hand. Time to hang on a man's arm. He had decided to pretend the previous night, and his defeat, had not happened. "Are you okay?"

"I need sleep is all." She needed so many things, putting any one thing into words seemed inadequate. "I failed."

"It's not a place for a woman. I'm just grateful you came back whole. I'll check on you in the morning."

She was so relieved to get away, she gave him a kiss on the cheek. He backed away for a moment, startled, then moved closer.

"Should we have a drink?"

"I need to rest," she said.

Robert stepped back into the restaurant, stopping at the entrance to light a cigarette. He hadn't taken her for the sort that fell for a guy like Darrow. Usually his women were the type who for one reason or another couldn't ask for much. With her intelligence, she must guess the string of women that Darrow discarded. The gold band on his finger a kind of shield against commitment. He watched Helen in the lobby, fumbling through her purse. He would take her down Bourbon Street; they would laugh and dance all night.

He liked her. A possibility for that house in his mind, filled with children. But Helen didn't move toward the elevators; instead she left the hotel and waved down a waiting cyclo. Of course, he thought, he could be wrong.

At the meeting place of silk and lacquered bowl streets, Helen found the moon-shaped entrance of the alley, still puddled from the rain, retracing her path as if she could return to the time before her failure that day. Reckless, she ran through water the color of ink at the alley's mouth while men stood at the corner and stared, ran through a cacophony of incense and spice smells she could not yet name. Past stores that sold only twine. What had before seemed strange now became soothing. We are hardwired for the comfort of familiarity, she thought. Again, the airless effect of buildings so packed together, the lights within storefronts dim, darkness and closeness smothering her.

She ran down the narrow, murky throat of the path till she saw the yellow building that listed to one side, darkened like a sweat-stained shirt. Looking up, she saw the glow of the lampshade in the window, and the weight on her chest grew lighter despite her anger. Wanting to forget the day, she pushed open the lacquered door, unable to see the peacocks and tigers painted on it, and felt her way up the black, groaning staircase that smelled of cedar and fish.

As she knocked on the door, the sounds of jazz inside and the high staccato of female laughter, made her feel like a fool—the idea that just the sight of Darrow would heal her childish wounds. She turned to escape before anyone came, but the door swung wide open to Darrow holding a glass of scotch in his hand.

"Helen of a Thousand Ships." He smiled, a victorious pleasure in his eyes.

She stood, unable to move. He was a stranger to her.

"Who's there?" a voice called.

"Come in," Darrow said, taking her arm, pulling her inside. The air thick with the grassy smell of pot.

"Jack, it's our new . . . intrepid girl reporter."

Nothing else to do for it, so she hauled back and punched Darrow in the face as hard as she was able, closing her eyes at the point of contact so that when he bent, she wasn't sure what she'd managed. His glasses flew off, and blood trickled from one nostril.

"What the hell?"

"You ordered me to leave. I had no choice. And then you come back and tell everyone I didn't take any pictures."

"I didn't."

"Everyone knows."

"Everyone knows because everyone's interested in watching you fail, girlie," Jack said.

Jack was sitting cross-legged on a cushion, a fat, hand-rolled roach pinched between his fingertips. Next to him, a Vietnamese woman was kneeling on a cushion. She had a wide, acne-scarred face, and she winked at Helen, her bright orange lipstick smudged.

"You ignored me. You didn't help me at all, show me anything."

"That's because I treated you out there like a man. No special treatment. Decide what you want."

"So that's cleared up," Jack said. "Introductions."

Darrow blinked, a napkin against his nose. "That is . . ."

"Tick-Tock," Jack said.

Darrow pursed his lips, and she could tell he was drunk. "Formal introductions, please. That is Miss Tick-Tock."

Jack patted the woman's thigh. "Just in time for the party. Here, Helen, have a puff of Cambodia's finest."

"Let me pour you a drink," Darrow said and led Helen to a chair. "Let's not corrupt her all in one day."

"If I was wrong, I'm sorry."

As she sat down, Jack pointed to her feet. "Didn't anyone tell you not to wear heels in the paddy?" He burst out laughing.

She looked down and saw her ruined suede shoes. Darrow went to the armoire and got a towel. He sat on the floor, took off her shoes, and rubbed her feet. No one had explained how to deal with the residual fear of physical danger; she felt five years old and in need of someone's arms around her. His eye was red and beginning to swell. Unable to stop, she reached out and ran her fingertips across his cheek. In the most illogical reasoning, she had chosen him because he wouldn't nurture her like kind, dependable Robert.

"Well, folks," Jack said. "I'll leave the joint with you, but I'm going to have to push off."

"You don't have to go," Helen said.

"Actually, we do. Come along, Tick-Tock."

No one said anything.

"No, please, don't try and stop me." Jack got up. "See you around."

Alone, Helen kept sitting in the chair, Darrow on the floor. He looked at her steadily, waiting.

"Are you okay?"

"No. Not okay. I froze today. Forgot the damn camera was there."

Darrow touched his eye and winced. "When I first started . . . You either get over it or you don't."

"I feel humiliated."

"I'll give you this—as scared as you were, tonight I thought you'd be on the first plane home."

She shook her head. The idea of sealing off her failure for all time was unthinkable. "I'm not going home."

"Why? You have a criminal record or something?"

She smiled. "Am I going to make it?" She was surprised at the calm and matter-of-factness in her voice.

"Try again. See what happens." Darrow stood, took her hand, and led her to the bed. "You aroused a bit of curiosity, you know. It's better for you if I don't protect you."

"No one will give me a chance now."

"It's always better to beat low expectations."

"I don't love you," she said. "Couldn't love someone like you." She kissed his collarbone, his chest above his heart. After all the elusiveness of the last few days, things slipping out of her grasp, this felt right. His skin cool under her lips. No magic, no heart pounding. Just lust, taken neat. Probably he would break her heart in the long run, but she did not quit. Would not give up this moment to avoid that future one. She did not think it was true that women fell in love all at once, but rather that they fell in love through repetition, just the way someone became brave. She did not love him yet.

Darrow said nothing, only kept pulling her in.

The sickle of moon angled down the narrow alley, lit the precarious room, the ramshackle bed. Darrow traced her profile with his fingertip. He was falling in love in his own way, building a legend that was not quite her. "When I saw you for the first time at dinner, do you know what I thought?"

She turned toward him, her body a smooth spoon of moonlight. "Tell me."

"I thought, There is a woman who has never been in love. And I wondered, Why? You could have any man at that table. Hell, Robert is ready to marry you and settle down in the bayou." He had wanted to say something romantic, but he had lost the knack for romance, if he ever possessed it.

On this night she would have preferred the tenderness of lies.

After she had fallen asleep, Darrow rose, put on his glasses, and lit a cigarette. His eye throbbed. Had to hand it to her: She had a good punch. He was a man who always wanted to reach the end of things, stories or people, to understand in order to put them behind him and move on. It had been like that since he was a teenager working in darkrooms in New York, when he heard for the first time the magical names—Pearl Harbor, Mount Suribachi, Tarawa— spoken in the hushed tones one would use in church. Those men who came in with unshaven faces, rumpled clothing, weary eyes. Smelling of leather. Their pictures harsh with white light like a stage: blinding white beaches and billowing, translucent clouds; shadows on palm trees, uprooted coconut logs; shadows on soldiers' equipment and along the folds of uniforms that gave them the density of monuments. So formative that ever since then he had distrusted oceans and beaches, had felt their menace, always found himself scanning the surf for danger. Many of those men had been past soldiers longing for the heat of battle. He had failed the physical exams—glasses, crooked spine. Photographs were his only entrée to this world of war, a pass to be in the center of the most important story in the world at any specific time.

Helen standing at the end of the table at the restaurant. Sprung from the monsoon outside. Appearing like a spirit in her dark blue soaked dress. Ridiculous, klutzy, sublime. Leaving a trail of wet footprints despite the towels the maître d' pressed on her.

Even after making love, she evaded him, disappeared under his fingertips. This night had proved only how much of her remained a mystery. A woman who didn't hate what he did, didn't begrudge him his obsession, in fact had her own that might be stronger, because more thwarted, than his own. After all the affairs he had had during his four-year marriage, this was the first time he had forgotten to feel guilty.

Helen shifted in her sleep, and he went to her, and her lips formed to his before she was awake.

Helen woke at dawn, bathed in sweat, a nightmare caught in her throat, barely swallowing when she saw the accusing fact of Darrow beside her. A mistake made because she didn't want to spend the night alone. As the nightmare drained away, it left behind a throb in her temples. Curt from Philly had become Michael on the evacuation helicopter, and the minor leg wound became a fatal evisceration, the blue and green and plum of his insides spilling out of him, and she bucking on the corrugated floor of the helicopter, trying literally to hold her brother together. Then they were on the ground behind the berm. Michael's eyes—the pale blue recognizable, but the whites yellowed from jaundice, marbled with blood. His face skeletal, hands crusted in dirt, black under his fingernails as he pressed her into the ground as if to bury her, her face in the mud, the helmet cutting her ear, unable to breathe, urine pouring hot down the inside of her legs.

In the soft dawn light, she rose and crept to the bathroom, closed the door, and stood under the trickling of the tepid shower to wash the fact of Darrow from her, the water falling rust-colored at her feet. Michael's fury, the idea that she was haunting *him* by entering *his* war. Her failure still raked against her this morning. Maybe she should give up, go home to California, take up the small life offered to her. Let everyone think it had only been a grand, misguided gesture. Running a washcloth across her throat, she felt her skin, tender and sunburned. She pushed the washcloth between her legs.

The water had a metallic smell, like medicine. She wanted to escape down to a café on a quiet street and sip coffee alone and think. Should she return home, tail between her legs? The last part of the dream, Michael and she were inexplicably prone on the ground beside the helicopter, and a group of Vietnamese children approached, circling the two of them, pressing in, circling around and around, touching, but when she tried to speak with them, they turned their backs to her. Stones began to fall.

When she opened the bathroom door, her hair wet, a towel wrapped around her damp body, Darrow was sitting up in bed. "Everyone was right about you. You're some kind of mermaid. Always dripping with water when I see you."

Defeated by the awkwardness of the moment, she turned prim. "I need to brush my teeth."

"There's a fresh brush in the drawer. Rinse with scotch, I'm out of bottled water."

She nodded, grabbed her clothes, and ducked back into the bathroom. Once dressed, she came out and edged toward the door. "I need to go."

He leaned over to the nightstand and picked up a key, tossing it to her. "So the door will always be unlocked."

Glad to have escaped, she was still not ready to go back to her own room. When the cab dropped her at the hotel, she walked through the streets of downtown and along the river walk, tired and overwhelmed by the strangle of noise, movement, and people. Beggars clogged the streets, and young ex-soldier amputees with sullen, closed faces lounged in doorways and along walls. The city bristled, full of dirty children and starving animals. The tension in the air unnerved her. Even the effort to decipher it seemed crushing.

She longed to return to her room, be cool and clean, close the curtains and lie in semidarkness, but she couldn't be alone just yet. Visions of home became more persistent, filled with more and more longing—the wide streets along the beach, the green mossy lawns, the Vs of pelicans flying along the cliffs. Along Duong Hai Ba Trung, makeshift vendors sold sodas, the dusty bottles lying in boxes of crushed ice in the shade. The heat made them tempting, but she was frightened by stories of ground glass put in the drinks by VC.

Walking on and on, she neglected to check street signs, indecipherable anyway for the most part. She wandered for an hour in a labyrinth, then found herself back on Tu Do and felt pleased to be back at the familiar. As she passed along a row of shops, a cool, mint green bedspread in a store window caught her eye. The smooth fabric glowed in the dimness of the store. Helen was sure that if she touched it, it would be as cool as stepping onto a dewy lawn in the quiet of early morning back home. She went inside to ask the price.

The woman behind the counter barely looked up from her bookkeeping. Dark blond hair coiled into a bun with two weaponlike black lacquered sticks to hold it in place. Her face was pale and dry and powdered, painted crimson lips. For a moment, the store was so quiet Helen could hear the buzzing of a fly at the window and forgot if she had asked for the price or not. Then the woman spoke with a French accent. "That is expensive. Hand-embroidered silk from Hong Kong."

Again she dismissed Helen's presence, scratching at her ink-splotched columns of figures with an antique fountain pen. After a moment, she reached under her desk and brought out a large flyswatter that she snapped at the window behind her. Then the store fell into utter silence.

Helen turned and was startled by the sight of two Vietnamese women sitting in high-backed, rush-bottomed chairs. Neither of them looked up at her, not slowing down or missing a single stitch in their sewing.

Although they both had deeply lined faces, their hair, identically done up in tight buns, shone jet black. They wore matching black silk dresses, perfectly fitted from a fashion in vogue in Paris forty years back, consisting of tight bodices and long, flowing skirts. Heads bent down, they embroidered with the tiniest, most delicate stitch on silk cloth. So intent, so silent, Helen had not noticed their presence on first entering the store, their chairs on either side of the door to the supply room like bookends in a museum.

As Helen turned away, one of them, the older woman it appeared, began to murmur under her breath in French to the other. Helen could understand them no better than if they had spoken in Vietnamese. What new event could possibly have occurred to prompt conversation in this tomb except her entrance?

She turned back to the Frenchwoman, challenged now by her dismissal. "I'll take it."

The woman looked up, penciled eyebrows arched. "Lovely, I'll wrap it with a large bow. I'm the owner, Annick."

Helen leaned against the counter, dizzy from the heat and her lack of breakfast. The seamstresses, self-contained as sphinxes, were oblivious to her distress. She looked down and saw that her blouse had half-moons of sweat under the arms, and she was even more depressed by her water-ruined shoes. The Frenchwoman had undoubtedly noticed all this; probably that was the subject of the seamstresses' conversation also. As she turned, she felt a warm stickiness between her legs, and realized that she had forgotten her time of the month. Simply too much to bear, and in frustration, to her horror, she began to cry.

"I need to use your bathroom. I have a problem."

Annick sized her up, determining if she passed some test. The two women could just as easily have become adversaries, but something had swayed her to be Helen's friend. "Come, let's take care of you."

When Helen returned to the showroom, she was sheepish.

"Have a seat. I'll get you some water," Annick said.

"The heat . . ." Helen mumbled as she accepted the glass.

Annick was as impeccably dressed as if in a store on the Champs d'Elysées. Helen stared at her dress—a soft peach-colored silk, with a Mandarin collar. Annick looked at Helen's slacks, decided something, and smiled. "I have a black skirt in your size. Borrow it. It's much lighter than what you have on."

"I'm sorry," Helen said. "Where did you get that dress? I don't have the right things. . . ."

"The unexpected social whirl, yes? The dress is made here."

"I brought all the wrong things." She felt humbled, broken, by the last days. "I mean, it's a war zone."

"There are tricks to living in the tropics."

"Really?" Helen was flooded with relief to have another woman to talk to.

"Watch the Vietnamese." Annick nodded her head toward the two seam-stresses. "They move slowly. As do the French. When you walk down the street, you can always spot the Americans because they are hurrying."

"I didn't notice."

One of the Vietnamese women dropped a spool of thread, and it rolled out of reach under her chair. Carefully she laid down the cloth she was work-ing on and stood up, gathering her skirt in one hand, the fabric rustling. Helen saw she was wearing dainty black boots with buttons going up the ankle like the kind worn at the turn of the century. The cloth she was working on was a silk hanging of a bacchanalia: figures sitting at a table with naked dancers swirling around it. Detail so fine that red thread formed the rubies in the dancers ears.

Annick laughed. "It's true. You'll never survive here otherwise. The place will wear you down. I've been here fifteen years. Very few Western women last. It's an art to master. But they never ask for help."

"I'm a mess, so I'm begging."

Annick was attractive in the Vietnamese way: simple attire, pulled-back hair, sparing makeup. Painstaking work to look so natural.

"Lesson number one: Move slowly. Lesson two: Bargain for everything. You paid double what that bedspread is worth. You didn't even find out the price. The difference will buy you a dress like mine. What do you do, Helen?"

"I'm a photographer. Freelance."

Annick frowned. "Lesson three: Vietnam is a man's world. We have to make our own rules, but always the obstacle here is the men."

Helen closed her eyes for a moment, remembering the disaster of Dar-row. "I've been here two weeks and made every mistake."

"And it's only noon. What you need is a nice lunch."

Annick took her to a favorite place, painted metal bistro tables and chairs on pea gravel in a courtyard garden. The heavy air was trapped against the walls of the building, the perfume of the fleshy, tropical flowers around them making Helen light-headed. She hid under the shade of a banana tree and drank down glass after glass of chilled white wine as pale as water.

During the main course of sautéed sole and julienned vegetables, they discussed the logistics of surviving as a Western woman in Saigon—how to find feminine products and the chronic shortage of hair spray, where to have one's hair styled, where to buy clothes, where it was safe to go alone, what kind of culture there was, how to handle the number of soldiers all around.

Demitasses of espresso and sliced mango with sticky rice were served, and Helen asked about the two seamstresses. "Do they work for you full-time?"

"Madame Tuan and Madame Nhu are sisters. They worked for a French couple who owned a plantation north of Saigon in the thirties and forties. The sisters made all of Madame's clothing so well that her friends requested dresses. The sisters put silk on the backs of all the *colons* during that time.

"It was the time before my husband and I arrived. The couple was returning from a party at a neighboring plantation when they were killed by the Viet Minh. They weren't politically important, just unlucky."

Just as Darrow had warned, better not to ask what had happened to someone. "How horrible. What a tragedy."

"Actually . . . quite common. Anyway, the sisters wanted to keep sewing but didn't want to open their own shop. Didn't want to deal with the foreigners directly so much. We met shortly after that."

"So how old—"

Annick giggled. "The madames? They are timeless. The great fat old *chats* perched on their chairs. They know everything going on in the city and yet never leave the shop, hardly talk. They knew all about you."

Annick lit a cigarette and watched a Vietnamese man in his late twenties, dressed in an expensive suit, pass their table, then she blew smoke out through her lips. "That suit is so fine it must have just arrived from Paris." Her eyes narrowed as she studied the man's retreating figure. "These wealthy Vietnamese around town. Him, the son of an important SVA general. You will never see such opulence and such corruption together. They can't help themselves. They made their fortunes with the help of the French, on the blood of their people. They're cursed."

"You sound like a revolutionary," Helen said.

Annick laughed, a deep throaty sound, her head thrown back and her graceful white neck bared. "Never. I love the high life. If you know how to play it, Saigon offers the best life."

"So you stayed?"

"I tasted freedom. We stay on, just hoping it will last a bit longer. The sisters will put silk on the backs of the Americans now. But they will remain long after all of us have been banished."

"I went on my first assignment in the field yesterday and forgot to shoot my camera, I was so terrified." The words come out with a rush. "So terrified I slept with a man last night I shouldn't have. Too scared to stay and too scared to leave."

Annick stared at her for a moment. "It seems I have become your friend just in time."

At first, afraid she had started something with Darrow she wasn't sure she wanted to continue, Helen was relieved when she didn't hear from him. After several more days of not hearing from him, she realized that she had been dismissed without knowing it.

She struggled to make her way around Saigon alone, avoiding Robert in her embarrassment. When she returned to her hotel, she skirted the front desk, afraid of messages from Darrow, more afraid of none. Impatient, she frowned at the elevator, waiting for one of the bellboys to run over to her with a note: "Very important message. Mr. Darrow say urgent." But not a single word came. It occurred to her that the drawer beside his bed might be full of keys; he relied on the fact that they wouldn't be used. But she had used hers. In a rush to make the night before not seem a mistake, she had dropped off the green bedspread she had bought from Annick, gone so far as to make the bed with it. Pathetic. One more colossal blunder.

After a week had passed, Helen found out through her room boy that Darrow had been on assignment and was back. The answer to why he hadn't called. He hadn't bothered to inform her of the fact of a trip, but she could forgive that. In her relief, she sprouted affection for him. He was at his room in the hotel. She hurriedly changed into a linen dress, brushed her hair, and applied the pale pink lipstick Annick had given her. She made herself walk, not run, to his room. When she knocked, he answered distractedly, "Come in."

Sunlight streamed through the dusty windows, opaque through the tape used to keep them from shattering from bombs. The air smelled of dirty fatigues piled on the floor, stale cigarette smoke. The desperate feelings she had talked herself into minutes before abandoned her. She again felt like a fool.

Linh, bowing his head at her entrance, sat in a chair by the window, going through contact sheets with a magnifying loupe.

Darrow didn't move toward her but stayed at a large table piled with bags of equipment. His face was drawn, eyes invisible behind the glare of glasses.

She stood in the middle of the room, fingering the rough material of her dress, searching for an excuse for her presence, cursing herself for having come there. Finally she offered up "I heard you were back."

"Yesterday," he said, continuing to unpack cameras from a muddied bag. "I spent last night developing film."

"Oh."

She noticed the tremor again in his hands as he lifted equipment. She was making a spectacle of herself, another Tick-Tock. She hated being the kind of woman to insist that a night together had meant something.

"You remember Linh," Darrow said.

Linh rose and nodded to her as she crossed the room to hold out her hand. Blinded with hurt, it was as if she were meeting him for the first time. He stood and took her hand awkwardly, and she noticed without thinking the scarred skin along one wrist. What had he done before becoming a photographer's assistant? It occurred to her that perhaps a woman wasn't supposed to shake hands with a Vietnamese man.

"I dropped some things off at the apartment. Just a thank-you for taking me along that day." Fool, idiot. Just get out of there.

"I saw." Darrow lit a cigarette and offered her one.

"Was the bedspread okay? I bought one for my hotel room. The one there was too depressing, and I figured why not get two for the price. . . ." She couldn't stop talking, sounded ridiculous. She should die on the spot, of humiliation and bad judgment.

Silence in the room as he let her hang herself.

"It was fine. Linh, give us a minute."

"Sure." Linh, bowing even lower than he had the first time, not meeting her eyes, quickly left.

She felt stranded as the door closed behind him; she wanted to go out also, instead of staying and listening to what was coming. The lock shut so softly one only knew he was gone from the tap of his footsteps fading down the hallway.

Feigning interest, she walked over to the table by the window and was heartened to see the photo of herself on top of a pile of prints.

"Let me ask you one thing." Darrow said.

"What?"

"Did you really come halfway around the world to a war zone so you could play house with a married man?"

She pressed her fingers into the table, stared at the photograph of herself while she tried to gather her thoughts, arranged her face enough to carry herself out the room. She picked up her photograph, crumpling it in her fist.

"Don't get me wrong," Darrow said. "I had a great time, but I'm just thinking of you."

She turned and looked at him. "You had me fooled."

"Why's that? Didn't you say you would never love someone like me? So what's it now? Our Lady of Doomed Loves?"

"You are a grade-A prick."

Darrow sat on the bed with his legs crossed and took a long drag on his cigarette. "Sad fact is, Helen, baby, I can't save you."

She slammed the door behind her, hating herself for the theatrics but grateful she had at least left before tears. Relief topped mortification. Plenty of time for that later. He was right—this wasn't what she had come for.

In the dim hallway, she leaned against the wall. Sick at the absurdity of the dress and lipstick, she swiped at her mouth with the back of her hand. The balled-up picture fell to the ground. When she looked up, Linh stood there. He kneeled to pick up her photo, smoothed it on his knee, and held it out to her.

FIVE

Chieu Hoi

Open Arms

Her bags remained packed in a neat pile in the middle of her hotel room, but the days passed by, one after another, and still Helen didn't leave.

She could not face returning home a failure. A mode of being so ingrained she did not even recognize it. Her mother had remarried a year after their father's death, a close family friend who had become widowed. As like their father as could be. When Helen cried before the wedding, in jealousy, in fear, in betrayal, her mother sat her down and gave her "the speech." The speech would start with the particulars of the situation and then boil up to the universal truism that failure was not an option. Ever. "This man will be a good husband and a good father to you two. End of subject."

When Michael and Helen were teenagers, they would hide on the beach and smoke pot and drink alcohol with friends and caricature their mother, her grim pragmatism, how she buried the second husband ten years later and declared that she was done with men. "'Failure not an option,' she probably told him in bed," Helen said, thrilled by her rebellion.

A friend of hers, Reba, curly red hair spilling down her back, who had a crush on Michael, laughed so hard at the impersonation of their mother that liquid poured from her nose.

"She sounds like a monster."

"No," Helen answered. "She's just that way." It never occurred to her that there was anything wrong with such demands.

In her effort to prove that she could survive in Saigon and function without Darrow's help, she befriended other journalists in town, went to official briefings, took the rickety blue-and-white Renault taxis out to Tan Son Nhut to photograph American and Vietnamese soldiers back from operations. She and Robert joined official army junkets that flew journalists out in transport C-130s to write and take pictures of scarred land and dead soldiers hours after the action ended. Robert was content doing his job, writing up his stories, but she found the whole process frustrating. Her pictures were no different from those of a dozen other freelancers selling photos to the wire services for fifteen dollars a picture.

The journalists were in a questionable fraternity while out in the field, squabbling and arguing among themselves, each sensing the unease of the situation. No getting around the ghoulishness of pouncing on tragedy with hungry eyes, snatching it away, glorying in its taking even among the most sympathetic: "I got an incredible shot of a dead soldier/woman/child. A real tearjerker." Afterward, film shot, they sat on the returning plane with a kind of postcoital shame, turning away from each other.

In terms of the present moment, they were despicable to the soldiers, to the victims, to even themselves. In the face of real tragedy, they were unreal, vultures; they were all about getting product. In their worst moments, each of them feared being a kind of macabre Hollywood, and it was only in terms of the future that they regained their dignity, became dubious heroes. The moment ended, about to be lost, but the one who captured it on film gave both subject and photographer a kind of disposable immortality.

The wires sent her to cover human-interest stories—hospitals, charities, orphans, widows—but when she opened the paper and saw combat shots by Darrow as well as others, she knew that she was being sidelined. Of course, the truth of the war existed everywhere—battle and combat only a part of the whole—but her truth pulled at her from out on the battlefields. With her failure out in the field part of the public record, she didn't know how to start again.

Another month passed; she grew more restless. Only skimming the surface of the land and the war, returning to her safe bed every night. The reporters that were satisfied at this level were like archaeologists piecing together fragments and guessing at the truth of something long since disappeared. She felt like a fake. She kept going on the after-battle junkets with Robert, embarrassed for them both, needing the drinks at the Continental bar each night.

At dinner with Robert, she tried to explain her dissatisfaction. Ever since the night she left with Darrow, Robert remained aloof, as if there were some irony that he alone was privy to. She understood he needed to save face. She had acted badly, and there was probably no fixing it. Outwardly they still joked and flirted, but they both understood that things had changed between them.

"Is it enough?" she said. "These pictures don't feel like enough."

Robert shrugged, bored and disappointed. A cruel thought ran through his mind that at least nurses didn't bring their work with them. "You're too earnest now."

"Sorry," she said, realizing her mistake confiding in him. She changed the subject by ordering another drink, but he wasn't fooled.

"The only way to get the picture you're talking about is to get so close you become part of it."

But instead of deflecting her, his words gave her an idea. Now she went hunting at the air bases for stories. To go around official channels, see what was really going on, she copped rides alone on transport helicopters dropping rations and ammunition at distant firebases. Since there was no ostensible story, no combat, there was no restriction on her movements, either. Whenever possible, she tried to visit Special Forces camps in the hope of running into someone who had known her brother. There were men at the outposts half-naked in the heat, bodies coated by the inescapable dust and dirt that caused small boils on the skin, eyes wild from the isolation and the threat of danger. A few refused to talk with her, simply watched from the edges of the camp like feral dogs, but most were glad for the company. She sat and shared cigarettes, took their pictures, and talked while the chopper unloaded. In between the most banal questions—*What's your name? Where're you from? How long you here for?*—she caught glimpses of what she wanted.

At one landing base high in the foothills, the pilot decided to put up for the night. Pleased, she didn't bother mentioning that it was against regulations for her, a woman, to spend the night out in the field. Inside the small sandbag-and-wood structure with the unmistakable barn smell of marijuana, Helen was introduced to a former Special Forces officer, Frank MacCrae, wearing an apron and cooking a vat of chili over a makeshift fire pit. At forty-five, he was considerably older than the other men, and unlike them he was at home there. He had lived in Vietnam more than seven years, spoke the language fluently, lived out in the villages.

When they sat down to dinner—a dozen soldiers, the pilot, and Helen—Frank was quiet at first, drinking down beer after beer in a few gulps, appraising her. The chili had a bright layer of orange oil on top, and the native hot pepper made her lips burn and then go numb. When Helen complimented him and asked for seconds, he flushed with pleasure and brought out a bottle of wine he had been saving. "I was keeping it for when we have a boar to roast, but what the hell." He eyed her cameras. "Nice. I used to have a good Nikon but banged it up . . . Miss my picture-taking days. So now they're sending girl reporters?"

"Not willingly," she said. "They didn't send me. I snuck out here on my own."

"How long you been in-country?"

"Two months."

"Two months. Oh, baby." He lit a cigarette and leaned back in his chair, his white T-shirt freckled with reddish chili spots. "You came too late."

"How's that?" The heat of the chili beaded her forehead with sweat, and she wiped it with a napkin. That was her fear, that she had missed the biggest part of the war already. Her stomach started to churn.

"The good ol' days are gone."

"Oh, not this again," one of the soldiers said.

"See . . . we were just learning how to do business here, but they screwed it all up. It's easier to send soldiers, easier to throw money at corrupt leaders who'll play ball with us. Easier for us to just take the damn thing over."

"Did you know my brother, Michael Adams? He was here two years ago; died last year. Plain of Reeds area." A deep burble rose from her stomach, and she regretted taking the second bowl of chili.

"Not familiar with. Who was his captain?"

"Wagner, I think? Project Delta?"

"It's a small world up here. Didn't get to meet him. A damn shame." Frank smiled as Helen's eyes watered, a belch escaped. "Not used to good home cookin'?"

The pilot, bored, got up and signaled the others to go over to another table for a game of poker.

Helen felt as if she would explode. "The report was just the generic 'Died a Hero' stuff."

Frank examined the ceiling and blew smoke rings. "Our government is creating a show. All that shit years ago about Diem being the Winston Churchill of Southeast Asia. Did the English riot in the streets against Churchill? Did he imprison or kill his opposition? That was all a PR campaign courtesy of *Life* magazine."

"Maybe Diem tricked us."

Frank shook his head, gently at first and then harder. "No! No, no, no. Everyone knew he was a crook from the get-go. That's why they chose him."

"So why?" She stood, clinching her bowels. She'd have to make a run for the outhouse in the dark.

"Now you're going!" He banged down all four feet of the chair on the floor and clapped his hands. "Start thinking like a reporter about your own side, too. Why aren't you satisfied with the pabulum they fed you about your brother? Friends of mine started poking around—it was not appreciated. Got stonewalled, their stories weren't considered credible, they were reassigned back to the States. Visas and military passes revoked. I'm impressed if nothing else by the single-mindedness of the enemy. I can't take their hate personally."

"You aren't one of those conspiracy-theory crazies?"

"Just remember," he yelled as she ran outside, "where there's smoke, there's usually a bale of marijuana close-by."

She groped her way in the darkness, and she didn't know which was worse—her stomach or the fear of sniper fire. When she came back, they talked several more hours into the night, Frank so full of information that Helen wished she had a recorder on because she simply couldn't absorb it all. Finally he stood and stretched. "Bye, sweetheart. I'm out tomorrow for a five-day patrol."

"Take me with you," she said.

"No way, baby girl." He leaned down close to Helen's ear, and she smelled chili and beer on his breath. "They want you to be part of their movie, don't ever forget it."

"Please let me go with you." She blushed. After all, she was the girl with *The Quiet American* under her bed.

He went off to a corner of the room and came back with a small stitched bracelet. He motioned her to stick out her wrist. "Here. It's from the Yards. Good people. Now you're one of us."

"That means no."

"Can I ask *you* a favor?" Frank asked. "A smell of your hair?"

She nodded, and felt a scratch of whispers and a peck on her cheekbone.

"I want to know what's really going on."

He inhaled with a deep gulp. "I'm a sucker for beautiful hair." He sighed. "I'll never admit I told you this. My little present for you, so you can sleep better tonight. Didn't know your brother, but I knew Wagner's unit went in to assassinate some local chieftain along the Laos border. They were dropped into this mud hole, didn't know that the dry area on the map became a lake at the wrong time of the year, heavy and thick like quicksand, and they were stuck; when the bullets started flying they realized they had been ambushed; sitting ducks, the whole unit wiped out minutes off the plane. Crying shame. Shit like that doesn't happen to us."

"Take me tomorrow," she said.

"I'll sleep on it. Be up at five."

But when she woke up at five the next morning, MacCrae had already left camp.

"So what's he involved in?" she asked, trying not to show her disappointment.

"What isn't he involved in is a better question," a soldier answered with a laugh. "Frank and The Cause."

She handed the soldier one of her Leicas. "Tell him he owes me. Tell him to use it and bring me back pictures."

Frank was right in one way: The knowledge about Michael's death released her as knowing the worst can. Although it was as horrific as anything she imagined, she no longer had to imagine. But she was just as unwilling to leave as before; the mystery of what drew men like MacCrae to risk everything was bigger than Michael's death.

She rode out with the helicopter pilots high over the land of the delta south of Saigon, trailing over the endless paddy fields that reflected up at them like broken pieces of a mirror. The dull green of choking jungle and sinewy-limbed mangrove swamp contrasting with the light green of the new rice; the land only rarely broken by signs of human habitation—small clusters of thatched roofs or an occasional one of red tile. From above, the land appeared empty and peaceful, only farmers bent in the paddies or orchards. She sat like a tourist, enthralled by the dirty green and reddish brown rivers, slow and thick-moving like veins pumping life into the land.

It felt safe looking down from high in the air, protected by the metal of the machine and the speed of its movement. The confidence of the pilots infected her. Many of them were her own age, some as young as her brother.

She went out on dozens of runs, routine and without contact. A fact of war that in both combat and photography there were great stretches of nothing, boredom, and the only thing left to contemplate was the land itself that had brought them there. For a time she was content to commune with the mystery of it. But once she relaxed to the fact of nonevent, of safety, curiosity began gnawing at her again.

On each assignment, she would question soldiers about what they had seen of Vietnam. Their answers were strangely resistant.

Mostly, their worlds were sealed by perimeter wire and bunkers, bounded by the luxuries of C-rations, sodas, cigarettes. They lived in a universe limited to their weaponry and machinery, their chain of command, and so in the most fundamental sense it did not matter in which country they fought. They were immune except to the most basic facts of topography and weather. Vietnam was not mysterious to them, not the history or the land or the yellow faces. Uncovering the secret of place was considered nonessential. The mystery that held them was their own survival, the beauty and inscrutability of battle, the shining failure of death. To them, Vietnam was nothing more or less than what they purchased during R&R in the bars and the streets of Saigon and Danang. It was generally concluded a secret not worth knowing. Helen concluded that coming to Vietnam was the best thing that had ever happened to her.

The first time she rode in a gunship, sitting behind the gunner in the open door of the fuselage, the wind howling like a hurricane through the interior as they dropped through the air in a combat-landing spiral, she grabbed the webbed walls for support, but all the fearlessness she had gained from the transport flights vanished. She made bargains: If she survived this one flight, she was done and would go home. Or at least stay in Saigon and cover vaccine drives.

The gunner pointed his big gloved hand down, and she saw an enemy fighter appear from out of the tree line. He bent down on one knee and aimed his BAR rifle at their plane. It would be a miracle if he could down a chopper with it. Helen couldn't hear the high scream of bullets, but quarter-sized holes appeared in the sides of the plane, splinters of sunlight like angry eyes. He had managed to hit them.

After months of hearing about the elusiveness of the enemy, this man in his dark pajamas seemed anticlimactic. Even though he was trying to kill them, Helen felt more afraid for him, fear rolling in her gut at the unevenness of the battle, the lone man crouched in the tall, burning grass, the spreading shadow of the gunship passing over him.

Helen got the photograph of him aiming at them as the gunner let loose a round. They were almost on top of the man, so that the force of the first spray of bullets made him fly up and backward like a wind. Helen kept taking pictures until the film ran out. While she sat down on the floor to reload, hands shaking so badly that she had trouble opening the camera, he blew into parts in the spray of bullets.

When she climbed out of the plane back at the airport, ears ringing from the deafening thunder of the engines, the pilot gave her a thumbs-up and invited her for a beer. He had soft, moist eyes, and said that the beauty of the country made the violence especially awful, like slashing a pretty woman's face. She sat in the officers' club, stiff with sweat and fear, and listened to him talk about a girlfriend back home, the hope of a job in the airlines after his service was up. Neither spoke of being fired on or of the killed enemy, except to write it up in the military report. Helen didn't yet understand that conjuring up the future was the duty of the living, what they owed to the dead.

She lied to herself, broke her promises to go home or at least to stay in Saigon after that flight because the whole event had been so surreal, so unweighted, so anticlimactic, because the pictures were too far away from the man and showed the horror in miniature, which carried meaning only when the events were explained. Pictures could not be accessories to the story—evidence—they had to contain the story within the frame; the best picture contained a whole war within one frame.

Her arsenal of supplies became her protection. She would triple-check each item because she believed that without any one thing she might anger whatever god was keeping her safe. She carried two Leica bodies on crossed neck straps, bandolier style, one under each arm, with three lenses, a 28, 35, and 90mm, all purchased on the black market, as well as her tailor-made fatigues and canvas para boots. Annick had taken her shopping and then to lunch as if it were the most natural thing in the world to go on a shopping spree for war. Ridiculous and comforting. She carried a film case on the helicopter, but in the field she fastened the film rolls to her camera straps. She counted the weight down to the ounce, wouldn't consider carrying the added weight of a weapon. Her only concession to vanity was always wearing her pearl earrings.

Only a couple of weeks after meeting MacCrae, word reached her that he had been killed. She felt a grief all out of proportion to the brief time she had known him. Maybe it was his age, but he reminded her of the generation of her father. So clear that they had had unfinished business with each other. The pilot who introduced her to him handed her a bag MacCrae had left for her, and in it was her camera and a KA-BAR knife in a beaded Montagnard sheath. She took the camera to Gary, asked if he would help her expose the film. One shot, the rest of the roll empty—a newborn, still smeared with blood and mucus, umbilical cord stanched, in large white hands. Behind, unfocused, a woman lay on the ground. The mother? She seemed peaceful, seemed asleep, but it was a worrying picture. Whose hands? Why outside?

"Let me buy it," Gary said.

"It's not mine to sell."

She walked with Robert through the bookstalls in Saigon as she told him about MacCrae's death, and he frowned. A young American civilian passed them and greeted Robert.

"Excuse me a minute," he said. The two men stood aside and talked quietly, heads bent.

Helen moved off toward the books, wondering if there was any truth to the rumors about Robert feeding information to the CIA. Probably it was her hurt feelings over his waning interest in her. Which was fine. What he did was his own business, but she didn't like his muddying what it meant to be a reporter. The table was piled high with weathered paperbacks in English. Many had pages stuck together, wavy with humidity. She opened a book, *Pride and Prejudice,* the pages brittle and yellowed. The incongruousness of reading Jane Austen in Vietnam made her smile. "Five cents," the boy behind the table said. Helen nodded and took out the change.

After a few minutes, Robert returned, clearly pleased but offering no explanation of who the man was. He could have an informant. "I didn't even know MacCrae was still around. He turned against the SVA. Against us.

Forgot whose side he was on. Insisted on living, eating, sleeping right there with the tribal people."

"Isn't that what Special Forces is supposed to do?"

"Forget MacCrae," Robert said. "He was an old crazy. Thought he knew better than we do how to win the war."

"I trusted him," Helen said, testing the words out and realizing they were true. "He's what I came to find."

A note at the hotel told her where to jump a ride to a hamlet for MacCrae's funeral. Since he had been operating in an area officially off-limits to the United States, his death and funeral were being hushed. She would not invite Robert; it pained her, the new distance between them. His own secrets and now hers.

By the time the ceremony started, darkness had penetrated the hamlet. Rain poured down on the tin roof of the small, open-air schoolhouse. It needled the metal roof with a loud, continuous hiss that depressed Helen. In the threadbare, damp room, she waited on a rough bench, staring at the plain pine coffin surrounded by candles. The circle of flame extended only as far as the concrete floor, only as far as the glistening, bowing banana leaves that crowded to form a wall of the room. She had been asked to bring a copy of his last photo, and now she placed an eight-by-ten print of the newborn on a small table by the coffin. The hurt inside her was unreasonable, but that did not help stop it. MacCrae had been killed with enemy-stolen American weapons; his will stated that he wished to be buried in the hamlet he had lived in those last years, all his money and belongings divided up among the villagers.

Various men entered in ones and twos to pay respects. These were not the military she had met so far. Like MacCrae, most were older; like him also, many wore the tiger stripes and black berets of the elite divisions. She read the crest insignia on a Green Beret who came in—*De Oppresso Liber . . . To Liberate the Oppressed*. Most were accompanied by Vietnamese and spoke the native language freely. She heard names of hill towns and base camps. Lang Vei, A Luoi, Duc Pho, and Plei Mei. MACV-SOG, marker of clandestine activities, whispered behind her. When a man wearing a Ranger uniform spoke to her, it was hesitantly, the rusty English words forming themselves slowly on his lips. She thought of her father, how he would have felt right at home in this group.

A voice behind her made her turn. Darrow stood with Linh in the doorway, talking to a Special Forces lieutenant.

When Darrow saw her, he bowed his head briefly, then came forward. "Why are you here?" He had hoped to hear news of her departure, heading back to California. Her presence irked him. When she was gone, he would stop wanting her.

"You treat this like your personal war. Think I'm crashing a funeral?" All of her longing for him instantly turned to dislike. She regretted Linh moving off to give them privacy.

Darrow stared at the coffin, kneading the back of his neck. She had gotten further than he would have thought. He couldn't imagine MacCrae befriending her, exactly the kind of amateur he loathed. "We were good friends."

"Robert said—"

"Frank," he said, "was part of the old guard. The men here are the last of it."

She fingered the beaded sheath on her belt. "He left this for me."

So Frank hadn't quite dismissed her. Of course, he was human, too. A pretty face must have appealed to him. "He must have thought you needed protecting."

"I left my camera for him." She looked around. A lonely way to end. As if he read her thoughts, Darrow reached out his hand and laid it on top of hers. An impartial hand. She let it sit there for a moment, warming her skin, then pulled away before she got used to it. She would stay a little longer because Frank had taken her aspirations for real, not wanting to let his faith in her down.

With a shock Helen realized she had stayed till Christmas, a disreputable and wistful holiday in the tropics. A large dinner party was organized for all the journalists stranded in-country. A hot and rainy afternoon, but the evening held a touch of coolness, a token of it being the dry season. As Helen waited in the hotel lobby for Robert, it could not have felt less like Christmas Eve.

The party was being hosted in one of the rented old French villas near the embassy. When Robert and Helen walked in through the gates set deep in the high walls surrounding the compound, the courtyard was crowded with overgrown plants—heavy, succulent leaves, overblown blossoms beginning to wilt, heavy rotting mangos and papayas fallen on the ground from the overhead trees—all of it lit by thousands of small candles flickering throughout the grounds. White-coated Vietnamese menservants greeted them in the doorway with silver trays of champagne.

Everyone in the expat community was there. The few that had them brought family. The majority brought doll-like Vietnamese girlfriends who wore either garish Western dresses or demure *ao dais*. They giggled like children and wrinkled their noses at the taste of eggnog. Helen had invited Annick, and Robert had brought along a friend as her date. The four of them sat on sofas and drank rum-laced eggnog while Frank Sinatra played on the record player. A pine tree from Dalat had been helicoptered in, hung with items from the PX: packs of chewing gum and cigarettes, tubes of lipstick, decks of cards.

Dinner was served at two long tables with white linen tablecloths that resembled long galley ships. The tables seated twenty each, while the rest of the people went through a buffet service and balanced plates on their laps. The prime rib, mashed potatoes, and candied yams, all cargoed in from Hawaii, weighed down and crushed with nostalgia all in attendance.

Someone down the table asked where Darrow was.

"Oh," Robert said, "probably in some foxhole below the DMZ, warming up C-rations with a match." Laughter from the table. "During incoming fire." More laughter. "In the rain." Everyone laughed. Helen gave a tight smile. She had not seen him since the funeral. "Making us all look bad," Robert continued. "Especially when he gets the cover of *Life* next week."

After dessert, guests went back into the living room. A Santa-dressed reporter handed out gifts, mostly bottles of scotch and brandy. Helen had gotten up to get coffee when Darrow walked in. His clothes so caked in dirt that only the deep rumpled creases were clean. His forehead had a few long bloody scratches across it, and the beginning of a brownish purple bruise was swelling under one cheekbone. She almost laughed because it seemed an extension of Robert's joke, and he saw her smirk and turned away with no acknowledgment.

"Where have you been, Darrow?" the host shouted.

"I have an announcement to make," he said, pausing to cough into his fist. "Jack was killed tonight. We were ambushed in a jeep patrol in Gia Dinh."

The holiday mood destroyed, the host clapped a hand on his back and then poured him a drink. They went off to the kitchen.

"The war doesn't stop for long," Robert said.

"It's been that way forever," Annick said, and finished a full brandy in one gulp. "A land of continuous siege."

"Jack knew that. He said it didn't matter who we backed, that the people didn't care. So why do we?" Helen said. She herself felt trapped, too scared to go out in the field, too scared to give it up and leave. "I mean . . . we have a choice. Why don't we leave?"

Nobody spoke.

"I'll be back." Robert went to the kitchen.

Annick leaned over. "Is that him?"

Helen nodded.

Annick shook her head. "Poor Helen."

Lights were turned off in the living room, and small white candles were passed out. " 'Silent Night.' In memory of Jack."

Helen looked at the faces around the room, at the makeshift decorations, and felt closer to the people in that room than to people she had known all her life back home. It had only just begun for her—people disappearing from her life. Not only people she loved, but people she knew only casually, people whom she knew only by sight. The familiar world chipped away each day.

After dessert, guests made excuses to hurry away. No one could rebound from the news. Robert came and said they should get back to the hotel before curfew. Helen nodded, hoping that Darrow would come out, would take her away again to the crooked apartment, but, of course, that was all over.

In her hotel room, Helen kept the lights off. With difficulty, she banged open the rusted window to let in fresh air. In Vietnam everyone wanted windows shut to keep things—heat, humidity, bugs, bullets—out. After midnight, the only noise the swish of a police jeep blading down the wet streets. The male reporters were still enjoying themselves inside bars or in the brothels that locked their doors till dawn.

She took off her clothing and, with the deliberateness that came from drinking too much, hung each piece on its hanger. In the morning, she'd go out to Ben Cat and tag along on a sweep made by combined forces. She would eat Christmas Day rations with the soldiers. The thought of the greenish half-gloom under the trees depressed her. Already sick of the war. The overhead fan creaked as she paced the room, smoking and drinking bottled water to stop the spinning in her head.

She had gotten used to water at room temperature. Annick could spot Americans across a room because of their insistence on having ice. Ice tinkling in glasses. Anything to deny the crazies-inducing temperature. The military had contracted out the manufacture of ice-making plants to keep up with the insatiable American demand for ice cubes, ice cream, anything frozen, and now the Vietnamese were beginning to have an appetite for it. Helen had taken picture upon picture of Vietnamese children eating ice cream, and those were the ones always printed—they made readers happy, an example of America's civilizing process.

She longed for the refuge of Darrow's room, but she denied herself its Spartan comforts. It was true—the soft beds and rich food and even the ice cubes, all of it a kind of game, keeping her from feeling things. The beginning of some kind of understanding had come as she sat in the tin-roofed schoolhouse at MacCrae's funeral, but it had been too ephemeral, had disappeared before she could get her mind around it.

A soft knock on the door interrupted her thoughts. She stood still, fingering her necklace, her mind flooding with horrors.

More knocking, more insistent.

Her heart jumped against her ribs. If it was the police, no one would be able to help her till morning. There were always rumors of arrests, people disappearing.

"It's me. Please open," Darrow said.

She grabbed a robe and pulled it over herself as she unlocked the door. Down the hall, her room boy with the long eyelashes was lying on his mat.

He propped himself up on his elbow and looked at them, a smile showing crooked, gleaming white teeth.

Darrow pushed her inside and shut the door.

"What is it?" she asked, but his hands gripped her shoulders, his mouth hard on hers. He had come straight from the party, clothes unchanged, skin still smudged with dirt and sweat, chin unshaven.

He pulled off her robe and pushed her back on the bed, his mouth on her breasts, her stomach, her thighs.

They made love urgently, without tenderness or words.

Afterward he buried his head in her neck, his arms so tightly around her that it hurt to breathe. A shaking in his shoulders. He wept, his head on her stomach, face turned away from hers in the darkness. Their first intimacy nothing, the usual wartime coupling of people escaping fear, but now they entered a place of their own, invisible and not describable. Words like *adultery* small and meaningless against where they now were. When she woke at dawn, her room was empty.

It became their ritual—his arrival in her room at night. Sometimes to make love, sometimes simply to sleep.

No promises. When she did not see or hear from him for weeks, it no longer upset her. She understood; the war consumed. Her bags were finally unpacked by her room boy, who carried the empty suitcases away for storage.

Something shifted, infinitesimal, frail as a hair root reaching down through soil, anchoring the plant; no longer were there thoughts of leaving.

SIX

Haa

To Civilize, to Transform

After months of pestering military command, she obtained permission to go out on ground search-and-clear missions. The military was not happy having a woman out in the field overnight, but they relented. She learned the art of shouting like a drill sergeant, cussing out officers with expletives when they tried to deny her access, realizing that it gave her a surprise advantage in making her demands. They figured any woman that tough could hack it on her own. They trotted out the worn-out old objections of lack of bathroom facilities and lust in the soldiers.

"It can't be worse than fighting them off in the officers' club, can it?" Helen asked.

Chuckles and permission granted. It was also a trick she played on herself: knowing that if she was successful, it would be too humiliating to back out of going. At first, with the newness of the experience, there was an undeniable excitement as well as paralyzing nerves. But even with that, the fear didn't stop. The hardest thing was to give meaning to what appeared to have none.

She woke at three in the morning and two hours later was riding a clattering helicopter through the dark. They were dropped in the Phong Dinh area in the smudged light of predawn. A known hostile area, as most of the countryside was now turning. The South Vietnamese troops insisted on flying in the next day straight to the village, letting the Americans patrol the surrounding area in advance.

The officers were unhappy having her along, so she knew if she couldn't keep up on patrol they'd use that as an excuse to send her back. The only way she could keep up in the heat and physical exertion was to lighten her load. She stripped out a normal supply pack from thirty to fifteen pounds. Although she was issued a flak jacket and helmet, she stopped wearing them out in the field. She sat on the flak jacket on the choppers like the men did, but then she left hers behind. The soldiers laughed that she was trying to out–John Wayne them, but it was just a matter of mobility.

The captain in charge of the mission was a twenty-six-year-old Swede from South Dakota named Sven Olsen. He was stocky and muscled, with a bulldog jaw and a smile that quickly flashed and then was gone. His eyes were a cool, hard blue that did not give away his thoughts.

"The most dangerous times for the FNGs are the first few times out. They get themselves killed by stupid mistakes. Stay in the middle of the formation, next to me, that's the safest place. Don't crowd up on the guy in front of you because if he trips something, we don't need two dead for the price of one. Try to walk in the footsteps of the guy in front of you. If he's okay, you'll be okay."

They waded through greenish gray paddy water the temperature of blood. Two hours later they climbed up to a dirt road and stopped for a break; the temperature was already ninety. When Helen took off her boots, her feet were bluish and shriveled, with a circle of black leeches feeding on her ankles. She pulled iodine Syrettes out of her pack and opened them, dousing the leeches till they dropped off. The point man, Samuels, came over and started burning them off her with the end of his cigarette. Olsen had given her an army pamphlet outlining VC explosive devices to be on the lookout for.

Helen buried her face in the booklet so she wouldn't have to watch the leeches spasm and smoke as they burned. "This says to bypass booby-trapped areas," she said.

Samuels paused and took a drag of his cigarette before he started on the leeches again. "Then we should be patrolling Wyoming because this shit hole is honeycombed with the stuff."

He had the wide-open face of the Midwest, empty and innocent, but his eyes reminded her of the men stationed at firebases too long. His tanned arms were knotted with muscles, a green dragon tattoo wrapping around the left forearm under his flak jacket. He had been in-country for eight months.

"Come up front for some real fun," he said.

Helen nodded but felt relieved that if she tried, Olsen would pull her back. They started again down the wide dirt road.

Helen had been briefed on the various kinds of mines and booby traps to be aware of, but now, thinking where to put each footstep while watching the terrain around them frayed her nerves. She should be doing five things at once; like learning to drive, it needed to all become automatic. Whatever Olsen said, she couldn't match her stride to the guy in front who was six feet tall. Constant guesswork whether a certain flat rock looked too inviting, if a patch of dirt seemed artificially mounded.

At eight in the morning, the day was so hot that her fatigues were soaked. Sweat poured into her eyes, forcing her to tie a bandanna around her fore- head to keep her vision clear. A soldier behind her, Private First Class Tossi, handed her a roll of salt tablets that she chewed one after another. One more supply she'd need to start carrying in her pack.

"If you run out of salt tabs, suck on a pebble," he said.

They approached a hamlet half an hour later, walking single file through a narrow break in the bamboo hedgerow that hid the village. The thatched dwellings were small, filthy, and sagging. The villagers looked at them with dead eyes and turned away, going about their business as if the troops were invisible. After they had passed, Helen saw a farmer turn an impassive face from the troops and slap his son so hard the child bawled.

The Vietnamese in the countryside seemed more foreign than in the cit- ies. Smaller and darker and more hostile, making the Americans moving through their village feel like awkward and hated giants.

Tossi stood near Helen. "They give me the heebie-jeebies, the creepies, the way they are."

After the hamlet was searched and secured, they sat in the shade of a grove of areca palms and pulled up pails of well water. Children peeked around the corners of huts and giggled as Helen took pictures of them. The men took off their helmets and poured whole buckets of water over themselves. Helen dipped her bandanna in the pail and wiped her face. Her vision swam. She opened a can of peaches, ate the whole thing in a few bites, and drank down the syrup. She bargained another can off Samuels in return for her ration of cigarettes.

As they prepared to leave, a young Vietnamese woman walked up to Helen and handed her a woven palm conical hat. She had a narrow oval face, almond skin; the soldiers growled out a few wolf whistles as she knelt down. Helen bowed and gave her the two candy bars she was saving as a bargaining chip for more peaches.

"Ohhh, baby, let me liberate you now!"

"Shut up," Helen said. The men ignored Helen like a sister, but this woman was fair game. The hat, finely woven, had a pale flower painted along the brim. The girl bowed lower. "You're scaring her."

The woman rose quickly and made off. Helen put the hat on and was amazed by how light and cool it felt.

Nothing suspicious, they left the hamlet half an hour later, at ten o'clock, and continued on the dirt path that went along the river. The soldiers grumbled and finally Captain Olsen came up to her.

"I can't order you, but the men want you to take that thing off."

"It's just a hat."

The way he looked at her left no doubt that it was a kindly worded order. With regret, she made a production in front of Olsen of laying it on the side of the road. When she looked back, the line of soldiers had detoured, each man taking his turn to step on it with clumsy, muddied boots. It was the first time she felt something pull back inside of her—a distrust of her own soldiers.

Samuels offered her his bush hat. "Part of our pacification program. Don't get on the wrong side of *our* hearts and minds."

She took the cap meekly. Later, she picked a yellow daisy at the side of the road and tucked it behind her ear. "Am I going to be accused of being a peacenik now?"

Another hour, and they came to a small stream. The peasants crossed in narrow pole boats or walked across on monkey bridges made of single bamboo poles. The American soldiers were too big, loaded down too heavily, to try them. But Tossi, showing off, rushed halfway across one bridge before

falling into waist-deep water. Everyone laughed and made catcalls. Even villagers stopped and hooted. The clowning was a relief, as if they were out on
a nature hike.

One of the privates shuffled down a bank into a solid clump of reeds
to wade across the stream. Next thing, the concussion from an explosion
knocked everyone flat: earth and shards of metal rained down. A pressure-
detonated case mine sheared off his left leg and buttock; he lay screaming in
the river, a sudden flush of red all around him as the water leaked his blood
away.

It was as unexpected and horrific as a traffic accident, and Helen sat frozen in place, stunned. But then, as a reflex, she lifted the camera and started
shooting as two soldiers jumped in and dragged the private out of the water
and onto dry ground. A Vietnamese man, close by the explosion, stood with
an icicle-shaped piece of shrapnel coming out of his cheek.

The medic shot the private up with morphine and tried to stanch the
blood with a large compress. The wounded man moaned and cried out. When
he saw Helen, he yelled to the medic, "I don't want a woman to see me this
way." Stricken, she moved out of his sight, her courage failing her. Nothing
left to do but wait for the medevac, the medic left to patch up the Vietnamese man.

The private's screams spooked them all; they stole looks at him, praying
for the dustoff to come faster. When the morphine took effect, Helen braced
herself and went over. "I'll leave if you want me to." His hand reached out to
her, and she held it.

"Would you take my picture?" he said.

"I did. The next one will be when I visit you in the hospital."

"Now. Send this one to my mother."

"You don't want your mother to see this."

"Do it."

Helen held her camera, wiping at her eyes so she could focus. He looked
straight in the lens—cheeks and chest pitted with black shrapnel. One leg was
straight out and ended in a boot, next to it there was a phantom space where
the other leg should have been. A blanket was bundled around his groin.

"Don't be so scared," he said. "You look so frightened you'd think it was your leg. You'll make it." He seemed satisfied and looked away. Ten minutes later he died.

"I didn't find out his name."

The medic looked impatient. "Scanlon. Private Scanlon."

Helen nodded as if the name were an explanation.

One soldier walked past. "Fucking Scanlon fucked up. And that's the whole fucking story."

His body was zippered into rubber. And then he was as gone as if he had never existed, and they moved on.

They crossed the stream in silence, for once walking in perfect formation, each alone with the new truth that if he died in the next moment, he would be as gone and as forgotten as Scanlon. The rage that filled her felt good, weighted her like a good meal or a strong drink, felt better than fear. The rage filled her so nothing else could get in.

Besides stolen American antipersonnel weapons being used against them, as they had been on MacCrae, they had to watch out for the enemy's handmade traps that showed a peculiar genius. She had been told not to pick up any valuables such as books or hats or watches, to avoid lighters and canteens, to make a wide berth around unopened beer cans. Not to touch discarded enemy uniforms or helmets, and especially not VC flags because the enemy realized their souvenir value and booby-trapped them. Watch for obstructions such as large stones on a path or fallen logs or broken-down wheelbarrows. Keep an eye out for any unnatural appearance in fences, paint, vegetation, dust. Most of the men refused to use the outdoor latrines out of similar fears. After enough time, even the palm fronds waving in the wind came to look like razor-sharp knives.

When the men stopped to rest, Scanlon's death unleashed their fears, and they passed around rumors they had heard: an officer sitting on a plush, mossy tree stump and blowing himself into a million pieces; a patrol coming upon an abandoned bunker and hearing the incessant crying of a baby, climbing down to investigate, and being incinerated. Endless war legends of booby-trapped hookers.

"These people simply don't value life like we do."

Helen heard that over and over. And, of course, after living through war for two generations, it seemed at some level to be true. Many of the Vietnamese seemed numb to the unrelenting death and destruction that was messing with these American boys' minds.

It was hard to know what was true from what was false. Mostly, it depended on whose side you were on. Most of the time, the reality of a situation fell into a gray no-man's-land in between. The Americans called it "the Vietnam war," and the Vietnamese called it "the American war" to differentiate it from "the French war" that had come before it, although they referred to both wars as "the Wars of Independence." Most Americans found it highly insulting to be mentioned in the same breath with the colonial French.

At three o'clock they stopped to eat at the edge of the jungle that they would soon have to work their way through. The temperature more than a hundred and ten degrees, and the humidity almost as high. The men ate their rations in silence, and like a dealer Helen expertly traded her Lucky Strikes and C-rations of meatloaf for cans of peaches.

After half an hour, they rose again, but two soldiers remained on the ground, sweat-glazed, their skin the color of unripe fruit, from heat exhaustion. Another dustoff, and Helen felt a flutter in her stomach as the planes lifted and flew off. After all, she had the burden of choice. The rest of the soldiers hefted their packs and started into the jungle.

Helen could have left—this patrol wasn't promising to yield any worthwhile pictures—but they had allowed her to come, had accepted her among them, and to her it was a point of honor to remain till the end.

Out in the open, the main danger came from the ground, but in the jungle danger existed at every height. Thick vines, accidentally touched, might swing back with a grenade at the end. Thin green bamboo, if tripped, was capable of whipping back with barb-point arrows.

She could see only a few feet in any direction, and claustrophobia made her long for the open paddies and roads they had just so gratefully left behind.

Under their feet the ground liquefied into a mud of vegetation that gave off a sour, green smell, like a thick, algae-filled pond. Behind her, Captain Olsen reached a hand out against a large green trunk and triggered a tiger trap from overhead. The board came crashing down with its rusted long spikes, but the new plant growth impeded it, and he just had time to roll off the path—only the edge of the board grazed his right forearm. They all squatted in place on alert as the medic bandaged him. He examined the rotting, rusting board and determined it had been there for years, if not decades.

"Probably had a Frenchman's name on it," Olsen said, laughing.

At six o'clock they broke through the jungle and found themselves on dry ground again. They had not encountered a single enemy soldier, yet it seemed the land itself, inhospitable and somber, was their enemy, bristled at their trespass, wore down their spirits.

They walked a quarter of a mile and stopped in a field at the side of the road, under an old French watchtower. The soldiers pulled out entrenching tools and dug in for the approaching night. Helen sat down, body aching, muscles quivering. Only the first day of a three-day patrol completed. She sat smoking a cigarette, a new habit, and watched the last golden light over the jungle. The air like velvet, filled with folds of pollen and insects. Once in a while, far away, she heard the sharp caw of a wild bird or the eerie wail of a monkey. The soldiers joked that you could throw a pit of fruit on the ground and come back a week later to find a tree, a week later and find it full of fruit, a week after that and find an orchard.

As the light faded to a deep purple, they watched a group of peasant women make their way home. The women talked animatedly until they saw the soldiers in the dark field, and then they grew silent.

"Well, boys, looks like we're on the map now," Olsen said. If the enemy didn't yet know their location, they soon would.

"Don't they know we're here to save their asses?" Tossi complained. "Whoever heard of being afraid of the people you're saving?"

"Maybe somebody forgot to translate that into Vietnamese," Samuels said.

Olsen, Samuels, Tossi, and Helen huddled in the shallow foxhole to smoke and sleep while a perimeter guard kept watch in shifts. At first Helen tried to stay awake but kept nodding off; she gave up and slept even after the rain started, merely pulling the plastic poncho over herself. The bottom of the foxhole filled with water, but she guarded her camera equipment in an airtight plastic bag set on her stomach. The guys had great fun with the fact that she stored her film in condoms.

At dawn, stiff and wet, they drank lukewarm coffee and ate canned ham and eggs before breaking camp and moving out.

"You okay?" Tossi asked.

"I'm fine," she said. "Just cold. And wet. And muddy."

Tossi handed her a flask and some pills.

"What?"

"The pharmacy is open."

She nodded and swallowed them daintily, an obedient child.

By eight o'clock it was again more than ninety degrees. The sun stiffened their wet uniforms. They arrived at their rendezvous point and waited for two Chinooks to bring in the company of South Vietnamese paratroopers to form a joint sweep of a *ville* consisting of nothing more than two dozen grass huts. The Vietnamese troopers jumped briskly out of the helicopters. They appeared small and clean and rested compared to the American soldiers. Their uniforms were freshly pressed.

"Do you ever get the idea," Tossi whispered, "that we're on the wrong side?"

"Hey, they know it's too dangerous out here at night. We're the only ones stupid enough to get our asses blown off," Samuels said.

The Vietnamese trotted along the dikes in textbook perfect formation. The Americans had to lumber along with their packs to keep up, like overly protective parents.

"Sorry, Adams, looks like no pics for you today," Captain Olsen said. "If they're eager that practically guarantees the area has been cleared of VC. No action today."

The Vietnamese troopers stormed the empty *ville,* M16s sweeping back and forth erratically. They stopped and struck heroic poses against empty buildings as if they were rehearsing a movie. Helen didn't take a single picture. Excited and trigger-happy, a few of the SVA soldiers shot at a pig, the squeals unnerving Helen. They missed the lucky animal, who escaped. The Americans hung back, not wanting to get caught in the line of fire. As predicted, the place was empty, save for stray dogs and chickens. The sun beat a harsh white off the dirt, the only shade provided by a few old fruit trees, the ground underneath them littered with rotting mangos and papayas that perfumed the air. A few old women, tending children, stood warily in doorways.

The SVA troopers abruptly dropped their guns and declared lunchtime. A dozen chickens were procured, butchered, and cooked over open fires. The Americans stood in a knot, watching, weapons at the ready, until Captain Olsen shrugged and told everyone to take lunch. Then the Americans dropped their packs and opened up cans. A few Vietnamese soldiers came over to bum cigarettes and practice their English, but for the most part the two groups stayed separate. Captain Olsen communicated with his Vietnamese counterpart through hand signals. Captain Tong was small, trim, and finicky, with a wisp of mustache and two gold incisors that flashed in the sun when he smiled.

The Vietnamese troopers took a siesta after lunch that lasted two hours, and as the American soldiers had nothing else to do, they also gratefully stretched out in the shade and went to sleep. The heat was unbearable and made everyone lethargic. Captain Olsen stayed awake with the radioman, communicating with headquarters and asking how to proceed. Orders were to accommodate Captain Tong at all costs.

Out of the corner of her eye, Helen watched an old man in peasant pajamas sidle up from the back of the *ville*. The guards searched him but found nothing. Had he come from the fields or had he been hiding in one of the huts the whole time? He walked to the main communal square, stared balefully at the pile of feathers and discarded chicken parts, and moved off. A few minutes later, he came back. The guards searched him again, found him clean, and again let him through. Now he seemed agitated, and he talked to himself as he approached the Vietnamese troopers.

Helen turned away until she heard shouting between one of the Vietnamese soldiers and the old man. She asked Captain Olsen what was going on.

"I don't know what they're saying, but my guess is that the old guy is unhappy about his 'donation' to the war effort. We've complained to headquarters about it. We're under orders not to take anything that isn't offered. But not to interfere with what the Vietnamese soldiers do. Let them work it out between themselves."

Helen held up her camera and framed shots as the soldier turned his back on the old man. Insistent, the old man grabbed his shoulder as another soldier approached him. Now the old man talked louder to the second soldier, frenzied, his hands flailing, pointing at the chicken remains when the first soldier spun around and kicked him hard in the leg. The old man was on the ground when Captain Tong strode over and barked some commands. The old man dramatically shook his head.

Unnoticed, Helen moved closer as Tong pulled out a .45 revolver.

The old man struggled to his knees, tears in his eyes, not frightened but agitated, and kept talking and pointing to the chicken remains.

Helen's heart knocked so hard in her chest that her breath came out shallow and rasping. No way is this happening, she thought. She crept forward, kneeling, as Tong's soldiers moved away from him, sensing his rage; she got closer to frame the shot when Tong, standing stiff, stuck his right arm straight out, the revolver against the old man's head. She kept shooting. Surely, she thought, it's only a threat, surely—until the deafening explosion, the gun fired at close range. She kept shooting—the old man's head shattered like the carnage of ripe papayas under the trees, body spread-eagled on the ground, thrown by the power of the blast, blood hosed up and down the front of Tong's pants.

"VC," Tong screamed at the Americans.

Helen was on automatic, shooting f/8 at 250, everything inside her shut down, no fumbling, just cold, clear, and mechanical. She didn't realize for the first moment—face behind the viewfinder, vision constricted—that now Tong was shouting and flailing his arms in her direction. He strode over and stood a few feet away from her, aiming his gun straight at her forehead. She fell backward, still in a crouch, framed the muzzle and his apoplectic face above it in the viewfinder, the gold incisors flashing in the sun, and kept shooting. Captain Tong, bent in half, waved the gun wildly in one hand, screamed, and the other Vietnamese soldiers ran over to form a half circle of menace behind him.

She heard Captain Olsen's voice, a long-forgotten presence, behind her, yelling back at Captain Tong, each in a different language, neither under-standing the other.

On a high, Helen kept shooting for what seemed like an eternity but was probably less than a minute. Captain Olsen, still behind her, still yelling over her head, took out his own gun. At that signal the American soldiers jumped up and formed behind him. Olsen took several steps forward, and in one bear-like swipe of his arm knocked the revolver out of Tong's hand. The screaming continued, Helen kept shooting, frozen to the camera—the tendons in Tong's neck bulging, his face purpled. The film ended, nothing to do but remain fro-zen on her knees, camera to her eye, afraid to move. If she removed the protec-tion of the camera's body so that it no longer shielded her face, she was sure she would be killed. In the far distance, the blowing of a water buffalo could be heard, which meant that Tong had finally quieted. He kicked at the dirt in front of Helen, sending dust flying into her face, spat at her, and turned away.

"Mother of Christ," Olsen said, grabbing Helen by both arms, dragging her back. "Are you crazy? Trying to get us fucking killed? By our allies?"

All she could think was how unafraid she felt. How gloriously unafraid. "That old grandfather was not VC."

"Radio for a helicopter *now*!" Olsen screamed to the radioman. "You are out of here."

"I didn't do anything wrong." She was thrilled by what she had just done, and it was inconceivable that she would be dismissed.

"Everyone, move out front."

Away from the Vietnamese soldiers and Tong, Olsen calmed down. "I thought I'd lost you."

"It's not fair to send me out."

"Look, he's a slimy little bastard. But he's our bastard. You made him lose face. I can't vouch that they won't stage a little 'accident' to get you."

Helen sat on the ground and held her head in her hands. Suddenly thirst was killing her. "Can I have a little water?"

Olsen slapped his thigh. "I don't want my guys getting killed defend-ing you."

"Fine. Okay. Water." The idea of going, against her will, didn't seem quite as bad as a moment before. She had film to develop.

"Look, you're one crazy *bao chi,* okay? You can come back out with me some other time."

"Put it in writing."

"I know." He laughed. "I know you will."

Despite the heat, Helen shivered, the skin on her arms full of goose bumps, as the helicopter flew her back to Tan Son Nhut. So drained from the patrol and her sleepless night that the danger of the incident with Tong still seemed unreal. Her fatigues were mud-encrusted and smelled; her hair a knotted ponytail; she was proud of herself.

The crew chief gave her a thumbs-up and passed her a flask, and she took a long drink of whiskey, drank it down like water, only the good burning sensation down her throat registering. They flew high above the jungle canopy, out of reach of danger, and Helen wished the flight would never end, that they would never have to come down and touch earth again.

When she got out of the helicopter, Robert was waiting for her in a taxi. "Tell me everything. Olsen already radioed the incident in. I'm writing the story while the photos are developed. The package needs to be couriered to Hong Kong ASAP. The censors will never transmit it out."

She stood in the darkroom, the size of a closet, bumping her head on shelves filled with plastic chemical bottles, watching Arnie, the wire's office manager, develop the film. He said it was too important to let her or the assistants do it. Arnie was potbellied and married, his wife and kids back home in London. The office's assortment of freelancers were his misfit orphans. He had spent a lot of time explaining composition technique to Helen.

"You're catching on, damn it!"

The pictures were properly framed and shot, a whole sequence from alive to dead villager, and then a muzzle below the outraged face of Captain Tong, the end of the gun pointed straight at the camera and the person behind it.

Looking at the pictures, Helen broke out in shivers again, seeing what had been invisible before, a devouring shade as if a cloud had passed before the sun—the mystery she was chasing, the one she'd glimpsed at MacCrae's funeral. Now she understood what he'd said to her that night: that the mystery came in its own language to each person, and you had to decipher it on your own. She had been so scared at the moment she might as well have been blind.

"Too bad," Arnie said. "This kind of work under pressure. Incredible. So good they're probably going to throw you out of the country, and I'll lose another promising photographer."

"They're good?" The tension in her body unspooling fast now.

"I wouldn't have believed it without seeing them. But I talked to the office in New York, who said if they were half as good as they sounded, they'd think over offering you a full-time job with the wire service."

"Are they half as good?" Part of the dread those last few months had been the fear that she was incapable of doing what she had come for, that she would be found lacking. As a freelancer, she could stay out as long as it took to get a shot. Captain Tong had just happened, her actions unpremeditated. Now would she feel the pressure to take such risks again and again?

"Two hundred percent as good. I might even have to give you a raise to thirty per shot. Don't get greedy."

She frowned. "They can't throw me out now, can they?"

"They can. They've done it to others."

"Okay." That was enough for now.

"I agreed to share the pics with *Life*. If that's okay by you. They can print the whole series in next week's issue. That philistine, Gary, pays a bit more than we do. You can actually survive on what they pay."

Helen nodded, unhearing, and left the darkroom for the office's tepid air-conditioning and lumpy couch. She stretched out and plunged into a dreamless sleep.

That night Helen met Robert in the bar of the hotel. He was a little bit amazed and a little bit delighted but mostly afraid for her.

The tables were crowded, spilling out along the sidewalk. The city's electricity had gone out, and the room was lit by oil lamps, opening out onto the dark street. After her night out in the rain, the city felt luxurious even in the dark in a way no city had ever felt before. Waiters floated between the tables with small flashlights. Everything seemed uniquely fine. She felt at ease, perfectly in the moment. The danger of the incident with Tong faded into the background, and all that was left was her shining invincibility.

A bottle of champagne appeared, and the old Vietnamese bartender in his white coat opened it with great ceremony, nestling it in a bucket on the corner of the bar. Robert and she toasted, and at her insistence, the bartender joined them for a glass. Ed and some of the other journalists came by and stopped to congratulate her.

Matt Tanner came and stood behind her. He was a recent ex-Marine who had re-upped so many times the joke was that the Marines had finally thrown him out. The rumor was that he simply loved war too much and brought his bloodlust along with him to journalism. He was always competitive when another reporter did well, as if they were stealing his chance at glory. When he was jealous and drunk, which he was at present, his face thinned to an even more wolflike aspect.

"Nice little publicity stunt this morning. Who'd you pay to snap the pics, huh?"

"Get lost, Tanner," Robert said, standing up.

"G.I. Jane, eh? Nice angle."

"Maybe you should take a break from trampling over other people's backs to get the story first," Helen said.

"Nice talking to you," Robert said to him. "Sorry you have to go."

Tanner squinted at Robert, deciding if he was in the mood for a brawl. "All I'd like to know is who she had to screw this time."

"Why?" Helen said. "Do you want his number?"

"That's enough," Robert said.

"We all know you're not getting it from Bobby here," Tanner said, and stalked out of the bar.

Robert sat back down on the bar stool, emptied his glass, and poured another.

"I wish the Marines would take him back," Helen said.

"I'm your friend. It's none of my business about you and Darrow. But you have to be careful. Tanner is a competitor. Not like me, too scared to leave Saigon and the official junkets. There's going to be sore feelings if you don't sweeten up."

"You're smart enough not to need the attention."

Robert stiffened. "You don't have to throw me a bone."

Helen drank down her glass and looked into the bottom as if she might find answers down there. "If I was a guy, you wouldn't tell me to worry about sore feelings."

"If you were a guy, I'd tell you to punch him out. But I'll tell you the truth, I probably wouldn't have bought this bottle of champagne, either."

Helen laughed. This charade of light flirtation was necessary for both of them. "Can I admit something? Just between us? This feels good."

"Enjoy it. You earned it. But be prepared."

"What for?"

"For what comes next."

In the morning her pictures and story headlined across a dozen front pages worldwide. *Life* magazine bought the series of photos and planned to use one as the cover for the following week; the contributor's notes touted her as their first woman combat photographer for the Vietnam war.

She stared at her name in print with a feeling of relief that now she could stay on, no longer a joke. Six months before, no one would have believed her capable of this. Her only background a high school photography class and some work on the college newspaper taking pictures of football games. In a way, she had not believed it herself, but now she felt a sense of belonging to a fraternity, even if it was one that wasn't sure it wanted her. As time went on, she would find herself welcomed and ignored in equal measure.

The nerve that she had hit was not the atrocity of the killing of the old man, which was a routine horror, nor the evidence that the SVA had run amok and was alienating the civilian population. Not even the angle that America was supporting dubious allies. Her pleasure started to chip away as she realized they were using Captain Tong threatening a woman photographer, an American civilian, to sensationalize the story. Her being a woman was the story.

The South Vietnamese government immediately protested to the American embassy, saying that the incident had been faked. Captain Tong denied

Helen's version, calling her a spy, although he couldn't explain why Americans would be discrediting their own allies, but the pictures and the testimony of Captain Olsen were ample verification. The company's mission was aborted because of the publicity alerting the VC of their movements. Olsen cabled her congratulations and said the company celebrated with brandy and cigars back in the safety of the base camp. There was even a movement under way to have an LZ named in her honor. Not Scanlon's.

That night she turned down Robert's invitation for dinner with the boys and spent the evening walking alone through the streets of Saigon. The adrenaline high of events now turning into a low of confusion. She had proved to herself what she hadn't known before: that under the right circumstances she could be brave. An unknown gift, strange and random, like the ability to play an instrument or be good at a sport. But the memory of the old man poisoned her. His balding head; the sagging, dark eyes; the thin, sinewy legs splayed out. She felt guilt that, outside of his village, she was the only one to mourn his death; an arrogant thought, perhaps, but he had already slipped into the realm of statistic. Maybe now was the time to leave, tonight, without a single good-bye.

She could see the potential for the war to undo her. There was hardly any way the incident could have turned out better, ways without number for it to have turned worse.

The street barbers closed up shop along the sidewalks, taking down the mirrors and shelves hung on the outside of building walls. Food smells made her stomach growl; she had not eaten since breakfast. Ducking down awkwardly at a soup stall, she pointed at what she wanted. The old man smiled and soon a large crowd stood watching her, giggling at the sight of a Westerner, a woman no less, squatting on the street and eating with chopsticks and ladle-style spoon. The official health brochures warned against eating the street food, but Helen was tired of obeying rules, tired of being frightened. This night she was immune. She slurped her soup the same way the Vietnamese man next to her was doing.

Finished with her soup, she rose to the claps of a few Vietnamese around

her, impressed that she had eaten the whole bowl. She bowed and made her
way back to the hotel.

In the lead article about Captain Tong, Scanlon being killed by a land
mine while on patrol had been mentioned only in passing; his death was not
newsworthy enough in the war. But, of course, his death was the only thing
that day that mattered. The old villager's death was another tragedy of unnews-
worthy proportion. She consoled herself with the thought that the pictures
were graphic enough to shake people up, stop them being complacent about
what was happening, and if that meant the war would end sooner, those two
deaths weren't in vain. As she hoped, with less and less confidence each day,
that Michael's had not been in vain. Too much waste to bear.

MacCrae's words never left her thoughts. *They want you to be part of their
movie, don't ever forget it.* Their prescience haunted her, and if there was anyone she needed to talk to that night, it was him. Appropriate that he was now
a ghost. Whatever victory she felt was cut neatly by the idea that her photos
would be used for purposes she had not intended. She pictured MacCrae's
face across the table that night. An even more grim possibility. Would discrediting the SVA allow them to bring in more American soldiers?

The only tangible effect of her photos was the number of requests that
came to cover Helen herself. Photo teams from the States wanted to go out and
photograph her photographing the war. If she let that happen, she may as well
go home because she'd be a spectacle. The journalist's cardinal sin of becoming the center of the story. It embarrassed her, and she had Arnie turn them all
down. And then an offer came from *Life* that she couldn't turn down—staff
photographer.

When Arnie finally got clearance to offer her a full-time position with the
wire service, she blushed. "Gary already made a big offer."

"Yeah, I figured. Good for you. Hell, this is small potatoes here."

"I'll miss you."

"Tsk, tsk," Arnie said. "You should find a nice soldier to marry." Over the
years, he had learned that each journalist had his own specific reasons for why
he went into the battlefield. He guessed hers worked as well as anyone else's.

She requested that her first assignment be to cover the Central Highlands and I Corps area, especially her brother's Special Forces unit. Gary promptly ignored her, and she learned the price of being bought.

That night as she brushed her teeth, getting ready for bed, she heard a light rapping on the door. Her heart lifted, all the emotions of the week rushing out, hoping it was Darrow. She opened the door in her slip, but it was Linh standing there.

"I didn't wake you?" he said, startled at the sight of her undressed.

"No, no. Is everything all right?" Helen asked, looking behind him.

"I'm going to work for you now."

"What? What do you mean?"

"Sam asks me to give you this." Linh handed her an envelope.

"Come in. Sit down." She motioned him to a chair and tore open the envelope.

Helen of a Thousand Ships,

Congratulations! Even though you bumped me from a cover and almost got yourself killed in the bargain. Since you're determined to play the boys' game, at least accept a life preserver—Linh. He will be invaluable to you.

Love,
Darrow

Linh stood by the window staring out. When she spoke to him, he kept his face turned away, and she guessed her slip embarrassed him. She put on a robe. Still he was pensive.

"How do you feel about this?" she asked.

"It's important to Sam that I work with you. I'm hoping you are strong. I am thinking this is going to be a very long war."

SEVEN

Hoi Chanh

Defectors

A week after the dinner where Linh was first introduced to Helen, he went to Darrow's hotel room and was surprised to see a picture of her on top of a stack of prints on the table. Darrow never joined his reporter friends with their Vietnamese bar girls at the various clubs. Linh knew about a few native women, including the one in Cambodia, but Darrow never openly had a girlfriend.

Perhaps Darrow preferred Western women, but there, too, Linh had observed a fair number try to capture his attention with no success. Was he struggling to stay faithful to his wife back in America? He never talked of her in the way a man talks of the woman he loves. But then Linh himself had never spoken of Mai until she was gone.

Which made the picture of the beautiful photographer all the more startling—a single bloom sprung up on a parched riverbed floor.

Linh examined more closely, saw she was wearing a flak jacket and camouflage pants, that the palms behind her were water palm fronds. Darrow had not mentioned going out on a mission with her, and Linh felt a pang of betrayal at the omission. He had become possessive over Darrow's company, as well as his confidences.

"Oh, you remember the freelancer from the States?" Darrow said, turning away, obviously irritated at Linh's attention and the necessity of explaining himself.

"A very striking freelancer."

"You're right. I've got to straighten myself out. Breaking my own rules."

"Everyone gets lonely. Even the great Sam Darrow."

"Don't make me feel worse."

Linh shrugged and finally forced himself to look away from the picture. He hated the fact that he had forced this admission; he was becoming a prude. Darrow had rescued him at his lowest point, and he was determined to repay the kindness.

The next time Linh saw her, she was sprung to life from the picture, pacing Darrow's hotel room. When she shook his hand, he knew she was blinded by Sam's rough treatment. Darrow was in the process of breaking her young heart, and Linh quickly escaped the carnage.

At the hotel bar he stood drinking a *citron pressé* and asked Toan, the bartender, an old man who had relocated from Hue, about his oldest son just drafted into the Saigon army. Toan complained that the cost of bribes to get a safe desk job had doubled from the year before. During the whole conversation, Linh imagined Darrow and Helen upstairs, negotiating their way through their love. Although he had seen and suffered much, he did not find them frivolous; in fact, he found it more than optimistic that in the middle of war, people could still think about such things. Didn't that mean the world could still recover?

Although Linh took his time finishing his drink, still he was too early returning and witnessed Helen, like a *tien,* fairy, crying alone in the hallway. As a youth, he had made a great study of all the Vietnamese myths, and a *tien* was often an essential feature of each hero's story. When she saw him, she fled.

Months passed and neither Sam nor Linh brought up the subject of Helen again, although now a new picture of her was framed on the table. In one of his favorite fairy tales, that was exactly what happened to the *tien:* She disappeared back into a picture. Probably Helen had returned to her country, the romance of the war quickly tarnished.

Linh and Darrow were both surprised by the pictures of the execution, and Darrow admitted he had been keeping track of her. The way he said it revealed even more.

"She has made an impression on you."

"I see her going through all the things I went through."

"Yes?"

"And I don't want her to do it. . . . I see each step where I could have stopped."

He had been with Darrow long enough to see that he was the best at his profession, and he cared passionately about it. There was the sadness, but he thought that had more to do with the personal. "I don't understand. . . ."

"Gary has offered her a staff position with the magazine. I don't want her getting herself killed making some stupid mistake. Work with her."

"What if she doesn't accept?"

"She will."

From the tone of voice, Linh understood it was a lover's assurance. "I prefer to work with you."

"It would mean the world to me, my friend."

When Linh came to her hotel room that night, she seemed embarrassed. She lit a cigarette, offered him one, then sat on the bed.

"We haven't gotten off to the greatest start," she said.

"Sorry?"

"Me making a fool of myself."

Linh shook his head as if shooing away a pest. These Americans still took getting used to, their bald honesty, their constant confessing of deficiencies. In Vietnam, etiquette prevented such things from being talked of. He had been married for six months, bringing Mai sheet music every week, but she never sang the new songs before having him sing them out loud first. When he got angry at her, she finally admitted she couldn't read; he thought she meant read music, but then it dawned on him she had also been memorizing his words.

Now he looked at Helen and was shocked by her naked admission. And yet it was disarming and made him feel protective of her as over a small child who was helpless and too trusting. "I saw you for the first time at the restaurant. You come in drenched from rain."

Helen made a face. "Another bad impression."

"No. A hungry woman, I thought." They laughed. Why had he omitted the true first time he saw her, getting out of the military jeep in front of the hotel, while he sat at the bar with Mr. Bao? Was it because he did not wish to be remembered in Mr. Bao's company? Or was it that he wanted to keep his first glimpse of her private? Or, worse, was it because the habit of deception had become so ingrained in him, he preferred lies to truth?

The next morning Linh walked to her hotel and spent the whole day seeing the city again through her eyes. This happened each day, day after day; the realization dawned on him that now he was showing her his home.

Her first request was to learn enough Vietnamese so she could put the people she photographed at ease. No other American, not even Darrow, had made such a request. During the monsoon downpours, they would duck inside small tea stalls. She would hold a ceramic cup laced in her long fingers, listening to the drumming of the rain on the tin overhang of the roof while they practiced speech. Often children gathered at the sight of the foreign woman in their neighborhood, still a novelty, and giggled at her mispronunciation. They sat on the ground around the battered table, loose pieces of plastic wrapped around thin shoulders against the rain. Helen called over a food vendor and bought *banh da,* rice cakes with sesame seeds, for everyone. Linh was sure they, too, felt as if they were in the presence of a *tien.*

"How do you say 'Thank you'?"

"Cam on."

"Come on?"

"Xin ba noi lai." Please say it again.

" 'Com on'?"

"Better." Linh laughed.

"How do you say 'Can she speak English?' "

"Chi ay biet noi tieng Anh khong?"

The words came in a flood, impossible to separate them, guttural stops and starts that she felt she would never understand. "Sorry I asked."

"We'll go slowly. Use the words every day. Listen to stories. That's how I learned English."

Helen poured more tea from a dented aluminum pot. "I know it's a letdown to go from working with Darrow to working with a beginner."

"What is 'letdown'?"

"A demotion. Step down."

Linh took his cup. Again, this stating of what should remain unspoken, and yet he flushed in embarrassment that she guessed his feelings. "When the words form on your tongue naturally, you enter the heart of the country, I think."

"But you've never been to America."

"Once upon a time. My favorite was Chicago."

But just as she started to question him, a group of children rushed in and swarmed them with questions.

After taking her back to the hotel that day, he walked along the river. How could he have made such an admission? Shameful. Yet he had been alone so long, had not talked from his soul to another person, that at the first sign of interest, his mouth flooded with words. No one should know about his years abroad.

His father had gotten caught up in politics at the university. He chafed under the unfair French restrictions for Vietnamese to advance to any real power. Studying the life of Uncle Ho, he was convinced of the importance of seeing the world. He spent a great deal of money and used many promises to get Linh a berth on a freighter going to the Middle East, and then on to Europe. Linh went one better in going on to America. Although those had been the happiest years of his life, there had never been a question of not returning, of not fulfilling his father's wishes that he be of service to his country.

He was still haunted by what he had seen. In Phan Rang, dockworkers drowned and floating like milk fruit in the port after being ordered to jump into the water to salvage ships. On shore, French officials laughed, jiggling bellies of fat. Linh became as lean as a dagger. In Dakar, he watched the same horrors of colonialism, watched as natives were ordered by the French to swim out to his ship in a storm. Helpless, Linh watched from the deck as they drowned like heavy, dumb animals in the water. Although he had been called Chinaman in America, the freedom had been heady. But then he had gone into the South. His experiences taught him the need of freedom at all costs.

Gary's first assignment for Helen was to cover the Buddhist strikes, visiting the pagodas around Saigon. At Xa Loi, the bonzes orchestrated protests against the Ky government. Linh described the marches three years before against Diem, telling her of the chaos then. Monks and nuns using their bodies as tinder throughout South Vietnam, horrifying and alienating the West. In Linh's village, a nun described how she had daintily tucked her robes around herself in the town square, how a circle of bonzes formed a barrier against outside interference. "What could the military do? Shoot them?" The absurdity in Saigon of antisuicide squads equipped with fire extinguishers patrolling the streets.

Gary wanted Helen to get pictures of daily life in the pagodas. They took pictures of boys in brown robes receiving instruction and old bonzes reclining inside dark rooms, sipping tea and strategizing. Young men ran back and forth in their orange robes like waiters in a busy restaurant, pamphlets fluttering, directing traffic and arranging interviews with the head monks as if they were rock stars.

The noon heat and the thick smell of burning joss sticks drugged Helen, slowed her movements to those of a sleepwalker. When everyone retired for the noon break, she photographed a more peaceful mood—a single white-clad nun sweeping the grounds in front of the carved columns of the building, the shadow of a Buddha statue inside barely perceptible.

Under a banyan tree, Helen leaned back into a cradle of gnarled roots. Her shirt clung to her back. Linh motioned to a vendor who brought them coconuts filled with sweet, brackish juice. When he handed her a straw, she hesitated.

"Drink it."

She nodded, emptying it in one gulp. "I'm tired of being afraid."

"The VC are cunning, but they haven't yet trained the coconut trees to grow poison."

They watched women, young and old, enter the pagoda grounds carrying prepared dishes or baskets of fresh vegetables.

"Does the community supply food?"

"The community is the pagoda. They bring food or money, whatever they can, whatever is needed."

"But they don't have enough for themselves."

"One is like a brick in a wall, interdependent; one has no meaning outside one's relation to family and others."

Helen sat up and pulled the fabric of her shirt away from her back. "Do you know why I came here?"

Linh shook his head, wary of more confidences.

"I wanted to be famous. I had dreams of being the only American to get pictures of the Ho Chi Minh trail. Stupid, huh?"

Linh smiled. "Darrow is very happy every time he gets a cover."

"Really?" Helen laughed.

"He sits in his room and drinks a glass of scotch and stares at the cover for a half hour. Then he puts the magazine in a drawer and doesn't look again." Linh shrugged. "But he's passed up shots that could have been his, too. And he mourns every death until it seems impossible that he can continue."

"That's why I love him," she said.

He couldn't stand hearing more. How could he go on day after day listening to this woman bare her soul to him? "I should go back to the office with the film."

"Where is your family? I mean, what you said earlier, bricks in a wall?"

"I don't want to insult. We are different from Americans. We only share important things with people who have earned our trust. Otherwise we dishonor our memories."

She flushed, chastised, and tried to brush it off. "I ask too many questions. Join me for dinner tonight?"

"I'll meet you in front of the hotel early tomorrow."

She turned back to the pagoda to hide her hurt feelings.

Linh walked down the crowded street and stopped at an outdoor café. He motioned to a busboy and paid him to run the film over to the office, then ordered tea and nursed it. He felt guilty about his gruffness toward her, but he had changed since coming to Saigon, grown a second skin that insulated him from others. It would have been smarter to be kinder. After all, that is what he liked about the Americans—their innocence, their willingness to share their life story with a stranger. After fifteen minutes, he crossed the street and surveyed the pagoda grounds.

The area was still empty, but he spotted her in a deserted courtyard. She sat alone, crying. He felt discomfited, her face so naked, as if she stood before him unclothed, and he knew the right thing would be to leave unobserved, yet he stood rooted to the spot. He recognized such pain. The reason—Darrow had told of her losing a brother to the war—was it enough to cause her to put herself in danger's way? A place not fit for a man, much less a woman. He made a show of reentering the compound and stood in front of her. When she saw him, she showed no surprise, simply held her hand out to him.

"I'm sorry about prying. I hate when people ask about my father. Having to say that I hardly remember him. Or my brother."

He pulled out a cloth handkerchief from his pocket and handed it to her. "I think telling a friend this story is a great honor."

She gave him a sly, crooked grin. *"Cam on."*

Before he could react, she stood and hugged him. No one had held him in a very long time. His head felt light, blood rushed hot to his skin. He made an awkward, panicked escape.

"I will be gone for a few days. A week at most."

"But we have the story to cover."

"Can't be helped. You'll be fine."

Back at the café, he ordered a whiskey. He was meeting with Mr. Bao the next day in Tra Vinh, and had to have his head clear. He would gather maps and stop by the American commissary and pick up Mr. Bao's new passions: two cartons of Marlboros and four loaves of Wonder Bread.

Linh allowed Mr. Bao to believe that they were having an effect on the American reporting of the war, although the reporters ended up being far more disillusioned by the truth than anything Linh could craft. "You just can't manage to stick to one side," Mr. Bao had said after finding him. Ironically, Linh's intelligence gathering now included Mr. Bao, too, and his new sideline of drug trafficking, using the military for protection. He was making millions. Besides his dabbling in small-time brothels. His corruption made him the ideal partner for Linh—a man always open to compromise.

A week later, the helicopter dropped Helen and Linh off at Pleiku in the early morning. The change in geography was startling: the sultry flatness of the Mekong, with its inland oceans of rice paddies and white-hot sky, all replaced by the thinner, cooler air of the Central Highlands with its burned gold of elephant grass, olive drab of bamboo and scrub, its ancient menace of mahogany and teak forests.

Inside the military compound, a mission was being patched together to rescue an earlier convoy headed for a Special Forces camp on the Cambodian border. According to the last radio dispatches, only a few survivors were holding out.

Helen argued with the head sergeant, Medlock, a hound-faced man, and finally got permission to accompany the rescue. She felt jittery but swallowed the fear, already getting used to having Linh at her shoulder.

"You willing to share some of that?" Helen asked a first lieutenant, Reilly, sitting on an ammunition crate eating a chocolate bar.

"Sure." He broke off a piece and handed it to her. "Need my energy for this baby."

Helen nodded and put a piece of soft, melted chocolate on her tongue.

"You and I better keep our hats on." He pointed to his own hair, the color of red-licked flame. "Our heads are like target practice." He pulled out a beaten-up bush hat. "This here is my lucky one. Some shaman or something blessed it by pissing on it."

Helen gave a short laugh. "No kidding?"

"Yeah, but he said whoever wears it won't get hurt. So far not a scratch."

"Makes up for having to put it on your head."

"I got two. 'Case I lose one. You want to wear it?"

"Already have my own." She touched the bush hat that Olsen had given her, that led to the Captain Tong pictures. She stood up. "Thanks for the chocolate."

"You find me if you change your mind."

Medlock gave a shout, and Helen searched for Linh, finding him with a group of Vietnamese paratroopers. "Let's go," she said. "We're on."

He looked at her and then looked back at the Vietnamese officers. He picked up the film and camera bags and followed her. In the background she could hear snickers from the paratroopers. "We're not going," he said under his breath.

"What?"

"This convoy will be ambushed."

"Well, a chance of that. But we're going." She couldn't let on that her stomach was sour, her hands clammy. Shouldn't she be getting over this by now?

He put the bags down. "This time, no."

Helen looked back at the paratroopers and then at him. Trucks lined up and loaded with supplies; jeeps filled with machine guns and grenades. A queer, unreal look to everything, and now Linh was spooking her. "Do they know something?" she said, pointing her chin toward the paratroopers.

"Let's move out," Sergeant Medlock shouted again.

"Listen to me this one time," Linh said. He looked her in the face because this was more urgent than his politeness. "Stay behind."

"I'll look like a fool," she said. "Gary's expecting pictures."

"Be a fool then." His throat grew tight. "*Here* you listen to me. *Here* I know better."

The sergeant came toward her with a clipboard. "Adams, you ride in the second jeep."

She stood for a moment looking at the ground. She hadn't expected this—not an assistant but a babysitter. Her confidence so fragile that she was afraid if she backed down now, she would always find reasons to.

Medlock sighed. "Look, don't give me trouble about the lead truck. I need my men on that one."

Helen kept silent, Linh's eyes on her. If she let him order her around now, there would be no end to it in the future.

"Adams? Am I disturbing you?"

"I'm going to have to pass."

"Hurray, one less problem." He walked away, already forgetting them.

Now that the choice had been made, she took off her bush hat and wiped her forehead, angry that she had given in, angry that she already felt the physical relief from fear. Failure pounded at her. "I doubt you would have kept Darrow from going."

"I wouldn't need to. He would know better."

"What would've he known?"

Linh shrugged, tired of the conversation. He could not endure this. He would go back and give Darrow an ultimatum—either he worked for him or no one. Certainly not this woman.

Helen glared. Without a word, she turned and stalked away toward the communications bunker. The rest of the morning she took pictures at the field hospital. Her nerves were badly jangled by the tension of the camp, the sight of the wounded, the thought of what she had avoided. Although they worked side by side, she didn't speak to Linh once. Her intuition told her she had missed something important, and far from helping her, he had talked her out of it. She planned on ending the arrangement when they returned to Saigon.

But the outgoing flights were loaded with wounded, and they would be forced to spend the night. At sundown, as she was lounging in the communications bunker reading a magazine, the radioman waved Sergeant Medlock in.

"The lead jeep set off a mine. Everyone inside got it."

Medlock shook his head, his long face even longer, and punched his fist on the table.

The radioman listened again. "Sounds like the rest of the convoy is blocked and ambushed. They want to know how to proceed."

"Damn it," the sergeant said. "Give me the phone." He looked around the bunker at the grim faces, then spotted Helen. "This is classified, sweets."

Helen left. An hour passed and the sergeant wheeled out from the bunker, short of breath. She approached him.

"The rest of the men caught it. We've got two left, hiding in the jungle."

She said nothing, tried not to think of the faces of the men she had joked with that morning. By nightfall, the radioman had lost contact, and it was concluded the two had not survived. Linh didn't stay with the Americans but went to sleep with the Vietnamese soldiers.

In the damp, stale air of the bunker, only flashlights were used for light. Sergeant Medlock sat on a crate next to Helen, hesitated, then passed her a flask; she took a deep drink. He asked why she had changed her mind about the convoy.

"I didn't. My assistant refused to go."

"Little coward saved your life. Bullheaded orders from headquarters. I grew up in the Oklahoma panhandle; worked the stockyards. Let me tell you, no difference. Waste of lives. I don't want to be giving the orders for it."

The night stretched long and bitter, her thoughts chasing from fear to self-pity to animal joy at being safe. Around midnight she left the bunker for fresh air and a smoke. She nodded to the perimeter guards and offered them a cigarette. When they hissed to her that it would attract sniper fire, the risk wasn't enough to keep her from squatting down against the sandbag wall and cupping her hand over the tip until she sucked it down to a stub.

Damp and still. Fog curled in the far-off rubber trees, overhead stars poked through the clouds, spiked and fierce.

She hated the night, the stopping of activity. Sleep out of the question, stomach churning, bowels watery. Looking around, she wondered how she had gotten there, why she needed this. Such a cliché to expose the war, or even wanting to test oneself against it. Whatever else, the place was a magnet for evil, or had they, Americans, brought it with them, like the European colonists brought pox in their blankets to the New World? Nothing she would do, including photographs, could have any effect on it. Such a nunnish urge to find purpose or clarity or even to bring ease. Since she had arrived, she had merely been running from illusion to illusion—by turns obsessed, deluded, needy, full of herself, thinking she had achieved some small understanding. MacCrae stoking her vanity, but now she was simply lonely and tired and confused.

Chilled, she returned to the bunker and lay down fully clothed on the dirty cot, boots on, cameras an arm's length away; her mind unable to stay on any one thing for long, a revving engine. At three in the morning, she heard machine-gun fire, then incoming artillery. Their own mortars began, the empty *whoosh* of the shell out of the tube, and for the next hour there was the regular pounding of guns, slamming of ground. No one spoke inside the bunker, vulnerable flesh wombed in earth. In the dark, Helen pressed herself on her cot, longing for the relative luxury of her hotel room in Saigon, of having a good meal and an iced drink. Creature comforts taking an importance all out of proportion to what they offered. Again, she made herself small bargains—buying a silk scarf she'd had her eye on—if she made it out.

At four thirty in the morning, she dozed off and was awake again at five. Mortally weary. She rose, stiff, and washed her face with a napkin and water from the canteen. The sergeant handed her a cup of tepid coffee. The thought of food nauseating, but she traded out rations for fruit cocktail, ate two cans, then drank the juice.

At dawn a third convoy was ordered to get ready to collect the bodies of the first two failed missions. Linh sat at a small fire with the Vietnamese soldiers, boiling tea and rice for breakfast. She hesitated, not sure about approaching him. But when he caught sight of her, he rose at once. He walked her over to a low wall of sandbags and indicated she should sit.

"I want to apologize—" she began.

"I got a message through the radio—Darrow's helicopter was shot down in the Ca Mau area. Darrow is fine."

She felt the ground swaying underneath her at the possibility of something happening to him. "He's okay?"

Linh turned away, the expression on her face too painful. He had seen that expression in Mai's face and taken it for granted. "He said only scratches."

When the trucks began to load, he stood, hefted the pack of equipment onto his back, and walked over to her. They boarded without another word to each other. Now she couldn't remember why she had placed such importance on the mission; she resented the time it would take to complete. If only they would call it off, she could take the next flight out. She had badly lost face with Linh and didn't know how to make it up.

The trucks grinded through their gears as they climbed into the mountains along muddy, hairpin-turn roads. The wall of trees and plants on each side provided a thick screen that could have shielded any number of snipers. Sometimes a hole in the foliage allowed a sight line twenty or thirty feet into the jungle, sunlight filtering through the dense overhead canopy, turning individual shafts of light the color of honey.

Linh reached out to touch small white flowers clinging to the trunks of trees as they passed. The trucks climbed sullenly up the red dirt road, engines drowning out every sound, the only movement the bouncing, swaying bodies of the soldiers. Some of them turned outward and squinted into the jungle, fingering the clips of their machine guns, the rings of their hand grenades. Others simply stared at the floor of the truck bed or closed their eyes or prayed, resigned and unconcerned, weapons splayed under their feet. Plenty of time for fear when the trucks stopped. But Helen was hardly aware of her surroundings, barely noticed the jungle or the soldiers, wondering if it was true that Darrow was unhurt. What if she got hurt now, before she saw him?

They reached a straight part of the road that leveled out, a slight depression muddied with the remaining trickle of a steam struggling across it. The abandoned trucks, noses buried in jungle, impeded their way.

Engines were cut and clips slammed home; the new silence rang in Helen's ears. She ducked at the shriek of a bird, and the soldiers in the truck snickered. Odds were good that the enemy had long since departed, but still they moved forward with slow, deliberate steps.

The first thing was the vinegary sweet meatlike stench. An elemental imprint on the brain one recognized without knowing why. The instinct was to run, but instead the soldiers crawled forward, and Helen reluctantly followed. Clouds of birds and insects flew up as they neared. The ground littered with the detritus of battle—ammunition casings, a destroyed radio, hastily moved sandbags, bloodied bandages; weapons stolen.

A swarm of translucent orange-winged insects rose up, a kind of locust, and underneath Helen saw a flash of strawberry blond that she at first mistook for a clump of flowers. Two thick, loglike shapes covered with leaves, and going closer, she saw they were the bloated legs of a body. And then a few feet farther the lucky bush hat. Two soldiers rolled the remains into a rubber poncho, but the body did not move away in one piece. She turned away and vomited.

"That's what you get, bringing women out here."

She rinsed her mouth with water from her canteen and let the tears dry on her face as she pulled the lens cap off the camera. Most of the scenes too horrific to be used, but she took the pictures anyway because she had to keep her hands and her mind occupied. The promises of leaving replayed themselves in her mind. In this place filled with death, it was impossible to believe that Darrow remained unhurt. She wanted to go to Linh and be reassured all over again, but she couldn't get him away from the other soldiers.

So she turned to the work. During their days wandering Saigon, Helen hadn't known more than loading the camera and shooting, centering the images so they could be cropped, but Linh taught her how to extract the meaning out of a shot. It seemed impossible to concentrate on light, shutter speed, and aperture in the middle of combat or even in its aftermath, but those were the peculiar requirements of the job. Now the distance of technique saved her.

He had told her to picture the image being formed; the idea of light going through the lens, striking the translucent emulsion, staining it dark. The more light, the longer the length of time, the darker the stain. Those areas most saturated by light—by intensity and duration—called latent images. No turning back, only advancing frame by frame by frame. All the grays had to be sorted out, lights and darks contrasted, even if it meant making them up. She saw that even pictures that purported the truth involved a great deal of discretion and taste and choice, that subject matter and angle and intent were as involved in image-making as they were in the military briefings.

After the area had been searched, Linh stood apart looking down a gully along the side of the road. Helen went to stand near him, hoping he would say something more about Darrow, but when he remained silent she squinted into the gully. "What is it?"

"Look at those white flowers. Everywhere on this hill. I noticed them while we were in the trucks."

Not understanding such callousness, she stared hard at his profile for a minute. "How did you know the rescue convoy would be attacked?"

"You mean do I have 'spy' knowledge? Do I have a secret phone to Viet Cong headquarters? Medlock knew it was a death mission. He had no choice. When the NVA leave a few alive, it is to lure more in. Guerilla tactics. I was a soldier once."

The Vietnamese troopers complained about having to load the bodies onto the truck. Sergeant Medlock and another officer argued with them. Voices grew pitched and strident. Finally the Americans, even though there were fewer of them, loaded alone, and then the Vietnamese grudgingly helped. By the time all the bodies were on the truck, tension was high.

Helen took a shot of the back of the loaded truck with its inert human cargo like a sculpture from a circle of the *Inferno*. She knelt and framed the truck like a mountain, the focus sharp on the tread of the tires, the matching tread of the boots of the dead. The darkness of the surrounding jungle and the light on the road made it seem the most forlorn spot in the world.

"Man, let's blow this place," one of the soldiers said.

The trucks rumbled back to life. Helen rode in a jeep with Medlock while Linh rode with the Vietnamese soldiers in the trucks.

When they arrived back at base camp, the Americans went into the mess tent to eat while the bodies were loaded into helicopters for transport back to Saigon. Helen didn't know what else to do, so she followed the officers and stood in line for hamburgers and more fruit cocktail. She sat at table and spooned peaches into her mouth although they tasted obscene to her.

"Did you see the price of the new radios they're selling down at the PX?"

"It's easier to buy radios and trade them for cigarettes. Sell them on the black market and make a fortune."

"I'll start my retirement fund right in Saigon," Medlock joked from down the table.

"Next time I'm in town, I'm going to load up on chocolate."

A pause, a moment of panic because Helen did not hear half their words, so lost was she in the memory of the strawberry-haired soldier's chocolate, but then Medlock asked if anyone had caught the football scores from the paper. The world went on.

When Linh came inside, Helen was drinking coffee. "Can I talk with you?"

She felt exhausted and not up to dealing with him. Their relationship was wearing on both of them. She sighed but didn't want to make matters worse. "Can it wait?"

"I told Darrow we're going back to Saigon now. He wants for you to fly down to Mekong Delta today."

"He's really okay?" Helen hesitated. "About yesterday . . ." She was mortified by what now seemed like a temper tantrum on her part.

"I check when we're okay for flying out." He walked away, brusque, but he didn't want to be tampered with any longer. Easier to keep a distance. With Darrow, that had been acceptable. She wanted more, wanted too much, pushed him past his limits. What she wanted, finally, more than he was willing to give.

EIGHT

Xa

Village

Helen and Linh flew low over the southern Mekong area to An Giang province, controlled by the Hoa Hao sect that opposed the Viet Cong. One of the few safe areas in the country, it was where Darrow had decided to stay and recuperate.

The air boiled hot and opaque, the sky a hard, saline blue. For miles the black mangrove swamp spread like a stagnant ocean, clotted, arthritic. Farther on they passed the swollen tributaries of the Mekong. Papaya, grapefruit, water palm, mangosteen, orange—fruit of every variety grew in abundance, dropping with heavy thuds on the ground to burst in hot flower in the sun. The soil so rich from the emptying of the Mekong that crops grew year-round, and the local food supply remained ample even during wartime, allowing villages and hamlets to unspool loosely along the canals and rivers instead of circling tightly in privation behind bamboo hedgerows as in the north.

As they made a first pass over the dirt airstrip, Helen could see Darrow standing by a jeep with two other civilians. He stood straight, slightly too formal in this loose, watery world. A white short-sleeved shirt, his right arm supported by a cotton sling, he looked thinner, his brown hair shorter, eyes invisible behind the glare of his glasses.

She ducked under the wash of the rotors and ran, embracing him so that he winced as she pressed his shoulder. Linh followed, forgotten.

The reality of Darrow's injury struck her with new force, frightened her all over again. "Are you okay?"

"Except from your manhandling," He smiled and held her off. "Meet some friends. They've offered to put us up while my shoulder heals."

Both of the men worked for USAID, handling rice production and irrigation in the area. The younger one, Jerry Nichols, had a sunburned face and blond hair so sun-bleached it was almost white, giving him an albino look. He pumped Helen's hand and smiled, his mouth crowded with large teeth. The other man, Ted Sanders, was portly, with buzz-cut hair, also retired military, polite and formal in front of her.

"How long are you here for?" Helen asked. Darrow's attitude irritated her, the presumption she had nothing better to do.

"An eternity. Four weeks. But I haven't had a vacation in five years, so I'm overdue."

His hesitation went unnoticed except by Linh. Only he would understand how Darrow must have bargained as the plane went down—how many times could one escape unharmed? The fear that the crash had paralyzed him again like in Angkor.

Linh came up, and Darrow moved to embrace him. Seeing the easy friendship between the two men, Helen thought how stupidly she had handled things.

"You took good care of her."

"But *you* have got sloppy without me, it seems." He would have given anything for it to be only him and Darrow in the village, the way it had been in Angkor. A woman changed everything.

"These damned helicopters can't seem to stay in the air."

They got into the jeep, Helen sliding across the hot and dusty canvas, stepping over the semiautomatics lying on the floor. Nichols drove them a short way along the washboard dirt road to the hamlet of thatched buildings straddling a wide bend in the Hau River. The jeep stopped in front of a small hut in a shaded grove of coconut palms and mango trees.

"Home, sweet home," Darrow said.

"Are you sure this shack's okay?" Ted asked.

"She's a girl with simple tastes."

"We don't all go native like Darrow," Nichols said. "If you get tired of it, we can offer steaks and hot showers."

"Go away, guys. If she changes her mind, we'll show up for dinner."

The two men ignored Linh; he had hardly gotten out of the jeep with his bag before it raced off, covering him in dust.

The front of the hut was a narrow veranda of dirt floor and thatched overhang supported by thick poles of bamboo. Large clay cisterns filled with rainwater formed the boundary with the outside. The framework was bamboo, walls and ceiling interlaced palm fronds with a layer of rice straw on top that smelled thickly of grass in the heat of the day, reminding Helen of sleeping in a barn loft as a child.

Inside was a single room with a dirt floor, a low wood table used for eating, sitting, and sleeping. Around the sides of the room were additional clay pots filled with rice. In the corner was a stack of woven mats.

A young woman in dark blue pajamas, Ngan, carried in a tray with small ceramic cups of mango juice. An older Vietnamese man entered, and she bowed low. He was the village chief, Ho Tung, an elegant man with flowing silver hair and features softened by time like soapstone. After he welcomed them, he stalled long enough to share a cup of juice before leaving.

"We are very cosmopolitan in An Giang, used to Westerners," he said. "After all, my granddaughter lives in St. Louis."

"Really?" Darrow said.

"We have not heard from her in two years, but her last letter said that in St. Louis it snows. That things move very quickly."

"I'm sure that is true."

"That is how I've learned most excellent English."

Helen pictured the granddaughter living alone in the great foreign city, working long hours in some invisible job, yet back in her village she was a celebrity. After Ho Tung left, Ngan carried in their bags.

"I'm supposed to take it easy at least a month. Not much use for a one-armed photographer. I'm hoping a couple of weeks will do it. So I thought we'd have a little in-country R&R." He wished it were that simple. Since the accident, night sweats, insomnia, shaking, everything back with a vengeance. He couldn't say aloud that he hoped to be saved by her.

"And you just assumed I'd drop everything?"

Darrow picked up her hand and kissed it. He hadn't counted on her being standoffish, prickly, and he almost wished for the company of his native women, their docile willingness. After saying good-bye to the chief, Helen went back under the shade of the roof, sat down, but it was hardly any cooler than standing in the road.

"How about it, Linh? You could use a rest, too," Darrow said.

"I need to do some errands," Linh said.

"Stay and relax. They've got a place for you up the road." He wanted to say, *Stay and keep me company.*

"I'll be back at the end of the month." The smallest intuition that Darrow longed for the days at Angkor also. Instead, he had saddled both of them with this woman. He remembered how Mai used to exasperate him, and yet now he would give almost anything to have that irritation back. Was it like that for Darrow?

"What in the world are you going to find to do around here, in the middle of . . . nowhere?" Darrow asked.

Linh spoke in Vietnamese to Ngan, and they both laughed.

"What's funny?" Helen said.

"That we are in the middle of nowhere. Everyone knows this is the center of the universe."

"Don't go all Buddha on me," Darrow said.

During lunch the two men talked about people they knew, upcoming operations that might be interesting to go on, although they agreed it all could change in a month's time.

"I'll keep an eye out for things," Linh said.

It struck Helen how differently Linh acted now, at ease and forthcoming to Darrow where he had been so strained with her.

Darrow sighed and pushed his plate aside. "I hear you two got a little trouble outside Pleiku?"

"Yes," Linh said. "They sent in a suicide convoy. We waited till next morning and then we went in."

Darrow turned to Helen. "Bad?"

Helen continued to eat. She burned with humiliation.

"It's okay."

When Linh was ready to leave, he stuck out his hand to her, but she moved around it and hugged him. A silent peace offering. "Come back soon. Let's have a little fun together, the three of us, okay?"

He nodded but was already walking off down the dirt path. He loved them each separately, but he was ashamed he did not want to see them together.

"Where does he disappear to, do you think?" Helen asked.

"Maybe he has a beautiful little bar girl that he keeps. Or he's a Viet Cong spy."

She laughed. "What? Linh?"

"You've got to start seeing underneath things. Finding the real story."

"You sound like MacCrae now."

"Once when we were in Cu Chi, my camera got . . . smashed, and he constructed spare parts out of nothing. I worried about the film, and he said he would process it in a bunker if I wanted. Since it was dark, we did it by starlight. He traveled with two porcelain plates—one for the developer, one for the fixer. Tied a small stone at the end of the strip and dipped it into the stream to wash it. Only the NVA are taught that."

Helen laughed. "You're joking. Not Linh. That's impossible."

At dusk, Helen and Darrow sat inside the doorway of the hut. Ngan served them dinner—bowls of sticky rice and fried paddy crab and shrimp—and then bowed away. The USAID workers had sent over a cooler of beer, and Helen pressed an icy bottle against her neck.

There was an element of performance when Darrow was around others, but alone, he seemed tired, distracted. Although she was happy to be there, she had not had time to wind down from the mission. She traced the scar on his good arm; the warmth of his skin made her realize how happy she was to be with him again.

"At least I'll know the cause of this new scar."

"It's a sign that something worse didn't happen. It's a sign that I survived."

"Linh stopped me going on that convoy."

"What're you talking about?"

"In Pleiku. I wanted to show off how ballsy I was. I thought he was a coward for not going."

"It's experience. But he's a guardian angel."

"So who guards him?"

Darkness fell; the jungle suddenly quieted. The only sounds the faint pulse of flame in their kerosene lamp, the lapping of water against moored boats along the river's bank. Small bats fluttered over the trees and river in loose rolls like drunks.

"I love . . . this country," Darrow said. "My dream is to photograph the North and South in peace."

"Why did you ask me to come down here? I mean, we could have met in Saigon."

"This is the third time I've been in a helicopter that went down. One time we ran out of gas and crashed into a hillside. One time we were rocketed. My mind was always clear before, ready; this time all I thought of was you."

"That's a good thing, right?" Helen took a long sip of beer. All his words were the right ones, but she wondered if they had just come too late for her to hear them. "What exactly did you think about me?"

"You've made me selfish," he said. "You've made me greedy for life again."

In the middle of the night, a rustling on the roof woke Helen. She grabbed a flashlight and poked it through the opening of the mosquito netting and onto the ceiling. In the corner, a greenish gold gecko turned to pose in the light, in his mouth the wiggling body of a scorpion.

Stealthy as a thief, Helen rolled off the straw mat and stood in the doorway, watching the night.

A golden moon hung over the outlying palms, casting a light so bright she could make out individual grains of dirt on the ground. A faint coolness to the air, more lovely because of the previous heat. The surrounding roofs of pale thatch gave Helen a feeling of calm and protection. Everything she had thought she wanted within her grasp, perfectly all right with her if time stopped at that very moment, but already something had changed. No turn-ing back, only advancing frame by frame by frame. The scene in front of her not just itself, but a potential shot: the widest aperture, the slowest shutter speed. Allow in every drop of light. Shallow range of depth, focus on one thing. But were they the thing to focus on?

In the distance she watched an old woman come out of one of the huts and stretch her arms over her head in the moonlight. She walked to the well, pulled up a bucket, and drank heartily from the ladle. A frame. She pulled a pin from the bun at the back of her head and let her long silver hair spread over her shoulders. A frame. She made her way to the riverbank and onto the wooden dock, hooked her bare foot on the edge of a boat that had been knocking against its mooring. It wasn't until the noise stopped that Helen was aware of its earlier irritating thump. With expert, practiced movements, the woman bent down and wound the rope more tightly. She then walked back up past the well and disappeared between a clump of trees. With a slow enough shutter speed, the woman would have blurred to nothing, become a ghost.

From around the corner of the house, Ngan appeared. "I get you some-thing?"

"No." The girl's sudden appearance annoyed her, breaking her reverie, but she tried not to show it. "Can't sleep."

Ngan folded up her leg and stretched it out, like the egrets Helen watched along the riverbanks. "Warm night."

"Who was the old woman down by the dock?"

"No one. Just old woman. You go back to sleep."

Helen watched Ngan disappear behind the house again until Darrow's voice broke the stillness, and she laughed, a great flood of happiness that she wasn't awake alone.

"Why're you up?" he asked.

"This place is like Grand Central. Promise we can stay here forever."

"Come sleep. All I promise is pineapple pancakes for breakfast. And a day of fishing."

She turned away from the dark mystery of the village.

At dawn they rose and, at Ho Tung's invitation, joined the villagers gathering to go out into the rice paddies. Helen asked Ngan to make coffee in the morning, but the girl only knew how to boil tea. When Darrow came back from a shower, he was balancing a pot of French roast and cups on a tray in his one good hand. He poured two cups as they watched the dawn color the tops of the palms.

"Where did you get that?" Helen asked.

"A good reporter never gives his sources," he said, bending, kissing her neck, her collarbone, her elbow.

Out on the road, the women gossiped as they walked along the half-mile of dirt road. Children flitted back and forth like sparrows. Two girls told the story of a ghost in a tree who gave out money. Their mother boxed their ears for lying but admitted that she had saved the coins. When the girls saw Helen, they screamed and ran away. The men remained solemn, smoking cigarettes, their eyes on the sky, divining the day's weather. At the edge of the paddies, the women kicked off sandals and waded into the brackish water. They tied on hats under their chins to free their hands, began the movement of bending and swaying, back and forth through the rows of green rice stalks, weeding.

A miracle that the war had not touched this place. One could almost pretend that it was peacetime, but they owed that to the cleverness of the Hoa Hao.

Helen took pictures, listening to Darrow's advice on framing. She motioned three young girls to move closer together as they bent over their work, faces hidden under identical conical hats, only the differing patterns of their shirts separating them from each other. Behind them stretched the sunlit water of early morning. Small, bright green rice plants surrounded them like the subtle brushstrokes of a painting.

"Here you have time to move things around. In the field, you have to find an anchor for the picture—a soldier's face, a background, and you just start shooting. You can never go wrong zeroing in on a face. Shoot all day, you might get one good picture."

As the farmers moved farther into the paddy, Helen and Darrow sat down under trees on the bank. High white clouds dissolved in the rising heat until the sky became hard white and as empty as an eggshell.

When no one was looking, Helen touched Darrow on the chest, the knee. His physical proximity made her feel content, and the great urgency she had felt when she first arrived began to fade.

"You stroke me like I'm your pet dog."

"When you were a boy, what was your favorite game?"

He watched her stretched out on the grass, her hair wrapped over her throat. "I don't remember being a boy."

Helen sat up, kissed his eyelids although the villagers would see. She didn't want to hear the sad details just then. "You are my pet dog. A golden retriever. Rover."

Darrow nipped at her fingertips. "Rover's hungry."

At noontime, Ngan appeared with a basket of food. After she had set it out, she sat in the shade some distance away, ignoring their invitation to join them. One of the women started a singsong chant, a *ca dao,* and the other women joined in the refrain.

"They think we're useless," Darrow said. "If my arm were better, I'd join them."

"Really?"

"Yeah, sure. Why not?"

Helen stood up, took off her own sandals, and rolled up her pants.

"What're you doing? Come back."

She waded in. The women stopped working and, pointing, talked and laughed excitedly. Ngan hurried to the edge of the water, giggling and covering her hands over her face.

"I was joking," Darrow shouted, but Helen waved him off. He was filled with enviousness, recognizing his old impulsiveness in her. "Showboat!"

The water and the mud squished warm between her toes. She sank several inches into the muck, then midcalf–deep, and could feel things squirming underneath her feet. Each time she lifted a leg, a pull of mud on her ankles. The vision of Michael rose, unbidden, his struggle against the suck of mud, helpless, shooting, betrayal as the helicopter took off, the pain and panic as he realized he was dying, but she pushed this away quickly. She could not lose face and return to the bank; she waved and moved farther out. After she joined the line of women, one of them showed her how to weed the seedlings along a row. When Helen accidentally uprooted a clump of rice, a woman grabbed it away, chiding, and replanted it. This was serious business— the difference between eating and not. These were not bad people, she and other Americans were not bad, only the war had made them appear so.

From far away, the scene looked graceful, but up close the work was grueling. The heat tore at her. Women's faces wet with sweat, drops running down their noses and chins into the water.

After an hour, Helen's back ached from the constant strain of bending. She stood to ease the pain, jamming a fist into the small of her back. Her sunglasses kept slipping off, so she had to put them in her pocket. One of the women handed her a hat, but still the glare off the water blinded her so that she had to squint to see the bank and Darrow. She was surprised how he appeared from far away—shoulders hunched, head down, almost convalescent.

As their feet dredged the bottom, a sour mash smell filled the air, a green smell of algae mixed with the reek of waste used as fertilizer. The chanting of the women was the only thing that kept her going—casting a spell. She remembered as a young child going with her father to the base for drill instruction, the sound of cadence as she waited sleepily on the grassy track field.

After half a day's work, blisters formed on her hands. She returned the hat and trudged sheepishly back to the bank. Even in this limited way, she had a feeling for what Linh had described—a brick in the wall, invisible except as part of the whole. When she stood on dry ground again, Darrow was leaning against a tree, reading a book.

"Blisters," she said, holding out her hands, palms up.

He smiled and closed the book. "Why? Token suffering?"

She smiled and wiped her wet hands on his shirt. "I'll never eat rice the same way again."

At first Helen was relieved to be away from combat, but as time passed, her thoughts returned to the soldiers she had met; what had happened to them; what it meant. The old curiosity gnawed, and she thought she wouldn't last, would need to make an excuse and rush back to Saigon. The seeming importance of events, and her desire to be there to record them. But with the passage of days, it grew difficult to remember the shape and taste of the fear that had enveloped her; she stopped believing in its power. Distance and the land worked on her. The lure of the war diminished, got quieter, lost its ravenous pull. The world shrank to the size of the village and then opened back up to the infinite in the same breath.

Their lives fell into a rhythm of sunrises and sunsets, of wind whispering through growing rice, of high white morning clouds dissolving to the metallic sheen of noontime heat. Their movements slowed to the speed of the thick, spreading rivers, the water buffalo's heavy footfalls. Their ears grew accustomed to the cocoon of Vietnamese, living like young children oblivious to meaning, only Ngan's painstaking, slow words requiring the effort of understanding; she, like a nurse, making every day comfortable. Their thoughts, too, slowed, filled with the sunlight through palm fronds, heat loosening muscles, tension unwinding from their bodies, until the war was something far outside both of them.

Monsoon showers came, and with it the percussion of water against the broad leaves of banana and rubber trees that lined the paths of the village. The heavy earth smell of rain. Drops pummeled against the thatched roof; rivulets curled down the inside corners of the walls.

In the afternoons they would lie in the darkness of their hut under the mosquito netting, wearing the thinnest of clothing, drenched in sweat. Darrow tracing a lazy finger along the damp of Helen's inner arm, her neck, down between her breasts, along the hollow of her stomach.

"I'm taking you to Switzerland."

"Really? Why Switzerland?" she whispered, reluctant to break the moment with her voice.

"To a small inn on the tallest mountain. Dufourspitze. So high there's snow in summer. We'll burrow under a thick featherbed in front of a roaring fire, and we won't be able to remember we were ever so hot."

"Let's go now." A revelation that they could be together somewhere else in the world, somewhere there was no war.

"Soon."

Helen shifted, aware she had gone too close to the edge, their tacit agreement not to discuss the future. Although she herself didn't exactly want to leave, his hesitation goaded her. "I'd miss Ngan's cooking. How she tucks us up in the mosquito netting at night. How she listens to us making love each night." She paused. "We shouldn't be here, should we?"

"What do you mean?"

"In this country."

"No."

"Then why do we stay?"

"We want to know the end of the story."

"How will our story end, you think?"

Darrow frowned. "I was in Eastern Europe, covering the Hungarians who were fleeing their country before the Communists took over.

"At night it was below freezing, and Russians with machine guns patrolled the borderland. It's flat farmland out there, no landmarks. People got lost crossing the fields in the dark, walking for hours in circles, getting caught or dying of exposure. So the Austrian farmers on the other side of the border started building these bonfires in their fields that could be seen for miles. Night after night, until they had to burn up their crops to keep it going. If people could get far enough to spot the fires, they had a chance.

"At the time building those fires seemed like the best thing you could be doing in the world. Shedding a little light. Being there I felt my life was bigger than it had been before."

Evenings, Ho Tung would invite Darrow to join the village men. They'd sit in the communal house in the center of the hamlet to drink beer.

Helen tried to read by lamplight, but she found it impossible to concentrate on the words of the page, so abstract and distant compared to the moonlight through the trees outside or the thick sweetness of grapefruit and frangipani blossoms. She closed her book, blew out the lamp, and gazed into the night sky. Words superfluous. She had reached a point of absolute stillness in her life, empty of wanting. Nothing could be added that would not unbalance the perfection of the present.

She fretted over Darrow's words because she halfway believed them. The picture of Captain Tong had created headlines. It had opened eyes, made the old man's death not in vain. In Darrow's words, it had made her feel her life was bigger, more important than before. But to repeat that, Helen would have to be willing to go out again and again on missions. She longed to be in that chalet in Switzerland, almost willing to turn her back on the Captain Tongs of the world for it. What was wrong with a small, selfish life?

Ngan came in on the nights that Helen was alone, bringing a bowl of scented water and a towel, insisting on sponging her down. When Helen at first refused, Ngan sulked until she reluctantly agreed.

The girl, only twenty, was already a widow with a small boy of two. She had bright, clear eyes and a high forehead, and Helen thought her quite pretty.

"Ngan, why no boyfriend?"

She giggled, squeezed water out of the sponge, let it run along Helen's arm. "No one interested."

"That's not what I hear." The other women in the village gossiped that a certain middle-aged farmer had proposed and been refused.

"Minh?" Ngan shuddered. "I study in Saigon one year. I want to be teacher. I learn more English."

"But no boyfriend?"

Ngan frowned, turned Helen onto her stomach, and made long strokes along her back. "Not farmer's wife. I go back to Saigon, back to study for teacher."

"No Minh?"

Ngan laid her head on Helen's back. "He is old and ugly. Smells like buffalo," she whispered, giggling, and Helen laughed.

"You want a young, handsome man?" She could feel Ngan's head nodding on her back.

"A good man, like your husband."

Helen did not correct her. "There's no one you like?"

"Linh."

Helen was silent for a moment. "Oh."

"His wife die. No family. No children."

Helen pulled the sheet around her and sat up. "He told you this?"

Ngan smiled and nodded. She stood up to throw the contents of the bowl outside in the bushes. "No woman friends, either. Very proper."

Helen feigned a yawn. "I'll go to sleep now."

The girl left the room, but not before Helen took new note of the straightness of her back, the small and delicate curve of her feet.

Alone, her breath slow and deep, she meditated on the tragedy of Linh's family. If one's meaning came from being a brick in the wall, what did it mean to have no one? To be unmoored? What did it mean in Vietnam not to be part of any family? Was that the answer to the sadness she sensed in him? The answer to his devotion to Darrow? Half asleep, she waited to hear Darrow's footsteps, waited for him to take off his clothes, to part the white netting surrounding their bed and close the folds behind him, for his lips to find her. A husband in every way that mattered.

Perfect stillness and perfect communion, and yet she struggled to stay in the present of her happiness, thoughts returning again and again to the puzzle of Linh. Of course, there was what had happened with the convoy in Pleiku. She probed that like a sore tooth, testing the impact of her mistake. But also, this news from Ngan. Was it true that he had lost family? What of Darrow's sanguine attitude to his possibly being a spy? Where had he gone off to now

while she was camping out in this village backwater? Darrow. She suspected
that even if she closed her eyes to the evils of the Captain Tongs of the world
to live her insulated happiness in a chalet in Switzerland, it was a fool's
choice because Darrow had already decided long before he met her.

The wariness of the villagers grew to friendliness—Darrow and Helen
enfolded within the life of the village. Grain by grain, Helen's restlessness
fell away; she became part of Linh's brick wall. A madness to consider going
back into battle. But as Darrow's arm strengthened, she noted he again listened to AFVN on the radio and read whatever newspapers he could cadge
from the USAID compound.

Each morning and evening, Helen joined the women to bathe in the
river, in an area upstream of the hamlet partitioned off with cotton sheets.
The women disrobed under the soft greenish light filtered through trees leaning over the bank. They slowly soaped while talking, the beautiful smooth
bodies of the teenage girls next to the sinewy dark limbs of the old women.
Many of the married women stood with jutting bellies while they nursed
babies at their breasts.

Ngan now kept far from Helen during bathing. The girl had been shy
around her ever since their talk, and Helen guessed that she regretted her
revelation. Two small girls stood naked in the shallows, washing themselves
while watching Helen. She called to them, but they ran away.

Helen handed out coveted bars of Ivory soap as gifts and created a sensation when she pulled out a razor and sat on a rock to shave her legs.

She had regained some of the weight she had lost out in the field. She
slept long hours, a deep and dreamless sleep fed by the rich life around her.

Twice a week Helen and Darrow went to the USAID house quartered in
an old French colonial building in the neighboring town, for both the
American food and the conversation. Nichols had just retired from active

military duty and now thrived on projects to increase agricultural productivity. He was in charge of building storage houses for fertilizers, pesticides, and improved grain for planting. Rumors were that he loved the lifestyle, including his young Vietnamese mistress, too much to leave.

The longer Helen stayed in the village, the more she made excuses to not visit the USAID house. She felt awkward in front of the Vietnamese servants, who were treated poorly by the American men. Darrow seemed oblivious; or rather, he chose not to notice. He happily listened to music and drank scotch while scouring the magazines and newspapers.

Nichols and Sanders were loud, both in their conversation and the music they played. Helen shivered in the cold gale of air-conditioning. The plate-size steaks grilled on the barbecue and the endless cocktails made Helen feel dull. At first, she brought a towel with her for the civilizing effect of a hot shower, but as weeks passed, she found she preferred the river.

During the long evenings, she watched Nichols's mistress in the background, the one whom the village women gossiped about. Only fifteen, the girl's family had disowned her because of the liaison but had just bought another parcel of land with money she sent. She received more spending money in a week from Nichols than her father could earn from farming in a year. Nichols didn't include her during the meal—like a stray, the girl stayed in the background, along the edge of their evening.

"Why don't you ask her to join us?" Helen asked, poking at a baked russet potato imported from the States.

Nichols turned and eyed the girl walking down the hallway in her unstable high heels. "Khue? She's happier on her own. Getting some time off."

"I bet." Helen cut at her meat with a large saw of a steak knife.

Nichols squinted, his skin flushing a darker red. "You said she had a sharp tongue."

"Actually," said Darrow, "what I said was that she was too sharp for you."

Nichols looked at him for a moment, weighing things, and then deciding to take it as a joke, broke into a barking laugh. "That's it. That's what you said, all right." He puddled ketchup and A.1 on his plate.

The room fell silent. Sanders, his food untouched, cleared his throat. He had lost a lot of weight since Helen and Darrow arrived in the village. They guessed he had developed a pipe habit. "You must be dying to get back to the life in Saigon."

"Not really," Helen answered.

"I'm ready to test this arm," Darrow said. "Send someone down as soon as a message comes from my assistant."

"You contacted Linh?" She felt betrayed not only that Darrow had been plotting his return all along, but also at her own feelings of panic at the prospect of going back. Why had he chosen this public setting to announce his intentions?

Nichols smiled. "Oh, boy, did I cause trouble?"

"They've already replaced me on a couple of assignments," Darrow said. "Pretty soon I'll be taking pictures of supermarket openings in Amarillo."

"What I wouldn't give to be in Saigon," Nichols said, swallowing a small bite of meat and daintily licking his lips.

"Looks like you're doing fine here," Darrow said, nodding his head in the direction the girl had gone. He intended the jab at Helen, his declaration at her possessiveness.

"Sanders gets the pipes, and I get the poon." Nichols looked in the direction the girl had gone. "But there would be so many more goodies to choose from in Saigon."

Helen excused herself and went down the hallway. She hated these men and hated Darrow when he was with them. This was her last visit. She applied her lipstick in the mirror, readying her excuse to leave.

When Khue came out of a room, she was startled, as if caught. Up close, the girl looked even younger. Pointing at the lipstick, she smiled, revealing a front tooth with a large chip. Helen motioned for her to try it. Self-consciously, Khue closed her lips and applied the color.

Why didn't Nichols take her to get the tooth fixed? Infuriated, Helen decided to take the girl to a dentist herself. Khue studied the rose sheen on her lips with great seriousness; too sad and wise for such a young girl. Forget the dentist, the girl needed to be taken away from there, put into a school. How would Helen manage that?

Khue handed back the lipstick, but Helen patted the girl's fingers around the tube. "For you." When the two of them entered the living room,

Nichols was sprawled out on a lounge, drunk. He took one look at Khue and yelled, "Come over here! Come now!"

A small, throbbing vein appeared along Khue's temple, visible as she stepped forward.

"Leave her be—" Darrow said, noticing that Helen had not come to sit next to him but remained standing.

Nichols grabbed Khue by the hip and pulled her down on his lap, wiping her mouth with his sleeve. "You look like a whore, honey. No good. Look like a little whore with that stuff on." He patted her cheek. "That's my girl. My good, clean girl."

Helen turned around and walked out.

"What's wrong? I just don't want you showing her bad ways," Nichols yelled.

Outside on the dirt driveway, Darrow stumbled getting his shoes back on. "We *walking* home?"

Helen marched down the road without a word. The darkness and the warm air were a relief.

"You mad at me?"

"Not at you. No . . . Yes. Why didn't you say anything?"

"If you're choosy, you're not going to have too many friends out here."

"I'm never going back there."

"Fine. But you're punishing the girl, too."

Helen slowed, shaking pebbles from her sandals. Darrow laughed and grabbed her arm. "What's funny?" she asked.

"What a puritan you were, how self-righteous. How outraged. I had no idea."

Helen said nothing.

"I lost that capacity some time back. But I admire it."

"You're ridiculing me. And you didn't tell me your plans to go back to work." As she said it she knew her outrage on Khue's behalf had also been for herself.

"That's the thing, I didn't want it official," Darrow said, suddenly serious. "All good things and all bad things come to an end."

Preparations for the summer festival frenzied the village, and Helen and Darrow were invited to take part. Ho Tung knew their plans to leave but insisted they stay through the celebrations.

Helen had been thrown out of her stillness. All she could think was that she was losing something she wanted. But she couldn't tell Darrow what it came down to—them or the war, no longer both. Apparent to her that she could no longer go through a village from the outside, as before. Impossible to cover the war with such conflicting loyalties. Was that what had happened to MacCrae, she wondered, too many angles of loyalty?

Pigs were butchered, the cries of slaughter haunting her till she escaped to the river. When she returned, the communal house had been hung with lanterns. They were seated in a place of honor next to the chief. He talked about how expensive it must be to send a letter from America, especially St. Louis, and Helen didn't know what else to do but agree. "I know young girls get distracted," Ho Tung said, "but how can she forget where she comes from?"

Women swayed under trays of food, delicacies such as glutinous rice, sweet boiled rice cakes, shredded pork with bamboo shoots. Toasts were drunk with fermented rice alcohol. Darrow spent long hours with a translator to figure out what they should contribute. Finally it was decided beer for the adults and ice cream for the children.

During the afternoon of the festival day, a decorated plow was taken to the communal rice paddy outside the village and a ceremonial furrow plowed. Later, the villagers gathered at the community house for the ritual enactment of the rice harvest, a fertility rite with four goddesses chosen from the village girls to represent Phap Van, the cloud; Phap Vu, the rain; Phap Loi, the thunder; and Phap Dien, the lightning.

Work was forgotten; paddies lay untended. The women wore their best clothing. Unmarried girls washed their hair in perfumed water and wore it long and dark down their backs. Platters of food were there for the taking; at almost any hour one could find a crowd of people busy at some game. Darrow's arm healed well enough to get rid of the sling, and he and Helen photographed boat races, kite flying contests, rice cooking and rice cake competitions, stick fighting, wrestling, and traditional dances.

"I love this," Darrow said. "We'll travel the world, do cultural layouts. Wildlife shots in Africa. No more wars."

"You promise?" she said, trying not to show how much she wanted the answer.

On the final night fireworks shimmered along the river, ribbons of light reflecting on the water as young couples escaped into the darkness. A leniency in behavior was allowed for the night, and Ho Tung laughed that many new marriages were celebrated shortly after the festival. He had urged Ngan to reconsider Minh's proposal. Helen saw the two walking awkwardly together along the river, Ngan frowning. But the chief shook his head. "Ngan refuses to settle down. She has caught the strange, unhappy-making new ideas."

The next morning at dawn, everything returned to its normal state—the women again hidden under their dark clothes and conical hats; the men bent under the weight of their plows. The paddies inhabited again, plaintive songs hanging in the air, the previous week as distant and separate as a dream. Helen dreamed of a third way for Darrow and her to exist other than Switzerland or the war—staying in the village for a full year until the next harvest.

She ignored the fact of Darrow's healed shoulder. But after her dismissal of Nichols, and all that he represented, Darrow went alone and spent his days at the USAID compound. He had already absented himself from the place. Something barely started, already ended.

As she walked back from bathing at the river one morning, Linh appeared on the road, and her heart sank. "You've come back," she said when they were within speaking distance of each other. She held out her hand and touched his arm. "I've been dreading this day."

NINE

Tiens

Fairies

Linh had taken a picture of Helen with him while he was gone, had stared and dreamed over it often during the whole long month, an impossibly long time to keep away, but he had forced himself. When he first caught a glimpse of her on the dirt road, he was struck by how she had filled out, how her skin had bronzed. She looked younger, a flushness in her figure he had not seen before. But as he came closer her face went downward and hardened as she recognized him, and he froze.

"Darrow said it was time to go."

"I know." She fell into step beside him, back to the village.

He was a fool, he berated himself. Wasting so much dreaming.

The afternoon Linh had delivered Helen into Darrow's arms, he was a tired man. After he took his leave of them, stowing his camera gear in the USAID compound, he dressed in the plain clothes of a farmer and hiked down a dirt road. Outside the village, he climbed down the bank of the river to an isolated grassy spot, took off his clothes, and went for a swim.

The grass along the bank was plush and long; it fell in swaths one direction and then another, like a hand-mown lawn. The spot reminded him of the place Mai used to lure him to during their school days to sing to him.

The water cooled his body, the solitude a deep pleasure. A relief simply not to have to speak. In his earlier life, he had lived so much in his imagination, writing in notebooks, that it was now a constant strain to keep his mind directed out into the world, trying to understand others more than himself, to rewrite his thoughts into a foreign tongue.

After his swim, he climbed back up on the grassy bank, put his clothes on, and fell asleep under the trees.

The sound of children's laughter woke him in the late afternoon. Two young girls trawled the shallows for crayfish and shrimp for dinner. More interested in splashing each other than in catching anything.

Linh sat up, startling the younger one so that she fell back and landed on her rump in the water.

"You scared us!" the older girl scolded.

"I'm sorry," Linh said. "Come closer here, and I'll give you a present."

The girls giggled and moved closer, and Linh handed them each a stick of Juicy Fruit gum.

The oldest girl had a smooth oval face like a polished river stone. Linh stroked her blue-black silken hair as she tore the first piece in half and handed it to her sister. She put the second piece in the waistband of her pants for safekeeping.

"Do you tell stories?" the younger girl asked.

"I used to."

"Please, please," the older girl said.

"There is one I've been thinking of," he answered.

"A poor woodcutter's wife passes away. He is very lonely, and in the market he sees a picture of a beautiful tien, *a fairy, whose image he falls in love with. He takes the picture home and hangs it on his wall, and he talks to it at night, setting a bowl of rice and chopsticks in front of it at meal times.*

"One day he comes home and his hut has been cleaned. There are delicious dishes prepared for him to eat. This happens every day with no sign of who is taking care of him. So the woodcutter decides to solve the mystery. He pretends to be going to work one morning and instead doubles back and peeks through a crack in the wall to find the fairy from the picture come to life. He rushes in and forces her to stay and marry him. As insurance, he locks the empty picture frame into a trunk. They live happily together and have three sons.

"The sons grow to adulthood and the woodcutter grows old, but the tien, *being immortal, is as young as the day she stepped out of the picture. The villagers begin to gossip and finally the sons confront the father. When he tells them the truth, they refuse to believe him. Angry, the father unlocks the trunk and shows them the empty frame as proof, but still they scoff. When he leaves for work, the sons confront their mother, who denies it until they mention the frame. She begs them to show it to her, and when they do, she admits the truth and bids them farewell and returns inside the picture forever."*

"Does the *tien* come back?" the younger girl asked.

"Yes. Actually, there is a *tien* in your village right now."

"Yes? Where?"

"Look for her. She has long golden hair."

"Who are you?" the older girl asked.

"I'm the ghost of this tree, don't you recognize me?"

"No."

"Every time you come by here, I know if you've been a good girl and caught fish for your mama."

"We've been bad today. We played and caught no fish."

Linh laughed. He reached in his pocket and took out a few coins. "Tell Mama you found these lost on the road. So you don't get in trouble tonight at least."

The younger girl leaned over and touched him on the knee. "You're a ghost?"

Linh nodded slowly, in his best guess at a ghostly demeanor.

"Will you be here tomorrow?" she asked.

"I'll always be here. You just might not be able to see me."

At sunset, Linh lay back on the long, cool grass of the bank and inhaled the heavy scent of grapefruit blossoms in the evening air. He closed his eyes, remembering the smell of Mai's hair after she washed it, adding a few drops of citrus oil to the rinse so that at night the fragrance permeated their bed when she lay down, making the room a dark grove in which to find her.

He rationed himself only one thought of her each day; otherwise he

would not be able to go on. He hoarded his memories like other men did cigarettes or chocolates.

Today was the third anniversary of her death, the period of official mourning over, but he felt he had lost her a hundred years ago and only yesterday.
He panicked at times, unable to remember a detail of her face as clearly as
before. Worried about the thousand small memories of body that had already
vanished from his recollection. Time like a chemical pushing a print too far, a
fog overcoming the detail. It pained him that he relied on a few poor photographs of her more and more; everything that made him love her absent from
the pictures. The images felt disloyal, as if he were dreaming over a stranger.

The next morning he rose at dawn, again washed in the river, then set off
toward Can Tho, hoping to bum rides there for his trip north.

Once he arrived, Linh went to a dirty outdoor café and sat at Mr. Bao's
table. He had last seen Bao a little more than a month ago, yet he had put on
the weight of a year.

"What took you so long?" Mr. Bao said.

"It took time to leave."

"There hasn't been anything as good as the Captain Tong piece since last
we talked."

Linh lit a cigarette.

"Why aren't they with you?"

"Darrow is wounded. And they don't go where I direct; it's the other way
around."

"You are their friend. Lead with sugar."

Linh hated Mr. Bao's stupid Confucian sayings, his peasant cunning.
These were the kinds of drones the party was filling itself with.

Mr. Bao changed tack. "How is your wife's family?"

"I don't know. I imagine not so good, since they got in touch with me."

Mr. Bao nodded. "You must go do your duty to them. The same as your
duty to your country."

Linh's anger flared. "What does your duty have to do with selling opium?"

Mr. Bao cracked a thin smile. "You forget your place."

"Darrow and Helen are in the village. Learning of Vietnam. I think this is a good thing."

"Agreed. Next time I see you, I have a shopping list: Wonder Bread, cigarettes, and maybe brandy this time."

Linh skirted his family's village, or what remained of it, never having returned since the night they were taken from him. His wife's sister, Thao, lived in a neighboring hamlet. As soon as they arrived in Saigon, her husband had been caught and inducted into the army; without an income she had been forced to return to the country. After she hadn't heard from her husband in more than a year, she had contacted Linh.

He didn't tell her that casualties among SVA soldiers were high. Officers threw poorly trained recruits into dangerous missions to please their American advisers while staying far away from any action themselves.

"Why does no one tell me if he's alive or dead?" she said. Always the practical one, not as beautiful or talented as her sister, Thao had made more out of less. "How can I remarry otherwise?"

She said that her husband's company had been patrolling the Iron Triangle region when last seen. The joke was that the main harvest of the area was mines; Linh guessed the body had been overlooked. After the false peace of An Giang, where he had left Darrow and Helen, the destruction in this area depressed Linh. Paddies choked in weeds. Starving water buffalo with washboard sides. He watched families bundling belongings, turning their backs on ancestral grounds. Clogged roads. Refugees formed an unrelenting river that poured into the coastal cities of Nha Trang, Danang, and Saigon. He was sorry he had acted so poorly with Mr. Bao.

Thao's village was in the process of being dismantled—huts torn down piece by piece and carted away to someplace with more luck. Some villagers packing to leave; others squatting among the ruins of their homes. The week before they had been subjected to a cordon-and-search, uncovering a substantial weapons cache under one hut, a large supply of rice under another. The huts and bunkers with supplies had been blown up, destroying their livelihood but sparing the people.

Thao's hut was still standing. Inside, she sat on the ground, haggard, her eyes red. She had two children, a girl of four, a boy still suckling at her breast. When Linh appeared in the doorway, Thao looked up at him, no surprise on her face.

"Good, you are here. We can still honor Mai's death anniversary."

"Are you okay?"

"We are alive, but for what?"

He put his arm around her shoulders. The shape of her face, the way she placed her hand on his, brought back with an ache his wife's absence.

"I'm ashamed," Thao cried. "Here you are, and I have no rice, no vegetables, not even incense to honor my sister."

"Get your things. We're leaving."

"For where?"

"I'm going to get a place for you in Saigon. I can look after you and the children better there."

She bowed her head. The baby had fallen away from the breast. Linh saw the nipple, raw and callused. From the thinness of the baby, he guessed she was going dry.

"How can you afford to take us in?"

"Americans pay well."

Thao handed the baby to the girl but left her shirt open. "You were always more practical than your brothers. Cling to the winners in war."

"We'll get doctors and medicine in Saigon," he continued. "We can buy milk."

She looked down at her breast, pressing it with a fingertip till a drop of milky-clear liquid formed. "I've eaten nothing for days."

This sudden contact with the world of women confused Linh; Thao's likeness to Mai inflaming him. He turned away so that she would not notice the heat in his face, as if she could sense the cramped, shaming tingle in his body. "Things will get better now."

She swayed as she got to her feet and spoke sharply to the girl, ordering her to ready the baby. She looked at Linh as she buttoned her blouse. "So you think he's dead?"

"If he is alive, he will find us in Saigon."

Thao gathered yellowed photographs of her and Mai's parents from the altar, a few chipped porcelain bowls, a jade hair comb, putting them in a basket.

"If he is dead," she said, shoving in clothes, "Mai would want us to marry."

"We need to catch the last bus. Tomorrow night we will be eating a steaming bowl of *bun cha*."

Thao let out a small laugh of relief and placed her hand on his thigh. He picked up her hand and held it clasped between his own two, then dropped it.

"I can try to get a singing job when I fill out again."

"Don't worry, Sister. I'll make sure you are safe. For Mai's sake."

Thao positioned herself in the doorway, in the most flattering light. "You get lonely for her?"

"War distracts me."

"Plenty of babies are born in the war. Haven't you noticed?"

Linh stood outside holding the small girl in his arms. He tried to still the shaking of his hands. Thao had never been like this before, and he knew that desperation made her throw herself at him in this way. Still, it sickened him. He looked off into the thicket of palms and wished he were back in the hamlet in An Giang.

Darrow had begun to radio Linh after three weeks, but Linh answered that he had business in Saigon and needed an additional week. After his arrival, the festival over, Darrow readied his plans to leave while Helen's mood turned darker and darker.

As a farewell, the village chief, Ho Tung, suggested a sightseeing trip. "You must see this, the heart of the province. Strangers do not know this." Two flat-bottomed pole boats appeared. Helen, Darrow, Linh, Ho Tung, and a couple of villagers to guide the boats made up the party. Helen sat in the forward position, her face turned away in brooding contemplation of the surroundings.

At first they went along various branches of the Mekong and Bassac. The rivers changed from green to red to brown, filled with the heavy alluvial silt brought down from the mountains. The boats angled next to seemingly impenetrable walls of water palm, and then one of the boatmen would edge the nose of the canoe into a crevice, push aside some vines, and suddenly they were traveling a thin ribbon of canal no wider than the canoe itself. The chief explained that only the locals could navigate here, the tides so unpredictable that four feet of water might drop down to mud within hours, stranding a boat.

The palms on each side brushed against the passengers, knocking Helen's hat off. The air was close and thick, filled with insects.

"Flies bothering you, love?" Darrow called good-naturedly, knowing her furor, feeling more comfortable in the knowledge that she was, after all, just like other women.

They passed lone thatched huts that fronted the water, doorways filled with chickens scratching in the dirt, naked babies, and old people pulling on pipes. The peasants here lived by harvesting fruit and flowers from deep inside the jungle and got around by boat. Travel on foot was impossible.

Everywhere they stopped, children and women rushed up to stare at the white faces.

Helen finished handing out the full bag of candy they brought long before they reached their destination, an island in the middle of a wide part of the Mekong made by two tributaries joining and depositing silt.

"The rivers in the delta change direction, get bigger or dry up. Land is created and then taken away. Everything always in a state of change," Ho Tung said.

"You look tired, Linh," Darrow said, grinning. Indeed, there were dark circles under his eyes, and his thinness had turned sharp. "Was she at least pretty?"

Linh smiled. He had observed them since his return, how Helen's eyes lingered on Darrow's face, questioning.

"Maybe you need to go back to the war to rest?" Darrow said.

"Maybe we go rest together," Linh said, and Helen burst out in laughter, the first since Linh had arrived.

When they tied the boats along the steep bank and climbed up, the heat was so intense Helen thought the rivers should be boiling. They drank water and ate cold rice for lunch, then the villagers stretched out under the trees to sleep.

"When will you return to America?" Ho Tung asked.

"Soon," Helen answered.

"Can you go to St. Louis, maybe? Check on my granddaughter?"

"It's a very big country," Helen said, and seeing the disappointment, added, "Give us her address."

Ho Tung smiled, relieved, his mission accomplished. The chief motioned for Darrow, Helen, and Linh to follow him to explore the interior. "There is a temple in the center of the island."

"Come on, then," Darrow said, grabbing Helen's hand.

They pushed aside the thick barrier of brush and edged along an over-grown path. Every inch of land filled with huge purple orchids. Abundant, dense, violent growth.

Linh lagged behind the others, but when he saw the flowers he stopped. "I'll wait back at the boats."

"No, come on," Darrow said. "It won't take long."

"I'd rather—"

"Come."

Flowers hung aggressively from trees and crowded on the ground and along rocks, thick and choking in a wild scramble for light in the semigloom of the overhead palm and rubber trees.

"This is an enchanted garden," Helen said, moving forward into the sea of flowers, her bad mood turned to delight.

She picked a small bloom and brought it to her nose, but there was only a faint scent of decay. She tucked the flower behind her ear anyway.

As she turned, Darrow snapped her picture. "There's my girl."

"No fair."

"Look over here again."

"No."

"Come on." Darrow took a step forward through the dense foliage.

"No!" Helen laughed and ran, crashing down the path through the flowers, trampling vines and leaves and petals.

"Come back," Darrow shouted, laughing, running after her.

Drenched, she ran as if in a downpour, sides heaving. Hearing the crash of footfalls behind her, she ran faster, careless, when suddenly a shadow passed in front of her face. She looked up into a huge banyan tree from which hundreds of orchids clung, choking the tree in a blaze of purple. One particular orchid hanging from a long branch seemed especially large and perfect. She took another step to reach for it, tripped over a tree root hidden in the underbrush, and fell down into the plants.

"You okay?"

Darrow stooped down next to her as she laughed and rolled onto her back. He bent over and brushed the dirt off her knees as Linh and the chief came up.

"Helen is hurt?"

Darrow shook his head. "Not yet."

She sat up, searching the ground for what poked into her back and picked up small white sticks. She brought them closer, her smile fading as she realized they were bones, and showed them to Darrow.

"Human?"

"This is a burial island," Ho Tung said, pleased.

"Why didn't you tell us?" Helen asked.

"They bury monks here. The first monk, a hermit, lived here by himself. When the villagers came to check on him after the monsoon, they find only his bones and a purple orchid growing out of the rib cage. The flowers are said to be a manifestation of his enlightenment. How do you say? They are 'right luck'?"

Helen dropped the bones on the ground.

Ho Tung waved his arms, motioning to Helen as he talked. "Keep. Brings right luck."

"What do you mean?"

"Come on," Darrow said. "You don't believe this hocus-pocus?"

Linh shook his head. "Right luck. Some women come here to pray because

they want children. Or they have only daughters. Others come for forgetting."

"Forgetting?" Helen asked.

"Their sorrows. If they grieve so much they cannot bear the land of the
living."

She stared at Linh, and he met her eyes. "I'll wait at the boats," he said.

"Me, too," Helen said. The mood broken, the small island now seemed
gloomy and claustrophobic.

"No temple?" Darrow shook his head. "You two are no fun."

Helen swept the bones under a bush with her boot. She stood and dusted
herself off. Ho Tung knelt with his hands together in *mudra* and chanted under his breath.

As if he had been waiting behind a tree for just this moment, an orange-
clad monk stepped out into the middle of the path and bowed to them. Linh
came back and talked at length with him.

"This is the hermit monk of the island," Linh translated. "He invites us
to tea."

They sat in the small temple that was no more than branches strung
loosely together overhead. The monk stirred twigs and placed his iron teapot
over them, looking at the foreigners sideways, giggling.

"He says he has never seen white faces before. He asks why you are here."

Darrow shrugged. "The war. Tell him we're photographers."

"Who would want such pictures?"

Darrow chuckled.

"He asked, 'Which war?' "

A pause. "Between the North and South."

"He says there is always war, but why are the Westerners fighting Vietnamese war?"

"To give freedom."

The monk shook his head, rubbed his hands over his stubbled scalp. He
talked rapidly to Linh, gesturing, then laughing. "That makes no sense. Why
die for Vietnamese?"

"Tell him . . . it's complicated. Tell him it's geopolitics, the movement of
Communism, the domino theory of the fall of Southeast Asia. . . ."

The monk stood up and yawned, moved off to a tree, and relieved himself against it. Linh laughed. "He says your words mean as little as his piss does to this tree."

Darrow blinked and then laughed, and the monk laughed louder, till he was red in the face, and came back to sit down.

"We're making bigger and bigger mistakes because we can't admit we made the first one. We can't lose a war to a small Asian country."

The monk giggled and covered his mouth. "But you'll have to fight till every last Vietnam man is gone."

Darrow looked at the ground and nodded. "The first wise man I've met."

The monk shook his head and poured tea.

"He is only a simple monk. He is afraid for the Westerners, that you will lose your own way by interfering with Vietnam's destiny."

The monk got up, bowed to them, and walked away.

"He hasn't talked so much in a year. He's tired."

After the tea, they walked back in silence. As Helen climbed into the first boat, she got off balance. Darrow was looking away down the river, frowning, but Linh reached out his hand to steady her.

The peace of night was broken by the sounds of jeeps driving into the village. Headlights glared as American soldiers and local Vietnamese militia jumped out swinging machine guns, cordoning off the hamlet, and beginning a house-to-house search.

Darrow threw on a T-shirt and pants, and ran outside. "What's going on?"

"You're here. Where's Adams? All Americans are ordered to the AID compound immediately."

"Give us a minute to dress. What's going on?"

"An American has been attacked and killed in the area."

"Who?"

"One of the AID guys, Jerry Nichols."

As they packed, Ngan appeared. She crouched in the corner of the hut, crying. Helen bent down to pat her back, reassuring her as Linh came in.

"I'll stay. Interrogations start, they need an interpreter," Linh said.

"Meet us in the morning."

They were escorted to a jeep as the village men were herded into the center of the hamlet at gunpoint. Their women clattered loud and angrily like birds disturbed in their roost. Harsh, unfamiliar sounds awakened the children, who began wailing. A helicopter hovered over the road, floodlights bathing the tops of trees in an eerie dust of light, the noise deafening.

"I don't think we should leave Linh," Helen said.

"He'll be okay," Darrow said.

When they reached the USAID compound, the courtyard glowed in the ghostly sulfer light. In the center, resting in a pool of rust-colored blood, were the trussed bodies of Nichols and his young mistress. Their arms and legs had been bound with wire; bodies mutilated either before or after being executed with one bullet, neatly in the back of each head.

Darrow slammed his good hand down on the hood of the jeep when he saw them, then cradled it in his bad one. The officers came over, concerned at the outburst, but he shook his head. Helen moved off. The violence after such a peaceful time jolted her. She felt as raw as she had after the last convoy mission; time had done nothing to buffer that. The sight of the girl an apparition. No places of safety in this country, just temporary escapes. Khue, who had lost one thing after another—home, parents, village—now lost her life. Not even so small a thing as her tooth could be mended. After a few minutes, Darrow went about the rote gestures of putting film in camera and took pictures of the bodies. Who would want such pictures?

Inside the villa, the black-and-white tile floor was muddied from the boots of the soldiers. Sanders sat on a sofa, being questioned. "Everyone liked him."

"Hardly," Helen blurted out. The officer looked up, and Sanders blushed.

Helen and Darrow were led to two rooms, but didn't bother with the pretense, entering only one. They lay down on the French carved wooden bed, fully dressed, unable to sleep. For the first time in more than a month, they didn't touch, each lost in thought. Their time in the village not simply over, but undone. All of it, including why they had unquestioningly accepted it, a delusion.

Finally Helen turned to him. "What do you think?"

"As in who?"

"You said the region was safe."

"I said it was overseen by the Hoa Hao. Whatever happens, it's under their sanction. They must have allowed it."

In the morning, Helen took no pleasure from the hot running water in the sink but longed for the cool green of the river. Linh did not show up. She remembered the women gossiping about Khue. Whose side were they on? The captain in charge of the investigation drove them back to the village for statements before they were flown out.

As they approached the village, the rice paddies were empty, as they had been during the festival. The hamlet appeared smaller and meaner from in-side the jeep. Helen could hardly remember her joy at having been out in the paddies; it seemed so indulgent. Now her actions simply seemed childish. Even their hut, while they packed up their equipment, seemed alien. In the center square, men, women, and children had been herded together, and squatted in the dirt in the full, hot sun.

As Helen walked by, she recognized individuals and nodded to them, but no look of recognition or greeting was returned. Faces stared out, sullen and closed. Even Ho Tung turned his back on them. The villagers feared show-ing friendship with the Americans in front of the Vietnamese military or spies for the VC. They knew better than to expect help from either side.

Then Helen saw Ngan, her face bruised, her clothes bloodied. Helen cried out her name and moved toward her, but the girl shuddered and slunk back into the crowd.

The American colonel sat at a table set up under the shade of the trees. His face was dark red from sunburn, cheeks and forehead pocked with small heat blisters. He kept pulling out a small tube of ointment and dabbing at them. When he saw Darrow and Helen, he put the tube in his pocket. "Damn things itch, driving me crazy. So . . . how long have you two been staying here?"

"Over a month," Darrow said.

"And it didn't come to your attention that you were in a VC hotbed?"

"Jerry Nichols . . . invited me to stay here. So it hadn't come to his atten-tion, either."

"There were no VC here," Helen said.

"That was a classic VC-style execution."

"How do you know it came from here?" Darrow asked.

"That was easy. The snatch he had living with him in the compound—strictly against the rules—she was an undercover VC operative from here."

"Where did you get that piece of shit information?" Darrow said.

"Interrogation of one of the villagers." He ruffled through some papers. "Actually, the girl who worked for you."

"Ngan?"

"Yeah, that's the one."

"Who got that out of her? The South Vietnamese?"

"They're in charge of interrogations. Your man was present."

"That's ridiculous."

The colonel cupped his chin in his hand and winced. "What I find ridiculous is that two reporters didn't notice anything suspicious all this time."

Darrow walked off.

"Khue, your operative, was a child. Nichols should have been arrested."

"Actually, we have a report on you. From yesterday. Your hostility toward the victim."

"Don't even try to go there," Helen said, getting up.

Linh caught up with them as they walked to the jeep. He looked pale, unsure that his papers would be powerful enough against this craziness. As they passed the villagers, Ngan broke through the guards and ran to them, clinging to Linh's waist.

"What did they do to you?" Helen said.

Vietnamese guards ran at them with guns pointed.

Ngan talked quickly, eyes wide in fear, spittle on her lips. Linh took her hands and spoke in her ear as he led her back.

When they were in the jeep on the way to the helicopter, Helen turned to him. "What did she say?"

"She wanted us to take her. She says she is not VC. They hit her till she said it to stop the beating. I could do nothing."

"Who did the executions?"

"Nichols was not liked. Villagers say Khue with baby, and he refused to marry her. He only tell her later about American wife. He threw her out with no more money. To save face, they are killed. Making it look like VC takes shame away."

"Shouldn't we go back and tell them the truth?" Helen asked. "Linh can report the beating."

Darrow leaned in close to her. "Don't ever put Linh at risk. Americans can get out of prison. If they put him away, there's nothing we can do. The South Vietnamese have their confession, and they'll stick by it."

"What about Ngan?" Helen said.

Darrow turned away.

The helicopter rose to tree level, and Helen tried to pick out their hut from the surrounding ones. Brokenhearted to leave, but especially with the villagers' fates uncertain. Impossible to find their hut, the thatched roofs quickly blending together, and soon they were too high even to be sure which hamlet was theirs among the infinite canals and rivers. Soon even the villages were indistinguishable from the dense vegetation and trees, the pattern of rice paddies making the view identical in every direction, the land closing up and becoming impenetrable once more.

The pilot turned around and yelled over his engine. "Want to go have a little fun?"

TEN

Thien Ha

Under Heaven

The day was a perfect jewel, and long after Linh would remember it as the happiest day of his life. Neither too hot nor too cold. The sky a soft azure, unmarred by a single cloud; the white sand of the beach on fire in the sunlight. The helicopter pilot flipped off the switch for radio contact, hooked a sharp right, and came in low over the palm trees, creating a wind that raised the sand into small whorls, chopped the waves into emeralds at the ocean's edge.

Half an hour later, Helen, Darrow, Linh, and the helicopter crew were seated in a beachside café in Vung Tau, the old Cap St. Jacques, drinking "33" beer and eating cracked crab. The proprietor, thrilled by his dollar-laden clients, had two tables with large blue-and-white striped umbrellas dragged out onto the sand. For the occasion, he even ran a greasy towel over the oilcloth tabletop. When they ordered more beer, a small boy dug around in a trash can filled with ice that housed both the bottles and that day's catch. As the meal went on, orange-pink splintered shells formed a jagged reef around the table.

After lunch Darrow set up a chess set and played Linh while the helicopter crew ran touch football on the beach, recruiting the local boys, who kept running off with the ball. One of the men turned on AFVN radio.

Maintenance of the M16 in the field is affected by conditions. In the upper altitudes only a light lube should be applied, thin and often, especially often. Down in the delta, areas with plenty of water, be extra careful that your lubrication does not get contaminated. Take care of your weapon and your weapon will take care of you. . . .

If you leave Vietnam on emergency-leave orders . . .

"Turn that damn thing off!" the pilot yelled. "Can't you see we're on vacation here?"

And, indeed, the relaxed faces of the people on the beach, the wet breeze and the lethargic waves, made the war seem somewhere far away. When Helen left to walk on the beach, Linh moved his knight so that his king was exposed.

"Hey, you can't toss the game!" Darrow said.

"Sorry, I can't concentrate."

Darrow looked around and spotted the pilot stretched out on three chairs. "Billings, you're up."

The pilot mock sighed, opened a fresh "33," and sat down at the table. Linh stepped over the reef of crab shells and made his way to the surf where Helen stood. They watched fishermen, their skin a dark, sun-cured teak, tug nets of beating fish up on the sand.

As they walked along the surf, a boy ran by, and when he was within feet of Helen, he reached down his arm and splashed her with water. She stopped and looked down at her soaked capri pants, then at the boy. She cupped her hand in the warm water and splashed him back with twice as big a spray. His eyebrows shot up in surprise, and he stood still and gave a loud belly laugh. Then began a tag game in earnest, Helen and the boy joined by his friends, running through the knee-high waves, catching each other in ropes of water. At one point, Helen was clutching Linh inside a ring of the boys who circled the two of them, pressed them in, splashing them with water, circling around and around. Helen had a sudden vision of her long-ago dream of the Vietnamese children when she had first arrived in Saigon, how threatening she had found them as they circled around her and Michael. Perhaps she had read the dream wrong, and they weren't menacing at all. After fifteen minutes, the novelty of the American woman wore off, and the boys retreated to a food stall. Helen stood drenched beside Linh.

"I'll tell you the truth, I hated it here when I first came. It was strange and frightening. But this time in the village . . . despite everything, this place moves me."

"I'm pleased."

"Since we're wet, let's swim out to that buoy," she said.

"I can't."

"Come on. What if I get a cramp? You'll need to save me."

Linh looked down at the water slapping over his knees but said nothing.

"What?"

"I cannot swim."

Helen sensed his embarrassment and took his hand. "Then you're in luck, because I taught swimming every summer during high school."

They walked together along the sand, away from the crowds, coming across dead jellyfish whose purple translucent flesh reeked in the sun. At a deserted stretch, they entered the water that had only a hint of oily coolness. Helen showed Linh how to hold his breath underwater, to float on his back, to move his arms for the breaststroke and the sidestroke.

She touched him, hand against hand, arm against chest, trunk against back, with a kind professionalism, like a nurse with a patient. Linh dunked his head underwater again, opened his eyes wide to allow the sting of salt, the excuse for tears. No one had touched him, except in the most incidental way—Helen's hug, the brush of strangers—since he had lost his family. He had numbed himself to the absence, but this strange baptism woke each part of him to a fresh agony. He dunked his head again, held his breath till his lungs threatened to buckle, surfaced to the shattering of light, spluttering, the far-off laughter of playing children.

Helen put her hand on his arm. "Are you okay?"

Linh shook his head. They walked out of the water and stood in the sand.

"Don't worry. It doesn't come all at once. You'll get the hang of it."

"Why do you dream to photograph the Ho Chi Minh trail?" he asked her.

"I did." Helen shook out her hair. "I still do. Not for the same reasons anymore." She brushed sand off her arms. "I'm beginning to admire them. Their fierce will. Do you understand someone better when you've sat down and eaten a bowl of rice with them?"

The sun spun low in the sky, turning the South China Sea into a long liquid field of bronze.

"I thought of you all the time in the village. You should have been there with us," Helen said. "I felt it, the thing you talked about, being a brick in the wall."

With those words, Linh knew without a doubt he loved her. He barely remembered walking up the sand to the café, how they stood shoulder to shoulder, how her hair dried to the color of light straw.

As they approached, Darrow stretched his arms over his head, smiling at them even as he cast a troubled glance down the beach. All Linh could see was the radiance of Helen's face as she gazed at Darrow.

"I only have that fierce will for those I love," she said under her breath to Linh. "I need to get him away from here."

Years later Linh would wish that there had been some sign that this moment was the perfect one, balanced on the edge of changing, that the three of them would never again be together and as happy as they were then. But even if he had known, how did one hold time? Instead, there was a shout from one of the crewmen: "Ice cream!" and Helen grabbed Linh's hand as they hurried through the white powdery sand, stumbling, laughing, blind.

The three of them returned to the war that had brought them together, but the war itself had changed. Saigon with it.

Helen and Linh went out to photograph the refugees crowded into the new slums overwhelming the city. The faces they met were weary—bones pressing against skin, hollow-cheeked, eyes sunken and stony from hardship— looking away, not into the camera. An indication the enemy was winning?

Life in the city remained as schizophrenic as ever: Each night Helen waded through dozens of quickly mimeographed invitations to dinners at posh restaurants and cocktail receptions at the embassies. As the war grew larger, the social life of the city expanded with it. They attended the official functions dutifully, knowing that nothing of interest would come out of it beside the line about winning the war.

Darrow and Helen returned a couple, and they now took their place in the expat life of journalists and adventurers. Many came from ambition, as Darrow had claimed, but just as many came to escape whatever bound them to home—jobs, family, boredom. Media stars mixed with journeymen photographers and freelancers who never took a picture, a movie star's son, and a Connecticut debutante. American teenagers washed up on the streets, straight out of high school or college dropouts.

They met at all-night parties hosted in dilapidated French villas or in seedy bars scattered through the city. They listened to Cuban music a wire-service stringer supplied; they drank rum and scotch, smoked pot and opium. Most of the men had Vietnamese girlfriends; the few women had a number of men to choose from.

The talk of the parties was about the price of brandy and the availability of hair spray and war; the latest restaurant and nightclub and war; divorces and marriages, war; romances and salaries, war; babies, the danger of the countryside, war; eventually they came back to the bedrock of their existence, the cause of the present Americanized incarnation of Saigon, and it was always war.

But it was her life with Darrow in the crooked apartment behind the Buddha door in Cholon that formed Helen's true history. What was between them balanced the madness outside.

Darrow and Helen were sent to cover a refugee exodus below the DMZ—a poisonous, sinewy, snakelike stream of old fuming diesel trucks, loaded-down bicycles, carts, wagons, and people. By the time they reached the convoy, a dozen other journalists were already there, including Robert. Then Matt Tanner appeared. Helen had not run into him again since their exchange over the Captain Tong pictures, and she considered that a good thing, and regretted seeing him now.

Tanner walked on, not acknowledging them. Robert shook hands, polite and curious. As soon as he saw them together, he realized he had lost all chance with her.

Darrow and Helen walked alongside the refugees while Linh asked questions. People had evacuated in a panic; there was a shortage of basic supplies. They passed Helen with slow, solemn steps, taking no notice of her camera.

Food and water were scarce. Although she was parched, Helen avoided sipping from her canteen, guilty that she had water and at the same time protective, afraid to be mobbed for it.

After the calm of the village, the sheer numbers of people overwhelmed; the scale of the disaster made her feel useless. Dry-mouthed, she licked her lips, tasting salt, growing more thirsty. When an old man collapsed on the side of the road, she stooped down, shielding him from view, and gave him precious mouthfuls of her water, but in seconds a crowd formed, and she had to move on.

The sides of the road, used as both kitchen and toilet, had turned to mud, the stench unbearable. Some of the older villagers so frail every step was a miracle of will. Darrow walked ahead and ran into Tanner and two other photographers circling a young man as he struggled to pull a cart loaded down with belongings. A tiny, aged couple—grandparents?—sitting in the back with three small children in their laps. The young man had taken off his shirt and wrapped it around his head. His ribs were sharp, etched, every muscle and tendon roped with the strain of pulling the cart. Tanner appeared especially bull-like as he towered over him, bending as he angled his camera to capture the young man's expression.

Darrow jumped forward, pushing Tanner hard in the back so that he braced his hands on the side of the cart to keep from falling. The wood wheels of the cart shuddered and creaked from the sideways thrust.

"What the hell—?"

The young man stopped and put down the stays of the cart. His chest heaved with hard intakes of breath. Indifferent, resigned to whatever would happen next.

Darrow motioned him to the back of the cart and picked up the stays himself and began to pull. The young man's eyes widened, but he followed the cart, speaking softly to the white-haired couple. The woman turned her arthritic neck to study Darrow's back.

"What the fuck stunt is this supposed to be?" Tanner screamed. "You lunatic!"

Robert watched the scene unfold. Let Darrow hang himself, but he couldn't stand Helen's stricken face. He shook his head. "Go on ahead, Tanner."

"He's a goddamned nutcase!"

"Go on!" Robert yelled.

Linh slipped the two neck straps from Darrow's neck.

"Put them in the cart," Darrow said. "Go ahead and get some pictures farther up."

Linh jogged ahead. Darrow's face tight, jaw quivering. Helen didn't know what to do, and in her indecision, she walked alongside the cart. A brawl averted, Robert dropped back down the line without a word to either of them. Whatever had gone wrong in Darrow's head was her problem to deal with now.

For two hours, not a word was spoken. Finally the young man ran up to the front of the cart and tapped Darrow on the shoulder. He pointed to a shady spot under the trees, and Darrow nodded and pulled the cart off the road. The moment he set down the stays, the old couple sprang up and began handing down the children. As the old man washed their faces with the corner of a handkerchief and some water, the old woman unpacked a basket of wrapped banana leaves.

Clenching and unclenching his blistered hands, Darrow stood awkwardly, not knowing how to leave them. What are the boundaries of charity? When started, where does it morally end? His upbringing had been a secular one, but how he longed to have the crutch of faith, even temporarily. Something had exploded inside his head, an anger he thought he had dealt with. *The cool thing for us is that when this war's done, there's always another one.* The placid thought floated in his head that he would have shot Tanner point-blank if given the chance.

Helen came up and, silent, handed him a canteen. Shy with him, knowing he wished she hadn't witnessed the act. No matter what came next, she had seen underneath the bravado. Deep despair. Does contradiction in the beloved make one love him less or more?

The old man untied a piece of bamboo and opened the banana leaf. Inside was a square of rice. He motioned for Darrow to have it, but Darrow shook his head, fished in his pocket for whatever chance money there was, and handed it over, a fortune of a few twenties, as if in contrition. The man's face lit up, but already Darrow had slunk away, disappearing up the road.

That evening Linh, Darrow, and Helen sat at a table on the terrace of the Continental. Both of Darrow's hands were wrapped in gauze, so he cupped his hands to pick up the slick glass of gin and tonic.

"Tell her how great Angkor is," he insisted.

Linh smiled, sensing a shift between them, a new agreement. "It is a nice collection of rocks."

"No, I'm serious," Darrow said. He took a large gulp of his drink and turned toward Helen. "I need to take you there."

"There's just this little war thing going on," Helen said.

"Don't worry. You're in luck. There'll be plenty of war when we get back." Darrow heard the cynicism in his voice, but it felt old and outdated; he had moved beyond it.

Linh finished his own drink and lifted three fingers to the waiter for another round.

"Someday," she said.

Exchanged looks.

"Phnom Penh is like the dream image—Vietnam before the war." Darrow nudged Linh. "Do you remember the quiet?"

"Everyone thought we were crazy. Working all day in the hot sun."

Darrow laughed. "But it was good, wasn't it?" He said it eagerly, needing it to be true.

Linh wondered what was going wrong inside him. Had the outburst with the wagon really been justified? "Yes, it was good."

The waiter set down three more drinks.

"How about ordering some food on the side?" Helen said.

"Not someday—now. You need to see it. Let's leave tomorrow morning." Frustrated that neither of them was paying attention, treating him like a cranky child, Darrow sulked.

She caught the waiter's eye. "Leave for where?"

"You aren't listening," Darrow said. "Mouhot forgot his homeland, his family, blissful in his exploration. He couldn't tear himself away."

"What a selfish man," she said.

"No, you've got it all wrong. He was like one of Homer's lotus eaters. He simply forgot all thoughts of return."

"But you don't need to go to Angkor. You already have the war."

The waiter stood ready for their order when Tanner walked in.

"Pass on the food. Bring the check," Darrow said.

"Anyway, we can't leave. Linh and I are scheduled out with Olsen's unit day after tomorrow."

Darrow drank down half his glass in one gulp. "I need to go back to Angkor. I've been here . . . too long."

"What you need is to eat. You're drunk." He was childish and petulant, and she was bewildered by the change that had come over him. She saw this as a version of her own fear, and she tried to help him with her own mantra, Fear is not an option.

"We need to get back what we had in the village," Darrow said.

"But the village was a lie, wasn't it?"

Tanner scanned the tables and saw the three of them, changed direction, and walked the long way to a table in the back.

"You know what your problem is?" Darrow said, hunching his back against Tanner's presence, running his finger down the center of the table as if tracing a line of thought. "You should have been an accountant. You can take pictures, but you take them like an accountant."

Linh stood. "I am busy tomorrow. See you early on Friday?"

Helen ignored his effort to escape. "You know what you have, Sam? The great white correspondent's ego. When did it all get to be about *you*? What *you* did today was all about you and Tanner, not those people. Poor you."

Across the room, Tanner's loud bark of a laugh rang out as people joined his table. Darrow flinched as if from a sharp slap and kept glancing over his shoulder. "He makes me feel like a ghoul. Feeding off people's suffering. I'm tired . . . sick to death . . ."

"I'm sorry, but I can't leave. This is my chance now," Helen said, and in spite of her pity for him, she felt strong.

"You're lucky. I was like you once. I didn't care for a long time."

Helen threw bills down on the table, wanting to leave before he caused more of a scene. "Help me out, Linh."

Darrow dropped his hands into his lap. "I made a fool of myself. I know that."

Linh laid a hand on his shoulder, then turned to leave, wanting no part in Helen's hardness.

One of the street children, a young girl who regularly sneaked in, ran through the restaurant waving a twenty-dollar bill. "Thief!" A waiter grabbed her, lifting her feet from the floor, and she shrieked.

"He give, he give," she cried, pointing. In the back of the room, Tanner stood and motioned the waiter over.

"Yes, I did. Just a little present, okay? It's hers," he said to the dining room at large, then turned and shrugged to his companions. "Maybe I should hire a cyclo to take her home? Or better yet, drive it myself."

They had to drag Darrow out, as he muttered expletives behind him. On the street, Helen waved down a taxi. They arrived at the mouth of the alley, the meeting place of silk and lacquered bowl streets. The depression in the road was dry, and they walked through it and on to the crooked building, Darrow's arm around Helen's shoulder, half protecting, half supported.

They lay under the mint green bedspread, the light of the lampshade warming the shimmering expanse of silk and the barren room beyond it.

"One mission is blending into another. It's time for me to leave. I have nightmares."

Helen laid her head on his chest. "Watching Tanner made me sick, too. Forget him." She wanted to say something that would help, but he was so far away from her now.

Darrow moved up on his elbow and put his hand across her throat. "What's there to do other than war? It's become my life."

Helen held his hand against her mouth, kissing each fingertip. "I'm your life."

"I don't know how to repair." He had never spoken like this before, and she wondered what she would do if he said the words she had so long waited for.

"My family's name was Koropec. . . . Hungarian. I was fifteen when I decided I was going to be a famous American war photographer. And famous American war photographers didn't have names like that. I made myself into Sam Darrow. Who am I if not that name? Now I have to live up to it."

"Says who?"

He lay back in the pillows. "If only I had met you twenty years ago."

"We met now. That's worth something. I'm the accountant, remember?"

Dawn lit the sky outside the bedroom window. The leaves of the flamboy-ant fluttered, somnolent in the last of the night breeze. Helen woke to a noise and saw Darrow sitting at the window, smoking, an ashtray full of cigarettes at his feet.

"Did you sleep at all?"

"Can't."

"Why?"

"I left a will at Gary's office a few weeks ago."

Now Helen woke up fully, scared. "Morbid conversation first thing in the morning."

"It's not. . . . The reason I'm telling you is that it caused a rumor that I had some kind of death wish. It's just that if something did happen, I don't want to be buried. A phobia."

"It's bad luck to talk—"

"My scaredy-cat. It's the reality. I'm wagering to live to be an old man."

She rolled off the bed and pulled clothes off the chair to slip on. Since the previous night she had been formulating a kind of equation: the idea that leaving to save Darrow would allow her to leave Vietnam without guilt. A chance. "Don't you wonder if it's worth it?"

"Every time I go out. Wouldn't be normal if you didn't. No one wants to say it, but husband, father . . . none of that stuff is important in the war. Oth-erwise, why are we here?"

"We'll take the next plane out. You said yourself you've been here too long."

Darrow nodded his head and stubbed out his cigarette. "We might," he said, then softened it. "We could. Soon."

ELEVEN

Bao Chi

Journalist

On the morning Helen was to go out on patrol with Olsen, she woke and packed, ready for Linh to pick her up at three-thirty in the morning. She opened the door to a soft knock.

"I have a problem," Linh said, standing there. "Family. Sister-in-law, her baby has croup. She is new to Saigon. I must help her find a doctor." He had never talked of family before, and she was surprised.

"Sure. Can I help?"

"No. Can you go without me?"

"Don't worry. I'll be fine."

Darrow struggled out of bed in the darkness behind her. "What's wrong?"

Helen picked up her camera bags. "Linh can't go."

Darrow rubbed his eyes and put on his glasses. "Come with me instead to My Tho this afternoon."

"I promised to cover this. Besides, I'll be with my old buddies, Captain Olsen's unit. I haven't seen him since the Captain Tong pictures." She felt confident that she could handle herself and also a small excitement proving she could go it alone. Now that it had been decided that they would leave soon, these final missions took on a feeling of nostalgia.

Darrow frowned and looked at Linh. "You sure you can't go with her?"

"I'm fine." She resented his treating her like she wasn't competent enough to go alone and now was more determined than ever. Besides, giving him some of his own medicine might make things move faster to leaving.

After Linh left, Darrow sat in the bed and watched her pack the additional equipment she would have to carry alone. "Don't go," he said.

"You're being silly."

"For me." He hadn't intended it, but now it was a kind of test.

A test she wouldn't take. "Remember asking why the people supposed to love us the most are the ones who try to stop us doing what we love?"

He had met his match and didn't much care for it.

Problems plagued the assignment immediately. At Bien Hoa, one helicopter after another was diverted or canceled so that she didn't make it to the small village where Captain Olsen's unit was stationed until late afternoon.

The village hugged the edge of the jungle; it had been evacuated and bombed the month before. Nothing remained but piles of rubble and stone, a few freestanding walls pocked with bullet holes. From the first soldier she encountered, she heard more bad news—Captain Olsen had a recurrence of malaria and had been evacuated five days before. No one had bothered to inform her. His replacement, Captain Horner, fresh out of officer's training, had been in-country only two weeks.

Samuels came around the corner of a wall. "I heard chow and our good-luck charm had arrived. Need any leeches burned off those pretty ankles?"

Helen hugged him, glad to see a friendly face. "How's it going?"

Samuels wagged his head toward the soldier standing next to her. "He fill you in? Hornblower. Already lost three men since he's been here. An idiot."

Helen tried to ignore the shiver climbing up her back. The first chink in her confidence. Her smile filled with doubt. Should she have listened to Darrow?

"We'll be lucky if he doesn't get us all killed. Bastard. Think about turning around and catching that ride out. Come back when Olsen's here."

"Then you won't have anyone to complain to." She wished it hadn't been

Samuels in front of her; otherwise, she might have jumped back on the helicopter.

"Be careful is all I'm saying. Work us some magic like you did last time."

"I could do with some myself."

A patrol was coming in along a path, and at its middle was a scraggly, lank-
limbed man who towered over the others, sweating profusely and swearing.

"That," Samuels said, putting his arm around her, "is our leader."

The captain walked straight up to Helen as if she were one more obstacle
to be overcome before the long day was accomplished.

"Meet my girlfriend, Captain," Samuels said.

Horner had a long, thin neck with a prominent Adam's apple that jerked
as he swallowed. "I guess you're the reporter I'm supposed to allow."

Helen slapped Samuels's arm off. "That's right."

"They just told me Adams."

"Not a very complete description." She already felt weary of the coming fight.

He puckered his face as if he had bitten something sour. "I guess they really do start you at the bottom. Second-rate soldiers and women reporters."

Helen was too distracted by what Samuels had said to take full offense.
Everything told her that she had made a mistake not turning around and
leaving.

"You'll have to keep up on your own. And no fraternizing with the men."

"Who am I supposed to talk to, then?"

"You're a photographer. Why d'you need to talk?" He turned his face
slightly to spit, then walked away.

"Told you," Samuels said. "A charmer. You still have time to leave."

Helen dropped her pack. "It'll torture him more if I stay."

That night, Horner ordered plastic ponchos strung in a triangle against the
crumbling wall so that Helen was "protected" from the rest of the soldiers. She
lay down in the darkness, wearing full uniform and boots. Stars pulsed overhead like the small spots of fire she remembered from bonfires on summer
nights along the beach back home. After the hamlet, the night sounds—
screech of birds deep in the jungle and hum of insects—felt familiar and
soothing. The two sides were not fighting the same war. For the Vietnamese,

everything was known, was home, even if they came from the north. For the Americans, even the sounds before going to sleep were strange and menacing.

The thought nagged at her that she had missed an opportunity with Darrow, insisting on going alone. But he took it for granted that she would give up anything for him. Unlike him, she hadn't been in Vietnam too long; she had barely started.

The plastic liner squeaked, and a man rolled in underneath it. "Shhh!"

Helen squinted, unable to make out a face but recognizing the voice. "Samuels, get out."

"A little Laos heaven? Or how 'bout a sip of dago red?"

"No thanks." A rotten smell came from him; they had been out for days, while she had showered that morning.

"Talk to me. Tell me about the big lovely world."

"If Hornblower finds you here, he'll can me."

"He's snoring away. And I have a lookout."

"Not a good idea." She was indulging him like a child, but it was too dangerous.

"So good to see you again . . . you have no idea. Just to touch something soft." He reached out and placed his hand on her stomach.

"If you don't leave when I count to three, I'll scream. Wake them all up."

He withdrew his hand. "Just remember this. I go to sleep every night dreaming about lying next to you in that foxhole. That's as close to a woman as I've been in a while."

"My heart breaks. Good night, Samuels," she said loudly, and he was gone in another squeak of plastic. In the dark, she heard chuckles all around.

At dawn they broke camp and walked, single file, along a narrow dirt road; tree trunks and leaves and vines and bushes on each side so dense they formed a solid wall, curving overhead, forming a shadowed tunnel.

Samuels avoided her all morning, walking point, while Helen trudged behind Captain Horner. If possible, the captain's face seemed even thinner and bonier than the day before. When he spoke to her, the sight of his Adam's apple made him seem oddly vulnerable.

Now that she had exiled herself from Samuels and the other men, Horner seemed to have a change of heart and was anxious to include her on the mission, bring her to see his side of things. "This area is a major trade route for supplies from the north. We're supposed to figure out where they are and then bring in airpower."

"Sounds tough." She wondered if he was too green to know that he was being sent out as bait to see what was in the area.

"I don't get asked for my opinion on operations, you know?"

"Sorry."

"My goal is to get all these guys back to base in five days."

"Gotcha."

His profile was to her, and she saw his Adam's apple go up and down, twice, before he spoke. "I didn't mean for those men to die."

Helen looked up in surprise, but Horner's small, stony eyes revealed nothing, and it seemed as if the words had not come from him. "Understood," she said.

"But you don't write. I mean, you're only a photographer?"

Horner enforced strict discipline on the men. No talking, five feet between each man, fire only when fired upon. Despite herself, she was impressed. They walked for two days in deep backcountry, not encountering another human being. Later, Helen would remember the patrol with the haziness of hallucination, the silence so complete it made one's ears ring. If one stood still, one could hear an undercurrent, a hum, to the forest, even the sound of water on leaves, trees dripping moisture as if they were perspiring.

Giant teak trunks blocked the sun, and the vegetation lay thick and snarled below; unseen animals crashed away through the brush while birds screamed overhead. A russet-colored dust floated in the air. The ground a springy compost that left behind perfect footprints; Helen thought of Hansel and Gretel leaving a trail. During the heat of the day, the air was so hot and thick it tasted green on the tongue, like swallowing a pond.

It was not Helen's job to keep track of where she was, only to follow the man in front of her, and so the days became a series of rutted paths climbed, narrow grassy valleys traversed, rocky dry streambeds to be crossed. In the morning, they woke to a thick fog that reduced visibility to the end of one's arm, muffling sound so that their voices seemed to have been snatched away. By noon, the sun burned away the fog. In a clearing, with blue sky overhead, the light emerged, harsh and chalky and forbidding.

Although their attention was strained, constantly on the lookout for an ambush or mines, the silence, as palpable as the sunlight, made them dreamy. Helen found long stretches of time when her mind was empty, her thoughts ceased; her present and immediate future and even her past, all receded. As free as she had ever felt in her life. The illusion grew within her that she had always been in this forest. At times it seemed as if they were the only human beings left on the earth, and it was simply a fantasy to think that cities like Saigon or, for that matter, Los Angeles existed.

Two nights after the incident with Samuels, Helen dropped off a pack of cigarettes on his bedroll. The next morning, she found a small pyramid of canned peaches on her pack. Samuels moved back in formation so that he walked in front of Helen again, taking back his role of big brother.

"You stay right behind me. I'm charmed. No mine is going to get me."

On the fifth morning they reached their objective, a small plateau overlooking a valley with a village below. The relief on Horner's face made Helen start to like the man. When they opened radio contact, they got orders to abandon their patrol and move as quickly as possible to the main road and head north. A convoy would pick them up en route and join them to two companies that had run into heavy NVA fire.

They fanned out and moved quickly down the gentle grass slope, their long, loose strides stirring up hundreds of greenish yellow grasshoppers that jumped waist-high in their path. Helen felt like the prow of a ship, grass brushing her thighs, flecks of green-gold insect life like the spray of water from a bow. The sun fell in heavy, flat planks, smothering sound, the great silence of the forest extending to the valley so that she felt they had been bewitched. Nature hushed and waiting for a misstep on their part to yawn awake.

They reached the rice paddies bordering the village. As far as they could see in any direction, no human being visible, their enchantment continued. The surface of the paddies feathered in the imperceptible breeze.

"Let's have three men go through the paddies," Horner said.

The men looked down or away. They weren't returning to base but were heading to combat; no one wanted the extra danger of the paddy. The men had told Helen that Horner ordered the men who had died to scout a paddy after a villager confessed it was mined.

"Who wants to volunteer?" Horner again asked, and the men, again, remained silent.

Helen felt sick to her stomach, the calm of the last week gone. For the first time in the five days, she desperately needed Linh or Darrow.

Finally Samuels coughed. "Captain, we need to meet up with the convoy. Why don't we skirt the paddy and village to reach the road quicker?"

"Negative. We will finish the original mission."

Samuels took a deep breath, and Helen wanted to reach out a cautionary arm but didn't.

"With all due respect, sir. An empty paddy in the middle of the day is a live one."

Two of the men shook their heads and began to hand off extra equipment.

Horner nodded, satisfied. "We'll need one more," he said, staring down at his map.

"Oh, fuck it," Samuels said, and threw off his equipment.

Helen crouched down and took a picture of the three men standing at the edge of the paddy. She got one picture of Samuels knee-deep in water, turning to give the other two a thumbs-up with his dragon-tattooed arm.

Ten minutes later she heard the shrill whistling of a mortar shell from the village. They all ducked, but Helen looked in time to see the explosion of water all around Samuels. The other two men in the paddy splashed through the water, reaching him as shells burst at their old positions. They all ran to the shelter of a paddy dike.

"Shit!" Horner yelled. He flattened on the ground, and when he saw Helen rise to take a shot, he screamed, "Down!" After a few minutes, the shelling stopped. The three men in the paddy scuttled back across the water and scrambled up the bank, collapsing next to Helen.

Samuels was panting. "Not a scratch."

The men chuckled and spread out, gulped water from their canteens.

Figuring she had enough shots, Helen took off her lens and put the camera away, intending to have a smoke.

"That was close," one of them said.

"Everyone's okay," Horner said.

"No thanks to you, stupid motherfucker," Samuels said and glared up at Horner.

Horner scanned the village with his binoculars but said nothing. The other two soldiers remained silent. The air tense, Helen almost wished another mortar would fire just to distract them.

"Goddamn West Point asshole," Samuels continued.

"Did you make it to the other side of the paddy?" Horner asked sadly.

Samuels blew air out through his lips in a slow hiss, the fight knocked out of him.

"No, I don't think you did." Horner looked tired but kindly, like a father urging his son to finish a necessary task. "Go back across."

The other men shifted, but Horner held up his hand. "Just Samuels."

No movement except for the scanning of Horner's binoculars over the paddy.

"No," Samuels said.

Horner sighed and put down the glasses. He brushed a dried weed off his shirt. "That's an order."

In a burst of energy, Samuels was on his feet, his revolver unholstered. "You go."

Horner's skin went red; he seemed more offended than frightened. "You're looking at a court-martial, mister, unless you put that thing down," he said, his voice almost a whisper. When Samuels didn't move, he leaned forward. "*Now,* I said."

"It's not even loaded, you stupid fuck." Before Horner could get close, Samuels turned the gun at his own head, grimaced, and fired. Everyone crouched for a minute, unable to comprehend what had happened.

As they laid him out, Horner got on the radio, ordering an immediate medevac. Helen knelt down next to the corpsman.

Samuels's helmet was still on, and as the medic pulled off the compress wrapped under his nose to his neck, a wave of black passed over Helen's eyes. The forehead, the eyes, the nose, all of it was the old Samuels, but the lower jaw was missing. Blood poured in luxuriant gushes down his chest. The entire crescent of his upper teeth was laid bare; she quickly turned away. The corpsman grabbed a large body compress and pressed it up into the hole beneath the nose.

"Hold this down tight, okay?"

Helen nodded and held, breath gone, pressure behind her eyes as if she were going to pass out.

"Don't press on the neck," the corpsman yelled as he punctured the skin, creating a trache hole. "You'll block his breathing passage."

Helen followed orders instinctually. She looked into Samuels's eyes, and his look said he couldn't believe in the reality of what had happened, either. She leaned down to his ear. "Don't you give up on me."

A few minutes later his body went into convulsions, the torso bouncing as if an electric current pulsed through him, legs stretched out and trembling, arms reaching, throwing Helen and the corpsman off.

"I need help to hold him down!"

One of the solders came, knelt on the other side of Samuels, and pinned his arms. The medic couldn't give morphine because it was a head wound. After a minute, Samuels's body relaxed, the tension loosened. His eyes, which had been wild and fierce with pain, now flattened out. When she looked into his eyes, his gaze was cool and impersonal, a great distance and solitude in them.

The medic wrapped an elastic bandage around the compress and over the helmet. "No need taking it off and having things spill out."

Helen moved off, hands covered in blood. She didn't want to dig out her bandanna from her camera bag, smearing blood on her equipment. Too afraid of snipers to get water from the paddy, she settled for wiping her hands on her pants. Horner sat on a rock alone, face crumpled and worn, years of training all unraveled in minutes.

When she returned to Samuels, she concentrated on his tanned arms, still perfect, the dragon tattoo still wrapped around the muscled left forearm. She took his hand and held it to her.

When they placed him in the helicopter, Helen got on also. "I don't want him to be alone."

The corpsman squeezed her shoulder. "He's not going to make it, okay? Nothing you can do either way to change that."

At the field hospital, stretcher bearers ran Samuels into the tent. An hour passed. The noise of the planes and jeeps, the rushing of the medical staff, unreal after the silence of the forest.

Finally a nurse came out to have a cigarette and offered one to her. "Honey, you need to clean up."

Helen wiped her hands against her pants and felt the dry crustiness of them.

"Over there," the nurse said. "The supply building. Hot water and soap, a cot to lie down in. You need it."

"Samuels?" Helen said, barely able to mumble the words, her mouth dry, tongue thick.

"Oh, sorry, honey. Didn't make it to the operating table. Somebody should have told you."

Helen nodded her head. Before, there had been this small, shiny thing inside her that kept her immune from what was happening, and now she knew it had only been her ignorance, and she felt herself falling into a deep, dark place.

"Come on," the woman said. "Let's get you cleaned up and fed."

After the nurse went back on duty, Helen returned to the supply building. Inside, it was hot, close, and dim, the only light from a row of exposed light-bulbs at the front of the building and the cracks of light through the rough, uneven seams of the metal walls. Racks of metal shelving stood eight feet tall, piled with supplies as tight as the stacks in a library. The air smelled of card-board and plastic. As promised, a small cot was made up in one of the rows.

Helen put her equipment underneath the cot, then stretched out. She rolled onto her side, dragging her muddy boots across the blanket, too tired to take them off. Her arms and legs and chest trembled so that she had to clench her teeth as if against cold, and yet her skin was bathed in sweat. Beyond tears. She longed for something, anything, even physical pain, to provide a diversion.

"Adams."

She did not know how much time had passed, but she woke to the sound of a helicopter coming in. The flights had been constant, the radioed battle that Horner's unit was joining, the wounded piling in. She prayed that Horner had delayed the unit but knew he wouldn't. Just as he wouldn't take blame for breaking Samuels. Although now he would die in shame, Samuels had simply chosen the method of his suicide. Horner's way would have earned him a metal for bravery. It sickened her. She heard a soldier calling her name again. This was her ride to rejoin the company.

She rolled off the cot and crawled on her hands and knees farther into the rows till she reached the farthest, darkest corner. She sat on the floor balled up, with her back against a box, her knees drawn into her chest, her forehead resting on them.

"Adams! Where the hell is she?"

The door opened, and her name echoed against the thin metallic walls. Helen breathed in, held her breath until she could feel her pulse throbbing. The door slammed shut.

"Where did the girl photographer go?"

Helen rolled down on her side, the ground cool and smelling of moisture like a damp basement. She tucked her fist under her chin. When she closed her eyes, she saw Samuels as he had been next to her under the plastic partition, and then she fell asleep.

Hours later, she left the supply building and searched out the air controller.

"We couldn't find you for the supply run."

"I've got enough film, and I need to send it out. When's the next flight to Danang?" She held her breath, the lie so obvious.

He looked at his clipboard, bored. "Cargo flight at sunset."

"I'll be in the mess tent."

She sat on a bench and stared at the table. She stood at the LZ half an hour before the plane was ready to take off. She had already boarded when a soldier ran up with her camera bags that she had left behind, forgotten, in the supply building.

When Helen returned to Saigon, she was relieved to find Darrow and Linh on an assignment in Cam Ranh Bay. In the apartment, she continued her hiding, camped under the mint green bedspread, trying to forget what had happened, including her own humiliating part in it. A pain throbbed behind her eyes—she could not put Samuels out of her mind, his death like a disease inside her. The more she thought about it, the less she understood what had happened or whom to blame.

The film in the bags was an accusation; if she could not figure out Samuels's intention, she couldn't in good conscience broadcast the photos, so instead of mourning the loss of her friend, she had to act as judge on his actions. Obviously Horner had been in the wrong, had demoralized his men, but Samuels was a veteran of two tours. He should have been able to deal with Horner easily. Had he just been showing off, a terrible, stupid accident? Or had Samuels snapped? Had the waste and stupidity up to that moment finally done him in?

There were worse alternatives to consider. Had the lines begun to blur so much that Samuels simply didn't care whether there was a bullet in the chamber or not?

In exasperation, Gary came to pick up the film himself, and she reluctantly let it go because to make an issue of it would be to convict Samuels. An assistant would develop the rolls. Gary took one look at Helen and called a doctor. He promised to return after the film was processed.

When the doctor examined her, he shook his head. "Exhaustion. Post-stress."

"You're *my* doctor, right? Call it vitamin deficiency."

The sheets were dirty; she hadn't changed them in weeks, too busy for normal life. Gingerly Gary sat on the edge of the bed. "What happened, honey bunny?" He didn't want to be responsible for his star girl photographer going down and that becoming the story.

Helen shook her head. How could she not betray Samuels and still let the photos go out? "I don't think the film's any good."

"They're great shots. You just need to rest, okay?"

She leaned over, her eyes slipping away from him. "I don't know what happened. Out there." She knew what had happened inside, Samuels's frustration. But hadn't he really meant it as a dare, a bit of drama, a boyish prank?

The room was hot, and Gary's forehead beaded with sweat. "Why do you stay here? I pay you a lot better than living here."

"It's the real Vietnam."

"Who the hell cares? Didn't you notice? The real 'Nam is a shit hole." Gary kicked at a pillow on the floor. Bad enough to witness all the military casualties, but now his reporters were falling apart. Every day he lived with the guilt, sending them out, knowing the dangers, the scars it would leave either way. Pretending, pretending, his cowboy talk that none of it was so bad, that they'd be okay if they took precautions. And here was his girl getting all messed up.

"Why's the place good enough to die for, then?"

"That's real philosophical and deep and all, but I got my own problems. Look, sweetie, I don't know when's a good time to tell you, so here it is. The new assistant was rushed and used too much heat drying the negatives. The emulsion melted."

The shock that the whole thing had been destroyed stunned her. "All of them?" Despite her doubt about releasing them, now the news knocked the wind out of her. It was clear now that she would never have sat on the photos. Samuels betrayed again, now by being forgotten.

"Of course not. About half. But listen, the ones left were good enough for another cover. And your fee doubled, too, so not so bad, huh?"

He was a sly one; she suspected he had tricked her into realizing how valuable they were.

"My fee just tripled. And I want my byline on each picture." She rolled back onto the bed, appalled with this small, hard ambition inside her. "What about the one with Samuels standing at the edge of the paddy?"

"Tripled, didn't I say that? I'll have to check on the name, greedy girl. Your soldier's the cover boy." He was relieved by her voracity. That bit of ruthlessness would serve her well and meant that all this bed rest was just theatrics.

"No, you didn't say."

"Of course," Gary said, running his hand up and down the bedspread, "knowing the outcome of the battle . . . well, he's immortalized."

She closed her eyes, weighing the decision. "Even if he shot himself?"

Gary paused, relieved now that he had found out the cause of her behavior. "I didn't even hear that."

"Are you *that* cynical?"

He glanced at her, a small, wan smile, then got up and moved away. "Man, it's boiling in here. What I *am* is a guy with a constant deadline. Samuelson—"

"Samuels."

"Whatever. Was a brave soldier—I have testimonials. *You* don't know what happened for sure. Things go on out there that can't be judged by the standards of ordinary life, little girl."

Even if Gary knew exactly what had happened, it would make no difference.

"Give this a thought. Fly to Washington and present a print of this Samuels to his parents, or girlfriend, wife, whatever he's got. That would be great coverage."

She shook her head. "I'm through."

"That's why you had your fee tripled? What you need is rest." He paced the room, sweating and wiping his forehead with a paper napkin. "How about me sending some meals over from Grival's."

"You can't buy me," she said into her blanket, but they both knew he had won.

"It's on the expense account, okay? And you'll get your byline."

"I don't care."

He studied her for a moment. "Even if the guy did flip out for a second— which I'm officially denying—what about all the times he's a hero and no one is handy with a camera? He's a brave SOB in my book just for being out there in Vietnam, another name for Hell." He picked up his pack to leave.

"At the field hospital—"

"I'll tell you something I shouldn't. I rescued Darrow out there in Angkor. Don't ever let him know. Hiding in the rocks. Flipped out, man. Scared of his shadow. I'm not sure what would have happened if Linh hadn't shown up." An exaggeration, of course, but one for a good cause.

Helen had never heard this version of their time at Angkor; all she knew was Darrow's obsession with going back there.

"Be one of my best photographers. The job won't betray you. I love Darrow, but he's headed in a bad direction again—the thing with Tanner was dumb. I'm relying on you and Linh to pull him through."

But Gary was wrong. Already the job had betrayed her. Or she had betrayed it, had fulfilled MacCrae's prophecy, and become part of their movie. Young boys like Michael would see that picture of Samuels and follow in the footsteps of a man who rolled the dice with his life.

When Gary left, Helen got out of bed, dressed, and took up life again. At dinner with Annick, she sipped at a martini, so icy it went down like water. The smoothness of the tablecloth, the ice in their water glasses, the laughter at the tables around them, soothed her. A man across the room nodded, and she smiled back. The waiter brought them a complimentary round of drinks.

"You're strange tonight," Annick said, and lit a cigarette.

Helen noticed the smudge of lipstick on Annick's glass as she moved it away from her lips, the pristine cleanness of the china (nothing in the field could be made that clean), the rustle of a woman's dress as she passed by.

"I was a coward."

Annick blew away a stream of smoke and shrugged. "You made it back to Saigon. The only victory that counts." She looked over her shoulder at the man. "I think he likes you."

"Maybe I should call him over." Helen pointed her chin in the man's direction. "A whirlwind romance. We'll get married, and he'll take me home to meet his mother. Why not?"

"You're drunk."

"That's the problem. I can't get drunk. I'd need elephant tranquilizer to bring me down."

Annick finished her drink and started on the new one. "But maybe you should marry him. All anyone can gossip about is Darrow's wife coming to town."

Helen set down her glass, sobered.

"She came for a surprise visit. Waiting for him in his room at the hotel. Word is that rumors made their way back home about a certain loose female photographer."

This mythical wife existed in a time and space so far away from the crooked apartment that Helen had been able to ignore the situation. Darrow himself gave the marriage such little credence that she couldn't grasp the reality of the wife's sudden presence in Saigon. But here it was, or rather, here the wife was, pushing herself into a place she didn't belong. Helen felt the scruples of her old life. If she had meet Darrow back home, the fact of his marriage would have kept her from seeing him, but the thousands of miles, the nature of the war, had seduced her, made life back home strange and unfathomable.

"You shouldn't care. He loves you, not her."

The idea of being the other woman so ridiculous. Compared to what she had just witnessed, wasn't Darrow right, wasn't this small and unimportant? She wanted her life to be clean and right; to have things of her own. This must be the first thing to change. Helen leaned forward, elbows on the table. "What should I do? Go home?"

"A woman's never the most important thing to a man like him. You are fighting over scraps. Why not just take your pictures?"

Helen waved her hand as if shooing off an annoying insect.

"Then stop," Annick said. "You've proved yourself."

"The more I go out there the less I know why. But there are moments . . . when I feel this is what I'm alive for."

"So take a little vacation to Singapore. A break." Annick stubbed out her cigarette. "Other people make a whole life out of avoiding pain." The waiter brought a bowl of fruit; Annick smiled up at him extravagantly till he left. "Distracting themselves."

Helen smiled at her open flirtation. "What about you? I know how you distract yourself."

Now Annick sat up and her demeanor became as businesslike as in the shop. "Speaking of—would you mind if I saw Robert?"

A stab of possessiveness, but Helen dismissed it. Of course, life had to go on, and it was no one's fault that she had messed up her own. "Someone should be happy in Saigon."

"Don't be silly. This is a small place; we have to reuse each other. You think he's an innocent, but you're wrong. He sees through you and Darrow. He's like me; he knows this war means nothing. Maybe a change would do us both good. Maybe living in New Orleans would be fun."

That night Helen lay in bed, restless. After the drinks with Annick, she had hoped to fall asleep quickly, but each time she closed her eyes the image of Samuels haunted her. She regretted things. Crazy thoughts, made more powerful because of their lack of logic. What she had done or failed to do. The arrival of Darrow's wife presaged a change, but to what? She fell into a fitful sleep, and again she had the dream; children approached and circled her, pressing in, circling around and around, touching, but when she tried to speak with them, they turned away.

After midnight footsteps on the stairs woke her, a key in the lock, and now that the change was close she wished he had stayed away longer.

Darrow felt his way into the dark room. "You awake?"

"Yes."

He flipped on the red-shaded lamp. "I was hoping you were here." He sat on the bed. "I drove straight in from Bien Hoa, screw the curfew."

In his arms, she let herself be still a minute, feel protected for the barest fraction of time. He smelled of sweat, dirt, and the fecund reek from being in the field. It repulsed and made her hold him tighter. His body strong, but he was no different from Samuels, the vulnerability of flesh.

"Your wife's in town. At your hotel room."

He let go of her. "Not now."

"Wasn't my choice."

"How do you know?"

"As in, have I seen her? No."

Darrow pulled off his glasses and rubbed the bridge of his nose. "She threatened something about coming."

Helen moved away and pulled the sheet up around herself. "You didn't mention me . . . no." He had let it come to this, having her here. Helen's feelings were suddenly clear. "I had my own little religious experience out there this last time. Maybe you didn't tell her about us for a reason. I need something of my own. Not you. It never was. You and I were just a diversion."

"Where's this coming from?" He was angry at how quickly she was willing to throw them away.

"That's rich—you're being jealous."

Darrow stood and shoved a chair hard across the room. It made a heavy thud as it fell on its side. "A war is on, you notice? What the fuck do my marriage and your hurt feelings mean?"

" 'The cool thing for us, baby, is that when this war's done, there's always another one. The war doesn't ever have to end for us.' What would you do without the war as an excuse?"

"Ask me to leave her."

"Very romantic, but impractical."

Darrow kicked the door, and it bounced back into the wall. She flinched. The knob left a fist-size indentation in the wallpaper. "I'm ending this marriage now, regardless of if you're here when I get back." Her back was to him, and he stood in the door frame, catching his breath. "Be here when I get back."

A military jeep roared past Darrow in the street. Three ARVN soldiers sat in the front, two squeezed in the passenger seat. They had just finished a good dinner, with ample quantities of beer, and insisted on driving him to his hotel so that less liberal-minded soldiers didn't hassle him for being out past curfew. Apparent that if he didn't oblige, *they,* in fact, would be the ones to hassle him. He got in and offered cigarettes all around. Satisfied, the soldiers forgot about him and gossiped among themselves. Darrow sat back in silence and smoked.

Helen was right, of course. He didn't reveal himself, or rather the limited facts of biography never seemed important, always giving an arbitrary, confining version of the truth. He smiled in the darkness, realizing this was a liar's rationale. His wife's father owned the major newspaper that he had first worked for; he knew that fact led to surmises about his integrity. What it meant in reality was that he worked much harder to prove himself, that he had doggedly achieved on his own merits despite that.

But the withholding had started even earlier. He had never even told his wife about his name change. At the time, he had felt it gave him a foolish and vaguely embarrassing vanity, an adolescent stunt. Now too much time had passed for the truth; they had been married six years, even though he hadn't spent more than a few weeks at a time with either her or the boy.

No, not telling his wife had involved something deeper that he wanted to hide. She fell in love with Sam Darrow, the famous war photographer, but he was still the insecure young man determined to create this mythic persona. When he told her the first time that he was leaving for the Middle East, she sobbed. Wanted him to move to features, take pictures of politicians and movie stars. Not understanding that the creation now demanded its due, demanded to be played out.

He sat her down on the chintz-covered sofa in the living room. The marriage a terrible mistake, he offered an immediate divorce—an annulment for her sake. But she insisted on waiting till after the baby. Which was the way she announced her pregnancy to him. Much to his father-in-law's displeasure, he jumped when the offer to work for *Life* came, no longer beholden to the paper. He had been gone since; if it made her happy to stay married, he had seen no reason to inflict more suffering on the girl than he already had.

As the jeep swung through the empty streets, the night air blew cool and damp; he was still grimy from patrol but in no hurry to reach his destination. No other place he'd rather be than Saigon, no other life he would choose.

He hardly knew the woman waiting in the hotel room for him. He supposed she was a nice, loving girl and that her marriage to him had been a terrible disappointment. He blamed himself for weakness. There was another reason for his marriage that he hadn't admitted to Helen, which had to do with his fear of not coming back; a kind of insurance policy at the time to leave someone behind, waiting for him. But this woman's love had not weighted him down to either safety or caution.

The jeep stopped in front of the hotel, and Darrow climbed out. He tossed the rest of the pack of cigarettes to the driver and received a happy nod as the jeep sped away.

He felt a hazy discomfort, as slight as a sore muscle, afraid that changing the status quo, no matter how unsatisfactory, would jinx his luck. Helen's love was difficult, took away his lightness, his fearlessness.

Sunlight, broken up and scattering itself as the leaves of the flamboyant tree moved in the wind outside the window. Helen hadn't slept, reconciling herself to the future of things, and now at late morning, she still lay in bed, heavy, half awake.

She heard the key in the door, and then Darrow stood in the bedroom. Studying his face under half-closed eyes, she imagined she had summoned him with her dreams. The thought surprised her that she would never love anyone as much. His expression defiant as he pulled the wedding band off his finger and threw it across the floor. They both heard the hollow roll of it as it circled down into silence.

TWELVE

A Map of the Earth

Months passed. Robert's assignment was up; he was being promoted and sent to Los Angeles as bureau chief. When he invited Helen for a last lunch, they sat at the patio tables of the Cercle Sportif as shy as young lovers with unfinished business. Helen pretended to sun herself, tilting her face and closing her eyes. Although she always enjoyed his company, she wanted to know nothing about his relationship with Annick, which had been going on for the last few months. Annick had indicated that the relationship was less than satisfactory. Out at the pool, the daughters of wealthy South Vietnamese families sunned in French bikinis and ordered drinks from waiters who had been there since the colonial era.

Robert's white shirt and khaki pants were freshly pressed, his face shaven and smooth. And yet there were circles under his eyes and a cowlick that wouldn't settle over his forehead. Something vaguely dissipated about him, as if the tropics had finally had their way. He had aged a decade in the year and a half Helen had known him.

"If ever there was a revolution," Robert said, "it should start here, don't you think? Hopefully that waiter over there is a VC operative, a nephew of Uncle Ho."

"How can you leave all this?" She was teasing but also curious. Reporters were beginning to consider Vietnam a must-have on their résumés.

"I've had more than enough of this place. Two years is a lifetime in Saigon." He looked at her and smirked. "When're you taking off?"

"Soon . . ." Her hand fluttered toward the pool, the city beyond, before running out of force and dropping back in her lap. Darrow had delayed their departure three times, and the fourth date of departure was still up in the air. "If things would settle down . . . it's been one crisis after another."

He felt bad for needling her, so clear to him the one-sidedness of the thing with Darrow. "You're both coming to my going-away party?"

"Do we ever miss a party?" The truth was if Darrow wasn't on assignment, then he was buried in a crowd of people, either at other people's houses or at impromptu get-togethers at the Cholon apartment. They were never alone anymore; no doubt he intended the buffer to keep him safe from her nagging.

"Annick and I didn't work out. It's easier this way. Hope that doesn't change your mind about coming." Robert stood up. "I'd better get back to the grindstone."

Helen pushed back her chair to get up. "What happened?"

"She's a crazy one. Another war casualty. But it's ungentlemanly to kiss and tell. . . . Stay and enjoy your coffee."

She sat back and shaded her eyes to look up at him. "That's too bad, but I've missed you. You haven't had any time for me. I'm almost a lady of leisure now. Feature work. I've been sticking close in."

He wondered if part of his attraction to her simply had to do with being rejected, but now that the possibility was long past, he thought himself probably lucky. "I worry about you. I've kept my mouth shut because it'll sound like sour grapes," Robert said. "With Darrow, the war's different. I've seen it in other guys. He can't let it go. He's searching for more than a picture when he goes out, do you understand?"

Helen picked up her coffee cup and held it in midair, then set it back down without taking a sip. "What are you saying?"

"He's taking risks he doesn't have to take anymore to get a cover," Robert said.

"You're wrong. He wanted to leave for Angkor awhile ago."

"For your sake, I hope I am."

"Anyway, we're leaving here right after you. He's got a replacement coming."

"But do you think he'll stay away? A man like him living in a house with a wife and a dog, taking the garbage out Monday nights?"

Helen shook her head. "There are other things to do. Stories that don't involve war, like the Angkor piece."

"His choice?"

"Our choice. We both want this."

Robert sighed. "So why have you stopped going out?"

Helen shrugged. Since Samuels, she had not ventured into the field, making excuses to Gary, which he all too readily accepted. Samuels's picture had gotten a lot of play and had been copied for numerous articles. Each plane of new soldiers coming off the planes at Tan Son Nhut a weight on her. "I'm taking a break. You know—do no harm."

"Just don't let him take you down with him." He bent to kiss her cheek, but she turned her face and kissed him on the mouth.

"Don't worry about me," she whispered. "I'll save both of us."

But days passed each other in a succession of delays and excuses, fights and lies. As if Robert's words, spoken aloud, had taken on a truth of their own. Darrow bewitched, enchanted, and nothing Helen could do.

As one of their last assignments, Gary had arranged for them to cover a Red Cross center for children. Darrow went there for a week while Helen made arrangements for their trip back to the States. The day he finally took her, she noticed a strange excitement in him.

The courtyard, a converted villa, was filled with the "healthy" ones, children merely missing limbs but who could still sit or crawl or hobble about. They threaded their way around children sitting in the fine white dust of the yard; Helen watched as a small boy picked up a fallen red bougainvillea flower and popped it in his mouth.

Inside, the unlucky were hidden away—the ones paralyzed by mortar fragments or burned from napalm or white phosphorous, flesh and muscle melted away.

"I was walking through the wards when I caught sight of Lan. You'll know when you meet her. What I'm thinking is narrow the focus to one child and stay with her through the entire rehab so that people get caught up in her story."

Darrow walked quickly, pulling Helen along by the arm. They entered a long, low-ceilinged room that was hot, like the dark insides of an oven, crowded with beds, two children in each one, sardine-style, head to feet. The sheets smelled of sweat and urine. One harried nurse, a Scotswoman with a sunken face and wide, maternal hips, was in charge of thirty children. The more fortunate ones had family who brought food and cleaned them; the others languished in institutional neglect. Lan was a single-leg amputee flown in from a free-fire zone west of Danang.

Darrow led Helen to a small cot by the shuttered window. He crouched down and spoke softly. "How's my sweetheart?"

A small mound stirred under a grayed cotton sheet and a delicate face peered out. The girl had enormous eyes and perfect almond skin, hair pulled back by a white lace headband, and thin gold hoops that accented her petal-like ears.

"Won't donations pour in for this face?" He smiled like a proud father.

Helen tried to see the girl in front of her, but no matter how lovely she was, Darrow saw something more than the child in front of him.

"I'm thinking we stay until enough donations are collected so she can make the trip to America with us. Document the prosthetics, rehab, the whole thing."

Helen sat down on the dirty floor between the filled cots and pulled out a bag of candy. "That could take at least another month or two. Or more."

"But this can make a difference."

"So why don't we pay for her plane ticket?"

Darrow shook his head. "No, no. Don't you see? We'll collect enough to send dozens of kids."

"So you're going to make her your poster child? Delay her rehabilitation?"

"What's another month? I want to accomplish something tangible, and here's my chance."

The girl rocked herself over to lean against Darrow's chest, her wiry, twiglike arms supporting all her weight. When she saw the bag of candy, she lunged across his knees and snatched it, scratching Helen's hand.

"Hey!"

Darrow laughed as Lan tore the cellophane and greedily unwrapped the candies, stuffing them in her mouth. The boy sharing her cot whimpered, holding out an unsteady arm.

"She's wild as a stray," Darrow said. He unwrapped a caramel and handed it to the boy.

"Do you think it's wise . . . singling out one child?" Helen asked.

He grimaced. "I know the power of pictures." Darrow held Lan's chin. "Some Iowa mother is going to fall in love with that face while she's feeding her family eggs and toast for breakfast. She's going to send ten, twenty dollars."

Helen got to her feet. "Let's take some pictures."

After several hours, they had finished for the day and packed up. A Vietnamese woman approached with a bamboo basket of food and spoke to Lan. She looked Helen over carefully.

"Is that her mother?" Helen asked.

"No. Linh's sister-in-law, Thao. I paid for her to care for Lan."

The words flew out of her mouth before she could think. "Don't you think you're getting a little too involved?"

Darrow stiffened. "This is one of the perks of the job. Being in a position to act."

"So why don't we all go to the States now?"

She had become like all the others, like his wife. He had worried when she went out alone on missions, but having her underfoot was worse, and now the jealousy. "We need to draw it out a bit for publicity. Then we'll have a story to work on in California. Maybe we'll end up helping a lot more kids. You can't be against that?"

"Of course not." He had pitted her against an orphaned child. How could she not look bad in the comparison? But if they were staying till every last orphan was tidied away, well . . .

When Darrow lifted his bags to leave, Lan let out a howl. He sat back down, and she clung to his chest. They rocked together while he hummed a song. But as soon as he tried to move away, she whimpered.

"I come back tomorrow, okay?" Darrow said. Slowly, the girl strained up and gave him a small kiss on the cheek.

Helen bent down to hug the girl, smelling the stale sweat and sour milk. Small sores from the dirt and heat had erupted on her face and neck. The girl looked deep into Helen's eyes, took a breath, and wailed, bringing the slow-moving nurse over.

"She's a temperamental one, that girl," the nurse said.

"She'll get used to the idea we're coming back. Let's go."

Helen was relieved to be back out in the courtyard, breathing fresh air. The afternoon sun flooded the yard with cleansing light. The smell of grilled meat over the brazier of a street vendor on the sidewalk outside made her light-headed with hunger.

"Let's eat."

Over a cold beer and grilled pork, Helen couldn't help probing the new situation like a toothache. "She's an orphan?"

Darrow took another bite, then wiped his mouth. "In effect. The family's too poor to come this far. As far as they're concerned, she's just a girl."

"You've probably got plenty of footage already. We could finish in California."

Darrow turned and signaled for another dish. "I want to show her full . . . progress. We'll do other assignments in the meantime."

"I thought . . ."

He stopped and looked at her. He understood the fear, and he also understood, as she didn't, that she would get over it. He reached across the table and took her hand as the Vietnamese at the nearby tables tittered. "Hey, time is on our side now."

Helen looked across the street to the center's walls, blinding, its aspect dull and impassive and unyielding.

Thao went home that night tired of the brattish girl she tended, filled with the certainty that the American woman was the reason she could not get Linh's affections. His duty was to marry her. It was not an unusual thing during the war for such unions of convenience. Linh appeared lost to her, and she could be a good wife, saving his money, caring for him, while he watched over her and her children.

That night, she invited him over for dinner. With the money she earned for Lan, she had bought a new smock and pants, new pillows for the apartment. She had never known such luxury. Thao and Mai had come from simple peasant stock; strong, healthy girls, Mai the beauty, Thao the brains.

She arranged for a neighbor to take the girl for the evening. The baby slept. She wouldn't wait Linh out any longer, whatever visions he had for himself. He was a man, after all, and she knew how to deal with a man.

When Linh arrived, the apartment was filled with smells of food cooking. It was uncharacteristically quiet.

"Where are the children?" His main reason for visiting was the joy he got playing with them.

"With neighbors. The baby sleeps."

Linh sat down. When Thao came out, his throat caught at the transformation: her hair oiled, face powdered, a pale pink smock of silk.

"You look beautiful," he said. What he meant was that she looked like Mai. She smiled and poured him a rice brandy she had bought for the occasion.

"What is all this?"

"Nothing. A thanks for all you have done for us."

The evening proceeded, Thao a perfect hostess, plying him with alcohol, serving his favorite crab and asparagus soup, heaping his plate with food, asking intelligent and flattering questions about his work. When the dinner was finished, she had him sit on the new cushions she had bought for the Western-style sofa that came with the apartment.

"I'm tired. Drunk," he said.

"Let me massage your neck," she said, and turned him away from her, lowered the lights, and began kneading into the muscles of his neck. "Lots of tension."

Afterward, they sat side by side and sipped tea. In the dimness, Linh looked over, and his heart skipped at the image of Mai. Although he knew better, he couldn't hold out against Thao, all these months of her seduction. He stroked her arm. But later, when she was naked and lying spread out on the bedding, when he felt his hardness begin, it felt like a desecration of Mai's memory. What type of a weak man was he? He pulled away from her, head hidden in hands in confusion and disgust. Thao got up, slammed a cup in the sink, went to check on the baby.

Weeks passed, and the agreed-upon time to leave drew further and further away as they approached it. Darrow, swept into the pull of the war, gave terse answers when Helen questioned him.

In desperation she accepted an assignment to go with him and Linh into the field. Four other reporters were joining them to Quang Ngai province. Darrow almost always chose to work alone, hated the "junkets," but he accepted this situation. To Helen, it proved Robert right in guessing Darrow's desire to cover anything, indiscriminately.

It wasn't until they had already boarded the cargo plane for the first leg up to Danang that they realized one of the four was Tanner. As soon as he noticed Darrow, he came over, cracking a tight smile over his small, yellowish teeth. He held out his large hand. "Let's forget that other day."

Darrow paused, then clasped the man's hand. "What other day?"

Tanner nodded his long, narrow head. "That's it, man. The war's bad enough, we don't need to fight each other."

The journalists divided up between two companies. Helen was irritated to see that Tanner had joined theirs; his presence would only grate at Darrow. Bad luck. The companies had orders to sweep three hamlets and meet back at base camp if they didn't encounter resistance.

When they met the commanding officer, Captain Molina, a slight, dark-complexioned, humorless man, he told them his company had been ambushed the day before, although it had sustained no casualties. The coolness of his report belied the tension visible in the troops. Helen saw spooked faces; the eyes of the soldiers hard and distrustful. Jumpy. Hot and without sleep, walking around with fingers tight on the triggers of their weapons. Linh's presence created a stirring, soldiers growling low to each other, casting long, stony looks. Molina went to talk with his NCO and returned.

"He can't come along," he said, pointing his thumb at Linh.

Darrow stretched his arms overhead, then bent to retie his bootlaces. "Do you have any moleskin you can spare? I think I've got the beginning of a blister."

Molina took off his helmet and wiped his face. "Sure."

Darrow untied the laces and began to pull off the boot. "He's accredited, and he's been my assistant for the last four years. I can't do my job without him."

Molina moved closer. "The men are a little wired after yesterday. Thing is, I can't guarantee his safety."

"Can I quote you? Their commanding officer?" Darrow pulled off his boot and his sock. "Besides, who speaks enough Vietnamese to question these villagers?"

Tanner had come up and stood listening. "Listen, Molina, these guys are okay," he said. "They'll make your little company look like heroes." The captain went back to talk with his men.

They waited in the shade of a large granite boulder, drinking warm sodas someone had scrounged up. Darrow nodded at Tanner. Linh stood to the side. "Too much, huh?" Darrow said, rolling his eyes. "Too much. What kind of captain admits he can't control his men?" Fifteen minutes later, Molina came back saying they reluctantly agreed.

"Linh's the best scout you could hope to find."

Molina grimaced. "He gets it first if he leads us into an ambush."

After he walked away, Helen tugged on Darrow's arm. "This feels bad. We should get out of here."

"You're skittish."

The soldiers moved out single file along the narrow trail of crushed shell that wound through the high sand dunes. Tanner walked point singing, " 'Hi, ho. Hi, ho. It's off to work we go,' " making the soldiers around him snicker. Midmorning, the temperature climbed over a hundred, the sky a low, gloomy, saline white. The soldiers wore flak jackets open over bare chests. Under their helmets, they wore bandannas to keep sweat out of their eyes.

The first hamlet contained fifty adults. The huts clustered at the base of a chiseled limestone cliff next to the ocean. The villagers seemed friendly enough; they smiled and went through the charade of carrying on as if the soldiers were not there. A thorough search yielded nothing, and the soldiers got ready to move out again.

Linh and Helen entered a hut at the urging of an old woman who waved them in. The room was small and dark, filled from floor to ceiling with paper flowers. Rows of reds and yellows and white lined up. Linh hesitated, wiping his face. "She makes these," he said, "for celebrations, for altars."

The old woman spoke in a low mumble to Linh.

"What is she saying?" Helen asked.

"She's afraid the soldiers will burn the village. She has a year of work inside. All on its way to be sold in Danang."

"Tell her we're on our way out."

As they gathered on the edge of the hamlet, bunched up in a group, sipping from their canteens in the smoldering heat, lighting cigarettes, a mortar whistled down between the palms. Everyone dove, but when they rose, four men on the left side of the tree were dead, while two others crawled along the ground.

When they heard the strike, Helen and Linh pitched themselves against a sand dune next to the old woman's house. All the fear that Helen thought she had recovered from came back tenfold. Her legs useless, acid in her throat. Darrow ran over, cameras hitting against his chest in his hurry. He put his hand on the back of her head. "You okay?"

She nodded.

"Linh, take care of her."

Darrow was gone back through the smoke.

Captain Molina ordered the casualties pulled down the road, and called in air power. Helen watched as he held the radio receiver, his face wet and tight. She saw the tremor in his hand as he handed the receiver down to the radio operator.

The helicopters would come in from the west, forcing the fleeing VC toward the ocean, where the other companies would block their escape north and south. A young boy, Costello, had frag wounds to both legs, his skin peppered with black holes. Darrow and Tanner together pulled him along with the other wounded to the road. As the shock wore off, the kid trembled but made no sound.

Helen felt nauseous from the heat and the blood and the noise, but she picked up her camera and focused through the viewfinder. Molina stood over the boy, his face a mottled red, his lips tight and pulled back from his teeth. In the viewfinder, framed, he had a terrible kind of power. Helen framed a shot of him on the radio handset while the operator crouched next to him, fingers stuffed in his ears at the sound of another mortar, face clenched, reluctantly attached by the umbilical of the cord. Molina waved his arm and brought it down hard on his thigh as if he could will the helicopter's appearance, oblivious to the flames snaking their way up a thatched roof behind him, oblivious to the comatose boy at his feet. If he had taken any more notice of Costello, he might have shot him.

Helen put down the camera, puzzled, when she saw blackened, fluttering shapes in the air like dark butterflies. The sight of his injured legs mesmerized Costello; Helen grabbed a plastic field poncho and draped it over his lower body.

"Let me see them," Costello said.

"You're not hurt that bad," the medic said.

But Costello was past hearing.

"You'll be okay," Helen said. She said the words by rote, as if comforting a child, but she felt angry at his squeamishness when there were dead bodies yards away. There was a sense of release in the coldness she felt, her lack of concern for the man. She didn't want his name and rank, or his picture. She wanted to forget him the moment he was on that helicopter.

Within minutes assault helicopters flew overhead and sprayed bullets and bombs over the village. An inferno, the fire created a hot wind that fed upon itself, heat upon heat, until Helen felt each breath she took scorched her lungs.

Linh pointed, and Helen again noticed a swarm of black fluttering shapes that looked like swallows or bats rising above the old woman's hut. "Her flowers."

Helen remembered when her father returned from duty in Italy. How he had brought her a red tin of amoretti. How he took the waxy wrapping as she ate each cookie, lit a match beneath it and smiled as it flew skyward like a spirit, to her screams of delight.

Although they watched the hut burn to cinders, the old woman was no-where in sight.

The action seemed to be mostly over, and so it was a shock when a dozen men burst out of a tunnel opening at the edge of the village, the heat from the burning hut above the entrance roasting them in the tunnel, parts of their clothing curling off their backs in flame. They ran down the beach to reach the water, wanting to plunge in the wetness and stop the burning, but the running alerted the soldiers, who opened fire.

Linh yelled, but Darrow grabbed him. "No!" He pointed to Helen. "Stay between him and the soldiers." She held Linh's shoulder, felt the quivering of his muscles.

"They're villagers, not VC," he said.

Darrow ran down through the sound of the automatic weapons' fire. So much smoke and the deafening pound of the helicopters—it was impossible to make out clearly what had happened.

Fifteen minutes later, the helicopters gone, the beach was strewn with bodies on the sand and down into the surf. An eerie quiet except for the keen-ing cries of the village women who had a view of the beach. The mood of the soldiers had turned murderous. They went back again and again to the bod-ies of the dead men, as if they feared they would resurrect. Tanner took pic-tures, moving bodies with his foot into more graphic positions. "Don't think this one is running anywhere," he said to a soldier, who glared down, bayo-net pointed.

Darrow's forehead creased, his head bent down as he walked over. "That's enough. Women are watching up there."

Tanner turned and narrowed his eyes. "Don't get jealous, Sam. You're not the only photographer in Vietnam."

A few of the soldiers glared at Linh as he moved along the beach with Helen. "How come he didn't warn us?" they asked over and over.

"Because he didn't know. He's on our side," Darrow said.

When the first medevac landed, Darrow joined Helen and Linh. "Let's take this one out. We've got enough."

Tanner stayed with the company.

As they walked by villagers placed under guard, Helen felt their eyes on her. The women clutched their children against their bodies, away from the guns. "Why aren't they releasing them?"

"Interrogation. Can't ask a dead man if he's VC."

"Maybe we should stay," Helen said.

"The company's out of control. More Tanner's style anyway."

Scared herself, Helen didn't have the heart to argue. Later, she would regret giving up so easily and leaving. The change in herself proved by how little she thought of the villagers' fate, how uneasy she was around her own soldiers. They flew to the field hospital and unloaded Costello, who floated on a large pillow of morphine, oblivious to their good-byes. The trip back to Saigon was a gloomy one.

That night, as she prepared to take a shower, she noticed the ends of her hair were stiff. When she brought the tips to her nose, they smelled singed. After staying under the shower so long the water ran cold, she came out of the bathroom in her underwear and bra, hair dripping, and sat on the bedspread beside Darrow. He was stretched out, eyes closed.

"You're dripping on the bedspread," he said.

"I don't care."

He opened his eyes. "Let's see Lan tomorrow."

Helen bent her head down. How could she admit what she felt all afternoon coming home? Still as clear as after they lifted off from that beach—the photograph wasn't enough. Helped no one. Soldiers still died, civilians suffered, nothing alleviated in the smallest amount by the fact that a shutter had opened and shut, that light had struck grains on emulsion, that patterns of light and dark would preserve their misery. No defense at all against the evil that had been perpetrated. Out on the beach that day, it had all been failure. Even the best picture would be forgotten, the page flipped.

"I can't do this anymore," Helen whispered, apologizing to the pillow, unable to meet his eyes.

Darrow covered her body with his. "That's the first thing that goes. Belief. You're better off without it."

Hard facts were difficult to come by—twisted and manipulated by each mouth they passed through according to need or whim. Buried deep in newspapers or government reports, perceived facts had no effect on truth. Rumor, though, caught fire, flew as fast as the events themselves. Lived on in the minds of the listeners, haunting them.

They had been back in Saigon only hours when the first stories about Molina's company began to circulate.

The official version was that a female VC climbed out of a tunnel and opened fire with an AK-47 on the soldiers, although no weapon or bullets were found, although after the initial attack, not a single American soldier was killed or even wounded by bullets.

Another version was that a village woman who had witnessed her husband gunned down on the beach below pulled out an old French-made hand revolver. Was it to kill herself or to kill the Americans? The soldiers panicked, opened fire, killing all the fleeing women and children. Later, said revolver was examined and found to be rusted out and empty of bullets.

Another, darker story was that Molina cracked, frustrated by the casualties and the defiance of the women, and ordered the soldiers to fire on them. The next day, on patrol, Molina walked point and stepped on a Claymore, killed, neatly ending any interrogation.

Whatever the truth, Tanner made the front page of a dozen newspapers documenting it. His pictures backed up military claims that VC and VC sympathizers had been gunned down in battle. Darrow threw the paper across the room.

"You couldn't have stopped it," Helen said.

"It doesn't matter. I should have . . . been doing my job, not—"

"Babysitting me?"

"I was distracted. I can't afford to be."

The battles dragged on. Tay Ninh turned into Bong Son, which turned into An Thi.

At night, Darrow edged closer to Helen in the dark of the bedroom, the wind through the leaves of the flamboyant lulling like the sound of the ocean.

"What do you say, Helen, we delay leaving till next month. Get up to the DMZ one more time. I've heard things are going on in Qui Nhon and in the A Shau."

Nothing.

"California will still be there a few months from now, huh? We'll go with a few more covers under our belt."

Later, Helen often thought about why she remained silent. Their love a riddle she couldn't explain, only that Darrow coming of his own volition was the only way. Otherwise, she would be forcing him; unbearable, especially when it was obvious to everyone that she had lost the stomach for the work while he was so clearly born to it.

So he pretended he would leave, and she pretended that she believed him, and each knew the other was telling an untruth.

Days passed, each a lure that Darrow went out and followed; Helen again took the human-interest assignments she had previously scorned. The radius of her pursuits circling tighter and tighter, with the apartment in Cholon eventually the only place she was absolutely at ease.

Robert threw his "Light at the End of My Tunnel" party at the broken-down Hotel Royale. The restaurant and bar were colonial-period shabby, in keeping with the party's theme. Robert walked through the palm-lined lobby in the white wool uniform and pith helmet of a French military commander. People overflowed the lobby, standing on the steps and out on the sidewalk, sipping champagne while a band played fox-trots and tangos in the overhead ballroom. A street boy, small and fast, reached his hand up like a periscope over the platters, stuffing his mouth with whatever he grabbed before it could be taken away. A crippled war veteran leaned against the building, his left leg missing, and sipped at a glass of champagne someone had handed him.

In the cab going over, Darrow hummed show tunes. Helen had borrowed a long, cream-colored gown with a large black silk rose pinned at the chest. "Nice," he said, uninterested. He had reluctantly put a suit on, and he sat in the backseat of the small car, knees to his chest, looking crushed and miserable.

They walked up the steps to where Robert stood in the doorway. "The luckiest man in Vietnam," Robert shouted and raised his glass. "Beware, I might try to steal her away tonight."

Darrow smiled a strained, polite smile. "Do it while I get drinks," he said, and made a quick escape into the crowd.

"As cheerful as always," Robert said.

"He's tired."

More and more people arrived, cars jamming traffic for a block all around.

"How many people did you invite?"

"Oh, five hundred, give or take. Everyone I've ever met in this country. But I don't recognize half the faces here, so I think it's taken on a life of its own. Appropriate for a war with a life of its own."

Annick had been right—she had underestimated him. "You're leaving in style."

"Leave with me."

Helen smiled and looked down. For a moment she thought he mocked her, but he understood how shabby her situation was. Besides, there was no sport in it, like shooting fish in a barrel. "Is Annick here?"

"With her new beau. She's not one to hold a grudge, especially at the mention of a party."

"No, she isn't. That's part of her loveliness."

"Such a pretty dress and such a sad face." Robert drew himself up and put his hand across his chest. "Marry me."

"You're drunk."

"That's right. That's the way men like me screw up the courage to ask for what they want. After the fact, when it's too late."

"It is too late, isn't it?" She bit her lip. "You'd fall down dead if I accepted."

Robert burst out laughing and drank down his glass. "Of course I would. That's what's so delicious about you. You think like a man. No, I need a sweet, marrying type who loves me and stays out of war zones."

"That's not me," Helen said, smiling, stung by his words. "What're you going to do with all of that peace?"

Robert shook his head. "I'm more in love the more you pull away."

Darrow walked between them, balancing three full champagne glasses. "Who's pulling away?"

"I am, if I'm lucky. All I care about is my departure time," Robert said. He winked at her and poked his finger at Darrow's chest. "You know what they say—'Old reporters don't fade away, they transfer to lesser bureaus.'"

"Don't give me that. Los Angeles is a kick up."

Robert drank down his glass in one gulp. "Not if you want to be where the action is. Not if you consider the work a calling." His sudden earnestness made all three fall silent. Although it was obvious Darrow didn't think much of him, Robert respected and disliked the man in equal measure.

Darrow shrugged. "Say no."

"Oh, baby, that's where you and I differ. I'm twenty-nine months, five days too long in this hellhole." The one thing Robert knew for sure was Darrow's stringing Helen along was shameful.

"We're leaving soon." Darrow looked down at his feet.

Robert raised his eyebrows and looked from him to Helen. She seemed equally surprised. "That's great. Really. I'm two hundred bucks poorer, but what the hell."

"You bet on us?" Helen said. "Against us?"

"I'm a reporter. I took the odds."

Helen wandered the dining room and found Annick at a table of Americans from the embassy. A large, beefy-faced guy with curly black hair protested as Helen pulled her away to the bar to have a drink alone.

"Isn't he beautiful?" Annick looked back at the man, who never took his eyes off her. "Two champagnes."

"How long have you been seeing this one?"

"This one is *the* one."

"You said that last time. Isn't it bad form to bring him to Robert's party?"

Annick wore a long, beaded red gown that sparkled as she moved. Now she pushed away from the bar and began to sway to the music. "Look around.

All the good men are either leaving or dying. What difference can it possibly make?"

"What if you end up alone?"

"I was married and ended up alone. Everyone leaves. Robert, Sam, and you. It makes me too sad."

"Then find someone."

Annick turned a tough, appraising look on her; the businesswoman face at the shop was the real her. "You count on the future too much. Tonight, just dance."

"Go get your beau." Helen laughed, pointing to the man at the table, his lips pressed together in a frown.

"He hates to dance. And he's jealous. If I dance with another man, it will be a bad night."

"Then let's you and me," Helen said, pulling her toward the dance floor.

"You're *fou*. Crazy."

"Now you've convinced me."

Out on the dance floor, the two women danced to cheers from the surrounding tables. Helen led, and they both stumbled, doubled over laughing so they could hardly stand. Slowly they worked out the rhythm for a box step.

Helen floated to the music, her mind on the silly spectacle of herself and Annick, a huge surge of relief not to worry and want. She was glad she hadn't drunk much champagne, that this was pure joy she felt. As Annick spun in a circle away from her, sparkling, Helen thought she was perhaps right, this was the only possible escape from the war.

The first sign something was wrong: the band coming to a ragged stop, stranding the dancers on the floor. Angry yells. Helen recognized Darrow's voice. As she made her way through the crowd, she saw Tanner first but could not make out his words. Darrow stood quietly across from him while Robert stepped between the men, trying to lead Tanner away. Instead, he jerked out of Robert's grip, lurching forward and again saying something she couldn't hear.

Darrow made a single forward motion, right fist connecting with Tanner's face, knocking him onto his back. Cartoonish. Uncertain laughs came from the crowd, and Helen saw a smear of blood under Tanner's nose as he

shook his head. He sat relaxed on the floor, dabbing at his nose with a handkerchief someone handed him. When he spoke, his voice was low and rea-
sonable, as if he were discussing politics over brandy.

"Screw you, Darrow . . . just as dead with or without my pictures."

"My problem is you."

Tanner stood up unsteadily. Men approached to restrain him, but he
shook them off. "I'm done here." He wiped his bloodied mouth and looked
at his hand. "Quang Ngai. I'm supposed to interfere with a bunch of wacked-
out Marines? They were VC in the tunnels. What if they killed one of our
guys?"

Darrow leaned against the wall, rubbing his hand. "Gunning down women
and children."

"We're not the morality police out there. Especially you, huh? As long as
you have the wife and kiddie back home, the piece of ass over here, it's all
okay, huh?"

Darrow lunged. It took Robert and three other men to drag him outside.
Although Darrow and Helen had been together openly for more than a year
now, the spoken words unleashed something. She felt looks from some of the
men, stares from wives and girlfriends.

"Forget Tanner," Robert said. "He's a shit. You've given him wet dreams
even taking him seriously."

"I'm sorry," Darrow said. "I shouldn't have come."

"Come back in. It's still early," Robert said.

"Not for me."

Helen searched for Annick to say good-bye. At the end of the bar she
spotted quivering red sparkles. When she got closer, Annick was crying.

"What's wrong?" Helen said.

Annick shrugged. "It's all coming apart."

"What is?"

"Everything. The war is ending."

"Where's . . . your guy?"

Annick tossed her head, annoyed. "He's nothing."

"I thought he was the one."

"Only the war is the one."

Darrow and Helen drove back home in silence. Helen hung up her borrowed dress, turned on the red-shaded lamp. They went to bed, lay side by side, not touching or talking, then rolled away from each other in sleep.

In the middle of the night, Helen awakened to the rumble of thunder, the sound of rain on the roof. From long habit, she hurriedly got up to put bowls under the regular leaks in the ceiling. Back in bed, she listened to the drops of water plink first against metal, then against water. Darrow rose and stood at the window, smoking.

"I guess you don't care we might drown in a puddle in our sleep," she said.

"Damned thing is he's right."

She stared at the water stain on the ceiling. "Who?"

"That SOB Tanner."

"About?"

"What pisses me off is seeing myself in him."

Helen sat up, knees folded beneath her chin. "You're nothing like him."

Darrow came to the bed and sat down. "I've been here too long. I hear something going down in Can Tho or Pleiku, I have to be the first one there."

"That's your job."

"I've been leading you along, too." He took hold of her arm, stroking the skin at her wrist. "I don't mean to."

"Don't leave because of me," she said.

Darrow shook his head. "Let's take our trip to Cambodia. I want to see the *apsara*s again. I had dreams there. . . ."

Lying in his arms, she realized Darrow spoke with other people's words. Words she wanted to hear but that were not necessarily the same as the truth. He created himself like a collage, bits and pieces that she would never come to the bottom of.

"I'm ready to leave with you," he said.

She had dreamed the words so long that she barely made sense of them, but she tried to convince herself that the long siege was over. He loved her after all, and now they could go home.

When he left early that morning, she was still sleeping.

It was this way in Vietnam during the war—sometimes Darrow felt all powerful, felt he could ride fate like a flying carpet, like a helicopter, will it to do his bidding. Other times fate reminded him that he was only a toy, blown this way and that, swept away or destroyed on a whim.

The difficult decision made, Darrow felt lighter than he had in years. Helen equaled life to him, and he would let all this go and follow her, follow life out of this place. As scheduled, he joined the crew of a gunship, spent the morning flying in Tay Ninh province along the Cambodian border, photographing a cross-border black-market operation. It was a good morning, a good helicopter. He felt in his element. The pilot flew contour, almost touching the tops of trees, what they called "map of the earth" flying. Hostile forces could hear the plane but didn't have time to draw a bead on it in the dense canopy jungle.

The pilot, Captain Anderson, was in his midtwenties, a big puppyish kid with a constant grin, unable to hide his pleasure in flying. Sunlight glinted off his blond, buzz-cut hair. Darrow smiled, and the sobering thought occurred to him that he was almost old enough to have a son that age. Where had the time gone?

After doing an aerial recon, Anderson got orders to drop in on a couple of forward firebases in the Parrot's Beak. Isolated, the area was considered bandit country, riddled with VC and NVA positions. The night before, bases were attacked, and now enemy bodies, strung up in the perimeter wire, bloated in the hot sun as trophies.

Darrow and the pilot sat on the ground, their backs against sandbags, and ate C-rations, ignoring the fetid smell blowing in from the wire.

"I'm shy to say this, but you were the photographer when my dad served in Korea. You took his picture."

"No kidding?"

"I swear it. Recognized the name right away."

"That's amazing. So he came home. And had you."

"And five others. Wait till I tell him you were here."

"That'll be good. Very good."

"Where you headin' to after this?" Anderson asked.

"Heading home." The words felt strange in his mouth, as if they had no connection to himself. After all these years, where was home? He felt at home right there, with this young man who could have been his son, but wasn't.

The boy blew out a breath. "Home. You are one lucky—"

"Your father should be very proud. Do you miss home?" Darrow asked. In the bright sun, he thought the young captain's face impossibly unlined, impossibly innocent. Had he ever been so young? Choked up, he pulled out a cigarette and offered one. Anderson took it but averted his eyes, and Darrow realized that he had missed that look, the toughness in the jaw, that the captain was boyish only in his joy of flying.

"I do and I don't, you know?"

Darrow chuckled. "I'm there, guy."

Anderson, egged on, sat up, nodding his head. "I mean, I'm in the groove here. Finally. I can *do* this. But there . . . it doesn't make sense anymore. I don't know if I trust it."

"Me, either."

"Then why you goin'?"

Darrow shrugged. "A woman. Couldn't help myself."

Anderson laughed out loud. "No shit? Well, good luck to you. You're a braver man than me." He took a long drag of his cigarette. "I'm supposed to be one of the best pilots. So they send me on all the tough stuff. Hero shit. So the chances of me eating it are better than if I was just a washout. How fucked up is that?"

"You don't have to be the best pilot."

Anderson laughed. "Wrong! I do, and they know it. Can't help myself." He thrust his hips lewdly. "Flying's the only *other* thing I've ever been good at."

The next day Anderson and Darrow were on their way to the firebase at Kontum.

The morning passed, uneventful, and Darrow spent the hours in a dreamlike mood, lulled by the closeness and speed of trees under his feet. Except for the earsplitting noise of the engines, it was a bird's-eye view of the world, like boyhood dreams of flying before other dreams, dreams of war, had taken over.

He would take Helen to Angkor and show her the expression on one particular face. Serenity mixed with savagery. Only she could understand—the history of the place showed both a great lust and indifference for violence. And wasn't that what they had become, Helen and he, interpreters of violence? A very twisted connoisseurship. They would sit on the warm stones in the evening, and he would whisper his greatest fears to her.

That the image betrayed one at last. It grieved and outraged, but ultimately it deadened. The first picture, or the fifth, or even the twenty-fifth still had an authority, but finally the repetition made the horror palatable. In the last few years, no matter how hard he tried, his pictures weren't as powerful as before he had known this. Like an addict who had to keep upping the dose to maintain the same high, he found himself risking more and working harder for less return. He would never again be moved the way he was over that first picture of a dead World War II soldier. Was his own work perpetrating the same on those it came into contact with? A steady loss of impact until violence became meaningless? His ridiculous brawl with Tanner when in truth Tanner was the logical progeny of their profession. Maybe they deserved to be charged with war crimes, too.

He worried, as the trees sped by beneath his feet, that Helen did not believe he loved her other than by his leaving. But he would prove it to her in a hundred thousand ways.

They were flying over the Plei Trap Valley when Anderson, whom Darrow now imagined as his and Helen's son, tapped him on the shoulder, yelling over the roar of the engine, the boyish grin absurd and comforting. "You okay?"

"Fine. The heat's getting to me."

"I got two wounded for emergency evac. We're the only free ride around. Okay with you?" he asked eagerly, as if he were borrowing keys to his father's car.

"Let's go." Darrow laughed and gave him a thumbs-up. He had gone a little deeper, and then not intending to, deeper still. Didn't every man in every war believe that he would be the one to make it, to survive, to return home filled with tales? Darrow was no different. The unspoken truth of how each of them survived their time.

Minutes later they dropped into a combat spiral, and he felt the familiar wrenching of the stomach, the mouth going dry. And then a terrible shattering, as if the helicopter had been hit by lightning, smote by a giant hand instead of a rocket. Now the boy turned all warrior, face grim and masklike as they spiraled earthward; a tearing sound signaled the rear tail torn away. The green of the trees roared toward them with a sickening rush, and between the branches Darrow saw flashes of light. The smooth, brown warrior from the Lolei temple, the eyes wild. Reluctantly, Darrow lifted his now gravity-weighted head and looked at Anderson once more. Son. He took leave of him and looked out. A rush of green and then Helen's face. The branches like arms reaching out. He calculated odds he had escaped from before as he heard the whooshing sound, the vacuum of air as the cockpit glass became as bright as a new sun. White knuckles and sunlight and her eyes. An infinity of green. Every shade of green in the world.

THIRTEEN

Ca Dao

Songs

Name: Samuel Andre Darrow

Rank/Branch:

Unit:

Date of Birth: 7 May 1925

Home City of Record: New York City, NY

Date of Loss: 14 November 1967

Country of Loss: South Vietnam

Loss Coordinates: 1412?N 1074920E (ZA045798)

Status: Missing in Action

Category: 1

Acft/Vehicle/Ground: OH6A

Other Personnel in Incident: Captain Jon Anderson

The mission to recover bodies had been denied for months because of enemy movements, the area considered extremely dangerous, but then recon reported the enemy had pulled out. An invisible veil lifted, and although nothing to the eye had changed—the hills remained just as green, the paths stretched out in their promise of innocence—the land officially became neutral again.

Linh and Helen went in with a Green Beret unit and two South Vietnamese rangers familiar with the terrain of that part of the Ho Chi Minh trail network. They went in on cargo transports, linking with a contingent of Montagnard mercenaries led by Special Forces officers.

After hiking through the morning, the main force went to destroy enemy bunker complexes, while their unit branched off and went on the five clicks to the crash site. Because the bodies had not been recovered, Darrow and the pilot were listed as MIA. The mislabeling of the truth angered Helen, and she climbed the hills in a spirit of righteousness. She had not wanted to bring her camera, but Linh insisted that they bring a minimum of equipment.

From a neighboring hill, Helen focused binoculars and saw the blackened smudge of the crash site, the surrounding vegetation burned to charcoal in the fire. "There it is," she said, feeling foolish at the excitement in her voice.

Linh watched her, his eyelids half closed in the bright sun. Without a word, he followed one of the rangers down a steep ravine. He had been angry at her insistence to come, thinking there was no point in endangering herself.

Helen stayed in close to the man assigned as her escort, Sergeant James. He was a tall man with reddish hair and fair skin. Whenever they stopped for a break, he would take out a zinc stick and run it along his face and neck till his skin was white with the stuff. "I've burned and peeled so many times, I'm down to my last layer of skin."

Absurd as it was, Helen rushed her steps, walked ahead of James and passed Linh in her frenzy, as if time were still a factor, could change anything that mattered.

The crash site lay near the top of the hill, a view of green mountains extending all the way to Laos and beyond. The afternoon light slanted through the sky, cast everything in shades of greenish gold. The scent of grass was blurred by charcoal. The wind came up, a faint rustling of leaves, a clicking of bamboolike chimes in a graveyard. The most sacred place she had ever been.

She remembered Darrow waking her at dawn, watching the sun pour slowly across the Cordillera. The mountains too far away to ever reach, but now, deep inside them, they still stretched out of her grasp, unknowable.

"Ever been here before?" she asked.

"Not likely. This is *beaucoup* dangerous bandit country. But recovery isn't bad. Once they're already dead, the enemy usually isn't interested in scoop-up."

Sergeant James joined the other soldiers surrounding the burned-out hull of the helicopter, already so weathered it looked as if it had been there decades. The men crouched over blackened mounds on the ground, unzipped a body bag, put on plastic gloves, and used spades.

Head pounding from a threatening migraine, Helen stood, her purpose gone. Of course, there was nothing there for her, but she had been unable to stay away. Her whole being unmoored, the excuse of going out was her only relief. A death to suffer through with no ceremony, no commemoration of who they had been to each other. A red drop fell on her shirt and then blood began to pour from her nose.

Linh was quickly at her side, pulling out a handkerchief, settling her in the shade of a tree.

"What happened?" she asked.

"Altitude. Heat."

She sat with her head tilted back, the metal taste of blood stripping her throat raw. "Don't be angry with me."

Linh was cleaning a lens with cloth. "For nosebleed? We all miss him."

"Then why the looks?"

"You have been here long enough but still you act like a child." Linh remembered Darrow's theatrics over Samang's snakebite death in Angkor. Why couldn't any of them accept fate? Why the long march out here? Of course, he must ask himself the same question. The answer that he feared for her and didn't fear for himself. More and more he believed detachment the only answer to the constant onslaught of loss.

"Just be my friend."

"I am always your friend."

Later she walked back and forth along the outside of the site, searching debris scattered a good distance from the crash. Between tall swales of elephant grass, she found small fragments of 35mm film, the emulsion burned away so that it had a milky, blinded look. Linh recovered a piece of the embroidered neckband that Darrow used for his favorite Leica; it had been wedged under a stone. Although he would have liked to have kept it, he handed it to Helen, and she held it carefully between her fingers, as if it still burned.

Sergeant James came over to her and handed her his canteen. "Miss?"

"Sorry," she mumbled. "Heat."

"We need to be pushing off."

Helen nodded. Her fingers still searched the charcoal ground for slips of film.

"Ready to leave." He took back his canteen and screwed the cap back on. "Sorry for your loss. They died like heroes. Trying to rescue two of our own."

"Khong biet." I don't know.

He crinkled his nose as if from a bad smell. "How's that?"

"Too many heroes in my life. All gone."

Her fingers were soot black as she pocketed three small pieces of film. When she wiped the sweat off her forehead, a black smudge trailed behind. The time of extravagant grief over; now she was dry-eyed and quiet. Something had changed, she feared, whatever connection she had felt for the land or the soldiers broken.

Linh came up to her and motioned to her forehead.

During those convalescent days he had nursed her in the Cholon apartment, Linh had decided the only tribute he could pay Darrow was to send Helen home safely. She agreed to go only once the body was recovered. When they got news of the crash, Gary insisted that Linh go with him to the apartment. As soon as Helen opened the door and looked into Linh's face, she knew. The worst part how little a surprise it had been, how easy to accept. She pulled Linh inside and closed the door on Gary. But even the fatefulness of the death did nothing to diminish her grief. The sound of her crying tore open his own wounds. An agony to stay with her; an agony to leave.

During those long days, she had asked him about his life, and for the first time he revealed parts. She had earned this trust. He told how his father had been a nationalist, simply wanting independence for his country. When Ho embraced the early promise of Communism, he followed. Linh had joined the NVA, believing his father. Soon, they both realized it was a false promise. The family had been willing to lose all, escape. But they found the South, too, corrupted, filled with puppets for the foreigners.

Now Helen untied her bandanna and wetted it from his canteen, wiping the charcoal from her brow and then spreading the wet cloth open to cover her whole face. Under torture, men suffocated this way.

"It's time to leave." He plucked the cloth off her face.

Sergeant James stood at ease with the other soldiers, facing the ravine they had come up, feet spread, arms clasped behind his back like a sentinel. Two improbably small body bags lay at the soldiers' feet.

Far away the hollow thrum of underground explosives could be heard like a heartbeat. Many hilltops over, delicate white puffs of smoke hung in the air.

The Montagnards were supposed to carry the remains out, but they did not show up. James said they were probably still blowing bunkers, so the soldiers decided to carry the bags themselves and not risk getting caught out overnight.

In single file the soldiers walked step by step down the dirt path, the ground loose and red under their boots, each of them shouldering the end of a splintery wood pole, and the unevenness of their strides and the small slips in the crumbling soil caused the bags to sway and squeak. Linh and Helen followed—the ravine plunging, hairpin and overgrown—alternately blinded by the sunlight and then plunged into dark shade as they made their way back down the steep mountain.

Thorn bushes crowding the path snagged at Helen's pants, and once, as she gazed out over the valley, a large thorn dug a long scratch along her arm. Beadlike drops of blood formed along the wound, but she was oblivious to it until Linh came up next to her and rubbed it roughly with a piece of cloth, his eyes glittering.

"You must watch where you're going. Be more careful."

When they made it back to the LZ it was sunset, and a helicopter was on its way to drop supplies and take them out. Helen ached to go back to the city, to the crooked apartment she had not moved out of, boxes half packed. She waited with her back to the two bags lying by the side of the clearing.

As they waited, four LRRPs, called Lurps, walked in from the bush. They high-fived the platoon digging in for the night, nodded thoughtfully to the bags at the edge of the clearing, then squatted under a tree and began to boil rice and dried meat. These types, MacCrae's kind of guys, worked in deep cover, adapting to native ways and language.

Linh went over and joined them. Exhausted, Helen sat on a box of rations. She was surprised when one of the men held out a plastic cup to Linh, and more surprised when he accepted, squatting down to drink with them. By the jerk of Linh's head and the guttural laughter of the soldiers, she guessed it was the local hill tribe moonshine, a fermented alcohol made of rice, lethal stuff.

The helicopter came in, and everyone turned away to shield their faces. The whole camp pitched in to unload supplies. Two of the Lurps jumped up, jubilant and drunk, and each took one end of the first body bag and swung it up on the floor of the helicopter, where it landed with a hard thud.

"Careful!" Helen yelled.

The two men stared at her with blank expressions. "They won't feel a thing anymore, dolly," one of them said to the howling laughter of his companions.

Helen stared at them and at Linh sitting there, a part of them. "I'll remember that when I carry your bag."

The soldier made a motion with his hand as if he had touched something hot. "Sssssss!"

Helen watched as the next bag was loaded in carefully, almost tenderly.

Linh staggered up to her. "We're not going out. We're going on patrol with them." He nodded his head back to the Lurps eating their dinner.

"You're drunk." Helen's gaze took in the group of men who were oblivious to their presence. "Do they know this?"

"Already arranged."

"By who?"

He wagged his head. "Me."

She rubbed her boot back and forth in the dirt, a long, tired arc. "I'm beat. You go. I'm going back on this ride."

Linh grabbed her arm. "For me, this time. Without questions."

She hesitated. After Darrow's death, she felt strange around Linh. The memory of the three of them together making the absence more painful. "I don't have enough film."

"Enough for the job."

"Which is?"

Linh studied her face, looking for something. "You said you wanted to photograph the Ho Chi Minh trail. Still do?"

After three days, Helen no longer thought of the crooked apartment or Saigon. Even Darrow changed from a pain outside, inflicted, to something inside, a tumor, with only its promise of future suffering. The fastness of the jungle struck her again in all its extraordinary voluptuousness, its wanton excess. It enchanted. Time rolled in long green distances, and she took comfort in the fact that the land would outlast them, would outlast the war—would outlast time itself.

They traveled straight west for three days, illegally crossing the border at some point, and continued on. They moved beyond rules; she, in her grief, was also beyond rules. Gradually, as happened each time, Helen was absorbed by the details of the patrol—the heat, the terrain, the soldiers—till nothing else existed. She was impressed by the obvious relish with which they went about their job, hardwired for it in a way other units were not. They lived deep in the land; traveled through it like ghosts. No base camps or supply drops. Understood there would be no mercy if they were caught. They made do with very little—whatever was on their backs or taken from the land.

Deep in the wilderness, Helen experienced the longed-for slipping beneath the surface, losing the sense of herself as separate from her surroundings. After five days all thought of the war was gone. Only movement and land covered, the safety of the men and herself. She lost her tiredness, lost her appetite. Simply ate and slept enough to have the strength to keep walking. The idea of taking photos small and beside the point. The Lurps mostly ignored her except for the one who had made the body bag comment. After a week he came up and complimented her: "You're almost invisible."

On the tenth day they received a click-hiss on the radio, a signal an NVA convoy would be passing within hours. They set up positions in the bush with a clear view of a wide dirt path that crossed a quick-moving river. The sound of the water concealed them against accidental noise.

Linh and Helen cut branches to create a tripod inside a large bush, then hid the camera and zoom lens with leaves. Linh attached a cable release for the shutter. "When they come, no movement. No framing. We have to be lucky. If your hands shake, no problem."

She listened and did what Linh told her without question. Enacting a ritual to summon a spirit, conjuring an enemy that had for the most part remained invisible and otherworldly. Beyond belief that such a force could be made up of individual people, and she wondered if it was the same for the North Vietnamese—did they fear the magic of the Americans, with their planes and bombs? Their endless machines. Each time the Americans came across fresh footprints of rubber sandals, they stared at them with a kind of queasy awe. The only tangible evidence of the enemy's existence so far was dead bodies, but strangely, the dead were somehow less, did not match the fear and terror they inspired, much like one could not imagine flight from the evidence of a dead bird on the ground.

Hours passed that held the weight of days. Ten feet away, Helen heard the click-hiss of the radio again as the Lurp nodded up and down the line and then shut it off. More hours, with only a minimum of movement. The day overcast and cooler, a thin fog curled at the top of the mountains, and the first enemy soldier materialized on the path without a noise.

How young they seemed.

Barely out of boyhood in their shabby khaki uniforms, thin so that their pants, rolled up, revealed the large knobs of knees. The AKs strapped across their chests looked too big for them to handle, children playing war with their fathers' guns. Their faces so serious and yet they moved with the energy of teenagers, confident in their steps. When the first soldiers came to the river, they stopped and scanned it up and down, but they were at the narrowest and slowest-flowing part—the Lurps made sure of that before setting up positions—and Helen pressed down on the cable release over and over, hoping that just by sheer numbers she would come up with a usable frame, the click of the camera inaudible over the gravelly sound of the running water.

The first soldiers waded in their rubber sandals halfway across the river, the rushing water reaching waist-high so that they had to raise their weapons. Behind the point guard, soldiers came with heavy loads strapped onto bicycles, a bamboo pole across the handlebar and another from the seat of the bike for steering. One of them said something to a soldier in the stream, and the young man again scanned the river up and down and shrugged.

The bicycles shuddered in the river, the rushing water tugging against the canvas bags, forcing the drivers to cross quickly, almost at a jog because the power of the current would tire them, soaking the bags heavy and making their jobs harder. More than fifty bicycles passed in an hour.

Next came a kind of crude wagon balanced on four fat rubber tires. Two soldiers directed it, one front and one back. Halfway across the river, a front tire caught on something underwater, and the force of the soldier pushing from the back made it go in deeper, splaying the wagon sideways so it was at a forty-five-degree angle to the bank. The two soldiers tried to straighten it, then back it up, but the vehicle wouldn't budge.

Now the soldiers closest to the Americans stopped on their side of the riverbank, laid their bikes down and slipped off their packs, and waded into the water to free the wagon. It took eight men to get it moving, and when they reached the other side, the steep bank was too slippery, and the wheels couldn't gain traction. An order was given to cut down poles to create a ramp.

Five soldiers, including one young boy, took out small hatchets shaped like half-moons and began combing through the surrounding brush. Four of them moved upstream, away from the Americans, but the young boy moved downstream, straight toward them.

Helen held her breath and moved her head in time to see one of the Lurps nearest her pull the pin out of a grenade and then the boy soldier was near them, but he was not looking for a pole. He seemed glad to stop marching, and he looked up at the sky and down the stream and reached in his pocket, pulling out something white that he quickly stuck in his mouth, and as he began to chew, Helen realized it was gum, and the surprise made her smile. An order was barked from one of the soldiers holding the wagon in the stream, and the boy soldier veered directly toward Helen and Linh, seeing the easy lure of their cut branches. He reached for one of the poles holding the camera, bringing his right hand with the hatchet up. When the pole came away in his hand, he found himself looking eye to eye with Linh.

The boy soldier's eyes grew big, and his chest inhaled a yell when his vision caught the movement of Helen's hand on the cable, and his eyes grew larger.

Helen looked at him and knew that it was probably the end for all of them, but something in his face and gestures made her unafraid. Gently she raised her hand and ran her index finger lightly across her neck, more a statement of the situation they all found themselves in than a threat, and the boy soldier exhaled without a sound, stepped back, his eyes traveling again to Linh, who raised his own hand to cover his face, palm down, slowly dragging his hand down his features, fingertips finally grazing his chin, a mime to erase all that had been seen, and the boy soldier turned quickly at the new barked orders from the men soldiers in the stream, and again he looked at the river, squinting as the sun reflected off of it, motionless for a moment before he moved away, blowing a big, sugary bubble.

Poles were cut and put under the wagon, and it tracked up the muddy bank. The last of the soldiers, including the boy, crossed, and then the clearing was empty, only footprints proving the whole thing had not been a dream.

When they returned to Saigon they did not stop to shower or change but went straight to the magazine's darkroom and kicked out all the assistants.

Gary got word of the pictures and left his apartment before curfew to spend the night at the office. "You're kidding, aren't you? How'd you do it?" He was grabbing at his collar around his neck as if there were a pressure there. With shock, Helen realized that in the last month his hair had turned white.

"Are you okay?" she said.

"I forbid you to take chances like that. Or at least, tell me first."

Helen looked at him coolly. She had long suspected that Gary cared more than he let on, yet it was in the nature of the business that they all wanted to please him, that he created, subtly, the competitive drive and risk-taking that produced the pictures. "We were on our own time."

"Do it again, you're fired."

"And get five better offers the next day." She was beyond the point where he could make demands, unspoken that she would take the same risks anyway and simply sell to another magazine if need be. The pictures didn't matter anymore.

"Don't make me go through losing another photographer," he said. And with that, she was chastened.

"The pictures all go under a dual byline, okay? No one else in the darkroom till we finish. No one touches the negatives."

"Let me have a peek, okay? At least the first contacts."

"We'll see." She worried about the quality of the exposures, the dim light and the lack of aperture adjustment.

"You're my top paid feature person now. Tell Linh I'm putting him on staff full-time."

Helen nodded her head and gently closed the darkroom door behind her.

Linh began with test clips. As Helen feared, the light had been too dim. Linh left the negatives in the developer longer to increase the contrast and sharpen the edges. His first test got better and better, but at the moment both of them thought the exposure perfect, fog developed over the shadows. "Too long," he said. "We'll shorten the next one."

Helen sat on a stool in the dark, the red light on Linh as he moved back and forth. "What do you think?"

He studied the next test negative, then turned the overhead light on. He handed it to Helen, and the air went out of her when she saw the poor range of tone and the weak edge markings on the film. "It's not going to work. These are terrible."

"We can fix it. We'll leave it in developer longer. Use two baths. I'll make it work."

Helen chewed her nail. "How'd you learn to do all this?"

"This is nothing. I used to work in the forest at night with only stars. I rinsed negatives by letting water run over the strips in the stream. Dried them by hanging them along small leaves."

"Gary is making you staff photographer."

Linh bowed his head a moment before he reached for the printing trays. "That's a great honor."

"Honor, BS. He's afraid to lose you to a competitor. It means that they can transfer you out of the country if you want."

"Yes."

"Thank you for taking me out there. To see that. It was a dream. After doing this for me . . . I'm keeping my word. I'm going home."

"Yes."

"Come with me."

Linh said nothing.

"Robert will give you a good job."

"I cannot."

"Not even for me . . ." Helen said, more statement than question.

"It is too much to ask."

Hours later they printed the closeup shot of the boy soldier. Linh burned in highlights, and as he promised, the picture was decent in quality, extraordinary in subject. They handed the print to Gary, who stood at the door like a nurse waiting to carry off a newborn, forgetting Helen and Linh as soon as he collected his prize. They sat in the darkroom, door open, the red safelight a dull star. Both were tired and heavy-eyed but unwilling to leave.

"We make a good team," she said.

Linh smiled.

"Will they hurt the boy when they see his picture? Will they think he's a traitor?"

"No," Linh said. "He'll think fast like he did with us. He'll survive."

"I felt good out there."

"Go to California. It will be better there for you."

She was hurt by his constant dismissal. "What about you?"

"Nothing to worry about. With you gone, I will be the best photographer in Vietnam. Maybe I will marry Mai's sister. She need a husband for her children." He kept thinking of his debt to Darrow, how Helen's safety would have mattered to him more than anything else.

Helen's back stiffened. "I had no idea."

"It's a Vietnam tradition. To care for family," Linh said.

"Darrow wanted you to be happy. Have a good life for him." Helen scrambled to her feet and turned on the overhead light. "I'm going to grab a couple of hours on the cot."

"We got good pictures."

"How can I top this? Go out on top, right?"

Helen moved out of the apartment in Cholon, handing the keys over to Linh, and went back to the Continental, where she had started. The next morning, she made arrangements to fly home. She did not feel more or less grieved than before she went out with Linh in the field, but something had changed. She knew it and suspected that Linh knew it, and they did not speak of it but instead acted as if nothing had shifted between them.

Late at night Helen stayed awake in her hotel room, sleep no longer a thing to be counted on, and she lay in bed, propped up by pillows, staring into darkness until she could see the patterns of the tiles on the wall, the blades of the fan above as they pushed against the heavy air. She stored a bottle of bourbon on her bedside table, and it slackened the thirst and loneliness she felt during those long hours, sure that there would be no knock on the door. Helen slowly trained herself to believe in Darrow's death. He had been her guide and mentor, as well as her lover, and she did not feel up to the challenge of the war without him.

Was it the same for others? Like children, did they all wait for the reappearance of a loved one, death simply a word, the lack of a knock on a door? She knew better, had seen the two bags on top of the steep ravine, had watched them sway on poles on the shoulders of the living.

And yet. The sight of the pale NVA soldiers had changed everything for her. Just when she thought there was nothing more but repeating herself, a whole other world, formerly invisible, appeared. No American had yet photographed the other side. As thrilling as exploring an unknown continent on a map. No one could understand except Darrow and MacCrae, who were gone. Only Linh, who now was determined to send her home. Frequently she dreamed of the boy soldier who had held their fate in his hands, who saved them and himself for another day, and how the Lurps sat, tensed, how one wet his index finger and marked it in the air, *one down,* like a sports score.

Helen woke groggy in the morning, her room too hot, mouth sour with alcohol. Her room boy served her Vietnamese coffee, thick and sweet with condensed milk, out of a silver pot, laid down fresh rolls on a china plate with three small pots of jam—marmalade, strawberry, and guava—both knowing she used only marmalade. She slathered the bread with butter but used the orange sparingly so that the boy could take the two unused pots home with him each day. Why, just as she was leaving, did she finally feel at home?

When Helen expressed the desire to see the crooked apartment one last time, Linh told her Thao had already moved in, that the whole building shook from the running of children up and down the stairs.

"Good," Helen said. "Something to break the bad luck."

After the remains from the crash site had been identified, Gary brought out Darrow's will stating he wished to be cremated in Vietnam, but his wife made an official complaint to the magazine, and they gave in to her wishes, shipping the body back to New York for burial.

Helen, ready to fly out, felt all the original grief renew itself. She was nothing to Darrow. She begged Gary to read Darrow's letter over the phone to the wife, but the woman remained unswayed, convinced that he had not been in his right mind the last year. In the end, the body went to the States, and the staff had a Buddhist funeral with an empty casket, done frequently as the numbers of dead grew and recovery of bodies became more problematic.

The procession began at the apartment in Cholon. Helen looked up at the window, hoping to see the sister-in-law and her children crowding the sill, but it remained empty. Was it possible that Linh had kept her away so memory would not change her mind about leaving? The Vietnamese in the procession wore traditional white scarves of mourning on their heads. Monks chanted and burned joss. They wound their way to downtown, stopped in the plaza next to the Marine Statue, beneath the office's windows.

Helen was dry-eyed. Her head ached. At the plaza, Gary leaned against a tree, facing away from them, and all she could see was the curl of his shoulders, his newly white hair. But she wasn't able to comfort him. Weren't they all children, pretending tragedy when it was clear the danger they placed themselves in? Shouldn't they just damn well accept it? When they passed the Continental, the head bartender carried out a glass of Darrow's favorite scotch on a silver tray.

At Mac Dinh Chi cemetery, Linh scattered a trail of uncooked rice and paper money. Clouds gathered and wind blew as a mat was unrolled at the gravesite. A plate of cracked crab flown in from Vung Tau, a bowl of rice, and the glass of scotch were laid out. Tangible things that Helen understood, compared to the generic funerals of flowers and coffins and organ music she had attended back home. A bundle of incense was lit and then it was over.

The clouds darkened, the longed-for rain fell, and people scattered for any available shelter.

Helen looked for Annick in the procession, but she had warned that she would not come. *Too many funerals,* she said. If she went to them all that's all she'd do. But Helen was leaving that night and wanted to say good-bye, so she walked, covering herself with the umbrella, moving through the flooding streets, skirting small moving streams of dirty water floating with trash. The rain kept falling, gray and hard, pounding the earth, and a gust of wind blew off the river, lifting the ribs of her umbrella inside out until she was gathering the rain rather than sheltering from it, and she let the umbrella fall on the road, knowing it would be picked up, repaired, and used within minutes. Each item reincarnated countless times. One thing she had learned in Vietnam—that reincarnation was not only in the hereafter but also in the now. She continued on, rain pelting her, and reached the milliner's and stood under the awning, wiping water off her face. In the display window was a wedding dress she hoped had been created for some jilted bride and not her.

Inside, the Vietnamese seamstresses sat on their accustomed rush seats, sewing away faster and with more concentration than usual. From outside, over the sound of rain, Helen had thought she heard talking and laughter, but inside, the store was as silent as a tomb. She stood at the counter, but Annick did not come out from the back where she usually hid out, smoked cigarettes, and drank wine. The seamstresses took no notice of Helen's presence, so she tapped the bell on the counter.

At the sound, the older one stood. She wore the same black dress Helen had seen her in the first time and each subsequent time she came to the store, so that Helen was convinced that the madames owned seven identical black dresses, one for each day in order for the worn ones to be washed and starched and made ready. Her head pounding, Helen felt feverish as she stood, dripping water onto the floor. The elder madame mumbled to herself as she made her stiff, slow way to the counter, all the while looking down to study her suddenly idle fingers.

"*Bonjour, madame,*" Helen said, and the seamstress returned the greeting in her singsong French, more as a refrain than greeting, still without making eye contact.

"*Ou est Madame Annick?*" Helen asked.

The seamstress sighed. "*Madame est parti.*"

"*Ou?*" Where?

The seamstress looked up, and her gaze startled Helen, the eyes the pale gray of cataract. "*Elle est parti.*" The woman bent sideways under the counter, pulled out a small flat box tied in satin ribbon. Helen opened it and saw a card from Annick on top of a gold scarf. *No good-byes. Bon voyage, ma chère.*

"*Merci. Au revoir,*" the seamstress replied, and with a small curtsey she returned to her chair in obvious relief to again pick up her embroidery.

At the hotel that evening, Linh apologized for not being able to take her to the airport. He made no attempt to give an excuse. He could not trust himself not to betray her departure. Beg her not to leave. They stood awkwardly at the hotel entrance.

"I'll miss you," she said.

As Linh walked away, a soldier was arguing with the doorman, and Helen was distracted by his loud voice. When she looked back to the spot where Linh had stood, it was empty. But as the cab pulled up to take her bags, he reappeared.

"Everything's fixed. I can come see you off."

They rode in silence. Again he offered no explanation for his change in plans, and Helen, hurt that he had not wanted to see her off, now wondered why he had changed his mind.

As the plane rose steeply on takeoff, the passengers remained quiet, but as it swung out over the South China Sea applause broke out. Helen was the only one not smiling. Below on the dark sea, squid boats floated like carnivals, bright with light.

After Helen left Saigon, Linh sat alone in the crooked apartment. No sister-in-law, no children. When he had turned down Thao's proposal of marriage, she had promptly set her sights on a mechanic and was now living on the other side of town with him and the children. Linh still sent them money.

Linh had stood helpless at the gate of the plane; he had broken his own discipline and confused her by his actions. In his weakness he asked Helen for something to remember her by, but it was too late. All she had was a gold scarf around her neck that was brand-new and not hers yet, but she took it off and handed it to him. Now he held it to his nose, but there was no scent of her on it. Slowly he twisted it and wrapped it tight around one wrist, when someone knocked at the door. He did not want to answer, did not want to endure Mr. Bao at this moment, but to continue to avoid him would be worse. He opened the door.

Mr. Bao walked through the room, now needing a wooden cane, taking in each object although only the bare furniture remained. "Now it seems I must come to you. It's been months since we've talked."

"There are no developments. Other than my being a staff photographer."

"That is very good. Keep your ears and eyes open."

"That's my job."

Mr. Bao looked at him sharply, his small eyes behind the glasses magnified. "Don't forget whose side you are on. Sentiment is turning to our side. Men like you are credited with helping that. Don't make us doubt you."

"Why pretend? It's not as if this has been voluntary on my part. How is the heroin trade? Prosperous?" It amazed Linh how naive the North still was about the Americans, not realizing Westerners' quest for news was more powerful than anything he could have ever led them to.

Mr. Bao picked up a figurine of a Buddha, a trinket from the markets, left behind. "So your little adventuress is gone?"

"Yes."

"Too bad. Why didn't you convince her to stay?"

"I have no control." The truth was, and he felt shame in his pride over it, that he could have persuaded her to stay. But his loyalty to Darrow outweighed his love and his anger. The Americans did not yet realize that they would lose the war. There was a kind of hopeless certainty in Linh that no harm would come to him in this war, that he was one of the charmed, although he did not particularly care about that survival. He was angry that he had not been with Darrow, thwarted his death.

"It doesn't matter. Better to not deal with a woman anyway. What if she falls in love with you?" Bao chuckled and eyed the scarf. "What's that?"

"She left it behind." He saw Bao's eyebrows rise, and quickly added, "She asked me to deliver it to a friend to send on to her."

Mr. Bao reached out and touched the fabric. "Then you shouldn't wrinkle it so. Too bad. It is good quality—my wife would have liked it."

FOURTEEN

Back to the World

Helen refused to attend the memorial service for Darrow in New York City. She considered it a hijacking of his wishes and would not be party to it. She would not be party either to her moniker of other woman. Gary and the others thought her callous not to go, to represent his colleagues in Vietnam. No. They expected her to be a good sport, to let the past stay in the past, but it was not within her to do it.

She flew from Tokyo to San Francisco, and felt a childish excitement as she looked down through the clouds, the idea of home suddenly real after such a long absence. Home would fix things. On the plane to Los Angeles, the last leg, she sat with soldiers still in uniform who had processed out of Travis and were going home. Could it be as easy as walking off a plane to leave the war behind?

Her mother, Charlotte, met her at the gate with a bouquet of flowers wrapped in cellophane. She saw her own face in her mother's, softer and more fragile now. How she had missed that smell of Joy perfume. She pushed away the guilt she felt, her mother resigned to the whole selfish tribe she had raised. As they hugged, Helen watched the returning soldiers heckled by a small group of antiwar protesters. A stringy brunette wearing tattered jeans and a suede halter top stood in front of the soldiers, blocking their way. Her long brown hair was tangled, a feather dangling from a braided strand of it. With barely a glance, one of the soldiers shot his arm out to shove her aside.

The girl's eyes widened until the whites were visible, and she yelled, "Who do you think you are touching me?" But the soldiers ignored her and moved off.

"Let's leave," Helen said.

"You're so thin," her mother said. "I hardly recognized you."

Helen put her arm around her mother's thickened waist as they walked by the brunette. She slowed and stared at the girl, who returned a flat, dreamy gaze. A look with no contradiction, not the smallest doubt. "Think peace," the girl offered, then turned to drink from a soda can.

Helen stopped, transfixed. Her mother tugged at her arm.

The girl looked back now, flushed. "What?"

"That's real brave . . . what you're doing here."

"I want to leave," Charlotte said.

"Gee, thanks," the brunette said with a nervous giggle and turned to the two men she was with.

"You're really making a statement . . . standing in an air-conditioned air-port."

"Look," the girl started. "My boyfriend was drafted. Were you there?"

"Yes."

The girl's eyes widened. "That's so cool. Did you see them bayonet ba-bies?"

Helen shook with a rage she didn't know was inside of her. Charlotte dragged her down the walkway.

"What was the point of it?" the girl yelled, gaining confidence at their retreat.

Helen stopped, unable to think. No one had ever asked her the question before.

When they reached the house, Helen first went around to the back and stood staring at the view she had grown up with—ocean waves breaking on the rocks down below. Then she walked from room to room, marveling how big and clean everything looked. Nothing had changed since she'd left ex-cept for herself. It was hard to imagine what had burned in her to leave this place and go halfway around the world. She wanted to return to what she had been before she left, but better, smarter, more content.

"Come and look," her mother said, and showed her the pile of magazines and newspapers with her photos. "This just came." She held the magazine with the NVA boy soldier on the cover. Inside was an editorial announcing Darrow's death with the picture Linh had shot of him in the Special Forces camp. "So horrible, so sad."

Helen said nothing. If she told about her relationship with Darrow, it would boil down to the elements of a dime-store romance. How she had wanted to bring Darrow here, to meet her mother and see where she grew up.

"Please put them away for now."

Her mom fidgeted with her hands, shy in front of her daughter. "What was it like there?"

"Scary and depressing. Alive. Parts were wonderful."

"I can't imagine."

"Yeah."

"Did you find what you were looking for?"

No answer.

"I'm just so glad you're back. I'm proud. People say things about Vietnam behind my back. But my brave girl went."

Helen stared at the floor. "That means a lot to me."

"I invited some of our friends over," she said. "Everyone is so anxious to see that you're in one piece."

"Not just yet."

Charlotte stopped in the middle of the room. "This part of life is important, too." She bit her lip. "All of you acted like the war was the only real thing that mattered."

Helen hugged her, then stretched out on the couch.

"Take your shoes off the sofa. Don't be a lazy bones. Come see your room. I haven't changed a thing." The comforting assurance one gave an invalid, when everyone knew that nothing at all stayed unchanged. Her room still had the white-painted twin bed, the flocked coverlet with pastel flowers sewn on. The walls papered with the pictures of Indochina she had collected as a teenager—broad swaths of the monsoon across the plains, long sun-drenched valleys, two figures wearing woven conical hats sitting in a fishing boat in the watery distance. Unreal and movieish; had this bit of fakery really started her on her way to Vietnam? How impossibly naive she had been.

Helen laughed, and her mother's face looked hopeful, but the laugh continued too long, became raucous and then bitter, and her mother's face fell as she escaped from the room.

Beneath the pictures was the box of Darrow's personal things from the Cholon apartment. Helen avoided the box for days, and then broke down one afternoon, tearing it open, savoring the faint, sweet-rotten smell of Saigon inside. As strange and unsanitary as a full-grown Cholon rat. She loved it now in direct proportion to how she hated it then. Helen sat by the box, transported back to her crooked apartment, the Buddha door, the creaky stairs, the faded lamp. She closed her eyes and dreamed she could hear the street noise outside, longing for that life in this silence and hum of air-conditioning.

The magazine had taken care of his official things in the hotel, but Darrow's wife made a request for all his personal belongings. "Do whatever you want," Gary said. Helen would have ignored the wife, but the idea of the boy made her pause. As a young girl, she had studied in detail everything that related to her father for some clue to herself.

She made her slow way through file after file of prints and negatives. Any combat photographer as far forward as Darrow ended up with huge numbers of unprintable photos—material so gruesome that no magazine would publish it. But the photographer had to take them, nonjudgmental until he returned to the darkroom. Looking through his whole oeuvre, she saw that he had gone from a mediocre photographer in his early days in the Congo and Middle East to what some called a genius. Something had come together for him by the time he arrived in Vietnam, and the place itself had spoken to him. An astonishing achievement bought at an astonishing price. Helen kept the gruesome photos back, selecting the ones surrounding his published spreads. He had been notorious for taking many rolls for each intended shot, and these showed his artistic method at work. A child should know that about his father.

She came across the photos done at Angkor, stunned by their loveliness.

So unlike anything he had done before. A photo of Linh among a group of Cambodian workers. Although he was smiling, he looked too young for the pain in his eyes. Helen also kept out all the shots of herself. She included his cameras, his equipment, his fatigues, holding back only one shirt with his name on white tape above the breast pocket. The sum of his life fit in one box.

When family friends came over for a homecoming, Helen walked out wearing a cocktail dress and high heels, and only her crooked gait, unused to dress shoes, gave her away that she hadn't just been off at a women's college. When the conversation turned to the war, she changed the subject, told jokes, asked about neighbors' children, vacations, anything to give the pretense that all was normal. She didn't want to be treated like a quarantine animal.

A former tomboy, she cooked for the first time in her life. Whole days lost in the kitchen, poring over cookbooks, pages dusted in flour or glazed in sauce. She and her mother sat down to feasts and staggered away from the table. Her mother laughed, only the lines around her eyes giving away her worry. They had so much food they invited neighbors over, a family of Irish redheads; the mother, Gwen, owned a catering business. After she ate three pieces of Helen's chocolate velvet cake, she sought Helen out in the kitchen, washing dishes. "This is so good. You should come work for me."

"This is therapy for me." The idea of the job so alien, so ridiculous to Helen, that she considered it.

But it was their teenage boy, Finn, who kept trying to get Helen's attention, who kept her from pretending. The boy's hair was a soft golden-red, his hands and feet puppyish, too big for his frame. Helen remembered that long-ago boy with the strawberry-blond hair, killed in that first ambush that Linh had saved her from.

"What was it like?"

Helen turned to him. "Don't let them draft you. Go to Canada."

"Well, I think service—" the father said.

"What kind of cocoa did you say you used?" Gwen interrupted.

Helen would not be deterred. "If you go, they will use you up like a piece of meat."

The tightness in Gwen's face revealed a conspiracy of women trying to keep the war away.

"Did you see real combat? Did you see anyone get killed?" the boy asked, tenacious.

So for Gwen and Gwen's son, Helen opened the spout, ever so slightly. She talked, her voice low and flat, the words themselves enough, the words fire.

With a hollow drop of her heart, Charlotte noticed that it was the first time Helen seemed alive that day. After fifteen minutes, the room emptied except for the boy, listening rapt.

"They don't learn," Helen said, after he had left. "The pictures and the stories—we didn't, either."

Sometimes Charlotte entered a room she thought empty only to find Helen there, staring off into space, her face broken apart, her daughter the Picasso woman. Helen sat on the couch, legs curled up, tears rolling down her face, and all the mother could do was take her child in her arms, rock back and forth for hours, pretend her daughter was still a child and could be soothed, merely frightened of the dark.

Darrow's wife requested Helen bring his belongings in person. Although Helen suspected some final score settling on the wife's part, she had not yet decided what to do. The easiest thing was to give the box to Robert and have the magazine make arrangements, but still she held on to it.

At first the house and the small beach town that she had longed for while in Vietnam had seemed calcified, dead, as white and clean as bone. But slowly it came to life, or she came to life within it. But it wasn't the life she wanted.

The sight of people going about their days, shopping in markets, eating in restaurants, playing with children in parks, laughing and drinking and talking, created a deep resentment inside her. Perfectly happy living their lives, Helen thought, which is all anyone should want, and yet how blind, how oblivious to the biggest story in the world. Didn't they see that Vietnam was the center of the world at that moment? Seen from back home, her pride seemed monstrous. Vietnam monstrous and the acts committed there inconceivable. Her face burned at the thought of the risks she had taken for those photos, burned at the waste.

It was in the dead of night when she felt most herself. Come three or four o'clock, she would be wide-awake in her bed, pretending to herself that she had to get up for a mission, and she would try to remember details—the smell of the room, the temperature, her sleepiness—until they became so vivid she actually felt a fluttering of adrenaline inside of her. Sometimes she would carry it to the point of rising and going to the bathroom, washing her face, and looking into the mirror. Had she gone crazy?

A letter from Linh arrived. In it a picture of Linh and herself. When she unfolded the letter, a sheaf of gold rice stalks fell into her lap. The letter detailed his new activities as staff photographer. She didn't know if it was his awkward use of written English, but the whole letter was disappointingly impersonal. Only the last line spoke to her so she could hear his voice: *Each night I pray life is coming back to you, a piece at a time, just as on the burned hills the grass reappears.* She studied the photo more closely. The day on the beach at Vung Tau. Linh staring not at the camera but at her. Of course. She had known but ignored what she knew. The war wouldn't be over for her until she saw that grass reappear on those scarred hills.

This is what happened when one left one's home—pieces of oneself scattered all over the world, no one place ever completely satisfied, always a nostalgia for the place left behind. Pieces of her in Vietnam, some in this place of bone. She brought the letter to her nose. The smell of Vietnam: a mix of jungle and wetness and spices and rot. A smell she hadn't realized she missed.

But what could she do with such knowledge? Even to her, the idea of going back to Vietnam was madness. So she trudged on through the mystery of building a life. She started at Gwen's catering business, baking cakes and pies. Woke up at dawn and went down to the shop early, made coffee and sat in the bright light of the kitchen. Gwen, heavy-handed, brought a cousin to buy rolls—a setup. His name was Tom, a real-estate agent, a former USC football player. They had made small talk over coffee and muffins, and he asked Helen out. Helen was not friendly. She took his number, not intending to use it.

But she wouldn't give up trying to live a normal life. In the evening she ran on the beach and noticed a family playing Frisbee with a dog, and, in a burst of inspiration, she went down to the pound and picked up a golden retriever puppy. When she brought him home, spilling over in her arms like a too-large bouquet, her mother held the door open and laughed, shaking her head. "A dog? A dog! Why not? High time for a dog in this house."

"Yeah, it is." She stroked the gold velvet ears and tried to ignore her mother's intent gaze.

"What'll we name him?"

"Michael always wanted a dog named Duke."

Her mother nodded. "Duke, then."

"How come we never had one before?"

"I don't think your father liked them. Didn't he get bit when he was a kid? Something like that."

"But you never thought of getting one after he was gone."

"Life ended after that."

The puppy whimpered to be let out nights; Helen up like a shot, carrying the dog outside on the lawn, standing sleepy, barefoot on the wet grass, staring up at the stars. She walked him up and down along empty sidewalks, enjoyed the upside-down quality of the world at night, the only state that matched what she was feeling inside.

After two weeks, Helen called Tom. He sounded surprised. "I thought we didn't connect," he said.

"We didn't."

A pause. "What're you up to?"

"Knocking away on that chip on my shoulder you talked about."

He laughed.

"Come for dinner about seven, we'll eat with my mom." A chaperoned dinner to take the pressure off her.

"Why not?"

During dinner Helen played hostess, passing salad and dinner rolls, smiling at his jokes. Tom pleased her mother beyond words; she glowed, hopeful that this was a first step for her daughter. Helen snuck scraps under the table to Duke.

When Tom asked Helen about her photographs in Vietnam, she spoke of the beauty of the countryside. "It's too bad you never saw it in person, Mom. It's so beautiful. Maybe we'll go after the war is over."

Charlotte frowned. "Why would I ever set foot in such a place? A place where they killed my son?"

Helen rose and took her plate to the sink. After dinner, Charlotte suggested Tom and Helen take a walk along the beach. Driving down the coast highway, Helen insisted on stopping first at the liquor store for a bottle of scotch. She drank out of the bottle and turned Tom's radio on loud. At the top of a hill, with the town spread out below, she moved her leg over the gearbox and around the shaft. Tom ran his hand along her knee as she jammed her foot down on the accelerator, bracing herself against the back of the seat so he couldn't dislodge her, and the car raced down the curving road. Tom held the wheel and slammed on the brakes. "Are you crazy?"

"Just having fun."

"Some fun. Getting us killed."

"Didn't it feel good, just a little? Kept you dying from boredom?"

They parked along the beach and walked in the sand barefoot, passing the bottle back and forth between them.

"You're a little wild, huh?" he said.

"That's me."

"How long did you say you'd been back?"

"I didn't." She stopped and dug her feet into the cold and gritty sand. Waves in the moonlight sharp and hard as the blades of knives. "Six weeks, four days."

Far up the beach, teenagers crowded around a large bonfire that threw light up on the cliffs, but where Tom and Helen stood it was dark and deserted.

"So what are you doing with your days?" he asked. He took a long pull from the bottle and let his fingers brush along hers when he handed it back.

"Baking for Gwen." She laughed. "Cakes and cookies, buns and rolls."

"No, long-term. When are you going to start doing photography again?"

"I'm done with that."

"I told all my friends about you, all your covers. They'd seen your stuff and were impressed as hell. That's why I came when you called, even though you were a jerk that day."

"Wow." His bluntness made her like him better.

"So why aren't you working at a newspaper? Or covering another war? Isn't that what you're supposed to do?"

"I just went as a lark. It turned into something else. What do you do if you have a hazardous talent, like riding over waterfalls in a barrel? A talent dangerous to your health?" After the question came out of her mouth, she felt embarrassed.

He stopped and took a sip. "I don't know. If I was that good at something, I know it'd be hard to stop. Baking . . . shit."

Helen moved back into the cave of shadows at the base of the hillside, tumbled onto her back in the sand. Was that the simple answer, that Darrow couldn't leave his work because he was good at it? That she loved the work more than this life that felt like a living death? No matter how she tried, the gears of her old life kept slipping; she could gain no traction. Her mind was always far away, whirring. She had not known how alive she was in Vietnam. How despite the fear and the anger, she had been awake in the deepest way, in a way that ordinary life could not compete with. She motioned Tom down and pulled him on top of her.

"All those guys over there made you a little crazy, huh? We can go to my place. I have a bed."

"Baking's not so bad. You have flour, butter, sugar. The smell of baking bread." She shook her head, squirmed from under him, reached for the bottle nested in the sand, and took a long drink.

He grabbed the bottle away. "That's enough. I don't want you passing out on me." He kissed her on the lips, the neck, fumbled with the buttons of her blouse.

She closed her eyes, but that made her head spin faster, so she opened them again. "There was this place on Tu Do that made the most wonderful croissants." Despite the pulsing of the waves, the times in high school and college, despite the smoky taste of the scotch on her tongue, this wasn't even a moment's forgetfulness.

"Come on . . ."

"No." She couldn't remember why she thought this would work, why she sought him out. He had unbuttoned her blouse. For a brief moment the pulse of warmth began, a deep pull, but instead of distracting, the arousal opened a deep grief inside her.

Helen jerked open his belt buckle, but the scotch suddenly created a wave of nausea welling up in her, and she pushed at his chest to get him off, unable to bear another minute, which he at first mistook for passion, pressing down harder, her slaps growing more frantic, powerful, convulsed, until he moved off, and she rolled away, crouched on all fours, and heaved.

He sat on the sand next to her. "Jesus Christ," he said. "Nice."

She sat with her knees up, her head on her arms, sucking down gulps of air.

He stood and took off his shirt, then his T-shirt. He walked to the waves, then came back. "Here," he said, kneeling down, handing her his wet T-shirt to wipe her face. He sighed. "I don't know what just happened."

"I shouldn't have called."

"Yeah, maybe."

"I wanted to be the kind of girl you think of when you go off to war."

"*You're* the one who goes to war, remember?"

"We better go home."

"I like you. But you're not that kind of girl."

The next day she took the box of Darrow's belongings and boarded a flight for New York.

She did not think about what she would find, did not know what she was looking for. Not until later did she realize that the addition of facts would simply dilute her own store of memories without bringing him closer, that as she became the biographer of his life, Darrow himself would move further and further from her grasp. Although she knew him deeply, now she could discover only the surface of his life.

She drove out of the city, onto long, winding roads shaded by the dying yellow and red of fall. Although it was only late September, already there was a chill in the air, and the low sun cast a somber light on the lawns and houses. Circling streets aimlessly, unable to place Darrow in this suburban environment, she came upon his street name and turned. She planned to drive by the house a few times, to reconnoiter the area, but when she saw a long, rising lawn that led to a white Cape Cod, she stopped. How to reconcile this house with the crooked apartment in Cholon? Could the same man belong to both places?

Helen parked on the side of the road and watched as a coiffed brunette in a floral dress unloaded groceries from a car trunk. Her own jeans and army T-shirt with a khaki shirt on top suddenly seemed shabby. This place, this woman, were impossible to put together with the Darrow she knew. Was the excuse of war a way to go live another, a second life? Were there closets filled with his clothes inside? If she brought them to her nose, would she smell him? She got out of the car and struggled to lift the box, balancing it on her hip as she closed the car door.

The driveway dipped before it rose to the house. A small puddle filled with fallen leaves had formed from an earlier rain. Helen walked around it, stepping on the wet lawn, almost slipping in a hidden dip. The driveway was long, the woman too far away for Helen to see her face. Once she saw her close-up, she would know if Darrow had loved her.

As she walked up the gravel path, a small boy ran around the corner of the house with an Airedale chasing him. The boy laughed and shouted to his mother, the dog jumping and nipping him in midair, and Helen stopped. His curly hair the exact brown shade of Darrow's. Her legs went weak. Suddenly she did not want what she had come for. Nothing could be added; nothing would change her facts. The woman called out to the boy a name Helen couldn't quite make out. Her blood pounded in her ears like waves, and she realized Darrow had never told her the boy's name, had kept him unreal.

The child pointed his arm down the driveway toward Helen. The woman reached out for him, but he ducked away and began to run full speed down the driveway with her in chase. When they came within speaking distance, the woman stopped, and her face became hard, a cool stare. "Can I help you?"

"I'm Helen Adams. From *Life.* I have your . . . I have Sam's things."

"You're late. You were supposed to be here hours ago." The woman shielded herself as if a wind had come up. "I'm Lilly Darrow. Come," she said, and walked back up to the house.

The interior was neat and dark, low ceilings and unlit Tiffany lamps, unused chintz-covered furniture. Gloomy, wood-carved antiques and marble-topped, sarcophagal tables, everything in perfect taste, fallow. It did not seem that a man had ever lived there, and certainly not Darrow. As they sat in the dim living room, Helen noticed Lilly's face had a professional symmetry to it—a broad, pale forehead, tight smile. A face more to be admired than loved.

"Would you like tea?" she asked, and Helen, not listening, was at a loss until Lilly pointed to a china service. "I love having someone to entertain."

"It's too much . . ."

"Not after you flew across the country."

Lilly lifted the tea tray and pushed at the swinging kitchen door. "Come on, if you want. It's more comfortable in here."

The light through the windows was murky, the sun hidden by tall pines that cast bluish, prone shadows on the back lawn. Copper pots hung from the kitchen walls. Stacks of dishes leaned in the glass-paned cabinets. She was right: Compared to the other room, this did feel more comfortable. Helen liked Lilly better for noticing the difference and admitting it. Her back was toward Helen while she filled the kettle. The fabric of her dress was expensive with a dull, heavy shimmer to the thread.

When the boy wandered in, Helen was unable to take her eyes from him. His brown hair was messed, a cowlick in front, the promise of his father's heavy-lidded eyes and long, slender fingers.

"Go to your room, Sam. This friend of your father's, who came all the way to see us. To bring you some of Daddy's cameras."

He looked at Helen with new interest. "Show them to me?"

Lilly interrupted before Helen could answer. "Not now. We'll look later, okay? Now scoot."

"That's okay, I don't mind." She wanted the boy to stay, wanted the buffer of him.

"He never came here, you know," Lilly said, taking out pastries from a box, and the evident effort that she had gone through belied her casualness. "We married in the city and lived in a small apartment before he left. My parents . . . live down the street. He told me family was important to him. So I made this home for him."

"It's lovely."

"So he would have a home to come back to." Lilly shook her head. "Someone to survive for."

Helen said nothing. A feeling of claustrophobia, of wanting to escape, overcame her, and her hands fidgeted in her lap. As much as she hurt, she was lucky compared to this.

Lilly set down a series of forks and spoons at Helen's place, put out individual pastries, berries and cream, small sandwiches, and sat down to pour. Up close, Lilly's two front teeth, perfect otherwise, overlapped slightly. Helen hesitated, embarrassed that she did not know which fork to pick up.

"I was engaged to a law student from my hometown. But Sam . . . was so passionate about changing the world." She picked up the fork farthest from the plate. "How could I not fall for him? I wanted to wait before we had children. Spend time alone." She smiled and leaned forward, as if in confession. "I even thought of becoming a photographer. Going with him. But he insisted it was no place for a woman. He wanted a family."

Helen used the small fork to tear apart her apple tart.

Lilly reached over and held Helen's arm for emphasis. "I'm not naive. I understand things. He hated the war, and the two of you took solace in each other."

Helen cleared her throat. "I brought everything I thought your son—"

"You're the first one of them he talked of marrying, though."

Them. So this was her purpose. Revenge posthumously. Helen put the tiny fork down and picked up the sandwich with her fingers. "He loved what he did."

"Oh, yes." Lilly stood and moved to the now dark window. She ran her hands over her hair and looked out into the dusk. A natural, unselfconscious gesture, it spoke of many afternoons spent alone. Helen could see only the pale forehead and curved line of her chin in the glow of the lamp. She imagined her as the young woman that Darrow had married. "He was ambitious, wasn't he? That's what I have to convince Sammy of. That he was a great man doing important work. That his death was a hero's death."

"Yes." It took everything for Helen to remain seated in the room, not to run. A terrible mistake coming here; this woman twisting everything around until it was impossible to determine what was what.

"Every year he told me he was quitting. Each woman was the last. Finally I figured out that he was going to stay till he got killed."

"We were about to leave."

"I got divorce papers out of the blue. He wasn't thinking straight."

"He asked you in Saigon."

"He never asked such a thing. We argued when he was coming home. What kind of father doesn't see his son?"

"I came for the boy's sake. You didn't even know him. Everything that was most important about Sam, you didn't know."

"I'd say neither of us was his first love." Lilly leaned back and spread her arms out, encompassing the room. "But at least I have this. His home. I'm his grieving widow. At least I have Sammy."

"Yes."

Lilly moved closer till Helen could smell her perfume, could see her eyes narrowed on her, and understood for the first time how angry she was, and how hard she was working at controlling that anger. "Women like you I can't figure out. Was that little part of him really enough for you?"

Dizzy, Helen shook her head. "We had the war."

"I loved him, you know. I loved him when he was himself. He lost himself over there, in that horrible little country, but that didn't make me stop loving him."

The kitchen had turned shadowy and cold. Helen shivered in her thin cotton shirt, she was always cold now, but Lilly had sweat across her pale, high forehead; she glowed with a mineral kind of heat. Finally Helen saw—this place had nothing to do with Darrow, except for the boy. It was their life, and the war inside it, that was real, and she had simply not understood.

"I hated you in Saigon," Lilly said. She seemed weary from the long afternoon. "But I don't anymore. You've lost more than I could ever take away."

A month passed. Helen had returned to working in the bakery. Something had been solved in her mind regarding Darrow, and she lived with the past more easily. When Robert drove down from Los Angeles, and they walked arm in arm along the boardwalk in the cool, damp evening air, life almost seemed normal. The street along the beach was lined with slow-moving cars, teenagers cruising. Robert looked ten years younger than he had in Saigon.

"Peace has been kind to you," Helen said.

"Can you believe we made it? Seems too good to be true," he said. "Every morning I wake up, and I feel so grateful for the smallest things."

She didn't tell him about opening Linh's letter. How the glow over the ocean was purple, the room dark, and as she opened the envelope, the pool of light from the reading lamp shone on the sheaf of gold rice stalks as they fell out onto her lap.

How instantly she was transported, and what relief she felt.

The paper on which Linh wrote had the faint outline of a lotus blossom in pale yellow, and his writing in black ink on top of the image reminded her of the streets of Saigon, the constant juxtaposition of beauty with necessity.

"It seems so far away." She eyed the crawling line of cars. When the one nearest them backfired, she flinched.

"Remember the first night I took you to dinner? And you tried to free the ducks of Vietnam?"

"How could I have been so stupid?"

"I thought you were charming. And that you'd never last."

"I went to see Darrow's ex-wife."

"Why?" He frowned, tired of her constant exhuming of the past.

"My whole experience was clouded over there. We were in a dream. It was so vivid, I thought it wasn't real. But it was. Truer than anything here."

"Peace is kind to everyone, Helen. Except you."

She led Robert out to the sand, and they sat against a large rock, watching as the waves dissolved from view in the near dusk. The kelp had drifted in, and a strong brine smell blew down from the north part of the cove. "Nothing compared to *nuoc mam,* huh?" The fermented fish sauce smell was a staple of any local Saigon restaurant one entered. She grabbed Robert's hand, intertwined her fingers with his. "It feels good to be with you. You know, someone who *gets* it. Don't you miss it just a little?"

Robert sighed. "Saigon? Happy to have gone through it and survived."

Helen rested her head on his shoulder. "I don't mean the war. Of course not."

"Come to work in L.A. The story Darrow and you did on Lan was a big success. They want a follow-up on her here in California."

"Local?"

"I'm not sending you back to Vietnam, if that's what you're asking." He had never been one of them, had not understood MacCrae, or even Darrow, for that matter. The war had never captured his imagination. "What happened in Saigon . . . what didn't happen . . . things were crazy. But I thought maybe we could try seeing each other under normal circumstances."

Helen gave a small laugh. "Is that what this is? Normal circumstances?"

"Yeah. Not a war zone." He pulled back, irritated. "You know, I don't buy the 'weren't those the days' crap about the war. The war was shit, Saigon was shit, and we're lucky to be out of it alive."

"Sure." She could not share, after all, waking up in the middle of the night and pretending that she needed to get up for a mission, could not share her midnight patrols of the neighborhood with Duke.

"I gave you the benefit of the doubt over there. That you were out of your element."

"Have you heard from Linh?"

Robert was silent for a long minute. "A couple of times. He's on staff. I offered him a transfer, American citizenship to boot. He turned me down."

"I thought he married."

"Linh? No, that's not it. He's either patriotic or really patriotic, if you know what I mean. Darrow always joked that he was working for Uncle Ho's side."

"Whatever he is, I'd trust him with my life."

Robert said nothing.

"Do you remember that first night? When I left you at the restaurant? I thought you'd hate me, but you didn't."

"Didn't we go to some lousy Chinese place . . . in Cholon? I don't remember." But, of course, he did remember each thing from that night, and he had hated her, but it didn't hold.

"Remember Darrow saying they were lucky because there was always another war? I thought it was just macho posturing. But now I wish he was here so I could tell him I finally understand."

They got up and walked back to the boardwalk. The sky overhead black, a pale moon casting a sterile light on the water, on the houses in the hills behind them.

"There are plenty of twenty-year-old guys thinking they're immortal. You and I know better," Robert said.

"I'll take the assignment."

"Good girl."

She nodded and took his hand again, brought it to her lips. "Sometimes I wish I could just be back there an hour. Just enough so that I could really love all this again."

That night she opened the window while she changed for bed. After seeing Robert, she was confident that the dreams would come that night. She undressed in the dark, listening to the sliding of the ocean as she pulled the white, veil-like nightgown over her head. She put her hair back chastely in an elastic. Only then did she turn on the light, look at the pictures on the walls that were already in her head, then quickly turn the light back off. The dreams had begun to go away, and when they did come, they were less intense, and she found she needed to jog her memory before she fell asleep to meet Darrow again in that vast darkness. But instead of Darrow, the dream of the children came to her. She was kneeling this time, an unknown man beside her, lying prone, and the group of Vietnamese children approached and circled the two of them, pressing in, circling around and around, touching, but again when she tried to speak with them, they turned their backs to her. Even while dreaming, she was trying to remember where the image had come from—it was a more threatening feeling than that day on the beach with Linh in Vung Tau—but she couldn't place it.

The rehabilitation center was down in the Wilshire district, and Helen circled the hospital block a few times, finally parking a quarter mile away at a coffee shop. The day was hot, the air crackling dry with Santa Ana winds, the usual smog-stained haze replaced by a sharpness that etched the trees and buildings on the landscape. Helen sat in the restaurant, her appetite lost in the smell of grease, floor wax, and disinfectant. She tried to focus on the assignment, to think of Lan as just another story.

She was late as she muscled her camera bags onto her shoulders in the parking garage and pushed through the pounding sunlight, the sour smell of hot asphalt under her feet. On the children's floor of the hospital, a whole platoon of doctors and therapists waited for her in their long, white, picture-ready coats. The head doctor on the case lectured about surgeries, using charts. His lab coat looked stiff and creased, as if it had just been taken out of a box. Samples of prosthetics had been laid out on a banquet table loosely covered by a long red tablecloth so that the display had the eerie feeling of an awards table, each flesh-colored appendage set apart and spotlighted from above.

"Where's Lan?" she finally asked.

"I thought you should see her progress first," the doctor said. He sulked at her lack of interest.

"How about I see her first," Helen said. "We'll talk after."

The room grew quiet, the doctor coughed into his hand. "Well then, let's go see her."

In a quick decision to brief her on the run, the woman psychologist walked alongside Helen. She was short and made a little skip every third step to keep up. Each time she spoke, she bit her lower lip as if the coming words might be bitter. They passed rooms filled with children. "Lan's by herself right now," she whispered. "She's had an aggression incident again with the other children." The woman narrowed her eyes so they disappeared in the flesh of her full cheeks. "That's not acceptable behavior. Biting."

"It wasn't ideal . . . her living conditions in Saigon."

"But we've saved her," the woman said.

"Actually *we're* the ones who hurt her."

The woman stroked her own cheek with a dimpled hand, as if the unpleasantness of Helen's words might bring on a rash.

At the end of the hall, she stopped and opened a door. At first the room appeared empty, but then Helen saw Lan sitting at a low table in the corner, shaping a ball of clay. The adults formed a semicircle around the table, but Lan acted as if she heard nothing, did not move her eyes from the clay figure in front of her. Impossible to believe she was the same girl from Saigon— now filled out with rounded arms and cheeks, glossy hair tied in ponytails with pink yarn, wearing a pink Cinderella T-shirt and pants.

"Lan?" Helen said. "Remember me?"

The girl looked up with a heavy, bored look, as if bracing herself for more unwanted attention. Helen moved closer, bent down to hug her. Her skin smelled sweet and medicinal, like cough syrup. Close-up, it was obvious that her face was bloated, her eyes dry and hard. Helen wondered what medications she was on. Lan's body remained limp in her arms.

Helen sat on a low plastic stool. The table was filled with toys, but Lan had attention for only the small ball of clay in her hands. She had the dull, listless behavior of an animal in the zoo. "You have a lot of toys," Helen said.

Lan grabbed her hand. "You bring me candy?"

Helen laughed, relieved at the shared memory. The doctors standing around them made her feel she needed to offer something up. "I brought her candy in Saigon."

Lan shook her head, impatient, with a sharp tilt of the chin. "Sam bring me candy. What you bring me now?"

"I came to take pictures again for the magazine."

Lan yawned. "I'm hungry."

The nurse stepped forward eagerly. "I'll bring you back some lunch, sweetie."

"I want hamburger," Lan said to her retreating back as the door swung shut.

Helen looked from Lan to the doctors. "Should we start taking pictures?"

"What are you giving me?" Lan shouted.

Behind her the doctors moved off, whispering and marking their clipboards. Under her breath, Lan began to sing a tune, the words getting louder until they could be clearly heard: " 'There was a little honey from Kontum/ Boy did she ever like boom, boom. . . .' "

"No," Helen said, bending down and hushing the girl. "Not in the hospital. Don't let them hear you." She felt a flush of parental embarrassment.

Lan shrugged and plucked at her hair, pulling out a few strands that she dropped on the floor.

"What do you want me to bring next time?" Helen said, figuring on bargaining with the child.

"A camera," she said. "Sam promised me a camera, and he lied and goes to die instead." The words froze Helen, and Lan noticed, becoming suddenly attentive. "He lied to you, too?"

"It was an accident, Lan. He didn't want to die."

"Mama says no accidents. I lose my leg because I was stupid girl."

"That's wrong. It wasn't your fault."

"I pick vegetables because they grow bigger and more easy than walking around to safe place."

"It was an accident."

The nurse came back carrying two cafeteria trays of food and put one down in front of each of them. She winked at Helen. "If you two finish your lunch maybe I can find you a dessert."

Lan's face turned red, her brow furrowed. "My mama's right. No accidents. You're stupid."

Helen took a deep breath, suddenly tired of the whole idea of the shoot, the effort too hard; she just wanted to escape from the girl's craziness. "You like America?" Helen asked, bending down and taking a camera out of its case.

"I want that camera."

"This is mine. I'll buy you your own."

"I want to go home. Why can't my parents visit?" Lan shoved the tray of food across the table, sending it flying over the edge and onto the floor. "I hate chicken. Lan is special girl, eat anything she want." She jerked herself sideways on her stool, grabbing for the crutches against the wall, moving so quickly she lost her balance and fell.

Helen made no move to help her, and when Lan looked up and saw her sitting back, she cried louder as the nurse rushed forward and kneeled next to her.

"Don't touch," Lan screamed. "No touch me."

Helen's face beaded with sweat; she couldn't breathe, the commotion bringing back the low, dark Red Cross room in Saigon, the close smell of urine and unwashed bodies.

Images clattered one after another in her head. Helen rose on unsteady legs as if rising from a heavy, drugged sleep. No matter what she did, she could not escape, that much was clear. Even a dangerous talent better than nothing.

She longed for cool air and quiet. Lan's screams grew louder, more out of control, but Helen saw only the wounded children of Saigon in front of her, laid out on their beds sardine-style, the little boy in the courtyard eating bougainvillea blossoms. The camera in her hand shook. Lan rocked on the floor with the doctors kneeling around her like a wounded soldier attended by medics. Helen grabbed her camera bag and ducked out the door.

In the hallway, the cries muffled, Helen leaned against a cartoon rabbit painted on the wall and closed her eyes.

The nurse came out. "Sorry about that. Today's a bad one."

"She's done this before?"

"Oh yeah. Back and forth. Shell shock for kids. Not pretty."

"She wasn't like that."

"You don't look so good yourself. Why don't you lie down, and I'll get a doctor."

"That's okay." Helen moved toward the elevator.

"Aren't you going to say good-bye?" the nurse said.

"I don't want to upset her," Helen mumbled as the elevator doors opened.

"I can tell her you're coming back, right?" the nurse shouted, but Helen was already gone.

Helen and her mother walked below their house with Duke, along the crescent of beach where she had grown up; in the sand she took her first steps in, stumbling into her father's arms; along the water where she and Michael spent innumerable summers building sand castles while their young mother sat and talked with the other mothers and prepared sandwiches and Kool-Aid for their lunches. They walked under the limestone cliffs, Duke's gold body weaving in and out of boulders, where Helen and teenage friends had burned bonfires late at night and talked and drank warm beer, the whole point to pair off and go into the dark, lie back in the cool embrace of sand and explore with lips and tongues and hands, to allow a first kiss, hands under a blouse, a bra to be unhooked, gentle kisses and quick straightenings, and then return to the group at the fire, and all that sweetness, all those boys smelling of shampoo that would later be transformed into the shapes of body bags. They walked in the late afternoon, the sun saffron-colored, and Helen's mother cried, her face punched-looking, pale and blotched, hands clutching.

"I forbid it. No," she said. "It isn't fair."

"But it's no good," Helen said. "I don't belong anywhere else right now."

"No!"

"I need to go," Helen said.

They walked past families having early dinners, small children and dogs running and chasing, Duke running and chasing, around picnic tables piled with food, people laughing and talking, the same people *they* used to be, and Helen stumbled, something sharp against her ankles, her balance upset, and without thought she was diving sideways, facedown, pitching over her shoulder in a combat roll into the sand, and when she looked up she saw it was a piece of line pulled taut to a fishing pole stuck at the water's edge, and two frightened little boys turned from their dinners, afraid they were in trouble, and because it wasn't a trip wire, because it was not an ambush with a mine or a grenade or death at the end, Helen lost her control, sobbed and screamed and pounded her hands into the sand that had cheated her, that had cheated all of them, and her mother froze, a premonition, she did not know this strange haunted woman at her feet, her movements as foreign as that far-off, floating, green country, and seeing with her own eyes the death of her little blond-haired girl who was as dead now as her son, she realized she had lost them all, she was powerless against this thing called Vietnam. The people at the picnic table stared, silent. A large-bellied man with a sandwich in his hand hesitated and reluctantly began to approach them, Duke with a ball in his mouth ran along the water, and the young mother ran to her two boys, pressing them into her hips, the reality of the war creeping up the sand, invading, at last coming home.

FIFTEEN

Hang Hum Noc Ran

Tiger Den and Snake Venom—A Place of Danger

November 1968

It was a prodigal's return. Helen arrived in Vietnam at night; as the plane approached the darkened runway of Tan Son Nhut, the lights on board blackened to avoid rocket or mortar attack. Blind, she could only feel the magnetic pull of the place, dragging her back to earth, and she suspected it had exerted itself, however faintly, all the way to California.

She stood in the open doorway of the plane, unable to see anything in the pitch-dark night of the tarmac, the air shrill with the sound of jet engines revving for night runs. The physical weight of the heat and humidity made her feel like a fish being released back into water. She breathed in deeply, and the scent that had teased her in the States came to her, forgotten and familiar, a third-world emanation of jungle and decomposition, garbage and dinner and unwashed skin mixed with the fumes of sewers, diesel, and rain. Home.

In the chaos of the airport stood Linh, unchanged, as if their months apart were nothing. Her relief to see him in the flesh, as if she dreaded that he, too, had become a ghost, was so great she dropped her bags and ran to hug him, kissing his cheek.

He pulled away, embarrassed, and looked around to see who might have been observing. She had forgotten too much already; all the difficulties and barriers to life in Saigon had disappeared from memory in her rush to return. Linh handed her the golden scarf.

She took it and wrapped it around her neck. "I missed it."

Linh shrugged. "It was always yours. It waited for your return."

"Good to be back." She tried to hide her disappointment at the formality between them. When she had wired him announcing her return, she took his answer that he'd pick her up as approval.

She saw there had been a change in him, his face more tired and drawn than she had ever seen it. The war had not stopped simply because she went away.

"Is it really good?" he asked, and picked up her bags.

"Believe it or not," she said. "It's more terrifying there than here."

"I don't understand," he said.

They rode into the city in silence with a new distance. Without the barrier of Darrow, the easy camaraderie between them strained. Helen was very aware of Linh as a man, and her former playful intimacy, up to the kiss she had just given him in public, embarrassed her. Clear that they had had a unique window of friendship because of Darrow, and this allowed her to know him in a way that would not have happened otherwise.

Things appeared smaller and dirtier and shabbier than she remembered. The car idled at the mouth of the alley in Cholon, dawn just beginning to lighten the edge of the sky, the first merchants stirring. They walked single file to avoid the large puddle, Linh ahead, carrying bags, until they reached the crooked apartment, its worn, stained stucco and tipped blue roof, the faded Buddha door. Helen stood in the alley and looked up, and her heart flooded at the sight of the red lamp in the window. A guilty pleasure like smoking a cigarette after months of abstinence. Her vision swam. Unreal to accept that Darrow was gone when she felt his presence here stronger than she had in months. Nothing was the same and yet a teasing that one could rewind time.

"Did you marry, Linh?"

He watched her face, not able to guess her feelings. "No." He stopped, but when she remained silent he continued. "Thao fell in love with a mechanic. They married last year. She is expecting a child."

"I'm sorry . . ."

"I'm happy for her."

Helen seemed far from him. So far he feared he'd never reach her; he half-expected that she would know the imagined conversations he had with her in the intervening months, the intimacy gained in his thoughts. "Sleep and I'll come by in the afternoon."

"Stay and let's talk—"

"It's better to rest, I think. Be patient. Good night."

At the press briefings, Helen was surprised how filled the room was, how many unknown faces. New journalists jockeyed for information and packed the restaurants and bars. She recognized a handful of veteran reporters, and when she caught their eye, they nodded, unsurprised by her return. For those who had the appetite, it was as simple as wanting to be where the action was. For the first time in months, Helen felt she was where she belonged. Doing what she was good at. Being at the source of history in the making and not reading about it in the paper. But she noticed there was no more talk at the parties and restaurants and briefings whether the war was being won or lost. It had ceased to be an issue.

When she first went back to the magazine's offices, Gary met her with a big hug and stony silence.

"Come on," she said.

"You weren't supposed to come back."

"I missed you too much."

"Liar."

"And Linh sent me a letter."

"Don't worry about Linh. He hasn't been exactly mooning around. He's my new star reporter."

"He didn't say anything."

"Things have changed. Be careful. It's getting uglier by the day."

Linh and Helen went out on patrol in the Bong Son. She could not wait to leave the hothouse of Saigon. Orders were delivered that she not shower with soap or shampoo, and not wear perfume. Ambushes had been discovered because the Vietnamese could smell the deodorized, scented Westerners from far away. That morning, in preparation, the platoon had purchased gallons of *nuoc mam,* fermented fish sauce, and amid laughter from Linh, they had smeared it all over the canvas parts of their gear and on their uniforms.

A nineteen-year-old PFC named Kirby slapped a big gob of it on Helen's back and rubbed it around. "If you'll allow me, ma'am."

Helen acted the good sport even though the smell sickened her and she'd have to throw away her tailor-made uniform afterward—no number of washings would get rid of the odor. "Aren't they going to be suspicious of a patch of jungle that reeks of fish sauce?" she asked. But she felt excited and alert for the first time in months, energized by the patrol; in her new confidence, the debilitating fear seemed vanished.

"Naw, after a few days we'll just smell like any other gook."

Helen looked to see if Linh had heard.

But instead of lessening, the odor of *nuoc mam* seemed to grow more rancid, more lingering. It rubbed off of the canvas and onto her skin, sank into her pores, until Helen was so overwhelmed it distracted her from the danger of walking patrol. Sweat reinvigorated the paste; it stuck in her throat and burned her eyes, permeated her hair like cigarette smoke until that, too, reeked.

Two days into the patrol they were deep in the jungle, hunkered down for the night under a canopy of umbrella trees. Hot meals and mail had been delivered earlier, and Kirby made his way over to Helen, who sat on a rock, staring at her serving of ham and beans.

"Not hungry?" he said. He had a slight frame and a sleepy expression; one could almost see the fear in him. "I'm hungry all the time."

"The fish smell makes everything taste bad," she said.

"If you're hungry enough, it doesn't matter."

"Want mine?" They sat in silence for a minute. "Get any mail?" she asked.

"From my parents."

"Miss home? I do."

"I hear you loud and clear," Kirby said, his face relaxed now as he settled back, resting his head in the crook of his arm, relieved at the shared acknowl-edgment of fear. "I dream of that plane ride home. Girls waiting to jump the war hero. People so grateful, they give me a parade. Life like one of those stupid commercials."

"It'll happen," Helen said, stirring at her dinner that now seemed more, not less, revolting. "You're one of the lucky ones."

He looked at her and crinkled his nose. "You're putting me on."

"No. Trust me." She did not want this new role, giving encouragement where it wasn't particularly warranted. She did not like knowing in advance the poor odds for a scared boy with no heart for danger.

"I can't exactly collect if you're wrong," he said.

She handed him her dinner. "You'll be on that plane."

Kirby studied her face for a moment and moved closer to her, and Helen smelled the strong odor of the *nuoc mam* mixed with something sweet like candy. He spoke in a low whisper.

"Can I tell you something personal?"

"Sure."

His face tightened. "That dream before was just a wet dream. I know it's not going to be like that. I worry . . ." He stopped talking for a moment and swallowed hard. "What if everything's changed? What if my parents are ashamed? What if I lose an arm or leg and my girlfriend goes off with one of those guys who thinks the war is a crock?"

Now she was the one scared. "You'll be lucky, lucky, lucky."

The next morning a fresh gallon of *nuoc mam* was opened with orders to swab down once more. They reached a supply road that showed signs of re-cent travel and set up an ambush. The renewed strength of the fish smell made her queasy; she couldn't get down her breakfast. She sought out Linh and together they curled behind a berm to wait. The lack of fear was a new experience, but she'd reached the point of being almost bored. After half an hour she decided to tie a handkerchief over her nose; she began to root around in her bag when a loud explosion went off to her left.

Her eyelids closed and behind them a bright flash exposed a pink-veined starfish shape. The vision had a floating calmness to it so that she did not want to immediately open her eyes.

The platoon around her rose to crouching positions, firing round after round into the surrounding jungle until the air was thick with the smell of fired weapons. The captain signaled for end fire, but it took another minute before the order was passed along, and another after that before the firing actually stopped. In the middle of the path they saw the body of a lone Viet Cong who had come up to the ambush and lobbed a single grenade.

"Put a hose in his mouth, he'd be one heck of a sprinkler, man," Kirby said.

Their cover blown, the captain radioed for an extraction. Helen, her ears still ringing, moved to get up when she felt a dull pain. She pushed up onto her knees and her head swayed hard to the left; a gush of warm liquid wet her lap. She reached down and gingerly touched her abdomen as the medic looked over.

"Oh," she said absentmindedly, as if she had misplaced something.

Compresses and bandages applied, she lay back in the dirt, aware of how quiet all the men were around her. She had felt so sure of her invincibility that day that it seemed a poor joke that she got injured. All the warnings she had heard over and over came into her head—the sight of a wounded woman demoralizing the men.

"I'm okay," she said to the medic. "Just a scratch. Cocktail time."

The morphine made its way through her limbs, cushioning and cottoning sensation. It frightened her to be so lucid about her surroundings and yet unable to care about the outcome. Her first time in-country she had been obsessed with getting hurt, but this time the possibility hadn't even occurred to her. In her grief she had felt immune. The hard jarring of the stretcher into the helicopter registered as pain, but too far away to have anything to do with her. The last thing she saw as they lifted off was Kirby's betrayed face. What kind of prophet couldn't predict her own demise?

Linh squeezed her hand, spooled back her attention like a kite that kept straining away. "You okay?"

"Bad luck," she said. "First time out."

"Just a scratch, I think," he said hopefully, but they both feared otherwise.

The initial surgery in the field hospital was a success, but that night she developed a fever, and by the next morning she was bleeding internally and was rushed back to surgery again, passing in and out of consciousness. All she remembered was waking up groggy in post-op, and the nurse shaking her head, saying it didn't need to happen like that, the surgeons were butchers who weren't used to operating on women. Later still, when she was more awake, the doctor came in and held her hand and said the hysterectomy had stopped the bleeding and saved her life; he wiped his face and said it had been a long night and then he left, and she was alone, listening to the clatter of incoming helicopters, the slow, labored breathing of the wounded in the beds around her.

When Linh came in, he bowed his head. "I'm sorry . . ." All the awkwardness between them since her return vanished.

"I survived." She forced herself to be nonchalant, not able to stand his pity.

"It should have been me."

"Much easier to be hurt rather than be the one watching it."

When she was strong enough to be moved, she transferred to the abdominal ward on the USS *Sanctuary* off the coast. The recovery took more than a month, the wound slow to heal. The doctors on the boat blamed the field hospital doctor, who cut too many muscles; the field doctor blamed the medic for not cleaning out the debris sooner. Linh visited every day. The smell of rotting flesh so pervasive in the ward that he took lemons aboard with him and cut them in half, holding them to his nose and squeezing juice on his hands before and after going in.

As soon as she was strong enough to leave, Gary and he took her home to the apartment in Cholon. It would have been easier to stay at the Continental, but she insisted on the quiet of those rooms.

"What you see in this dive, I don't know," Gary complained. "I'll have to have meals sent from the hotel."

Linh and Helen looked at each other and laughed.

"What's so funny?"

"Everyone knows this is the center of the universe."

———————

Linh had a single shelf of books given to him by Darrow. In her confine-
ment, Helen pulled down a volume, the cover splayed, the pages swollen and
wavy with humidity. She read at random, her concentration shaky, following
Darrow's scribbling in the margins and his underlined passages. In Tacitus
she found:

> Fear and terror there certainly are, feeble bonds of attachment; re-
> move them, and those who have ceased to fear will begin to hate. All
> the incentives to victory are on our side. The Romans have no wives to
> kindle their courage; no parents to taunt them with flight; many have
> either no country or one far away. Few in number, dismayed by their
> ignorance, looking around upon a sky, a sea, and forests which are all
> unfamiliar to them; hemmed in, as it were, and enmeshed, the Gods
> have delivered them into our hands. . . . In the very ranks of the en-
> emy we shall find our own forces.

She closed the book quickly. This was the way she dealt with books now,
plunging in and out of passages as if they were glacial rivers too cold to be
endured long. She could not imagine reading a book from cover to cover, the
idea of narrative old and quaint, like a tea cozy in this new fractured world.

This was not a book she would have chosen; to Darrow such a book had
still seemed valid.

But something in the passage made her think not about the obvious anal-
ogy to the American soldiers, but instead about Linh; since her return she
found herself wondering about him often, speculating. Wasn't Linh without
wife or family, except for the brief, mysterious appearance of Thao? What
had happened? He never spoke of them, although Helen left many opportu-
nities when she told about her own family. Linh was in his own country, but
he was not part of that brick wall. Where, she wondered, was his heart? How
did one reconcile being on one side, then the other? What went through his
head on patrol when American soldiers distrusted him? Or worse, when they
tortured Vietnamese? Didn't he still have more in common with a fellow

countryman, even if he was the enemy, than he did with them? What did he feel when he heard *gook* and *slant-eye*? Whose victory, finally, would constitute winning for Linh? Maybe the only real victory for any of them— peace.

When he walked through the door with dinner, she turned and moved away guiltily, dropping the book, as if she had been caught doing something private and self-indulgent.

Each day Linh brought something to interest Helen. One day, a smelly durian like ripe cheese, the next a box of incense, then a lacquered river stone. She took a childish delight in the new, waited eagerly for it. He brought a re-cord of classical Vietnamese music, which they listened to each evening. One night, they were playing cards, and Helen said she was tired.

"Would you like to sleep?"

"Tell me a story."

And so Linh began with all the fairy tales he had grown up with. When he ran out of those, he brought the epic poem *The Tale of Kieu,* and trans-lated it to her a page at a time, explaining this was the most beloved of all Vietnamese tales. During these weeks, they began to understand each other in a way that had not been available to them before. Without telling her, one night Linh read aloud the play he had written for himself and Mai, the last one they performed together. When he finished, Helen held still for a moment.

"That was so beautiful—what was it called?"

"It's not well known."

"Who wrote it?"

He hesitated. "I did."

"I had no idea you could write."

"Before . . . I dreamed of being a playwright."

Helen nodded. "You would have been a fine one. You can still be."

"Those things are unimportant during war."

"Maybe that's when they're most important."

"Maybe."

"Do you have other stories?"

For the first time, Linh brought out the writings he had worked on, off and on, starting with the spiral notebook Darrow had given him in Angkor. Each night, they ate dinner, then Helen waited to hear more. Linh had not felt such intoxicating attention in a very long while. When the stack of pages grew thin, he began composing again. In this way, he came back to his real life.

After a month, she had recovered sufficiently to stay alone. Linh went for longer periods to check assignments downtown. One day, although he left her with food—sweetened rice and fresh oranges and pomelo—she longed for a spicy, hot bowl of *pho.* At the hospital she had endured a diet consisting solely of bland starchy foods, Jell-O and mashed potatoes. As she lay in bed hour after hour, the thought of the clear, pungent broth obsessed, and she was convinced that one bowl of it would bring back her strength.

She did not want to admit that the real reason for her planned assault on the *pho* stand might be that she did not want to be alone with her thoughts. The injury and the hysterectomy had happened so quickly, and she had not dealt with the aftermath. She had hoped eventually to have children in the distant future. Now the option had been taken away. She avoided writing to her mother with the news, showing what she had done to their family's future. But that mourning seemed indulgent when so many lives were being lost all around her, so many children, so many mothers and fathers. Her own pain slight in the ocean of grief all around her.

Helen dressed carefully, the pain in her belly a stab each time she moved. Using a cane, she slowly climbed step-by-step down the two buckling flights of stairs. When she was halfway down, it was obvious the trip was a mistake, but sheer will pushed her to continue, like a soldier carrying out an order, the most important thing not to admit defeat. Sweat beaded her forehead, and her legs wobbled, threatening to go out from under her. She gripped the cane tighter, rested against the wall. Now she could get in real trouble, fall and break a leg and be stranded for hours. The painkillers had worn off, but she had resisted taking more, worried about dizziness until she returned from her journey. Her plan was to swallow a pill when she was back in bed with a stomach full of soup. Panting, she braced herself on each step until finally she reached the Buddha door at the bottom.

From the dim stairwell, she noticed for the first time that the wood at the back of the door was black with oxidation; one of the panels had a hairline split through which sunlight showed. From outside the door had appeared sound, unbroken, and it was only her unlimited time that allowed her to notice this.

On the street, the heat and sunlight stranded her again, but at least she could shuffle along the even ground. By the time she made her tortured way through the alley and onto the main thoroughfare where the soup stall was, her whole body was shaken by tremors of pain and fatigue.

The soup vendor recognized her, patted the empty stool, and made soup the way Helen liked, with plenty of chilies and soy sauce, but when she handed over the bowl, Helen hunched over, rocking, and could only shake her head.

The old woman studied her face for a moment, then barked out orders to her young nephew who worked for her. He took off at a run.

Half an hour later, the boy reappeared in a cab. Linh jumped out, leaving the back door hanging open, the driver unpaid, and ran behind the soup stall to where Helen was curled on a mat, under the shade of the vendor's umbrella. Kneeling down, he placed his hand on her forehead.

"Are you okay?"

"Dizzy. I shouldn't have gone down. . . ."

"Can you sit up?"

Helen moved delicately, fearing she had ruptured something inside, the effort making her grind out her words as her forearms gave out, and she slipped back down, a black wave coming over her, threatening, then receding.

"Can you put your arms around my neck?"

Pulling herself up, she made the effort to concentrate on Linh's face. She nodded. Lifting her as if she were broken, he carried her down the alley. Helen laid her head on his shoulder, her hair winding around his wrist.

The body, he knew, has a memory all its own. The shape of a baby in one's arms will be imprinted forever, the cup of a lover's chin. The weight of Helen in Linh's arms broke his heart open. He wished the journey back to the apartment was ten times, a hundred times as long, wished that he could walk with the weight of her in his arms all day and all night and still keep walking. To repeat the journey of that night until it ended with a different outcome. He would gladly die walking for that, and he knew this desire was wrong, but kept looking down at her face.

With the snap of a grimy plastic sheet over the counter, the old woman declared her stall closed; she, the boy, and the cab driver, who shut off his car and took the keys, walked ahead, yelling at people to step aside. The boy was caught up in the drama; the old woman was scandalized; the cabdriver wanted to get paid. When they reached the building, the old woman opened the Buddha door and followed them up the two flights although her bad leg kept her from climbing any faster than Linh under his burden.

When he laid Helen down on the mint green bedspread, the old woman shooed him away and drew the curtain between the rooms, changing Helen's clothes and washing her face. Men had no place there, even if this was one of those loose Western women.

Linh went to the door and paid off the driver, in his worry forgetting to tip until the driver reminded him. Half an hour later, the pain pills in effect and Helen resting, the old woman got up to leave. Linh offered her money, which she refused.

Helen turned her head, sleepy. *"Cam on ba. Chao."* Thank you, Grand-mother. Good-bye.

The old woman broke out into a black-toothed smile and asked Linh, *"Co ay biet noi tieng Viet khong?"* Can she speak Vietnamese?

"Da biet, nhung khong kha lam," Helen answered. Yes, but not too well.

Grandmother shook her head in amazement and told her nephew to go run for some tea. "I have to read your fortune, daughter."

Linh frowned. He wanted to be alone with his new feelings, not stuck with some superstitious old woman. "Not now. She's tired. Anyway, she doesn't believe in that hocus-pocus."

"It's okay," Helen said. "Let her."

Grandmother looked at him in triumph. "She might be a foreigner, but she is wiser than some who were born here." She stared around the bedroom as she waited, and saw a plate on the dresser that held earrings and necklaces.

After the tea had been poured, Helen watched as the old woman took her cup and studied the insides, frowning, then went to the window and threw the contents into the courtyard below. "There is someone who loves you. You must be careful his love doesn't cause this person harm."

Helen, her mind drifting, said nothing.

"I told you it's all nonsense," Linh said. He turned to Grandmother. "Let's give her some quiet to sleep now."

"No, she's right," Helen said. "Maybe for Westerners their fortune is only clear after the fact. Backward."

"This nonsense keeps this country backward."

"Toi di." I'm going. She glared at Linh. He was a tricky one, but she wasn't afraid of him in spite of the rumors of powerful connections with both Viet Cong and the drug lord Bao.

"Xin loi ba," Helen called. *"Ten ba la gi?"* What is your name?

"Thua, ten toi la Suong. Ba Suong." Grandmother said something to Linh that Helen couldn't understand, and he chuckled, exasperated, as he shepherded her out the door.

"What did she say?"

"She said she is Grandmother Suong, who will bring your *pho* every day so you won't break your neck going down the stairs."

Each day after that, true to her word, Grandmother made the journey down the alley and up the stairs herself; her nephew carried a lidded container of soup while she carried a newspaper sleeve of flowers she got from a niece who worked in the market. Everyone heard the story of the American woman who risked her life for a bowl of Suong's *pho,* and no matter how long she took visiting, there would be a line of people waiting for her return. Business had never been better. Some fool had even started the rumor that the *pho* had a medicinal herb that returned fertility and that was why the American had wanted it so badly. Business was booming, so much so that she considered opening another stall a few blocks away to handle the overflow. Fate worked in mysterious ways.

She sat for a moment in the chair by the open window, her legs spread far apart in their loose pajamas, her calloused feet dusty in sandals. Helen and she exchanged the same few sentences that they shared, always receiving them as if new. Grandmother was insulted by tips above the price of the soup but was not averse to occasional gifts of packs of American cigarettes.

She fingered the necklaces on the plate on the dresser, holding them against her neck in the mirror. Once, when Helen was looking away, the old woman considered pocketing a thin gold chain, but at that moment Helen turned and offered her the necklace if she liked it. Perhaps this one was only American on the outside, Vietnamese on the inside, like people said. Grandmother quickly put the necklace down, almost ashamed. It was a reflex, mostly, a bad habit, taking advantage of foreigners.

On the days when Linh was away, Grandmother heated up water for a pot of tea, poured the cup, and allowed Helen to handle it. Each time she frowned over the contents, the fortune always the same.

"No, no, I want to know the *future*, not the past," Helen said.

Grandmother nodded. "Will be."

"But the man who loved me died."

The old woman shrugged and got up to leave. "Is. Now."

When Linh returned to the apartment and found Grandmother's flowers, his face froze. He grabbed them up out of their vase and threw them out the window.

"What are you doing?" Helen asked.

"Makes me sneeze."

Helen said nothing. The next day when Grandmother came, she stopped and stared at the scattered flowers on the courtyard brick. The day after, she brought yellow paper flowers, which Helen stuck in a bottle next to her bed. Linh spotted them as soon as he walked in. He grabbed the blossoms, crushing the paper, and then tossed them in the coal brazier and set them on fire with matches.

"Don't tell me you're allergic to paper," she said.

"Tell her to stop bringing them," he said, his face grim. "Never mind, I'll tell her myself."

"Give me a hint what's going on? What's wrong with flowers?"

He stubbed out the last of the ashes. "You wouldn't understand. It's a Vietnamese thing."

"That's what you always say."

"Ask me something else."

Helen sat back in bed and thought. Her face lit up with a sly smile. "There are jokes about you working with Ho Chi Minh. That you are some kind of spy and that's where you disappear to. That horrible man I've seen you with, Mr. Bao. Where do you go?"

"It's complicated," he finally answered.

"Make it simple."

"Sometimes one's past makes it harder to understand the present. I love Americans, but I don't know if they are good for the Vietnam people. I want them to stay and to leave at the same time." Linh took a deep breath, then shook his head. How could he make her see? His relationship with her, with all the Americans, genuine and false. He had wanted her to leave and had lured her to come back. That division inside him the same as his father's uneasy relationship with the French. How could she understand? Even through all her hardship, she still saw the world through privilege. How could she know how it felt to be on the outside? Especially in one's own country? That the Americans, in their optimism, had backed the wrong side. A side that could not hold without them.

After Helen recovered enough to return to work, Gary assigned her to do another follow-up on Lan, who had been sent back to her family. She had avoided seeing the girl, but now bought bolts of cloth and cooking pots, the most valuable commodities other than food, for the family. She pushed away the thought that these were bribes. For Lan, she got a simple automatic camera with lots of film. The plan started to form in Helen's mind of bringing

the child to live in the crooked apartment in order to be close to medical services and schools. During the war, it was common for families to farm out
children to those who could offer help.

Linh didn't approve of her traveling in the countryside; he worried it would
be too difficult physically. He argued with Gary about the assignment, and
Gary looked at him in surprise but said nothing. He had not realized Linh was
so far gone. "You're not responsible for her anymore. It's up to her to go or not.
You or her, doesn't matter to me who covers it. People made donations, they
want follow-up." When Helen was determined to go, Linh gave in.

He sulked on the plane ride. "You answer a question now. Why do you
push to do this?"

Helen was tired of his interrogating her. "It gives me a reason to get up in
the morning, are you satisfied? And yes, it has to be me. A woman sees war
differently."

They made their way to the family's village in Quang Nam province, only
to find it had been burned down. The military didn't have records of the clearing. Linh discovered the village's name only by accident, walking through the
charred remains of houses when he stumbled upon a small wooden sign in
Vietnamese staked into the ground—THIS IS WHERE QUANG BA VILLAGE WAS.

During the last year all Linh saw was his country being destroyed, faster
and faster, in larger and larger bites. He couldn't explain to Helen the sense
of physical sickness it gave him, the sense of despair. The desperate idea that
anything that stopped this destruction was better than its continuing. What
she didn't understand was that both sides were willing to destroy the country
to gain their own ends. Whose side was he on? Whoever's side saved men,
women, animals, trees, grass, hillsides, and rice paddies. The side that saved
villages and children. That got rid of the poisons that lay in the earth. But he
did not know whose side that was.

When they contacted MACV in Danang, they were directed to a reloca-
tion center the villagers had been sent to. After another day's jeep ride along
rutted roads, Helen stood, dusty and aching, in front of a wired-in prison—
villagers from different locations herded together, living on the open ground

under a tarp after more than two months. Without work, they queued each day for food handouts from the military.

No record of Lan's family, but after walking through the sections that had self-segregated into their original villages, Linh found a neighbor of the family. For a few dollars he whispered to Linh that they had fled early, not trusting the American military, and moved to the next province, Quang Ngai. "They were smarter than I was," he said. "They said nothing is for free."

Over a period of a week, Linh and Helen traveled from hamlet to hamlet, driving along bumpy roads, each day ending with no luck. At times, they heard wisps of the truth, at times lies—the family were Viet Cong and had disappeared into the north; the girl had magically grown a new leg; the girl had died; the mother had run off—each new rumor seeping into the last until their heads were as dusted with possibilities as with the dirt that blew across the valley and plain each afternoon.

"What is the difference?" Linh asked. "This is just one more girl."

She didn't answer that it was because the child had mattered to Darrow. But it was also something else. As the war grew larger, her sense of futility grew with it. Since coming back, she had been unable to focus her experience except by narrowing it down to one soldier at a time, one child, one village. This was how she could tell their story.

As the search prolonged, the rough travel and poor food weakened her. Gary, troubled at the delays, called them back to Saigon, telling them to give up, but she refused. She leaned on Linh's knowledge of the country to unravel the truth. Tell me, her eyes pleaded, as one more villager began yet another story, what to believe in and what to ignore.

Linh worried what would happen if they didn't find the girl; he also began to worry if they did.

At a roadside tea stand along Highway 1, he gossiped with a man about his punctured bicycle tire, only to find out he was a cousin of Lan's mother. He told them to go to a village an hour south. It seemed there was a falling-out in the family over money. They drove to the village and after asking around, Linh discovered that the biggest, most lavish house belonged to Lan's family.

When they knocked on the door, a young girl holding a broom greeted them. Lan's mother was out on business and the father was busy holding a meeting in the dining room. They were told to wait. As they sat on a bench in the courtyard, a dozen people came in and out on errands. After half an hour, the father strode out, a short, bowlegged man with the rough hands of a farmer, and shook Linh's hand.

"We'd like to interview Lan," Linh said.

"Fine, fine. But there will be . . . gift?"

"We have things to distribute." Linh waved his hand across the house. "You are doing well."

The father looked at the house, puffing his lips. An expensive gold watch hung loosely from his wrist. "Hard work. Very busy. The girl will take you to Lan."

He left, and the girl with the broom came back, took the cloth and pots from Helen, then led them to a back room. Lan sat on the floor with a stack of dolls. Other girls sat around her, wearing plain clothing, but Lan sat in a shiny satin dress, a black patent leather shoe on her one good foot. Her prosthetic was nowhere in sight.

"Lan," Helen said.

The girl looked up, puzzled. She had grown fat, and the satin of the dress stretched across her stomach

"Remember me? Helen?"

The girl nodded. "You never bring camera."

"I did today."

The girl's face brightened. "Let's see."

Helen pulled it out and handed it to her, but after a quick look, Lan put it down, unimpressed.

The servant girl came and brought soft drinks and peanut butter spread on crackers. Lan's parents had used the money from the magazine, plus donations that came in, to start several businesses and were thriving on the black-market economy. When Linh asked about the relatives in the camps, the servant girl whispered that the parents got angry when they had come with outstretched hands.

After they finished the soda and crackers, Helen asked Lan to put on her prosthetic so they could take pictures outside; the girl answered there wasn't one.

"Why not?"

"The old one hurt," Lan said.

"No one have time to go to Saigon," the servant girl whispered. "She's grown too big."

"People bring me things now," Lan said. "Much better." After pictures were taken, Lan grew bored and returned to her game with the other girls. She didn't bother saying good-bye.

As they packed their equipment in the jeep, the father reappeared. "You get good picture?"

"Yes," Linh said. "Many thanks."

"I know other children with problem. More pictures."

Linh, red-faced, shoved the last bags in.

They drove in silence. A convoy ahead of them stopped, the road had washed out; at least an hour before traffic moved again. They turned off the motor, left the jeep in its queue of vehicles. At the edge of the road, a farmer plowed the rice paddy that abutted the ditch. As a reflex, Helen took pictures—it would be decades before the market needed more scenic shots. Maybe decades from then, these pictures would be historical, like the ones hanging in her bedroom, showing a vanished world.

Linh stood off to the side, his hands in his pockets.

"I wanted to rescue her," Helen said. "Rescue fantasies. I needed to rescue her."

"She wasn't yours to save."

"Of course not." She wasn't Darrow's, either. He had been just as naive, thinking that Lan would give him meaning after all these years of feasting on war. No, better to just kick out all the props, to be clear-eyed about one's reasons for being there.

Linh shrugged. "When my father was a young boy, the French wanted the people to forget their country. They taught us that our ancestors, the Gauls, had blue eyes. Now we forget with gold watches and peanut butter."

They stared in silence at the rice paddy, the late-afternoon sun sending sparks off the water, the farmer and the water buffalo gone home.

"My mother told me," Linh said, "if I got up very early in the morning before everyone else and went down to the rice paddy, I would hear the hum of rice growing. The women sing a *ca dao,* a work song:

> *For a single grain of rice*
> *So tender and scented*
> *In your mouth . . .*
> *What effort and bitterness!*

Helen stretched. "I'm taking you out for a big dinner when we get back to Saigon." She had felt ashamed at Lan's house, so obvious that the American's beneficence simply corrupted.

Linh began to refuse but stopped when he saw her look of disappointment. After their intimacy during her illness, he didn't know how to act with Helen in public. He didn't know what to do with this woman.

"Good. It's settled," she said.

He smiled, at a loss.

"Where do you want to go?"

"I am thinking I would like to sit at the Continental and drink a very cold gin and tonic and eat a club sandwich."

On assignment as part of a "pink team," a hunter/killer helicopter team, Helen and Linh squeezed together in the observer seat of a tiny Loach on their way to join Cobra gunships going out on a mission. The pilot was early and asked if they wanted to run a little "scenic recon," a joyride through the mountains along the Laos border.

"The two of you together aren't as heavy as the gunman." The pilot laughed, finding the idea especially hilarious that morning.

They sat pinned against each other, the front of the helicopter a bubble floating over the land, nothing blocking their view but the metal floor and control panel. The razored mountaintops tangled in fog. The observation helicopter hung, birdlike, over trees and wrapped itself between rocky peaks plunging hundreds of feet into narrow ravines, dark even at noon. They hovered over giant waterfalls, bamboo thickets, hardwood forest, broadleaf jungle, all interlaced with small, jewel-like fields of elephant grass. In an hour, the only human they spotted was a lone Montagnard tribesman.

Helen's eyes hurt from the strain of searching for movement in a sea of green, the ride so vivid it was like a dream of flying, a magic carpet ride. Trees flew beneath her feet. The rush of green and sunlight lulled her, the pilot pulling up and the machine shuddering against gravity. She had a vision then, an infinity of green, her body tingling with heat despite the cool air in the helicopter. She burned and closed her eyes.

Linh, sitting next to her, scanned the terrain through binoculars. He placed his hand over hers, then gave her the glasses and pointed to a rocky cliff. "See, Helen? Come back now," he said in her ear above the roar of the engine.

As she focused the glasses on the dirt track under the cliff, a tiger stepped out into full view. The orange and black stripes burned against her eyes after the torrent of green. The animal stood calm, detached, eyeing the land below him. Only total isolation would give him the arrogance of ignoring the pounding machine overhead. He stood for another moment, head lifted, testing the air, as the helicopter swung around to pass over him, the pilot maneuvering for a closer sight line, his hand reaching for the M16 at his feet, but in a single flex of movement the animal stretched, his body attenuated long and thin, a wisp of smoke blown away, and the rock ledge was empty.

"Damn, did you see that?" the pilot shouted, elated.

Helen smiled at the pilot and looked ahead, but what she felt was the brief second Linh's hand had covered her own. Like a single jolt of electricity. He was right. She had been far away, closed off, but now she could see. She leaned and whispered, "I'm here with you now."

SIXTEEN

Tay Nguyen

Western Highlands

The war changed, and she was changed within it.

A major battle was mounting in the Dak To valley area in the Central Highlands, the same area that had seen horrific battles years earlier in the war. A paratrooper squadron that Helen had covered several times before had been defeated, and now infantry companies were being sent up to fight entrenched enemy positions.

Rumors were that the handful of remaining soldiers had called down strikes on their own position, hoping that if they missed a direct hit, they might escape in the chaos.

To Gary she insisted on covering the story—they were her soldiers and her area—but when she went to the bathroom afterward, she could not stop her hands from shaking. Foreknowledge a curse.

"You don't have to go," Linh said.

"I want to. The soldiers don't get to choose." What she meant was that she *needed* to, that the tension she felt was the thing she had been missing in California. That adrenaline coursing through her.

"You've already proved you're brave."

"Every good war picture is an antiwar picture. Why am I here otherwise?" She laughed at Linh. "Stop worrying. Anyway, I've become one of the charmed, haven't you heard?"

The Vietnamese called them the Tay Nguyen, the Western Highlands, because in their minds they still saw the country as a whole, not accepting the artificial divisions of north and south.

Names were important.

Names, finally, were the only thing the Vietnamese had left. For a whole period of history, Vietnam existed only on the tip of someone's tongue, forbidden to be said out loud.

Geography became power.

Names given to pieces of land or sea or mountain told who was in control. The Vietnamese were irritated by the Americans' sense of place. Especially irksome was the name South China Sea, locating their Eastern Sea in relation to their traditional enemy, China. Another irritant, the Far East—far east in relation to what? They had had this problem before.

The French referred to the Highlands as the Hauts Plateaux, a sensible descriptive name for the plateau stretching from the southern border of North Vietnam to within a hundred miles of Saigon, from a thin strip of cultivable land on the east to the fierce mountains of the Annamese Cordillera. Annamese another slap in the face—a French colonial fantasy meant to obliterate the original Vietnam. They called their mountains the Truong Son. Why, they asked, should Vietnamese use foreign words to rename their own land?

Helen had her own geographies. She knew the land by its colors—the Mekong always greens and golds and blues, the light soft, opaque from the water on the earth and in the air. Soldiers inevitably covered with dirt, the dirt of the delta heavily mixed with clay along the waterways so that it dried whitish on the faces and bodies of both the living and the dead. The Central Highlands were a land of chiaroscuro, sharp shadows, subtle gradations so that green could range from black to the most delicate shade of moss. Forests of browns and blacks, hardwood torn up by B-52s, moonscape tracts of gray, uprooted trunks and roots creating surreal sculpture. The soil a deep, rich laterite red that rouged uniforms and faces of the soldiers and faded over time to the rusted color of dried blood.

Her geographies, too, were full of dangerous curves and valleys; she had to remain constantly in flight, never alighting in one place too long, never putting weight on the crust of the earth that might give way. A line from Tacitus was continually in her mind: *In his sorrow he found one source of relief in war.*

They made their way up on ammunition drops and convoys until they reached field headquarters in a dusty, barren valley in the foothills. The press tent was in chaos, and in the command tent radio reports came in that helicopter after helicopter was being shot down. No evacuations in the last twenty-four hours. Calculations had ammunition on top of the hill running out by morning.

Infantry companies would go on foot through the jungle and fight their way to the pinned-down men. The surrounding hills echoed with NVA regiments, a nonstop barrage of weaponry.

Food was served to the departing soldiers but because of conflicting departure orders, they got a mix of breakfast and lunch. The men piled the food up on their plates, carrots against scrambled eggs, prime rib coupled with pineapple cake and grits. All fuel, it seemed like a good idea to fill the belly, another armor to survive. The food flown in that morning cheered up the young, scared faces; they took it as a demonstration of their value. Helen grew queasy at the sight of the bounty, knowing the perversity of military thinking, that the best food was reserved for the doomed. Literal last meals, but even with that knowledge, Helen chewed her food, not tasting, but sure that days or even hours from then, the idea of not eating would torment her. She chose to be full only in order to have the issue of hunger not interfere.

When Helen made her request to accompany one of the relief companies, the PIO flatly denied her. "This is critical stuff. Way too dangerous to allow a woman."

"I've covered these companies before—"

"Don't bother. I can't spare a man to escort you."

"I've been covering combat for two years—"

He made a long, sour face. "Regulations."

"Not for me. I covered this area in—"

"Regulations, understand?"

"—in 'sixty-six, before you even knew where Vietnam was."

"We don't need a dead woman."

From behind her, she heard a loud voice and felt a heavy hand clap down on her shoulder. "Helen Adams."

She turned and came face-to-face with Captain Olsen. Unchanged from two and a half years before, as if that dreary day in the Mekong were only yesterday.

"You must have made a deal with the devil," she said. "You look younger than when I last saw you."

"Just a little malaria and desk work."

"I went out with your replacement, Horner."

"That was a cursed mission. A damned shame."

Helen didn't mention Samuels, but he didn't need mentioning. She could see the responsibility for it in Captain Olsen's eyes. No Dorian Gray after all.

"This man here"—Helen pointed at the PIO—"is denying me clearance. My company is already moving out."

"Lowen, you giving this girl a hard time?"

"He said I'd be demoralizing dead."

"A real lady's man, huh? This is the girl who made me a hero. The eight-hundred-pound gorilla of picture takers. Let her have what she wants."

The PIO made a face. "Go. Get a .45."

"I won't carry a weapon," Helen said.

The PIO paused, his face scrunched up. "If she's your friend, I'd brief her."

Captain Olsen took Helen's arm and moved off toward the mess. Helen motioned Linh over. "I want to cover this," she said.

Olsen nodded and shook Linh's hand. "Lowen's an ass, but he's right on this one. Things are bad up there. Take the gun."

Helen shook her head.

"Serious. No one is going to help you up there."

"I'll carry it," Linh said.

When they came back, the PIO was smoking a cigarette.

"Smoking's bad for you," Helen said.

"If we're carrying weapons," Linh said, "I want an M16 *and* the .45."

The PIO turned red. "Shit, I don't believe this." He glared at Olsen, who ignored him. "You ever shot one of these?"

Linh didn't hesitate. "Many times."

Hours later, climbing from dense jungle to hardwood forest then back to jungle, they reached the base of the mountain at dusk. They squatted in place along the path, Helen resting her back against a tree. Usually, they'd set camp for the night, but time was essential; in the morning there might not be anyone left. Artillery barrages and air strikes on the surrounding hills deafened them; ground shook as they climbed over fallen trees blocking the narrow, steep dirt path.

As they approached the crest where the company was pinned down, parachute flares illuminated the landscape in an eerie light. As far as the eye could see, trees splintered and burned, a whole forest of devastation. Heavy smoke forming a fog. The flare died into a deeper, more eerie darkness.

As the company marched the final distance of several hundred yards in the dark they passed fallen logs, singly, then in clusters, then in mounds, discovering to their horror in the illumination of another flare the shapes were not logs but bodies. Stripped of uniforms, boots, weapons, resembling splayed and disfigured trees.

In the middle of the night, the relief company stumbled the last few feet to reach the Americans occupying a small circle of abandoned enemy bunkers. Out of a force of more than a hundred, only a dozen men remained. They had been without food for a day, strung out along the shallow forward observation bunkers.

After they briefed the new troops, the men devoured rations, then fell asleep on the bunker floor. One of the men, grimy faced, still held a spoon as he slept. Helen attached a flash and took his picture. Another picture of the sign made from the top of an ammo crate at the bunker entrance: WELCOME TO HELL.

A black soldier, PFC Simmons, stood next to Helen. "Looks like we're none too early."

"They hung them out, sending them up here alone," she said.

"Then what about us, lady?" he asked.

Nothing for Helen and Linh to do until daylight but sit and wait, the air rotten with the smell of bodies in the woods around them, smoke from the fires dotting the surrounding hills. Her eyes stung. She tried to wash them out with water, but it was no use, so she closed them and tried to rest, pressing against the damp dirt wall of the bunker. She dozed through the night, grabbing fistfuls of minutes, only to be startled awake by the slamming of rockets, the hiss of metal shards driven into whatever they came into contact with, the overhead dirt roof slowly trickling down on them.

After several hours, she slid down until her head was in Linh's lap, and he placed his hand over her ear to muffle the sound so that although she still could hear the barrages, the noise was distanced by the thickness of one hand. His cupped palm gave her the buzz of blood, the pulse of the ocean, the childish certainty that nothing could happen to her while she was protected in this way.

At four in the morning the frequency of the mortars increased, and a sergeant ordered Helen and Linh to move to the deeper back bunkers. Unfamiliar with the area aboveground, they asked to take their chances and stay put, but the sergeant wouldn't argue the point.

They crouched and scuttled across the broken, debris-strewn ground. The opening was supposed to be only ten feet from the observation bunker, but they traveled at least thirty feet until they ran into the tree line. They retraced their way back and veered to the left, finding a larger entrance than the sergeant described, but the shriek of incoming made the decision for them. Helen threw herself onto the ground inside, Linh at her back, the fall of several feet knocking the wind out of her while a mortar exploded twenty yards away. Underneath, in the darkness, she felt something smooth and clammy and realized she was sinking into human flesh.

Helen jumped, taking her chances outside rather than trapped in the ground. She doused herself with her remaining water, took her soiled shirt off over her T-shirt. She huddled against a low wall of sandbags. Mortars rang in her ears, strangling sound, and she could make out Linh's words only when he came close.

"Go back." He pointed to the observation bunker.

Nervous tears ran down her face. She couldn't stop them although she didn't feel afraid, didn't feel anything at all. The constant bottoming fear of being hurt or worse gone. But the biggest danger was after the fear left. She yelled at Linh, "Go ahead. I'm better out here."

He sat down next to her, and she shook her head, pushing at him to go away, but he stayed at her side. Later, when she calmed down, they crawled to another empty bunker for the rest of the night. The shelling continued until dawn. At first light they made their way back the observation bunker. The sergeant took a look at Helen and handed her his cup of lukewarm coffee made with a packet of instant and a heat tab.

Half an hour later, in the gray foggy light of morning, she saw American soldiers approaching through the trees. The sergeant took out his binoculars. Helen felt relief that the ordeal was over; her head dull, she felt something was wrong, but still no fear. Linh said the soldiers were coming from the wrong direction, not from the trail they had used. The sergeant trained his binoculars through the fog. When the soldiers were less than fifty yards away, Helen saw a lead soldier raise his machine gun. Her thoughts slowed. She felt cool and divorced from what was happening in front of her. Maybe the soldiers thought that Vietnamese were in the bunkers? The soldier opened fire, a spray of bullets, and Helen frowned, unable to comprehend the sight before her eyes. The sergeant screamed words to the other men in the bunker who opened fire on the men walking through the trees.

When the fog burned off, B-52s dropped canisters of napalm that set the surrounding hills on fire, the sky swirled gray and blue. Next came gunships, and this time they were able to get in and out unharmed. They had either broken the enemy or he had retreated.

Helen stood outside the bunker, looking at the area that she had only been able to grope her way through in the dark. In the white light of fog and smoke, she could make out the charred remains of trees and bodies. She brought her camera up to her eye, a relief. She followed the soldiers through the trees and took pictures of the dead Vietnamese in American uniforms. Those wounded lying silent, uncomplaining, resigned to their fate. Not expecting any help. Helen was struck by the foreignness of this reaction, the extreme capacity for hardship, and she couldn't help feeling a disagreeable respect. The Americans hated the enemy's willingness to use civilians, to dress in the enemy's uniforms, and yet playing by conventional rules would have lost the war.

American soldiers crawled out from beneath the ground, faces lean and dark, eyes like sharp knives from being afraid too long, uniforms molded to their bodies, patinaed by sweat and dirt. As they stretched stiff, cramped bodies and moved through camp, they grew more animated until Helen captured a shot of two soldiers lobbing a C-ration can like a football, a moment of relief at surviving the night.

She walked the camp and took pictures, simply a matter of composition and aperture and shutter speed. This was a bigger battle, with more casualties than she had ever before witnessed, and yet she felt less, actually felt nothing.

PFC Simmons walked beside her. "You here to make us fucking famous?"

She tried to sound normal, although she felt like a ghost floating above the scene. "Yeah. Sure."

"Fucking A. Ought to be some kinda reason for this. Besides you getting your pictures to Danang and having a scoop, talkin' about how brave you were."

After Helen had the film she needed, she sat on a rock and waited. She had not eaten for twelve hours, had not slept in twenty-four. Sound still came to her muted, as if she were underwater. Linh photographed a mortar crew who had been there the whole three days. Since her return, a new dynamic to their professional relationship: Linh, a photographer now in his own right. They traveled together, but when they reached their destination they went through the professional courtesy of pretending to be invisible to each other.

As they made their slow way back down the hill, following the wounded, they passed living soldiers with dead eyes who did not even glance at them; Helen felt reinforced in her ghostliness. The piles of the dead had not been moved but were powdered in lime, which hid the features, making the bodies anonymous, making the living feel they were moving through a bizarre kind of catacomb.

They waited hours while the wounded were loaded and flown away.

As the infantry stretched chain-link around the LZ secured only hours before, peasant girls drifted in singly or in pairs from the nearby hamlets. They stood barefoot, dressed in faded cotton tops and black pajama bottoms, shifting their weight from one leg to the other, wordlessly soliciting. When a helicopter came in they forgot themselves, rushed up to the fence and poked their fingers through in their thrill to see the flying machines. Their fingers were as tiny and delicate as children's, a few with chipped nails painted in gaudy pinks and reds.

One of the guards went up to the fence and said something to a young girl with jet shoulder-length hair and a shiny turquoise shirt too large for her slight frame. Curious, Helen raised her camera as he took something out of his pocket, and as he unwrapped it, she saw it was a roll of Life Savers. He pushed his fingers through the fence and fed the candy to the girl, placing it directly on her tongue.

That was the shot. Helen had endured the previous hours of terror to reach it, and yet when it came it satisfied her that the sacrifice had been worth it. Only in her stripped state would she have noticed something so small and so fraught. Later it turned out to be a cover and then led to her first award, but for her the value of the picture was that it returned her purpose—to find small glimmers of humanity.

Helen and Linh caught the last helicopter out and were dropped at a supply base that was supposed to be running more cargo flights from Tan Son Nhut. By the time they landed, the last flight had left, and they had no choice but to spend the night. The whole Highlands was in a state of emergency, and press seating was not a priority. Soldiers waiting to go in joked that the military powers were trying to get as many of them killed as possible before the rumored troop withdrawals.

The next day they waited again, Helen in the mess tent nursing a coffee, Linh stationed next to the air traffic controller, supplying him with cigarettes and sharing a flask of bourbon.

Their location was in a depressed bowl with ragged foothills all around, allowing only a short runway. The jungle seemed to bear down on their small patch of denuded territory, its tinsel of concertina wire, its hastily scratched-out bunkers. The jungle stood dense and majestic and unapproachable. The land itself against them; rice paddies and jungle and plateaus and mountains, all conspiring and waiting for their demise and disappearance.

Linh came in the mess tent and walked over to her table. "You doing okay?"

"What do the flights look like?"

"No one getting in or out now. We could be days."

The wind was knocked out of her. She had to admit she was more shaken up than she thought; she needed to escape, although escape was getting harder to come by.

"The good news is that nobody else is getting in or out, either. The pictures are still in play."

She could not blame him—this was their life—but the private's words about a scoop echoed in her head in a nasty way. By late afternoon, she despaired that they would get out that night, but Linh came running into the mess after having talked his way onto the last cargo plane headed for Tan Son Nhut.

As they approached the plane, one of the flight crew came up to her with a white scarf, but the roar of the engine and her own muffled hearing made it impossible for her to make out his words, and finally he motioned for her to tie it over her nose and mouth.

"I don't understand," Helen yelled over the roar, and he pinched his nose. The scarf was greasy, and she brought it to her nose and smelled the sharp smell of Tiger Balm slathered in the center. She shook her head and handed it back to him.

Linh walked up the cargo ramp and stopped at the sight in front of him. Inside the hold, body bags filled the space from floor to ceiling. He walked backward down the ramp; speechless, he pointed. He stood on the ground, arms wrapped around his sides, while Helen found the harassed air controller who had not told Linh what the cargo was on the flight. He shrugged, unimpressed. If they refused this flight, he said, they would spend at least another night or two out.

"It doesn't matter," Helen said. "One more night."

"Let's get out of here," Linh said.

They sat in the three feet of cleared space at the forward-most section of the cargo cabin. The smell penetrated, and she wished she had taken the offered scarf. A solid wall of broken bones and sliding flesh, the sight cleaned up and made civilized by being zipped away in rubber bags. She had to put something between herself and this sight and so she raised her camera. The great dark mass in front of her had power, but it was not her picture anymore. It had similarities with the photo she had taken years ago of soldiers piled on the convoy truck. Then she had been in shock at the carnage, determined to show it. Now each of the bodies before her were no longer anonymous, each was Michael, Darrow, Samuels, and all the others. The image valid, but she was unequal to it and lowered the camera. She had to find the smallest bit of redemption in a photo, otherwise taking it would begin to destroy her. Even if it meant risking the misconception that war was not as horrific as it was.

They sat and waited, cameras useless in their laps. Linh had made no motion toward photographing the scene.

Once they were airborne, the wind whipped through the open doors, diluting the stench but also creating a frightening ripple of bags, a hard flapping and flaying that was as bad as the earlier smell. Helen closed her eyes and tried to think of anything but where she was.

During the steep descent into Tan Son Nhut, fluids from the seeping bags sloshed forward in a small wave, and Linh felt a cool, viscous liquid soak through his pants. When the source of the wetness became evident, he put his hands down to try to stand up, but the slickness was like egg white against the metal floor, and he slipped back. Everything blacked in on him. He opened his mouth, but the engines drowned out sound.

Helen pulled him to her, her arms a vise around his waist, turned him away from the sight until they both stood clinging to the webbed wall, but even after he had regained his balance, still she kept her hold tight on him. This she could do. She would not let him go.

SEVENTEEN

Nghia

Love

His heart had been locked away for a very long time.

From the moment he shifted the weight of Mai's body from his own arms to the earth, he chose not to feel again. He hadn't held another woman in his arms until he picked up Helen from the sidewalk and carried her back to the room in Cholon.

One came to love another through repeated touch, he believed, the way a mother bonded with her newborn, the way his family had slept in the communal room, brushing against one another, a patterning through nerve endings, a laying of pulse against pulse, creating a rhythm of blood, and so now he touched others, strangers, only fleetingly, without hope.

The weight of Helen in his arms broke open memory. She invaded his heart, first in Darrow's pictures, and then later through the casual touch of her hand, the smell of her hair, and finally the weight of her pain in his arms.

After she returned to Vietnam, he would wait for her in the crooked apartment, and while waiting he would roll an earring of hers in the palm of his hand, comforted by the thought that it had been against the delicate skin of her earlobe. He did not intend for Helen to know of these feelings; he was perfectly content not acting on them. The invisible carrying just as much weight as the visible in his world.

After Dak To, Helen asked Linh to take her back to the hamlet in the delta where she had stayed with Darrow. She wanted to recapture that sense of serenity she had glimpsed there. But the hamlet was nothing but ashes now, the villagers refugees. "They declared it a center of enemy activity."

"We were there. It was safe."

Linh shrugged. "Maybe we were wrong; maybe they were wrong. Either way the village is still destroyed."

Helen was silent for a moment. "Don't you care what is happening to your country?"

He turned away, angry, intending to leave until he regained possession of himself, but instead, for the first time, he turned back. He'd been around Americans long enough to get used to their blurting out feelings, and the desire in him to do so was overwhelming. "My war has been going on for nine years so far. I can't take a vacation from it and go home and come back. The war is in my home."

"I didn't mean—"

"It is like a medic performing triage. You determine who will die anyway, and you move to those you can save. *You* want to stand over the dead and cry, but that helps no one. That's a tourist's sensibility. Day after day I go out with photographers who are tourists of the war."

"Why are you any different than us?"

"I was on both sides. Left both sides. Only they don't let you leave. Being a photographer was my only choice."

"And they allow it?"

"I pretend that I'm influencing coverage. I give them bits of information I pick up after the fact. Only to convince them I have value alive."

Now Helen was the one to turn away. Her face burned at the memory of herself playing at war when she first came, how Linh and the whole country had merely served as backdrop for her adventure.

"I will take you to a place that is peaceful," he said.

They caught a ride on a cargo plane to Nha Trang, then took an army jeep to a small village of a dozen houses tucked against a crescent of beach. The sand was bone white, the ocean the color of unripe green papaya. The houses closest to the water stood in the violet shade of a thick grove of coconut palms. The quiet of the place was the first thing one noticed—no sounds of war, no sounds of people—so rare.

The house was owned by Linh's aunt. It was large, made of stone with a red tile roof. Sheltered by trees, the front garden contained a half-moon pond of stone. Inside, the two rooms were bare of furnishings but clean.

"Where is everyone?"

"They evacuated the village six months ago. The old people escaped the center and returned to care for things until the rest are released."

"Where is your aunt?"

"Visiting relatives."

By the quick way he said it, she knew he was lying. "She didn't have to leave. I would have liked meeting her."

Linh nodded. "Maybe it's better for her to pretend she doesn't know I brought an American visitor."

It was the end of the dry season, only afternoon showers, the sun baking the sky into a hard mineral blue each morning, the air heavy and wet as if it could be wrung out. The rains were late, refusing to come. To the east the sky remained empty over the ocean; to the west, by noon one would see a lone tall cumulus cloud hang over the mountains, gathering others around it until by midafternoon a white-cloud mountain range lay on top of the solid one of earth. But the clouds did not spread; the sky remained hard and dry.

Helen spent whole days hiding in the lukewarm shade inside, sleeping on a woven mat on the floor. She stripped down to shorts and T-shirt but still woke in the late afternoon drenched. Her dreams stopped, and she felt a relief in the black denseness of sleep.

Something had broken inside her. No past or future, no sense of time, each day as endless as it was to a child. Linh had been right about her being a tourist of the war in the beginning, but with that detachment there had also been a kind of strength. As Darrow had said, there was a price to mastery. Now she was in a limbo, neither an observer of the country, nor a part of it. For the first time since she was a child, she considered praying, but it seemed small and cowardly this late in the game.

At dusk Linh came with a tray of food prepared by a neighbor woman, Mrs. Thi Xuan, usually grilled fish or shrimp, a bowl of rice, and eggplant in soy sauce. They ate at the open doorway, waiting for the evening breeze off the ocean, sitting cross-legged on mats. They stared out at the garden and the ocean beyond it until it grew too dark to see. Then Linh would strike a match and light the oil lamp between them and bring out a deck of cards.

A few months before, Helen had taught him gin, and they played at every opportunity. At first Linh had lost every game, but gradually he racked up wins. Now he was obsessed. He kept a notepad and pencil by his side, recording wins and points with the precision of an accountant. They played deep into the night; at particularly close games, one or the other would let out a loud laugh or howl that would wake up nearby villagers.

In those evenings he learned the intricacies of her face—the curve of her mouth, the laugh lines that ran lightly from the corners of her lips to her nose, the delicate arch of eyebrow, the vertical furrows between her brows when she frowned, which was often, as if she were studying a problem located deep inside her.

Although conversation had been easy between them, here it moved clumsily, by fits and starts. They both praised the food and the night to excess. Neither dared look into the other's face unarmed with words. Moments passed, absorbed in eating or card playing, the only sounds the waves and the soft scurrying of geckos running up and down the walls.

"Thank you for this," she said.

Linh nodded, peeled an orange, and laid a section into her outstretched hand.

It occurred to her that even when Darrow had been alive, she had spent most of her time in Linh's company. Now there was a new weight when they were together, each conscious of a pull toward the other that had been hidden before. She thought back to the time in the delta, the only time she had been alone with Darrow and away from work. Although they had been in love, there had always been a sense of jealousy, her suspicion of where his thoughts were. Always he had seemed focused elsewhere. Always a small element of friction and competition between them. Darrow had not wanted a relationship of smoothness and satiety.

After their meals, Helen took her bath, pulling a screen around the half-moon pond. Then, still damp, she would be asleep again before the first stars appeared.

Still the rain did not come. The water in the cisterns scraped low, then became brackish with silt along the bottom of the clay jars.

At night, the air did not cool but remained hot and prickly, weighted with rain that would not drop. Linh chose a hammock strung between two palms in the garden, hoping to catch any breeze that came off the water. The thick, overlapping fronds of the palms sheltered him from both the sun and the rain, if it came.

This is how the invisible became visible.

The sound of waves filled his head before he drifted off, and made its way into his dreams so that he was surprised one night at the sound of splashing water that woke him. Although his hammock was in the deep shade, a place of perfect darkness, the full moon illuminated everything around him. Again, splashing. He turned his head toward the half-moon pond.

Helen was submerged in the pool, only her head showing, her hair slicked back. She bent back and stared up at the moon, her face a lily pad on the water's surface. For a brief moment, Linh had the image of a Vietnamese princess out of legend who drowned herself from sorrow in such a pond, sorrow for a missing lover. He had not told Helen this legend. He pushed it from his mind. Americans didn't do such things.

He felt strange, confused, sure that Helen knew where he slept but guilty nonetheless for being there. Could it be a dream? Resolutely he turned over, his back to the pond, and squeezed his eyes shut. Still, he held his breath, straining for the sound of splashing water. He grabbed his shirt from the end of the hammock and wadded it up, putting it over his head to muffle the sound. He longed to see her body once, but he willed himself not to. Lines from *Kieu* came into his mind:

> *In the fragrant water of her bath*
> *Kieu immerses her body, a spring flower*
> *Purity of jade . . .*

He woke, shocked that he could have fallen asleep, then certain again the whole thing had been a dream. How long had he slept? His shirt fallen to the ground, he turned over toward the pond and saw Helen still there, standing with her back to him, the long blade of her body in the moonlight.

She turned, face in her hands, then looked up, straight to the darkness where he lay. She hungered, and felt guilt over the hunger. "Cover me."

Was it the sound of the wind in the palm fronds, perhaps his own desire playing tricks on him?

And then she said it once more. "Cover me."

If he went to her, his life would change, and if he didn't go, his life would change also, withering away. He had no choice but to go to her. He rose, the wrist of one hand braceleted by the fingers of the other. Five years since he had lost Mai. He walked into the pond, the water cool on his burning skin, and covered her shoulders in the wings of his shirt, holding her to his chest, tight under his heart.

He didn't expect more than this moment, already more than he thought he would ever have again.

His hands trembled as his fingers traced the tender cliffs of her collarbone. She reached with her fingers under his chin, brought his eyes up to hers.

"It's okay if you don't love me," she said.

He shook his head at the absurdity, it being so obvious that he had loved her from the moment he first saw her, the love only growing and deepening in time. Darrow's greatest gift that he never mentioned the obvious infatuation so that Linh did not have to remove himself from their friendship.

Desire made them again strange to each other. They walked hand in hand to the house, Linh leading, and lay down on the mats. Urgent, after all this time, suddenly intolerant of another passing moment without knowledge of each other. A whole Braille of touch—tooth on lip, eyelash on nipple, pubic bone on swell of calf. He explored her body in the smallest of increments, the width of a finger, as if she were the unknown space on a map, and he knew it was her he desired, and not simply his desire for desire. She cradled his head in the hollow of her hip bones. He ran his tongue along the scar on her belly that sealed the future.

He heard the rough breaths that passed through her lungs, cries that no one else could hear, meant only for him. The frailty of her closed eyelids, the blue veins visible underneath the skin; he was protective of the long curve of her back, the soft indentation of the spine. He bandaged his fingers and then his wrists in the healing strands of her hair.

They woke each day in the tangle of each other's limbs. Relieved and content simply to find the other within reach. Long hours spent in the shade of the palm trees, watching the movements of the villagers among the houses and down to the ocean and back. They didn't speak for long periods of time, talk unnecessary. This new stage of intimacy simply the fruition of their prior ease in each other's company. In the late afternoon, they went down the beach, away from curious eyes, walking separately until they found a deserted strand. Entering the water the temperature of blood, swimming easily in the warm salt liquid, tunneling toward each other like electric sea animals. Touches glancing: hand against hand, arm against chest, trunk against back.

Spent, they returned to the house, fell on mats, warm and heavy-limbed. Passion a narcotic. Linh rested his head on her lap, feeling the heat of her through the thin sheet, pressing his nose against the fabric to inhale the salty scent of her.

"What will we do after the war?" he asked.

"What do you mean, 'after'? Wars don't end anymore," she said. She rolled away from him and laughed. "I think Mrs. Xuan is spying on us. She and her friends stand very close to the fence during the afternoon."

This happiness would have to be paid for. Irrefutable evidence for Mr. Bao to use against him. Linh pulled her back to him and pressed his head into the softness of her thighs. Any price for this moment. "Gossiping old women."

"Maybe they don't like you here with an American."

"Gossiping old hags."

She stared at the ceiling and ran her fingers through his hair. "Tell me something about Linh. Something I don't know."

"Why?"

"Because we're lovers. Because it's time. Who was Linh before Darrow?"

He shrugged and sat up. "I've told you about the NVA and the SVA." He had caught the long sideways looks of Mrs. Xuan during the last week but had ignored her. Probably paid to spy by Mr. Bao. "If you don't know me now, how will you find me in the past?"

"Tell me about your wife. How did you meet?"

Linh slumped back down to the floor. "My family were city people, demoted to living in the village after the partition, when we left for the South. So the customs were strange to us. In the village, the boys would go down to the river on a full-moon night and sing songs to the girls on the opposite shore."

He remembered eating shrimp with hot red chilies no bigger than the tip of his finger, leaving his mouth burning; he and friends drinking beer his older brother, Ca, had bought for them. His stomach tightened at the memory of the colored lanterns hung along the river so they could see each other better, the reflection of the lanterns on the river. He squinted to see the faces of the girls, each bathed in a pool of pure color. But Mai's face was perfectly clear, the blue lantern showing her features like moonlight against the night.

"And the girls would sing a song back in reply. Back and forth all night long. We were both fifteen when I saw her singing to me across the river."

"She picked you."

He bent his face into Helen's lap. "She picked me."

"That's a beautiful story." She caressed his shoulder and neck lightly with her fingers. "How did you and Darrow meet?"

"I went to Gary for a job. He needed an assistant for Darrow."

"Amazing."

"He flew me to Angkor the same day."

"That's when he fell in love with the place?"

"Gary said no one else would work with him."

Helen laughed. "I'm glad you stuck it out."

Linh stood up and excused himself. Helen had almost fallen asleep when he came back in, dripping water.

"Did you go for a swim?"

He shook his head. "I met him once before."

"Darrow?"

Linh nodded. "He came to photograph a joint movement with my SVA regiment and American advisers."

"Oh."

Pulling away, Linh told the story he had been unable to tell, the only story that mattered. Wide-awake now, Helen shivered, knees drawn up, face cupped in her folded arm. Without thought, Linh grabbed both her ankles as anchor, one in each hand, fingers tight around the sharp knobs of bone, grounding himself or her, he did not know which.

Danger that after the telling he would not be able to stand being with her any longer, the wound too deep to share, but her tears fed him. His anguish had grown skeletal in its solitude. He wished it didn't have to be so, that one could ingest pain and keep it from others, but instead it seemed one could only lessen it by inflicting little cuts and bruises of it on another.

"Forgive me," he whispered.

A miracle how she appeared beneath him, how she unfolded and folded him into the wings of her arms and legs. He kissed the bony globe of her knee before descending.

Our company had been near the paddy fields settling in for the night when scouts ran into a camp of VC. Quickly, we pulled back toward my village while the American advisers stood alone in the field, yelling at us to stay put. But we abandoned our positions, and the Americans, cursing, called firepower in to target the adjoining forest. Planes came, bombs dropped that shook the earth many kilometers away, so powerful the villagers sent up prayers that the world would not end.

After a shaky perimeter guard had been set up, I slipped away to see my fam-
ily and reassure them.

My mother and father were bundling belongings, ready to flee with Mai, my
older sister, Nha, with her baby, and my brothers, Toan and Ca. My mother was
more weary than frightened. She cried that she had been leaving one home after
another since she was a young girl in the North. Tears ran down Mai's face, and
she held the sides of her belly as if it pained her. She shook like an animal sens-
ing the approach of the hatchet. Begging me to take them away to someplace
safe. To her sister, Thao's, home. "Please, take us. Take me away."

"I can't." For a brief moment, Mai's selfishness angered me. For all her girlish
charm, if I had to pick again I would have chosen the practical Thao. My mother
had worried that Mai would be too fragile, too high-strung, to make a good wife.

"You promised to take me to Saigon," she said.

"My company knows I'm here."

"Doesn't matter." Mai shook her head, her eyes wild and glittering, not see-
ing me. "I'll go anyway. Alone."

Nha, listening, turned away, embarrassed for her sister-in-law. Her own
baby whimpered in her arms, still feverish after a cold. Nha, as homely as Mai
was lovely, took comfort in her virtue and self-sacrifice.

I promised that the bombs were to protect us, that the VC would have re-
treated by now, nothing to fear, trying out the words in my mouth as I said
them, not knowing myself if they were believable. "I met an American. I don't
know why, but they are helping us."

"The eyes and ears in the trees see soldiers retreat here," my father said, shak-
ing his head.

My family was still frightened, but as the air grew quiet, nerves calmed. My
mother built a small fire and boiled tea and fresh rice for a meal. When Mai of-
fered to help, she slapped away her hand. "I remember in Hanoi, the servants
made a full meal, even mang tay nau cua, *asparagus and crab soup, as the Com-*
munists rolled into the city. No matter what, one must eat."

Mai rolled her eyes, a steady private complaint that the old woman turned
everything into a story of her former wealth.

"Wouldn't it be nice to have some asparagus and crab now?" my mother
went on.

Incense was burned for the ancestors. A bowl of rice held out as an offering. I bowed my head to the ground three times at the altar. We ate in silence.

"Did you notice," Mai said, "during the play, at the song—"

"Please," said Toan. "Stupid girl, can't you think of anything more important than that wretched play?"

Mai's lips puckered, and I refused to look her in the face, certain she would burst into tears again. She struggled to her feet, unable to stand until Nha came over and lifted her under her arms. Mai went outside with her bowl. I could say nothing because Toan was my older brother, bitter at his own unmarried state, but nothing would have pleased me more than to talk about the play. Anything to forget the present fear.

Because they had no choice, they tried to share my faith that the Americans were different. I knew I should report back to the company but couldn't. After a year's absence, what could one more night matter?

By midnight everyone fell into a fitful sleep in the communal room, within touch of one another. Later, I would remember dreading the coming morning, when I would be alone again. I woke and heard the suck of Nha's baby. I wished, and was ashamed to wish, that I could be alone with Mai one last time before our separation. Was Mai right? Should we have escaped when we could to Saigon? The thought of desertion was always present, like uncooked dough in my stomach.

A terrible howling noise. Like a roar from inside the earth. We woke, disoriented, in the middle of the night. Outside, mortars bit at the edge of the village, shards of fire and metal and earth flying. Palm trees, thatched roofs of houses, in flames. I could hear screams, could hear Mai's shrill sob rise up, her breath catching, and then another sob. Where had the mortars come from? Which side? A sound, pull, puff, *and then another three mortars landed all around the hut. Plumes of earth rising more than double the height of the tallest palm. Soldiers from my company ran by, abandoning their camp and leaving the village exposed. The enemy attacking from close by if not from inside the village itself.*

"Quick," I yelled. "We must leave."

Now the Americans would call in airpower and raze the village. My father, still in the vigor of middle age, ran and brought back a long rope that he used to tie our buffalo to the plow. It was stiff and heavy, the fibers scratched. Parts of it thinned and softened from rubbing against the wood stays, other parts caked in mud and manure. He cut off part of it and tied each member of the family together, each person's left wrist becoming communal, no longer one's own, a sacrifice so that we wouldn't get lost or separated, so that in a panic the weak would not get left behind.

Nha refused the rope, saying she had to hold her baby. She swayed in indecision. I said I would carry him, but she only looked down. "Things have to be looked after," she whispered.

"No."

"The baby's fever . . ." She shook her head. "A rope?" She let out a sad laugh and turned away. Father said we would return for her. As we escaped through the front gate of the village, a woman came asking for help to lift a sack of rice into her cart. Although he had not been in a classroom in over ten years, had spent more time buried in paddies than in books, Father still felt the obligation to set an example. He untied himself.

"What are you doing?" I asked.

His jaw was braced. "Toan, come with me."

"No," I said as Toan undid the rope from his wrist. "It's too late."

Father and brother left. Minutes passed. The whistling of shells came more rapidly. Earth and flesh being ripped like paper. Fire fed and burned on fire. Bullets flew like hot, sharp insects. People we had spent our whole lives with pushed past like strangers.

Although we might die standing in place, I didn't dare disobey. "Should we leave?" I asked Ca, but he remained silent.

"There," Ca said and pointed to Father and Toan jogging toward us. They retied themselves, and we had begun our walk on the path when a mortar screamed over our heads, striking two huts on the other side of the village, the thatch blazing up in a hiss of fire like a match. As quick as a bolt of lightning. Father wanted to turn back again, both of us sensing where it had landed, but I held his eye, shook my head. Move quickly. Save what is left.

We ran in the dark, confused by sounds all around, following in the wake of my fleeing company, who would stop to take random shots behind them, imagining that would stop an enemy they couldn't see. Many of the wild bullets struck villagers seeking them for safety. A family ahead of us was struck by a grenade, all five scattered like dolls in the field. I worried about my mother and Mai, but they were dazed, in shock, stumbling forward. I recognized this from being with soldiers in battle, how the mind shuts down and there is only instinct.

We came to a rice paddy and plunged into the cold mud, crouching, bewildered, going on. Mud squelched around our feet. The rope, soaked in water, grew heavy. No matter which way we turned, a spitting wall of gunfire from every direction. We had taken the wrong way, straight into a fire field. I cursed myself for not being a real soldier, for only pretending, for not taking control. More frightening for me not to be among my fellow soldiers. Instead, exposed with my family, who had no expectation except for obedience to my poor, blind father. My hand groped emptiness at my side, and I was defeated by the realization that I had left my gun behind in the hut during our hurried escape. What kind of soldier forgets his gun? Courage emptied from me again. I could barely lift my legs. Our progress was slow, the women slipping, falling in the mud, dragging the men's arms down till we stood bent in half. The only hope to get on the other side of my panicked company, but the soldiers, unburdened, moved away faster than we could approach them. The rope chafed and tore my wrist.

I always wondered what if—What if I had taken charge, turned left, not right . . . What if I had taken them to hide in the forest and not in the paddy— but in the middle of that night, fear itself hunted us. Because I was not sure, I did nothing.

It was while we were in the paddy bordered by trees that Toan was shot in the throat. The noise around was so deafening, the darkness broken only here and there by the ghost light of a flare, that we noticed only because of the inert weight on the rope. Mai in front of him pulled down on her knees. My mother crouched in the mud, trying to sop up blood with a piece of cloth. Toan, whose favorite sport was catching frogs in the paddy as a boy and dressing them in crowns of palm husk. Toan, my brother, who was afraid of the dark. Father untied him, and I saw ten years of age suddenly line his face. No choice but to leave the body half-submerged in its gentle blanket of mud, his head propped up on a dike.

Time stopped or raced on. Minutes or eternities spent lost, running. Rain trembled in the air, drops coming at first lightly, then pounding on our backs.

Our feet wore heavy boots of mud, stretching already bruise-weary muscles. A bullet punched its way into Ca's chest with a small ripe sound like an arrow hitting the heartwood of a tree. Ca, whose greatest joy was bringing sweets to Mai. His body jerked backward as if blown by a hard wind, dragging Mother onto the ground. Father groaned, grief squeezing his chest. He fumbled with the long, slippery rope, losing his knife in the mud. He bowed his head, face aged to that of an ancient man, and said to me, "You must take over now."

I ordered the women to turn away and took my knife, cutting the rope that bound us. I paused, then moved to each family member and cut through the knot on each wrist. If we survived, it would be each alone. The rope fell in pieces to the ground like a serpent.

Mai moaned and pulled at her hair in fistfuls, crouching in the mud. "Get up, Mai." She shook her head. I lifted her to her feet, her belly large and hard and jutting, but she buckled her knees and went down again. "Please, my love." She moaned louder, eyes on Ca, hands pressing against her sides. I pulled her up and slapped her across the mouth. "Enough! You will walk." My first harsh words to her since we married. She nodded, chastened, took one somber step and then another. We did not look back.

This is the way one learned to survive.

Two hours later, the fighting was more sporadic, only sniper bullets and the occasional faraway thump of mortars as they drummed into the earth. The rain had stopped; our bodies soaked and cold and tired. Easier to move without the rope, but I felt its loss like a missing limb.

Mai let out a soft cry and sat down hard on the ground, leaning against a splintered tree, heavy pear belly listing toward the earth like a magnet. In the dark night, her blood black as it poured from between her legs. She squeezed her legs together and remembered aloud how we had laughed only that morning at Ca mimicking her dance. "How long ago it seems." A deep, dragging ache pulled at her. She had been wrong, she said, had selfishly prayed for her own and my happiness, even to the point of secreting away money to buy a gold necklace for the baby. She had angered fate. "I wanted us to go to Saigon so you could see . . . I am not a useless wife."

I rubbed her feet, frozen hard like small river stones. "We'll go now."

Mother whispered with Mai, laid a hand on her belly. She took a blouse out of her bag and told Mai to press it up between her legs, stop the baby coming out on such a night. Mai was calm and quiet, suddenly matured from girl to woman, nodding wisely. So unlike her I worried.

"We are going to Saigon," I said louder, and began to make a sling with the remaining coil of rope across my chest like a pack animal.

Father came and touched my shoulder. "We must return to the village."

"You can't."

"Better for you two to go on alone. Maybe later, with Nha . . ."

Too exhausted to argue, I nodded. Mai sat wearily in the saddle of the rope sideways across my back, leaning her head on my shoulder. As I made my way off, Mother and Father remained standing by the splintered tree, and even now, in my mind's eye, that is where I still imagine them.

"Forgive me," Mai whispered, "my foolishness." But I didn't listen. I started the walk south, in the direction of the army and safety, the direction of illusion.

I lost track of time, but during the night Mai laid her fingers along my neck, my only comfort, my only goad.

I walked through the night. I lost my sandals in the mud, walked on blisters, and then on bloodied, raw feet, not daring to stop even when I grew thirsty, until my throat cracked like a riverbed with dryness, but still I kept walking. I would die walking. During the night, Mai fell asleep, her hand falling away.

And then like an angel, a bodhisattva *of compassion, the sky lightened to a pearl gray in the east, and the great tired face of the sun appeared. As if the day itself were shamed to light the earth. So quiet that I heard the singing of a single bird in a tree as I passed, a miracle that day could follow such a night, and I reached the highway south, joining a throng of refugees like ourselves draining from the countryside. I murmured, throat like an open wound, over my shoulder, "We are close now."*

I walked until I felt a tug at my sleeve and looked into the wrinkled face of an old grandmother. She shook her head sharply, as if shrugging off a ghost. I could not make out her words, so tired I simply noticed her sunken lips and the few blackened, betel-stained teeth in her mouth. She motioned with her hands to lie down, and the idea of sleep was suddenly overwhelming. I would have walked till I dropped over. I struggled to the tall grass at the side of the road, and only as I worked to loosen the knot of rope around my chest did I notice the cold heaviness of Mai's body, and as I slowly knelt down to let her off I realized I had felt no movement all night long, no warm breath, and now as I laid her in the long, lilac-tinted grass, and as her long hair draped down to the earth, I saw that she had the pearl gray pallor of death, and I knew, as the grandmother shook her head, quick as a bird, and handed me a small spray of yellow paper flowers before she turned away, that I had carried a corpse the whole night through, but somehow Mai's spirit had saved me.

This is how the world ends in one instant and begins again the next.

I crouched in the grass and saw that we were both covered in blood, that she had bled to death with our child. I looked up and down the highway, saw other bodies fallen by the side, and when I looked into the faces of the people, I saw we were all the living dead, no one had escaped.

I bowed my head, the spray of flowers still gripped in my fingers. The paper ones the poor bought to place on family altars. Petals faded yellow and dusty from long use, the paper crumpled in places where the old woman had clutched them. But when I brought the spray to my face, I smelled the fresh orange blossoms of Mai's hair. And so I buried my wife, Mai, under the tree the bird sang in, placing the spray of flowers in her mouth. The blossoms were paper, yellow faded, already dusty from mourning, but they were all I had left to give.

EIGHTEEN

Cat Cai Dau

Cut Off the Head

The next morning Linh sought out Mrs. Xuan, who was feeding garbage to the catfish in the large village pond.

"We need a lacquered box of betel and areca. And gold earrings. Can you prepare a small feast—at least six dishes—for the entire village?" he asked.

He was pleased to see Mrs. Xuan's eyebrows shoot up, her gossip suddenly gone stale. She chewed on her lips as Linh gave her dollar bills. "For when?"

"Soon. A day or two at most. We must return to Saigon."

"Too soon," she said, figuring that time would allow her to dole out the information to Mr. Bao for greater profit.

He knew the old woman would not give up the tidy sum she would make. "Then we'll have the ceremony in Saigon instead. She prefers it—"

"No, no. Hungry bridegrooms. So impatient." Mrs. Xuan scrunched up her eyes in a failed effort to appear good-natured, quickly withdrawing her hand filled with dollar bills.

When Linh told Helen of his plans for a ceremony, she was quiet. The implications of their time together had not sunk in for her, yet after hearing his story, she knew that he was dead serious. Only Americans thought that Vietnam was as permissive as the brothels and G.I. bars in Saigon. The society was conservative, a relationship outside marriage unheard-of. At times Linh seemed even more foreign now that he was her lover than before when they had been only friends. "Does this have something to do with Mr. Bao? Will he be angry when he finds out?"

"It's important to save face. But it's important for me also," he said. A wild gambit, but he thought the idea of lust would be understandable to Bao and protect Helen. For the last year, Mr. Bao had been consumed with his drug business, Linh with his work, and their reports to the NVA had been empty for a long time. In desperation to appear busy, Bao had slowly pieced together the idea of Helen being captured by the Viet Cong, taken prisoner. Maybe even allowing her to take pictures of the other side, leaking some of them out. He thought that would create new interest in his assignment, quell the talk of his being reassigned to a less lucrative post in the North.

"Why not have a civil ceremony in Saigon, with Gary and the others?"

"This first. A Buddhist ceremony for us."

"You know I can't have a child."

"You are my family," he said.

Helen rubbed her forehead. She had been living in a dream world in the hamlet, and now he was forcing her to think fast, but her thoughts came sluggishly. How could she explain the infidelity of her heart, that asleep in his arms she couldn't help if her dreams were still of Darrow. The pain of being in the war with Linh and the pain of being away from him were equal, were driving her mad. She had broken, become something else. She didn't know what yet. Could you love someone in the process of changing? She did love Linh. As much as a ghost loved. The mind treacherous.

The ceremony was simple, only a dozen people comprising the whole village attending. Both the bride and groom decades younger than the youngest guest. A quiet, subdued afternoon, the clouds having finally spread, wind speeding overhead and spitting raindrops. The times were lean in the countryside no matter how much money one had, and Mrs. Xuan could not buy a proper pig for the feast, so she had made do with catfish, shrimp, and buffalo.

Linh stood with Helen before a small altar of joss sticks, borrowing his aunt's pictures of his parents, brothers and sister, and Mai. A glass of rice alcohol and a plate of food offered in celebration. He bowed over the lacquer box of betel leaves and areca nuts, to signify unity and faithfulness in the marriage, then gave Helen the traditional set of gold hoop earrings to complete the marriage vows. It scared him to feel so hopeful for the future.

The old village women stood huddled at the back of the house, Mrs. Xuan in the middle. All during the brief ceremony, they eyed the plates of food brought and placed on the center table. When Linh clapped his hands and invited everyone to eat, they fell on the food with ravenous eyes and clawing fingers.

After they had eaten, their stomachs as tight as drums, the villagers settled down in the garden for a long night of drinking, but Linh scolded them away, pushing them out of the house with the remaining dishes of food, out of the garden with bottles of beer. The three old men grinned and said he was an anxious groom, but one of the women, Mrs. Xuan's best friend, said that he had already been at the duties of a groom for the last week, and they all burst out laughing.

"Enough," Linh said. "Leave us alone."

Helen, oblivious to all the talk, sat near the pool watching the clouds chase their way in front of the moon. When everyone was gone, Linh came out to her. "Don't you feel the drops? You're wet."

"I'm happy."

He carried her into the house, and they made love, past desire, past hunger, past exhaustion. His thirst for her had changed, grown greater, like drinking sea water only to feel more parched with each drink. He woke the next day, late in the afternoon, his face thinner, dark circles under his eyes like bruised fruit, but as soon as he touched her skin his desire again became electric, and he wanted to conquer each part of her all over once more.

Now it was Helen who searched out Mrs. Xuan for meals. The old woman approved of the American's new wifeliness. Helen brought food to Linh while he slept, and she sponged him off with cool water after they both were soaked with sweat, sore down to the muscle and bone. It gave her a deep pleasure to take care of him during those days, something that he had never allowed before. Finally, like a fever, their passion broke, and they floated in the calm left behind.

It became more and more clear in the intervening days that Helen and Linh could not love each other fiercely, selfishly, as young lovers. They loved each other like secular saints, too selfless for reckless passion, too aware of each other's pain and the avoidance of it. They loved with a middle-aged caution.

They returned to Saigon, and Linh moved into the crooked apartment in Cholon. She could have brought no other man there, it being both sacrament and sacrilege.

Within days Linh received the expected message that Mr. Bao wanted to have a meeting. He had anticipated as much. He sent back a message that the situation was too risky to meet in the city. Instead, they would meet at the house in the Ho Bo woods.

Linh took military trucks up to Cu Chi, then rode on civilian motorcycles and bicycles the final leg of the journey. On the prearranged night, he stopped for a leisurely meal at a street vendor's, making sure to get several men in conversation, periodically dipping his hand into his pocket, reassuring himself with the smooth touch of wire. After eating, he walked alone the final hours to the deserted cabin set deep in the woods.

The wind started up at sunset and blew with force, shaking leaves from trees, bending branches, dropping fruit not yet ready to fall. Linh had found great happiness during his weeks with Helen, but now he felt the weight and drag of that love. Ashamed at his relief to be alone again, walking on the deserted road, it occurred to him that he could keep walking and never turn around. A coward's thought. The wind wiped away the clouds; the sky burned sharp and glittering with stars like broken glass on blacktop. Linh hurried his step.

Mr. Bao lounged at a crude wooden table, drinking from a bottle of expensive Napoleon brandy. In the light of the lantern on the table's edge, he looked tired and smaller than Linh had remembered him. The graying at his temples, too, was more pronounced, and there were dark circles under his eyes. A pewter-topped cane was propped beside him. Many years had passed since they began their meetings. When he saw Linh, he smiled, revealing stubby brown teeth.

"Didn't hear you approach," he said. "Join me."

"Why not?" Linh sat at the chair opposite.

"I hear we should be making nuptial toasts."

Linh said nothing, only smiled.

"Indeed, when Mrs. Thi Xuan told me the whole village was invited, I wondered if my invitation had gone astray."

Again Linh said nothing.

"Come, we don't have all night. The question, it seems to me, is what do we do with the situation now."

"This is good brandy," Linh said, looking into his glass.

"You like the taste? Maybe your American can buy it for you now."

"Why do anything? I'm still your eyes and ears. I influence coverage as I can." Linh was confronted again with knowing how a situation should be handled but hoping against hope that it could be otherwise.

Mr. Bao laughed out loud as if he'd been told a good joke, then wiped at his eyes. "Things can't remain as they are. Uncle is waning, the powers are realigning themselves, some will go up and some down, loyalties will be re-assessed."

"I see."

Mr. Bao wiped his hand across his lips, jabbed his index finger on the table between them to emphasize his point. "Let's be frank, my friend. Neither of us are political men. I've been on a loose rein, some would say overlooked, and I've allowed you the same. Now is the time to show your loyalty."

"What are you saying?" At long last, marrying Helen, he had shown his loyalty, and they both knew it.

"What do we do with her now? What do we do with you for so blatantly acting on your own?"

Linh drank his glass of brandy down in one gulp. Mr. Bao raised his eyebrows but poured another round.

"My job was nothing more than providing whatever information came my way. We are going here; we are going there. Very little," Linh said. He studied the hut, saw a tail of dust blowing through a crack in the wall, illuminated across the lantern's beam as it settled on the table, on their glasses, on Mr. Bao's wrinkled and sickly face.

"True, most of what you give us is useless. What you did was infiltrate. You are in place. You are trusted. We never gave you credit for being much of a soldier or a spy. Mainly a lover." Mr. Bao giggled.

"Then let me go on."

"We are both men of the world," Mr. Bao said, his voice low and purring. "Women are hard to ignore. You and I have never believed in the war so much anyway. It is our sideline. But now we will show our allegiance, to survive."

"What do you want me to do?"

"I'll say the marriage was to gain her confidence. Take her back to the border. Another exclusive like the one you arranged on the Ho Chi Minh trail. This time have her captured. Let her be in on it or let her believe as she does. She takes pictures that are smuggled out."

"Too dangerous."

"Otherwise . . . the obvious choice . . . a dead woman reporter would demoralize the Americans."

"Think of something else." He had let Mai down; he would not let harm come to Helen. "Let me talk with headquarters."

"Headquarters doesn't know who you are. Think I'm a fool? Those are your choices. Prove you're not led by your pants. And you've had your bit of fun, too. Tell me, what is she like in bed?"

Linh laughed and drank down his glass. Mr. Bao had already been suspicious about him before this, so the marriage was neither good nor bad. But he was wrong about Linh. He had changed in the intervening years, had become what he wasn't before: a soldier. "Pour us another, and I'll tell you things. Her eyes."

Outside the wind howled so that the thatch of the hut rustled and whispered.

"Forget eyes. Tell me about her breasts. I knew when I saw you with her scarf that time." Mr. Bao laughed. He unbuttoned the top two buttons of his shirt from the heat of the drinks and the heat of the lantern in the small room.

"It was so obvious?" He knew how Mr. Bao's mind worked; he would rather find a dishonest route than an easier, straightforward one. He would rather steal a dollar than be given it. Like so many of the Communists, he did not particularly love his country or his people, but he used the system so he could steal from them. "Milky white breasts of a goddess. What else?"

Mr. Bao sighed now and became businesslike, forehead and neck glistening with sweat. "We might convince her to come over to our cause. Help get stories sympathetic to us. But it doesn't explain why you married her." Mr. Bao poured another round, but this time his hand was slower and unsteady with the bottle, leaving a small ring of spilled liquid around one of the glasses.

"Maybe I did it for love," Linh said. The truth was far, far more intoxicating and dangerous than any amount of brandy, and his heart beat hard against his chest at the released words.

Mr. Bao paused, his glass against his lips, as if considering this possibility. "That . . . would be the worst thing."

Stupidly, now that the outrageous truth had been told, he wanted to insist upon it. "Why? I mean, if it was true."

Mr. Bao looked at him now, the alcohol held in check, his reptilian eyes dark and cold. "A greedy man, a corrupt man, a man filled with lust, that's understandable. That can be accounted for. But you can never trust a man who falls in love with the enemy."

Linh stood and stretched, catlike. The brandy made the room seem to expand and contract as if it, too, were stretching, breathing, unsheathing its claws.

Mr. Bao reached out for Linh's arm and grabbed it. "I mean, how lost would a man have to be to do such a thing? Uncle's words: 'We are from the race of dragons and fairies.' "

Resolved, Linh jerked his arm free. He was a soldier. "We'll plan another trip to the Parrot's Beak next week then," he said, slowly moving back and forth in the small room, thumping his hand against the flat of his stomach. "Sufficiently risky area. She'll be captured for a week. Take pictures that are released to all the newspapers. Then she'll be released unharmed."

"Good," Mr. Bao said as he finished his glass.

"We'll divorce, and she'll go back to America. And then I'll start building a future for myself in the party—since there is no longer any choice," Linh said. "Maybe you can help me learn. Since no one knows who I am, right?"

"Young bull, huh?" Mr. Bao laughed.

"No one knows who I am to protect you. I can't report on your activities."

"True," Bao said thoughtfully.

"Don't you have unmarried daughters? I'll be in need of a new wife."

Mr. Bao was silent.

"Wasn't the youngest a real beauty? Or no? Am I wrong?"

"Yen is beautiful," Mr. Bao conceded.

Linh walked around the table and stood behind Mr. Bao's chair. Yes, he was a soldier now. A soldier did what he had to do to survive. As he reached inside his pocket and pulled out the coil of wire, wrapping it across each palm, the wooden ends tucked in closed fists, Linh was surprised at how thin Mr. Bao's hair was on top. Not even hair at all, really, more like the memory of hair. An old man already, ready for death.

"But," Mr. Bao continued, "she could never be given to a man who could not be trusted, a man who married the enemy. You know that, don't you? But—"

The air went out of his throat so fast that the sentence hung in the room, waiting to be finished. Mr. Bao's stubby hands raked the table, digging slivers of wood, then at last stretched out, relaxed. Afterward, Linh gently dumped him forward until his forehead rested against the table. A dark pool of blood shaped a halo around his head before it spread and encircled the lantern, the brandy bottle, and glasses. He picked up his own glass, shattering it against the stone floor.

Linh leaned against the wall and buried his shaking hands in his pockets. Yes, a soldier. Not fear but adrenaline. Mr. Bao looked like the old bureaucrat he was, taking a quick nap that he would never have allowed himself in real life. When Linh first learned of Bao's corruption—his percentages in drug and prostitution houses—he had despised him, but quickly he had seen its uses, how such a man would overlook lapses in others. In truth, Linh had grown, if not to like, at least to tolerate Mr. Bao. But no one would come looking for Linh if Mr. Bao disappeared; in the new coming order, old-time greed was an embarrassment. They had been two con men, and Linh had merely drawn the lucky card first.

The wind died down to a whisper outside as he blew into the hurricane shade, extinguishing the light. In the darkness, he missed Mr. Bao already. A silly man, a petty crook, but not a particularly evil one. His sin was not to understand the meaning of the weight of a woman in a man's arms.

Linh opened the door and walked out onto the moonlight-scarred path, but now he was a less free man than when he came.

NINETEEN

The Ocean of Milk

April 30, 1975

It was late in the war, and she was tired.

Helen had not slept long in the dead grass of the embassy compound. The night before she had grabbed only a few hours while keeping her vigil over Linh. If the Communists were going to kill her, it might as well be while she slept in her own bed.

By the time she reached Cholon, she walked like a sleepwalker—inside the crooked building through the now smashed Buddha door, up the rickety, cedar-smelling stairs that had lasted another ten years since the time she doubted they would carry her weight. The end had arrived with a sputter, and although she had prayed for an end to the evils of war, now that it had arrived she couldn't deny being strangely brokenhearted. Like a snake swallowing its own tail, war created an appetite that could be fed only on more war.

Somehow, Linh and she had eked out a happy life here. They had come back from the hamlet married, but Linh insisted for their safety on keeping it quiet. Too, there were professional repercussions, although quite a few American men had married Vietnamese women. In fairness, they felt they had to tell Gary, in case it came out. He, ever the diplomat, broke into a huge smile that could have meant anything. "There's a certain poetry to it, that's for sure." He took them out for a fancy dinner. But the person who was really joyous was Annick. The war had begun to take its toll on her. Gossip was that she took opium more frequently, and her pale skin and thin frame suggested its truth. In her store, she gave Helen a beautiful gold-and-pearl choker.

"I can't accept this."

"It is my wedding gift. Because finally something true has come out of this war. I predict you will be very happy."

And they were. Even as the war moved from the front to the back pages, bumped by the antiwar protests back home, Helen played wife, decorating their apartment, taking long meals with Linh, learning the city from the inside. Their time together was rich and precious. They continued covering the war, although the assignments were fewer and fewer, which suited them for a while. In America people had seemingly forgotten that soldiers in Vietnam were still fighting and still dying. And then came the drawdowns. Dwindling American troop numbers. Even less of a call for war photos. They covered the humanitarian crises caused by the country being at war so long. The effects of the defoliants on agriculture. Food shortages and lack of schools. In 1973, as the U.S. military pulled out, they classified their service dogs as surplus equipment and had them euthanized, claiming they were too dangerous to go back home. A few soldiers got in trouble trying to smuggle their dogs back to the States. Political stories in Laos, Thailand, and Cambodia began to take precedence, and they traveled with the news. Gary even talked of moving the bureau offices to Singapore, but then a flare-up in military action caused everyone to scurry back to Saigon. Helen hoped that some kind of compromise would be reached, a permanent division of the country so that they could stay. But Linh knew they all had underestimated the North.

Now the building stood hushed. Had it been abandoned on account of an American woman living there? And if so, where had the families gone in this city that was now as isolated and cut off as a quarantined ship on the high seas? These people had been their friends, had shared meals with them. Helen was godmother to five children. And yet the fear destroyed all of those bonds.

Although it was daybreak, the sky hung sullen with low clouds. Helen walked over to the red-shaded lamp and turned it off, intending sleep. Until these last few days the lamp had been invisible in its everydayness, but now she noticed the shade bleached to dull terra-cotta, like blood imperfectly washed out, the fabric so brittle she could poke her finger through it. It had simply outlasted its time. But the gloom unnerved her, and she turned the light back on.

Their belongings had been sent to Japan weeks ago, when the first news of President Thieu abandoning the Central Highlands came, the cities so familiar to Helen disappearing—Kontum, Pleiku, and Ban Me Thuot.

The rooms had the empty, threadbare feeling of that first night she had come there with Darrow. But it had long ceased to be his. Linh and Helen had shared so many memories in those rooms, they had excised the curse that she had feared was on the place. But now it was slipping away from them also. Already it felt as if the apartment, the city, the country, was in the throes of forgetting them.

Helen undressed, body stiff and aching, and she swabbed at the nail marks on her arms and the bruise at her temple. Because she had refused stitches, there would be a scar near the hairline. This worry over a small vanity would make Linh smile, but perhaps that was how one remained sane. She pulled on her new red kimono, the only piece of clothing she still had other than what she wore, but the joy she had taken in it was already gone without him to appreciate it. Now it was simply a covering, and she walked past the mirror, not wanting to confront herself in it. The rooms felt thick with ghosts, and she realized that she had hardly ever been there alone. Linh always filled them with life, banishing any spirits to the corners.

She pictured him at that moment out on the dawn-pink sea. Probably not sleeping, although he had slept only fitfully through the night. Had he forgiven her? He must know that she was coming shortly. A simple matter of days, photographing the new victors of the city, then being booted out. What was going through his mind? What would he miss the most about his homeland? Of course she knew. She was his country; *she* was what he would miss until they were back together.

Helen frowned and looked at the map on the wall. Linh understood.

Once one took a picture like Captain Tong shooting the old man, one inevitably started down the road of taking more and more. Bloated with self-importance, with the illusion of mission. One stayed at first for glory, then excitement, then later it was pure endurance and proficiency; one couldn't imagine doing anything else. But there was something more, hard to put her finger on—one felt a camaraderie in war, an urgency of connection impossible to duplicate in regular life. She felt more human when life was on the edge.

It had never been that way for Linh. Something kept him aloof, safe, but he understood her addiction. Allowed it but also kept her from going too far. Like she was doing now. She ran her fingers down the map—Quang Tri, Hue, Danang, Quang Ngai, Qui Nhon—each name recalling a past, each name a time of year and a military assignment, defeat, or victory. But now each name was being erased, exploration in reverse, the map becoming instead more and more empty, filled with great white expanses of loss.

Her mind, again, became a treacherous, circling thing.

A water glass full of vodka in order to sleep; she hoped she would pass out before reaching the bottom. Her mind skipped and jumped, a needle on a worn record, and she pulled down one of Darrow's old books to calm herself, a dip in the stream of a dog-eared passage:

The temple of Angkor . . . making him forget all the fatigues of the journey . . . such as would be experienced on finding a verdant oasis in the sandy desert . . . as if by enchantment . . . transported from barbarism to civilization, from profound darkness to light.

She had never understood Darrow's obsession with Angkor; it had seemed strangely indulgent and romantic given his character. She fell asleep with the book in her hands, her question unanswered.

Hours later, Helen woke, panicked she had missed something. She stumbled onto her feet and dressed in the clothes from the day before. At the door she hesitated, not afraid, yet the outside seemed newly forbidding. One fell in love with geography through people, and when the people were gone, the most beloved place turned cool and impersonal.

At the presidential palace, she took out her camera and framed the columns of Soviet tanks slowly grinding their way down Hong Thap Tu Street. Fencing them in the box of her viewfinder calmed her. They turned up Thong Nhut Boulevard, pulling up bits of the broken street in their tracks and slapping them back down like mah-jongg tiles.

As a tank approached the front gates, Helen's camera stuck. She pulled back and forth on the lever, but nothing happened. Jammed. She yanked the strap off her neck as the sound of crunched metal could be heard, clamped the camera between her knees and pulled out a lens for the second body, but by the time she had it ready, the tank had rolled over the gingerbread gate with a hollow tearing of metal. Later, she found out that there had been offers to open the gates, but the NVA insisted on breaking them down. Showmen. She cursed, the camera dropping from her knees, clattering on the pavement. Kneeling on the ground, she rubbed the lens with a tissue to see if it had been scratched. She looked up just in time to see the unfurling from the balcony of the huge red flag with the gold star of the North.

Within hours, once the Saigonese realized that their city would not be bombed, that the rumored bloodbath would not occur, people came out and tentatively waved and clapped at the passing North Vietnamese soldiers. If she knew anything about the place, it was how quickly it switched allegiances, a fickle paramour, and yet in spite of herself she felt betrayed.

Walking down the street, she was surprised to see noodle shops already reopened. At one, she spotted incongruous white-blond hair and recognized the new Matt, the young reporter she had run into the day before, slurping a bowl with a group of NVA. He had a day's-old beard and wore the same black T-shirt she'd seen him in last time. When he saw her, he motioned her over.

"I've got a scoop for you this time. Check these boys out, Helen. We're having a picnic."

A group of five young soldiers looked up at her and giggled. They were young and skinny in their loose, mustard-colored uniforms, unsophisticated compared to the jaded, sleek SVA. They reminded Helen of polite and well-mannered country children. She wished her boy soldier would reappear, blowing his bubble gum. Most had never been in a city before, and Saigon, even in its present disheveled state, was a marvel of riches. The new rulers got lost on the way to the palace and had to stop their tanks and ask a frightened civilian for directions.

"Get this. They think ceiling fans are head choppers." Matt laughed, his mouth full of noodles, his hand making small hacking motions against the side of his neck. "Choppy, choppy those bastards, huh?" he said, elbowing a soldier.

The fear was too fresh for Helen to sit down next to these men and slurp noodles. Matt was a fool, but he had the advantage of no history. "I've got to get some more shots," she said.

"Hey, wait, I think I've talked them into giving me a tank ride. You could take pictures of me."

"Maybe next time," she said, walking away.

"What next time?" he yelled.

In the next few days the Communists did not take over the city simply because they did not know how. But given they had already won an impossible victory, no one doubted they would soon learn.

The Saigonese quickly regained their confidence when they met these naive soldiers and began to ply them with the same cheap watches and fake goods they had pawned off on new G.I.'s. Secretly they wondered to themselves what they had been so afraid of. The most obvious hardship of the takeover on Tu Do was the absence of prostitutes, not allowed under Uncle Ho's rules of clean living.

Soon jokes were traveling the city about the new *bo dois,* how they used a modern toilet to wash rice and were outraged when they pushed the handle and their food disappeared.

Helen went up and down the streets taking pictures of shopkeepers tearing down their American signs, crowbarring off neon and metal, and replacing them with hastily made Vietnamese ones. A Vietnamese man stood on top of a swaying ladder, pounding at a neon tube sign that read BUCK'S BAR, with a picture of a naked girl in a cowboy hat with a lasso that moved up and down her body in red and green loops. His calves were thin and ropey, his feet in their sandals calloused, the toenails thick and yellow. A life of hard work could be seen in those legs. She filled the frame with his body, the sign behind him a blur. Glass fell in small, tinkling chips like snow, and he brushed the splinters off his cheeks and shoulders and pounded harder till the whole thing fell in the street; his face drawn with pain like he was beating a favorite child. When he saw the camera, he scowled and almost lost his balance, waving Helen off.

She made her way to the wire service offices, where Gary was camped out, a skeleton crew transmitting stories throughout the morning.

"Where've you been? Beating up some NVA? Or joining Uncle Ho's army? War's over, Helen!" Tanner said.

"Thought I'd hang out with you."

Gary walked over to her. "Your credentials were pulled a week ago. You officially don't work here. You're supposed to be gone with Linh."

"Fine. I'll go. And take my pictures with me over to AP or UPI."

"Don't be that way. Let's see them."

"Am I back in?" She held the camera bag just out of his reach, teasing.

Gary hesitated, then laughed. "Just be careful. It's weird out there."

"It's *Alice in Wonderland* time out there," Tanner said.

She developed her own film, and Gary sent out all the prints because they might be among the last to go out. Her byline would be on the majority of the pictures of the takeover, her name joined with the crumbling city's last hours. At last her stamp on a part of history. Everyone was waiting for the inevitable—communications lines to be cut. That was when the victors would show their true hand.

Early evening, the machines fluttered and went dead at last. A ripple of fear traveled the office.

"That's it, people. Vietnam is closed for business. Let's go to dinner."

A mixed group of nationalities among the dozen journalists dining on the roof of the Caravelle Hotel. Tanner raised his glass to Helen in a private toast. Although they had never liked each other, there was a mutual respect for time served. Waiters in white coats carried food out from the restaurant as if it were just another night. The Westerners were surprised that the place was still operating but remained quiet in front of the staff, as if bringing up the war were in bad taste. The maître d' stopped by their table and politely informed Gary that this was the last night they would remain open. They could not put the bill on account but had to pay by check or cash. Before dessert, the waiters had disappeared. Gary and a French writer rummaged in the abandoned kitchen for ice cream. The final bill never came.

After dinner, they "liberated" cigars and drinks from the now self-serve bar. Helen was lying on a lounge chair, drinking a glass of champagne and looking up at the stars.

The young Matt came and sat next to her.

"You should've hung around yesterday. I scored a lid off them," Matt said.

Helen knew he was a liar but didn't care. At this late date, personal preferences were a nicety. Should she start thinking other wars? South America? What would Linh think?

Matt's hair was back in a ponytail, and he wore a fresh tie-dye shirt with a peace symbol on the chest. He looked almost presentable for an antiwar protester. He lifted Helen's wrist and looked at the Montagnard bracelet. "Where'd you get that?"

"Years ago from a Special Forces guy. Before you ever took your first picture." She lifted her chin toward his shirt. "You actually wear that to cover combat?"

"Sure. It's a disguise."

"It's working. You don't look like a photographer."

"I totally dig this old-guard, ballbuster stuff." Matt chuckled and refilled her champagne glass as it dangled in her hand, but she remained reclined, looking up at the stars. "And my mentor, old Tanner, with his Graham Greene vices and his Marine crap, too funny. It's like you all read the same book."

"Isn't it amazing," she said.

"What?" he asked.

"The quiet. No planes, no artillery. I never knew the city any other way." A wave of nostalgia and history and failure overwhelmed her, and she drank down her glass.

Matt poured her another and signaled to Tanner over her head. "So did the bracelet bring you luck?"

Helen shrugged. "I'm still here. Is that luck?"

Tanner came and sat down at her feet. "Tucked your VC partner safely away and now you're ready to play with us, huh?"

"The two Matts have a proposition for you."

She looked at the young man more closely. A boyish face, unlined and unknowing, a long thin nose with the sunburned skin peeling. He licked his lips, which were thick and pouting and didn't match the rest of his face, and she realized he was wired up on speed. "Proposition away."

He grinned a smirky kind of smile as if he were letting her in on some great prank. "It's just a matter of time now before they kick us out, right? The excitement's finished here."

"So?"

"So . . . we'll leave before they kick us out. But our way. A little car trip through Cambodia, stop off in Phompers. The only Western journalists to get pictures of what's going down in the countryside. All the other reporters have been herded up in the French embassy."

"Wow. That's pretty risky."

"That's why we're inviting you along," Tanner said. "A bit of nostalgia. Our personal swan song."

Tanner took risks, but she supposed he was most interested in saving his hide, vulture reputation notwithstanding. Matt had covered the Rangers in Hung Loc and gotten a good story out of it. Not so bad. Not so desperate.

"Cambodia?" she said, staring at him. The oldest of seductions—falling under the spell of one clearly more innocent than oneself.

"We go out through Thailand," Tanner said. Now that she seemed actually to be listening to them, he was straightened into considering his own proposition.

"When?"

"First thing in the morning."

Darrow had won the Pulitzer before he got to Vietnam. But he continued on, his fame growing to legend status as he became associated with this small, problematic Southeast Asian bush war. Always he wanted to cover one more action. She told herself she was not as obsessed as Darrow. She was a professional, accessing a potential gig. Tanner was seasoned; he knew the risks; he was going. So if it was doable, was she simply too afraid to push out to the limits as Darrow had done? A total shutout of the media. A once-in-a-lifetime thing. That puritan instinct. How could she let them—the bad guys, the ones who wanted to do their dirty work in the dark—win, when it was nothing more than another car trip on her way out?

As dinner broke up, Gary took her aside. "I heard what those two clowns are up to. You're not going with them?"

She grimaced. "Of course not. What kind of fool do you take me for?"

At noontime, they were already on Route 1, getting close to the border.

Foreign employees at the wire services who had already abandoned the country left keys with directions to their cars, and the three had been able to take their pick. Nothing military because one couldn't be sure that isolated pockets of VC didn't still believe the war was on. They settled on a custom-painted pink station wagon with peace signs and the graffiti YOU ONLY LIVE TWICE on the side. They would try to pass themselves off as hippies or small-time drug smugglers—anything was better than being press if they were stopped.

All three sat in the front seat and filled the back with scavenged tires from other cars and cans of petrol. With their equipment on top of that, the car was filled to the roof and made it impossible to see out the rearview mirror. Starting at dawn, they had already stopped to repair three punctured tires. The car had no air-conditioning, so they rolled down the windows.

The hot air battered Helen's face, her lips, turned her hair into sharp lashing wires, but it felt good being in motion and having a purpose. Her mind skated, full of dangerous curves and valleys, a grand adventure. Once she got to Thailand and flew to Linh, they would take some time off in California. There would always be other wars. All in the service of this excitement that was commensurate with the risk one took. At times she had the dispiriting notion of needing to remain constantly in flight, although after all these years, she was growing tired, never alighting in one place too long, never putting her full weight on the crust of the earth in case it gave way. Her job was to get pictures, but sometimes she forgot why.

The countryside appeared empty. When they did pass villagers, there was more a look of surprise in their faces than anything else. Helen didn't know what she expected to see, nothing had changed—only the same barren fields and plots of banana trees and patches of scrub that had always been.

Matt sat in the middle and rolled a joint, passing it back and forth among the three of them. He wore metallic blue-tinted sunglasses that reflected Helen's image back to her.

"When did you first come here?" he asked.

"Why're you wearing those glasses?" she asked.

"You should have seen her. A schoolgirl practically wearing bobby socks," Tanner said.

Matt took a deep drag on the joint and held his breath for a minute. "When?" he finally squeaked out, still holding smoke in his lungs.

"We need to stop and eat," Tanner said.

"I'm starving. What did you bring?" she said.

"Whatever I could find. Some chips. Mangoes. C-rations," Matt said.

"Who would bring C-rations?" Tanner yelled.

"They'll keep," Matt said.

"Jesus."

"You know what—you do it next time, Mr. Gourmet." Matt turned around with his knees in the seat and burrowed in a bag behind the seat. A can flew out the open window.

"What're you doing?" Tanner yelled.

"You said you didn't want C-rations."

A bag of potato chips flew out. Helen pressed herself into the door. "I came at the end of 'sixty-five. I dropped out of college to come. I worried the war would be over by the time I graduated." She shrugged, but Matt and Tanner were still arguing. "I wanted to find out what happened to my brother. The pilot refused to land so the crew pushed the men out from ten feet up. He broke both ankles and while he was stuck in the mud the enemy shot him. He died like an animal." MacCrae had shielded her from the ugly details but over the years, she had found them out. The relief of feeling nothing at those words.

"Fucking pigs." Matt took a long drag off the joint. The smoke emptied out of his mouth with a gasp.

"You're like, drawing attention to us, throwing things out the window," Tanner said to Matt.

"I'm hungry," he said, flinging himself back down into the seat.

Her story, told at long last and at such cost, seemed already forgotten by both of them. Minutes passed.

"So why'd you stay so long?" Matt said.

Helen was silent. "Because it seems like you're doing the most important work in the world. Leaving was like dying."

They drove on in silence until they heard the soft *thunk, thunk, thunk* of another flat tire.

"Jesus," Tanner said.

They pulled off near a small hut, hidden from the road by a bamboo thicket. Tanner pulled out the jack and a new tire while Matt wandered off toward the building.

"Where are you going?" Tanner yelled. "Why don't you help me?"

"I'm taking a piss, okay?" Matt said.

"Why's he going to the hooch? Asking for a bathroom?" Tanner shook his head. "He's resourceful, that boy."

A few minutes later, Matt reappeared around the corner of the hut and waved them over. Up close, Helen saw that his eyes were marbled with red veins from lack of sleep and smoke. They followed him to a small dirt yard in the middle of which lay a struggling but still alive goose.

"His wing and his leg are broken," Matt announced in a dreamy voice.

The animal labored to get away but only made dusty circles in the dirt. Its black eye looked dull, but when Matt moved closer, the bird made a gritty, hissing noise at him.

"How can you tell?" Tanner asked.

"I grew up on a farm, man," Matt answered. "And it's about lunchtime."

Tanner snorted.

Helen looked from one of them to the other. "Don't we need to get going?"

"We need to eat," Matt said. "Give me an hour."

"I'm still working on that damned tire. Go ahead," Tanner said. "Are you sure that thing's not diseased? Doesn't have rabies?"

"Birds don't have rabies, man."

Helen regretted coming with these two, couldn't stand their squabbling any longer. Their recklessness made her afraid. She had lasted this long because she took only calculated risks. With the fall of Saigon, she'd done her bit. Covered the takeover, and should have gone home. Cambodia was a whole other thing. "I need to get out of here. I need to get to Linh."

Both of the men turned to look at her.

Helen wiped her face. "Never mind."

Matt's attention went back to the goose. "Maybe he fell out of a cart or was run over. He'll be dead in a few hours and then he'll go to waste."

Helen walked off and sat in the shade of the hut while Matt made quick, expert work of beheading the goose, plucking the quivering body, then chopping it up to cook over an open fire. The whole spectacle disgusted her, but after the pieces began to fry, releasing the smell of cooking meat, she felt a stab of hunger and realized she was starving. The body always betrayed one's best intentions. Memory of the recently flopping body, the head and neck thrown a few feet away in the tall grass, vanished, and instead she remembered Sunday dinners at home when Charlotte cut slices of white meat and put them on china plates as thin as flower petals and passed them down the table.

Matt grinned and brought Helen big, dripping chunks of breast and thigh wrapped in paper. She ate it down fast, laughing with the two men over how good it was, wiping the grease off her mouth and chin, then wiping her hands against her pants but unable to get the oily residue off.

Matt sat next to her holding a drumstick and attached thigh in both hands, biting off enormous mouthfuls of steaming meat.

"So how did you end up with a Vietnamese?" he said.

She smiled and took another bite of meat. "Ask Tanner. He's made a hobby out of analyzing my love life."

"Not bad chow, huh?" Tanner asked, taking a long drink from a bottle of whisky.

Helen nodded. "It's good." Matt gave her another handful of breast meat. She took a long pull off the bottle and handed it back.

"Linh's okay in my book," Tanner said. "He's a good photographer, and he keeps his nose clean. Doesn't seem to resent the fact that he's treated like a second-class citizen in his own country. That most of us suspect him of being a Red."

"That's big of you," Helen said.

"What I'm saying is that Linh is a realist. Of course he loves you; he got the prize. Darrow thought it was all owed to him. He kidded himself he was here for a higher purpose when he was just grubbing around for a byline and an award like the rest of us. Darrow would have put you on that chopper and come out here himself."

The truth of it stung Helen.

The sky was a high, pale blue with long wisping tails of cloud. The only sound their chewing and the rustling of paper.

"Where the hell did you learn to cook like that?" Tanner finally asked.

Matt looked at the two of them. "Truth time? My old man beat me so hard I decided I better run away if I wanted to stay alive. Went to North Dakota at fourteen years old and cooked in a greasy spoon till I was eighteen."

"Why North Fucking Dakota?"

"I once heard my mama say nobody in their right mind would ever go to North Dakota. So I thought the odds were good they wouldn't find me."

"Did they?" Helen asked.

"Never even looked. Best time of my life." Matt bowed his head. "Found an Indian woman who worked the cash register. Made love to me every day for four years until she found out I lied about my age. Kicked me out, can you believe it? She did things—"

"We don't want to hear about your squaw," Tanner said.

Helen's mind was buzzing with alcohol. The sense of urgency pouring out of her. "So then what did you do?"

"Came to Vietnam," Matt yelled and clapped his hands.

She didn't want to know but had to ask. "How old are you?"

"Nineteen." He arched his eyebrows. "Why? Interested?"

"We need to go."

"Best way to go to a genocide is on a full stomach," Tanner said, and Matt and he burst out laughing. Helen smiled. Clowns. Gary was right; she was glad he didn't know where she was. But after the pictures came in, all would be forgiven once again. It was always about pushing the envelope.

"This is the big one," Tanner said. "I can feel it. We're going to be famous."

"Interviewed by Cronkite," Matt said. "The TV guys will fight over us."

"Fuck the TV guys."

Helen almost envied them their glee, their lust for fame, their complete and unblushing lack of empathy.

"So, what was it like back in 'sixty-five?" Matt asked.

"You came too late." Helen smiled. "The good old days are all over."

Bellies full, they drove in drowsy silence until they approached the border. The guardhouse appeared abandoned, but they slowed the car anyway. The road ahead was littered with rocks and leaves, but otherwise empty except for a lone old man walking toward them, down the middle of it, carrying a suitcase in each hand. He stumbled as they passed him, refusing to look up, either from fear or exhaustion. They stopped the car.

"Can we help you, Father?" Helen asked.

He stood still, unsure in the bright sun, squinting behind black-rimmed eyeglasses like the old Vietnamese man's.

"*Teuk? Nuoc?*" Water? she asked, making a drinking motion.

He dropped his bags, exhaustion now evident in shoulders that remained stooped, and he shuffled over. He wore a tattered, dusty white shirt and khaki pants. His feet in rubber sandals were cracked and bleeding. Tanner dropped the tailgate for him to sit on, then went into the front of the car and got his camera. Helen handed the old man a canteen of water, and he gulped it so quickly he retched.

"Whoa, take it easy, old man," Matt said.

"Where did you come from, Father?"

"Prek Phnou, outside Phnom Penh. I am a teacher."

"That's far away on foot."

"I walk week. More. I don't know. Lose track of everything. I hide in the day in forest, but Khmer Rouge leave me alone. They think I will die on my own."

"We are going to Phnom Penh," Tanner said, crouching down and snapping pictures of the man as he drank.

"*Te!*" No! he shouted. *"Te Kampuchea! Te Phnom Penh!"*

"It's okay, Father."

"They empty the city. The hospitals. Terrible. I see things I did not wish to live to see."

"Are you a person of Vietnam?" Helen asked.

He bowed his head and nodded. "I go back after many years."

She knew better than to ask about his family. She went to the front of the car and got another canteen and handed it to him. "Take this. Do you have food?"

He shook his head, and she grabbed sandwiches, cookies, and C-rations.

"Here. And some bandages and ointment for your feet. The border is here," she said, waving her hand at land without demarcation, except for the guardhouse in the distance. "The next village not far." What was far to an old man on the verge of collapse?

"Don't forget an opener," Matt said, coming around the side of the car, for all the world like a polite schoolboy.

The old man kept sitting. *"Aw kohn, aw kohn."* Thank you, he said.

Tanner came back. "Let's hit the road."

Helen nodded. "I'm sorry, Father. Can I take your picture?"

He stared up at her with a blank look. "Daughter, there is no one left who will care." He stood uncertainly, looking down the road. Something passed across his face as she focused her camera, a shudder, and after the picture was taken she felt embarrassed at the intrusion. The image she wanted was her first sight of him—a small, anonymous figure in the distance with the two suitcases. She couldn't stage it. He felt around in his pockets and pulled out a sandstone medallion no larger than a small coin with a Buddha carved in relief. He handed it to her.

"I can't accept—" she said.

"I have one, too. It has given me hope." He pulled out another one from his shirt pocket. "Put in your mouth, like this." He opened his mouth, revealing a few lone teeth, and placed it on his tongue, then closed his lips. He spit it back out. "It protects you from harm. That is why I escaped, why they didn't kill me like they killed the others." He made a chopping motion with his hand. *"Vay choul."* With the back of a hoe.

Helen took the small Buddha, hand trembling, and bowed to the old man. "I hope it protects us as it has you." As they drove away, she watched him pick up his suitcases and limp down the road. She leaned out the window and took the picture she had wanted from the back.

"I wouldn't put that in my mouth, birdie," Tanner said. "No telling where that little medallion's been."

Like a pair of hyenas, Tanner and Matt laughed as she watched the old man grow smaller and smaller in the side-view mirror until he was only a shadow that disappeared on the horizon.

They had been driving long hours, a tortured skirting of crater-size potholes made by B-52s years before, riding through dry stretches of rice paddy that were smoother than the road, making slow progress, when they came upon a roadblock.

From a distance, it seemed just clutter, but up close its message was stark—a skull, a helmet, a gun, a shoe. They had entered a land before language. A clear meaning that beyond lay only danger. Beyond be dragons. The scorching air now seemed suddenly to crackle, dry and treacherous, incendiary. Helen stuck her head out the window and looked back the way they had come. Had the old man made it to shelter? When Matt and Tanner were preoccupied with the map, she slipped the medallion in her mouth, the texture gritty like pumice, tasting of salt and dirt and iron.

"Looks like we've caught up with our quarry," Matt said.

Helen turned back to the parched landscape ahead, the ground and sky a series of harsh reds and yellows, the trees stunted and full of prickling spines, the place like tinder, waiting for conflagration.

The first shape seemed to be only a pile of rags at the side of the road, but when the station wagon slowed down it turned out to be the corpse of a small boy, curled on his side as if in sleep, a tiny hand covering the gap where an ear was missing. Helen felt the courage pouring out of her, despair and fear taking its place. A quarter of a mile farther on, more bodies: a woman in her twenties with her hands spread out at her sides as if in surprise; a man with his arms folded behind him as if he were relaxing. Then the bodies began to crowd the road—families, groups of men, old people, women— struck down in rows like scythed sheaves of rice, so that Tanner had to slow the car and swerve back and forth along the road, until finally the bodies became so numerous and thick he had to stop to avoid running over them. Tanner and Matt got out while Helen sat loading film in her camera. When she was ready, a Tiger Balm–smeared handkerchief over her nose, they moved forward, cameras clicking. Tanner motioned to her, and she walked to the edge of the road and saw the sunken field piled with hundreds of bodies, many decapitated and bludgeoned, so that they knew the stories of *vay choul* were true, killing with hoes to save bullets.

"We are the only ones who have this on film," Matt whispered, his jaw tight and quivering, and then he turned away and vomited.

Helen put her hand on his back. "It's okay. It happens. Get some water."

"Not to me." Matt shrugged her hand off and wiped his face.

She bit her lip, annoyed at his petulance. "It's the first time I started to like you," Helen said.

"Then you've got some weird criteria," he said.

"We have enough," Tanner said. "Let's go."

The two men ran back to the car. Without thinking, Helen edged down the embankment and took more pictures of the piled bodies, framing the picture from a lower vantage point, with sky behind them, so the massiveness of the piles could be felt. *If the picture was no good, it meant that you weren't close enough.* She did a close-up of a young girl's face that was as peaceful as if she were asleep, a single flower tangled in her hair. Five minutes later, Helen climbed back up and ran to the car. Inside, she pushed down the lock on the door, then laughed at her own foolishness. "I'm going crazy. Get out a bottle of something."

"Whiskey time," Matt said, and burrowed in the bags again.

Tanner put the car in drive. "Forward?"

Helen took a long drink, wiped her mouth, then took another. The scale of this depravity like something out of World War II. She shook her head. This was clearly beyond them. "We'll never make it to Phnom Penh. And if we do, what then? They'll confiscate the film." Helen studied the map. "Let's go back a few miles and take this secondary road. It's probably a cow trail, but it'll hook up with Route 6. Route 6 goes to Thailand."

Tanner let out a yell and banged his hand on the dashboard. "Do you two have any arguments to sharing the Pulitzer three ways?" He laughed. "We have it. How lucky can you get?"

Helen tried to hold the whiskey bottle, but her hand couldn't grip, the shaking was so bad. She stuck it between her knees so the two men wouldn't notice. The irony was that she could have no better company for this trip; they were insulated from the horror by their own ambitions. She didn't have the strength at that moment to question her own motivations. Why, indeed, was she there? She could only pray their ignorance would carry the three of them to the border.

"They thought they would get away with it. Pol Pot denying the whole thing. No pictures, no proof. Won't make us too popular around here, huh?" Helen said.

"Smoked if they catch us," Tanner agreed. "Hand over that bottle and let's celebrate."

"They have to catch us first, Helen baby," Matt said.

After spending the night out, and another day of bruising roads, they reached the Mekong River. Tanner argued with and then bribed the ferryman to carry them across. The man, named Chan, had small, pig eyes, and one cheek puffed up nearly double from an infected tooth. He kept stirring at a pot of something green over a burner, spooning a paste into a dirty poultice he held against his ear. His left hand was missing three fingers, severed below the knuckle. After Matt asked to look at his cheek, he turned away quickly. "Abscessed."

Finally, Chan agreed to take them across for an exorbitant amount, ten times the usual, and insisted the station wagon be camouflaged under palm fronds. While Tanner and Matt covered the car, Helen walked down to the water to wet her handkerchief. A pink, checkered shirt floated in the water, and as she got closer she saw it covered a swollen torso, the fabric pulled tight, splitting the seams. Another body in black swayed at the bank, face-down, long hair twisting in the reeds.

During the crossing, the water lay still like liquid metal, the ferry suspended on its surface, unmoving. Helen stared down in the water, her image as sharp as in a mirror.

The ferryman sat at the very-most edge of the boat, poultice pressed tight against his face, and glared at them. Matt and Tanner smoked a joint. "To protect our cover." Helen slipped the Buddha on her tongue, growing used to the iron taste till the bitterness comforted her.

"I don't trust him," Helen said.

Matt shrugged and stared at Chan, his dour, squatting image reflected in the blue sunglasses. "What'd you want to do? Kill him?"

"He's going to report us," she said.

"Too bad. We'll be across the border in a day. But I'll kill him if you want."

She felt light-headed, as if there were too little oxygen in the air.

Once they got off the ferry, Tanner paid Chan again as much for a tip if he would forget their meeting. The ferryman eagerly accepted and smiled for the first time, breathing in their faces, his breath like sulfur, but his eyes remained hateful. He delayed pulling the rope gate away for the car to pass. His pidgin English suddenly improved. "Khmers bad. Americans rich, the goodest."

"So how do we get to the Thai border? With no running into Khmer? We take—" Matt pulled out a Baggie of marijuana to show him. "No *problemo?*"

Chan talked and gestured as Matt wrote down his directions. Tanner again pulled out a thick stack of money and peeled off more bills for him. Chan pointed to the car and Helen, and then motioned taking a picture.

Matt nodded sagely and motioned to Helen. "Girlfriend. Wants to take pictures of Phnom Penh and Angkor Wat." Matt grimaced and took him aside. "How far to Angkor? Otherwise no—" He made an obscene poking gesture with his hands, and the ferryman laughed. He gave another set of equally convoluted directions, taking Matt's pen and drawing part of a picture on the paper. Tanner peeled off more bills and handed them to him.

"You go Phnom Penh. Much goodest."

"No dangerous?" Tanner said.

"Much goodest." The man insisted. He slapped Tanner's stomach. "Womans."

At last he moved to take down the rope barrier, and the three men pulled over the ramp to drive the station wagon off. "You go Phnom Penh?" he insisted like a worried mother hen.

"Yes, Phnom Penh."

Matt wagged his head lazily and waved as they drove off. He lifted both hands off the wheel and again made the poking gesture so Chan laughed.

"Definitely avoid Phompers," Matt said.

"So we go up and over the long way?" Tanner asked.

"Chan expects us to do that."

"No, Chan expects us to double-cross him. Take the shorter route under."

"So we triple-cross him and do what we said."

They set off in high spirits, convinced they had thoroughly confused the ferryman, but the trip became a horrendous series of wrong turns and dead ends. "The little bastard lied to us," Tanner said, pounding on the steering wheel.

"I should have offed him," Matt said. At dusk they stopped because of the danger of being spotted by their headlights. Not wanting to be taken by surprise, they hid the car in the trees and slept in a ditch.

Helen settled down into a pile of leaves. "Listen," she whispered.

"What?" Matt asked.

"No sound. Nothing. No birds even, or insects."

"You're the lady in love with silence."

No one spoke for a few moments.

"Bizarre," Tanner said. "Tomorrow at lunch we'll be in the best hotel in Bangkok, popping a bottle of champagne."

Helen stared up at the sky, but even in the pitch black of the country, not a single star appeared. A blanket of lead; even the heavens had been extinguished. "I'm ready to go home," she said.

"What took you so long?" Matt asked.

She shrugged to the darkness. "I got lost."

Helen closed her eyes. She thought of the rolls of film in the car, the images cradled in emulsion, areas of darkness and light like the beginnings of the universe. She herself full of latent images taken over the years, and yet what she had seen would stay inside her, hidden. Linh had covered her eyes during the mission out of Dak To, because he understood that for them the eye was the most important thing. We close our eyes to spare ourselves or those we love. To see demanded responsibility. To gain power over their enemies, armies blindfolded prisoners. In the fields, the Khmer Rouge had the people turn away so that the executioners would not see themselves in their victims' eyes.

Tanner was probably right—the pictures were good and were taken at great risk, they had a shot at some of the prizes—and so she was catching up to Darrow. It was like chasing the tail of a comet. She had done her final job for the war and was proud of that. But even as she got closer, she understood his contempt had not been feigned, that by the time one earned such accolades, one had paid many times over what they were worth. And yet she was still there.

As she fell asleep, she wondered again where Linh was—still on a carrier or already on his way to California? She saw herself back in the embassy compound, smoke and burning paper swirling in the air. Then she was on the roof, tucking Linh into the cocoon of the helicopter, but this time she stayed on, felt the familiar weightlessness as they flew over the dark city and then over the darker water. She held Linh's hand, free for the first time in so many years, maybe for the first time ever. Somewhere out in that darkness the future was rushing toward them. Had she tricked her fate?

She thought of her brother, not the imagined, damaged Michael of the war, but as he had been before, laughing and dancing around her. His hands up in a mock-boxing stance, his hair slicked back, white teeth shining. She had forgotten that he had a life before the war. In guilt and rivalry, she had given away the chance to have her own. But then Michael tossed his head like a horse throwing off the bit, refusing her memory of him.

Helen saw the young Cambodian girl she photographed in the mass grave earlier. Imagined tearing at the gossamer fabric of her shirt, brushing the long strands of hair like threads of silk, like the tendrils of morning glories in the spring, plunging into the hollow cave of ribs and the small dried grottoes of eyes. The dead entered the living, burrowed through the skin, floated through the blood, to come at last to rest in the heart. Stirring through the bits and pieces of the mystery of the young girl, Helen imbibed her, would leave transmuted, brave and full of courage, knowing her fear and determined enough to ignore it, courageous enough at last to return home. Time to give up the war.

At dawn, Helen woke before the men did and felt as rested as if she'd had eight hours in her own bed. She snuck over to the car and pulled out a clean shirt from Matt's bag. An unlikely baby-blue with a peace symbol emblazoned on it. As she tugged her old one off, she brushed the scar on her belly. Linh had traced his fingers over it, the glossy raised skin as pale and iridescent as fish scale.

"No more bikinis for me."

"This makes me love you more," he had said.

"Why?"

"It proves that you will be brave in the future."

But she no longer felt brave. Since she had first arrived in Vietnam, she had been obsessed with courage. Such an ancient quality in modern life, called for only in extreme circumstances. She had admired it in others, in Linh and Darrow, but found it only sporadically within herself. A combat journalist's life measured in dog years. She felt old compared to these young savages like Matt. She was softening, but she pushed that thought away, too. As she turned, pulling the T-shirt over her head, she saw Matt watching her.

"That was beautiful," he said.

She picked up his bag and threw it at him. "Pervert."

Trading cigarettes for directions to isolated villagers working the fields, using their smattering of Cambodian and French, they reached Route 6 by midmorning. They let out whoops of joy. "Bangkok here we come," Tanner yelled. "I'm getting me the prettiest hooker I can afford." Helen thought of the images rocking in their cradles of film, gestating in emulsion. She would insist on doing her own darkroom work. The road ahead was empty, leaf strewn, unused. Depending on driving conditions, Tanner figured they were a day's drive from Thailand.

When Helen couldn't put off emptying her bladder another minute, they stopped in the middle of the road. She made the men turn away and peed behind the car, too dangerous to go in the bushes because of mines. As she squatted, she saw a few feet away a pair of black-rimmed eyeglasses like the old Cambodian man's, crushed.

They were half an hour away from Angkor when a loud explosion created a small hurricane as the back windows were blown out by automatic rifle fire. Splinters of glass flew through the car like steel filings, most absorbed by the equipment, enough reaching them to nick arms and faces.

The back window blocked, Helen couldn't see behind, and she peered through the side-view mirror, but the car was bouncing too hard; she caught only a glimpse of a boy, then sky, the boy, earth. Tanner floored the accelerator; the station wagon lurched forward as another round of bullets swept through the car doors. The tires blew, and the car skidded into the ditch.

"Shit, shit, shit," Matt moaned. One blue lens of his sunglasses was shattered, and he pulled off the glasses, revealing a gash around his eye.

"Shut up. Don't look worried," Tanner said.

"Are you fucking kidding?" Matt said.

The car was surrounded by two dozen boy soldiers. Circling the car, they pounded on it with small, violent fists. They wore tattered uniforms with red-checked *kramas,* scarves, wrapped around their heads or necks to signify the Khmer Rouge. AK-47s hung off their small shoulders. The leader was barefoot but wore a bowler hat and orange-tinted aviator sunglasses that matched the fiery sky, a getup so strange it made him seem less dangerous. He banged the butt of his rifle on the hood of the car, leaving long, elliptical dents, while two other soldiers flung the driver's-side door open, motioning with their hands for the three to get out.

First Tanner, then Matt, and then Helen wiggled awkwardly out with their hands folded up behind their heads. Using rifles, the soldiers pointed up the road. Helen hoped that they would simply take the car and let them go, all she could think of was the lost pictures, but when the three had walked about twenty yards, she could hear a barking of orders, and one of the soldiers ran up behind them and used his rifle like a baseball bat to hit Matt in the back of the knees.

The soldier, no older than ten or eleven, had a narrow face and large, crowded teeth, and when he yelled, his voice was high and girlishly shrill. He motioned for the other two to kneel in the middle of the road. When they did, he smiled broadly, pleased, and patted Matt on the back.

"You're welcome, filthy little fuck," Matt said.

Helen closed her eyes. The whole thing unreal, make-believe. She wanted to stand up and tear the gun away from the boy and slap him. So unlikely, it felt like at any minute someone should laugh and admit it was all a game.

At the sound of a groan from Matt, she opened her eyes to see the soldier miming for them to bring their hands down and take off their shoes. The boy soldiers were so inexperienced they had not even known to frisk them for weapons, but the gun Matt carried was safely back in the car. Not that they'd have a chance of shooting their way out. All three sat in the road and worked with numbed fingers at shoelaces, exchanging looks. Helen dipped her fingers in her pocket and slipped the small Buddha into her mouth, unseen. The saving bitterness of iron. Then, barefoot, they were ordered to kneel again and put their arms behind them, elbow to elbow. Other soldiers ran over and bound their arms with a crude rope made of twisted vines. Helen cursed herself for not bandaging her chest down as two of the boy soldiers stood in front of her, giggling and pointing. The smaller boy, with a spiky shock of hair, looked furtively back to the leader preoccupied with the car, then bent down and quickly tugged at her breast.

Matt made a lunge for him, and the other soldier aimed the butt of his rifle at Matt's temple.

"Don't," Helen said. "Whatever happens, you can't stop it. I need you alive." Her knees trembled, and she tried to cave in her chest. Thoughts came in fragments, pulling themselves out slowly and with great effort. No use to announce they were press because that would be a death sentence. The color of their skin, the fact of their car, its contents—everything was against them. Her mouth filled with saliva, and before she could think, she pulled up to her full height and spat at the soldier who had touched her.

The boy looked startled and then burst out laughing. The others joined in.

Helen looked back and watched soldiers swarming over the station wagon. Such a terrible mistake to come. So unfair that one did not get a magic wish, that one could not undo at least one mistake a lifetime. Her biggest regret in dying in this way its effect on Linh. At the car, the soldiers pulled out all the equipment and lifted each camera over their heads and dashed them one by one against the pavement. One soldier flipped open the canisters, yanked the rolls of film from their dark cradles, screaming out in long, wet ribbons, exposed, the images flown off. And seeing that, Helen felt delivered, her job done, released as if from a spell. Endless destruction. War destroying objects, land, and people indiscriminately, with its appetite the only thing that was eternal. She watched, detached, as the soldiers piled up the rest of their belongings and threw a grenade on top of the stack, laughing at the explosion and scattering debris. Jumping up and down on the bags of food even though they probably had little to eat themselves. Smashing open the cans of C-rations. Next they poured gas inside the car and set it ablaze, but it only smoldered, releasing a heavy, black, oily smoke into the sky.

Then their vicious attention turned back to the three kneeling figures.

Helen looked up the road and tried to picture reaching the Thai border. She imagined it came to a dead stop at a river, although she couldn't remember from the map if there was a river, but in her mind's eye it was a clear and rushing one, and she knew she would have to swim across it if she wished to be saved, and the impossible price of that swim would be to leave everything that had happened during the war behind. She heard the words Darrow had recited their first night but that she had not understood till now: *Let her go home in the long ships and not be left behind.* She wanted to go home; she did not want to be left behind. She pictured a flimsy bamboo gate and Linh standing at it, waiting for her. It was his waiting that had always saved her.

A gun went off at close range, but she would not turn to look. She pressed the Buddha against the roof of her mouth, clamped her teeth until she thought she felt them cracking, a salty wash of blood in her mouth mixing with the iron that had become a part of her. Her reporter's mind registered surprise that they were using bullets, always special treatment for the foreigners. She heard a whimper—Matt's—but still would not look, looking would make it real. No sound from Tanner; now it was just two of them. The air thick with the mineral smell of blood.

Far away a rumbling sound, but she was in a trance, searching for god or peace or grace or void, making amends for things she had or had not done. The sound grew closer, like a dream, and she wondered if it was her own heart, the sounds of her body rumbling apart.

The hard crack of another shot made her ears ring, and afterward silence, and she was alone. As alone as one could ever be in life, and bad as it was, she endured long enough to take another breath. In that moment, she mourned the loss of those two innocents more than all the other lives that had been lost because she had known better. A hot wetness at her groin as her bladder released.

She bit down on the Buddha, pain a relief, a trickle from her lips as her mouth filled with blood, when suddenly there were hands at her sides, and she was yanked by her hair roughly to her feet. Legs so weak she fell back to the ground, afraid of what they planned to do with her before she was killed.

A new voice entered her consciousness, and when she braved turning her head, she saw a dusty pickup truck had pulled up next to the smoldering station wagon, and a middle-aged man had taken command of the group. Helen closed her eyes again. Her greatest wish that death would simply come fast now.

A hard shove at her back with the length of a rifle, and she was lifted to her feet. She stumbled forward, took one step, then another. Gravel bit her feet, but she did not register it as pain but simply as life. Life, beyond good or bad. No one followed her, no one at her side: They were playing with her, forcing her to march with them and have her later, and she wished to move faster, to run, but could barely manage a slow stagger of a walk down the middle of the empty road. Her ears still rang with the distancing sound of the fired shots, her two innocents gone, and she could hear the soldiers arguing behind her, and she willed herself to move faster but was unable.

She closed her eyes and saw herself rising into the air until she was flying. Had the winged thing already come? Ahead Angkor. Everything below— the road, the soldiers, the burning car, the two prone bodies—as faraway and unreal as the tiger that had appeared below the Loach that long-ago day. Time permeable. As real as the burning road under her bare feet, Darrow standing at the entrance to one of the temples, appearing as he had when she flew down to the delta to meet him. He wore his white short-sleeved shirt, eyes hidden behind glasses, and raked his good hand through his hair, his other arm still unhealed in its sling.

Helen took a bigger step forward and tripped over a stone, losing her balance, but she would not stop or open her eyes, afraid to lose her vision of him, afraid to look behind at the boy soldiers still arguing, but if she had, she would have seen two of them separating and jogging toward her, easy and carefree as two ravenous young wolves.

She choked on the Buddha, sharp gravelly pieces in her mouth that felt like bits of teeth or clay. Dust to dust, and weren't the teeth always the last to go? Her eyes closed so small and tight she could barely see. Afraid of death and yet not afraid, already inside it and moving through it. It would come and had already come a thousand times. She breathed relief at the thought that she was soon done with it.

She remembered the pictures of the Angkor bas-relief "The Churning of the Ocean of Milk," which Darrow and Linh had photographed years before she had loved either of them. Devils and gods churning the waves and fighting each other to extract the elixir of immortality. Violence had poisoned them all, Linh the least.

Poisoned Darrow.

And she, become Darrow, poisoned her.

A sudden clarity that he had been poisoned before she met him. His spell on her broken. She didn't want to join him on the temple steps; she knew what that burning brightness ahead was, death, and an invitation to join him in it. During her blindness, Linh there from the beginning, guarding her, and now she wanted only to live.

Would Linh know—she wanted him to know—that she did not go lightly, that she was not willing, that despite what it looked like, he had changed her and made her brave in all the ways she wasn't before, and if there was one last wish granted, she wanted him to know that she did not choose this.

She struggled to a half jog, determined that she could survive from mere desire.

The sound of running footsteps behind her, the flat slap of peasant sandals made of tires. A hard swing of a metal object across her back threw her facedown on the ground, unable to move. Her cheek and forehead burned. Air filled with blood. She was lifted to her knees. A soldier from behind grabbed her hair and pulled her head back, ripping out a fist of golden strands.

And then she closed her eyes, and they could no longer touch her. She no longer embraced what they threatened. Linh was there, and when she reached for his hand, her own had become stiff and brittle, her arms become branches, and from her knees to her groin to her belly to her breasts came a covering, an armor of gnarled bark, and her hair, when she reached for it, had the aspect of leaves. She opened her eyes, alive, and she turned to look deeply and without fear into her boy soldier's face.

She was in a state between dream and reality when she heard the chanting. They carried her back to the prone forms of Matt and Tanner, the new leader giving directions, and a miracle she couldn't fathom, Matt no longer dead but now sitting up, pressing his bleeding arm against his side. She huddled against him as the boy soldiers approached and circled the two of them, pressing in, circling around and around, touching, in some kind of victory ritual, chanting. The riddle of the dream at last—a premonition.

Then the leader came and knelt down to look at Helen, and her mouth so full of liquid she gagged, spitting out Buddha and fragments of stone. The man picked up the small medallion and stared at her in wonder.

TWENTY

Dong Thanh

One Heart

When Linh arrived at Camp Pendleton, he was weak in body and spirit. Helen's mother, Charlotte, recognized him from pictures, and they hugged as if they had known each other for ages, grief providing an instant history and bond. He was her only real link left to family. She had buckled him into the passenger seat of her Buick and driven up the coast to her home.

The wideness of the freeway, the speed at which the car traveled, dizzied him, and he forgot his tiredness, he was so taken up by his new country. More than its differences, he was struck by its likenesses. Just as in Vietnam, this was a place of land, *dat,* and water, *nuoc.* Ocean on one side, the grassy, burned foothills on the other; they passed all the things that Helen had promised him they would see together—dark groves of avocado and orange, small towns of white houses with red-tiled roofs, signs with the names of towns he remembered from her lips: San Clemente, Laguna, San Juan Cap- istrano. And then without warning they rounded a gentle curve, and as far as the eye could see were golden poppies.

"Gary contacted me, Linh. He overheard two other reporters talking to Helen about driving through Cambodia to get out of Vietnam. All three were gone the next day. No one has heard a word since then."

"Stop," Linh pleaded, and Charlotte, alarmed, pulled over on the gravelly shoulder. He tugged at the seat belt and threw open the passenger door, and she thought he was going to be sick, when he ran into the field and fell on all fours and bowed his head. Confused, she warily got out of the car, but he was oblivious to her, eyes filled with the flowers, his hands tearing at the soft orange petals within his reach.

On his first day in California, despite his exhaustion, he begged Charlotte to take him to Robert's office in Los Angeles.

Robert stood up from his desk, smiling, came around to give him a hug, but Linh was all business, not acknowledging the view out the window, twenty stories up, the highest building in the biggest city he had ever been in.

"I need to go to Thailand," Linh said.

Robert winced. "You look like you *need* a hospital." It had been more than seven years since they'd last met, and yet Linh acted as if it had been only yesterday. Was it the effect of the war that collapsed time? Robert could not account well for the last years in Los Angeles, yet his two years in Vietnam were as deep as a full lifetime. While Robert had grown plump, Linh was thin as a wire, as if all excess had been melted off him. The intensity of his eyes made the room suddenly too small.

"Helen went to Cambodia," Linh said in a tone like defeat. "I have to find her."

Robert had never gotten to know him that well; he had never really gotten to know many of the Vietnamese well during his time there. The whole country had remained a cipher to him. Too, Linh was always part of Darrow and Helen, and he recognized their willfulness and determination in him. For the first time, it occurred to him that the three of them were alike and had merely found one another in Vietnam. They had shared some understanding and obsession about the war, and he had never had a chance of befriending any of them. They had merely tolerated him.

"No way I can send you. It would be criminal in your state."

"You cared for her, too." Linh said it as accusation, but Robert's failure with Helen had been part of a larger failure of nerve.

"Her choice to stay on and then go to Cambodia. If that's what she's done."

Robert treated him with a politeness that masked disdain, a condescending sense of him as the Other. But he was a man of honor. Linh could bargain on that. Even at the beginning, Linh hadn't understood his letting

Helen go without a fight, although the fight was clearly lost. Only a madman insisted on a fight impossible to win. Yet what kind of man used logic in matters of the heart?

"Over the years, I've developed contacts," Linh said. "I'll need your help now to use them."

Robert said nothing. "There always was gossip."

"People love rumors, plots. They always prefer the more complicated explanation."

"I'll say it again. It was her choice."

"It's my choice, also, to go. I need a press pass and a plane ticket. I need you to send some messages."

Robert sighed. Suddenly he felt less good than he had in all the time since he had been back; something about Linh's passion that was like a burning, the timbre of his voice in the room, how it changed the room physically. The thought, sacrilegious, crossed Robert's mind that perhaps he *had* missed something during his years in Vietnam, that perhaps by protecting himself too well from being involved, he ended up not being involved in the world at all. But he hurried away from this line of thought because it was indeed too late; as much as he might have loved Helen, he would be loath to consider getting on a plane now. He realized with a shock of sadness that he was incapable of action. "*If* I sent you, you'd have to promise to stay in Thailand."

"Do I strike you as the kind of man to take unnecessary risks?"

"For her," Robert said, the answer too quick. "Give me a hint what's going on."

"Certain people will be interested in the death of a drug lord, a Mr. Bao, seven years ago."

"Old news. Who cares?"

"Mr. Bao was a businessman. An associate transferred all his drug money to a bank in Thailand. Lots and lots of money. A fortune. Blood money. Revolutions need financing."

"You are that associate? I could get fired," Robert said. "The magazine could be discredited."

"Yes, you could." Linh sat back for a minute, grimacing at the pain in his side that had started up again. "I lied to Helen. I told her that one needed to perform triage during the war, save what could be saved. But now I know differently. Sometimes you have to try even when there is no chance."

Robert nodded and turned away. "Find her."

The ostensible story was that Linh was sent to cover the exodus out of Cambodia after the Khmer Rouge takeover. He grabbed it like a lifeline. But breaking back into the NVA network proved all but impossible. Mr. Bao had made certain that Linh officially didn't exist. The NVA would never trust a contact with him.

Linh had lost his faith long ago. But now something worthy of faith occurred. For a time after the filming at Angkor, Linh had kept in touch with the boy Veasna, followed his fledgling photography career with the gift of Darrow's Rollerflex. They had become lost to each other since, but as Linh began to dig and grasp at any straw that might save Helen—a miracle. Veasna had become involved with the nationalist movement, the Khmers. Anyone on the outside would assume his anti-Americanism, but Linh understood about the gray areas of patriotism. Veasna had risen to a fairly high position. And he remembered their kindness. A camera and money when his family had nothing. Contact to the Cambodians had been achieved; he had found out that Helen and Matt were being held hostage. Money was discussed. There was never any guarantee what would actually happen. The original idea of holding the money until Helen was given up had to be abandoned. Now, bribes paid, it became an act of faith.

In Thailand, Linh went to the border and looked through his binoculars at lands now as inaccessible as the dark side of the moon, the blank part of a map. Looking for something more elusive than a tiger. The remaining Westerners in Phnom Penh, mostly diplomats and journalists, were being convoyed to the Cambodian border town of Poipet to be turned over for release. Helen and Matt were supposed to be thrown into this group and be smuggled across. Hours later, when the group crossed to freedom in small, defeated clusters, they were not among them.

Linh stayed at the border long after everyone else had left. His eyes smarted from staring down the dusty, hazy road, willing her shape to materialize on the horizon, as if his very wanting would make it so. He planned to cross into Cambodia that night under cover of darkness to find her. It was not his country; he was unfamiliar with the land and the language. Chances were he would not survive beyond a few days.

Returning to town, trying to bribe a guide, he sat in one of two restaurants on an empty street in town, ordered a beer and a meal, and as he waited for his contact, he overheard one of the Westerners from the release talking loudly as he stuffed food in his mouth. Linh heard a few French-inflected sentences and turned to stare at him, at his young face, with long brown hair and beard. As he listened the restaurant grew unbearably hot, the beer tasted bitter, and finally he set down the bottle and stood unsteadily and walked up to the man's table.

"Did you see a woman named Helen?" Had his contacts lied to him? Taken the money and run? Had something gone wrong?

Frightened, the man looked up at him, and Linh realized he had been wrong, that despite the youth and loudness, this man cared enough to remain at the border waiting for those who had not come out. "No. No one by that name. Still some of our Cambodian people haven't been released. I don't think they will be. We wait. There is a rumor of another release tomorrow morning."

The guide that Linh had paid never came.

At dawn, Linh waited with a small group of foreign press. The table of people from the previous day, including the Frenchman, arrived, and he nodded glumly at Linh. A funereal quiet in the group, readying itself for the bad news they expected.

Just as the first rays of sun lit the distant treetops, a dusty pickup could be seen in the far distance, a plume of dust ranging far behind it, marking its progress. It stopped a couple of hundred yards away from the border, whose stone-faced guards, as ferocious as those carved figures on the temples, faced the small, motley crowd of Westerners. They held their weapons at the ready, and Linh smiled at the ridiculousness of their guarding a country no one in their right mind wanted to enter. Soldiers jumped out of the truck and rolled a body out that hit the ground heavily; a collective groan went up in the crowd. The Frenchman rushed to the makeshift gate, but the guards stepped forward in warning. Another person came from the back of the truck, standing up, swaying. Wearing a light blue T-shirt he didn't recognize. Linh's breath caught as he recognized Helen.

"That's her," he said.

"But there's only two," the Frenchman said.

Slowly, Helen bent down and pulled at the prone form. After interminable minutes, the man stood, and supported by her, he began to move with her toward the gate. A cheer started in the small group, but their progress was so slow that the cheer grew ragged and stopped off before they could reach the border. Another bit of cruelty to make them struggle the last few steps to freedom when help was so near. As they got closer, Linh could see the white-blond hair of the man, his face sunburned and bruised, one eye closed, his arm in a makeshift sling. At last, when they were close enough, a guard kicked open the small rickety bamboo gate, and the two stumbled through.

Linh touched the purpled bruises of her cheeks, the swelling of her eye. This body that had come to stand for everything that had been lost. Hard to trust that after so much had been taken, so much could still be received. But she was there, alive, his truth. Helen come back from the dead.

Author's Notes

This is a work of imagination, inspired by real people and events, but I've given myself the fiction writer's prerogative of blending and mixing, outright distorting and making up. I have been an eager reader of every book and movie on Vietnam I've come across since I can remember, so influences are many and impossible to pinpoint. I first became aware of female journalists and photographers in Vietnam when I read about Dickey Chapelle in Horst Faas and Tim Page's *Requiem*. In the course of my research, I found a few others who spent significant time there, among them Katherine Leroy, Kate Webb, and one photographer I only came across in preparation for publication, Barbara Gluck.

In the strange way of fiction, I had been writing the novel for several years, having one of the characters developing into a spy, before I read about the true case of Pham Xuan An, a North Vietnamese intelligence agent who also was working undercover as a journalist for *Time* magazine. That much information was validation, the rest imagination.

When this particular story began to come together, the following is a list of works I read and consulted, instrumental not only for facts but for immersion in the atmosphere of that time and place. It also might make a good reading list for those unfamiliar with the history of the country or the war. If I have forgotten or left off anything, I apologize, and any omission will be added in the future if pointed out.

Specifically for the Fall of Saigon, I'm indebted to:

Butler, David. *The Fall of Saigon*. New York: Simon & Schuster, 1985.

Dawson, Alan. *55 Days: The Fall of South Vietnam*. Englewood Cliffs, N.J.: Prentice Hall, 1977.

General Bibliography

Bourke, Joanna. *An Intimate History of Killing*. New York: Perseus Books, 1999.

Browne, Malcolm W. *Muddy Boots and Red Socks: A Reporter's Life*. New York: Random House, 1993.

Chapelle, Dickey. *What's a Woman Doing Here?* New York: William Morrow, 1962.

Duiker, William J. *Ho Chi Minh*. New York: Hyperion, 2000.

Emerson, Gloria. *Winners and Losers*. New York: Random House, 1972.

Faas, Horst, and Tim Page, eds. *Requiem*. Introduction by David Halberstam. New York: Random House, 1997.

Fall, Bernard B. *Street Without Joy*. Introduction by George C. Herring. Mechanicsburg, Penn.: Stackpole Books, 1961.

Fitzgerald, Frances. *Fire in the Lake*. New York: Vintage, 1972.

Halberstam, David. *The Making of a Quagmire*. Introduction by Daniel J. Singal. New York: McGraw-Hill, 1964.

Hofmann, Bettina. *Ahead of Survival: American Women Writers Narrate the Vietnam War*. Berlin: Peter Lang, 1996.

Huu, Ngoc. *Sketches for a Portrait of Vietnamese Culture*. Hanoi: The Gioi Publishers, 1997.

Huynh, Sanh Thong, ed. and trans. *An Anthology of Vietnamese Poems*. New Haven, Conn.: Yale University Press, 1996.

Jamieson, Neil L. *Understanding Vietnam*. Berkeley: University of California Press, 1993.

Karnow, Stanley. *Vietnam: A History*. New York: Penguin Books, 1983.

Keegan, John. *The Book of War*. New York: Penguin Books, 1999.

Kulka, Richard A. et al. *Trauma and the Vietnamese Generation*. Foreword by Alan Cranston. New York: Brunner/Mazel, 1990.

Laurence, John. *The Cat from Hue.* New York: Perseus Books, 1992.

McAlister, Jr., John T. and Paul Mus. *The Vietnamese and Their Revolution.* New York: Harper & Row, 1970.

Melson, Charles D. *The War That Would Not End.* Central Point, Ore.: Hellgate Press, 1998.

Moeller, Susan D. *Shooting War: Photography and the American Experience of Combat.* New York: Basic Books, 1989.

Mouhot, Henri. *Travels in Siam, Cambodia, Laos, and Annam.* Bangkok: White Lotus Ltd., 2000.

Nguyen, Du. *Kieu.* Translated by Michael Counsell. Hanoi: The Gioi Publishers, 1994.

O'Nan, Stewart. *The Vietnam Reader.* New York: Anchor Books, 1998.

Plasters, John L. *SOG: A Photo History of the Secret Wars.* Boulder, Col.: Paladin Press, 2000.

Reporting Vietnam. Part 1: American Journalism, 1959–1969. New York: Library of America, 1998.

Reporting Vietnam. Part 2: American Journalism, 1969–1975. New York: Library of America, 1998.

Salisbury, Harrison E., ed. *Vietnam Reconsidered.* New York: Harper & Row, 1984.

Shay, Jonathan. *Achilles in Vietnam: Combat Trauma and the Undoing of Character.* New York: Simon & Schuster, 1994.

Sheehan, Neil. *A Bright Shining Lie: John Paul Vann and America in Vietnam.* New York: Vintage, 1988.

Taylor, Keith Weller. *The Birth of Vietnam.* Berkeley: University of California Press, 1983.

The Traditional Village in Vietnam. Hanoi: The Gioi Publishers, 1993.

Thompson, Virginia. *French Indo-China.* New York: Macmillan Co., 1942.

Walker, Keith. *A Piece of My Heart.* Novato: Presidio Press, 1985.

Webb, Kate. *On the Other Side: 23 Days with the Viet Cong.* New York: Quadrangle Books, 1972.

Young, Perry Deane. *Two of the Missing.* New York: Coward, McCann & Geolhegan, 1975.

Acknowledgments

I would like to thank Nat Sobel, a true gentleman in publishing, who still believes in fighting the good fight for a book. My gratitude also to my brilliant young editor, Hilary Rubin Teeman, who poured her passion and intelligence into the project. For assistance on parts of the manuscript in its earlier incarnations, I'd like to thank Adria Bernardi, Robert Cohen, and Megan Staffel.